KISS ME, KILL ME

A Novel of Suspense

Allison BRENNAN

BALLANTINE BOOKS • NEW YORK

Kiss Me, Kill Me is a work of fiction. Names, characters, places, and incidents are the products of the author's imagination or are used fictitiously. Any resemblance to actual events, locales, or persons, living or dead, is entirely coincidental.

A Ballantine Books Mass Market Original

Published in the United States by Ballantine Books, an imprint of The Random House Publishing Group, a division of Random House, Inc., New York.

BALLANTINE and colophon are trademarks of Random House, Inc.

This book contains an excerpt from *If I Should Die* by Allison Brennan. This excerpt has been set for this edition only and may not reflect the final content of the forthcoming edition.

ISBN 978-0-345-51169-0
eBook ISBN 978-0-345-52547-5

Printed in the United States of America

www.ballantinebooks.com

For Toni McGee Causey

Thank you for your unconditional love,
support, and friendship,
above and beyond the call of duty

ACKNOWLEDGMENTS

Writers write in a vacuum, spending hundreds of hours writing (and rewriting) that we sometimes forget that after the book is done, there are many people involved in making that book the best it can be. Editors, the art department, sales team, marketing team, copy department, production, and more. I particularly want to thank, as always, my editorial team—Charlotte Herscher and Dana Isaacson. I am so blessed to have you both.

Other amazing people at Random House: Kate Collins, Scott Shannon, Gina Wachtel, Kelli Fillingim, and the production team. And Linda Marrow, who bought my first book for Ballantine. Without her continuing support, this sixteenth novel wouldn't exist today.

My agent, Dan Conaway, who must have been a diplomat in a previous life, deserves much credit for his support and advice.

One of the best things about being a writer, other than the love of writing, is talking to experts across the country about their passion while learning in the process. I particularly want to thank Nathan Kensinger, photographer and journalist, for his *amazing* online photojournal. I spent many hours reading articles and viewing pictures, enhancing my love of New York City. Nathan also answered numerous questions about the many abandoned buildings and warehouses around the city. I took some liberties with his information. If you're interested in some of my inspiration, visit his website at: kensinger.blogspot.com.

A special thanks to Diane Lind for her wealth of information regarding tracking cell phones and identifying phone numbers. Also Wally Lind and his group of experts at Crime Scene Writers for answering numerous and odd questions about decomposition, missing persons, and jurisdiction. Any errors are mine alone.*

The Sacramento FBI Citizens Academy, which has been a continuing source of information and inspiration for many of my books, deserves a shout-out, particularly retired SAC Drew Parenti and media representative Steve Dupre, who always found time for my questions. I also want to thank the FBI Training Academy at Quantico for the time and information they shared during my tour in 2009. I hope to return later this year for further research.

A warm thank-you to Kirsten Benton, who won the use of her name in this book at the Helping Hands for Hank fund-raiser. The real Kirsten is nothing like the fictional character; only the name is the same!

And lastly, my family. My husband, Dan, for keeping the house functioning, bringing me Starbucks in the morning, and adjusting to my intense writing schedule. My mom for her attempts to keep me organized and being my number one fan and promoter. And my kids, for putting up with my deadlines and the haphazard meals that go with them. I am so proud of you all, and I love you.

*I also want to thank Teena Maness for her help with parole and probation issues in this book and the previous book!

PROLOGUE

The deafening music thundered through the warehouse, drowning out the howling wind outside and the raucous crowd that had gathered in this desolate spot in Brooklyn after midnight.

Any other night, Kirsten would be going wild on the dance floor until she collapsed from exhaustion or was whisked away by an unknown guy for anonymous sex that left her feeling both exhilarated and ashamed. For months, she'd lived for these weekends, complete freedom, the chance to be someone else, but tonight she just wanted to go home.

What home? You don't belong anywhere.

The pounding music made her feel sicker than what she was drinking. She knew better than to drink from the bar, but she'd been so thirsty, and she needed something to take the edge off. She'd built up a tolerance for most of the drugs that flowed with the spiked punch, and she always brought her own water. Maybe it was her nerves, or the fact that Jessie had sounded so strange, that set Kirsten on edge. She wasn't even supposed to be here this weekend, but Jessie had begged her to come. And where was she, anyway?

A tall, skinny blond guy came up to her with the

smile she knew all too well. She hadn't been in the mood for sex when she'd arrived an hour ago, but whatever was in the punch had definitely loosened her up. The guy wasn't half bad, probably in college. And Jessie was *late*.

"You want to party?" he asked, his hand rubbing her arm.

"On the dance floor."

He glanced skeptically over at the thick crowd. Not everyone came to the underground parties for sex, though the night often ended that way. Most came for the drugs and drinking and music.

She laughed and took his hand, rubbing her thumb lightly across his palm. "New?"

"Just thinking of logistics."

Her phone vibrated and she almost ignored it. She looked at the number and saw a message from Jessie.

"Hold that thought." She tapped her phone to see where her friend was.

i see u with that guy. we need 2 talk now. im getting worried. outside 10 min.

What was with the cloak-and-dagger? Kirsten looked around, but didn't see Jessie anywhere.

She replied.

What's going on?

"Hey, you want to screw your phone or me?"

"What's your name?"

"Ryan."

Jessie sent an immediate reply.

plz, k, need 2 talk 2 u. im freezing.

"I need to talk to a friend first, then I'm all yours."
She wrapped her arms around his neck and gave him
a full-body kiss.

He pushed her against the corrugated metal wall
and pressed his pelvis against hers. "You're hot," he
said in her ear.

She kissed him hard, his mouth different and unknown. The thrill of the moment hit her, and she forgot everything else. She forgot who she was, where
she was, losing herself in the right-now, any-how moment. She smiled as her mind wandered, her body almost forgotten.

"You like that?" a voice whispered in her ear.

"Yes," she said, though she didn't know why. Her
arms were tight around his neck. Who again? *Ryan.*

Her phone vibrated. She shook her head to clear
her mind, and over Ryan's shoulder she read Jessie's
latest message.

Don't be such a slut and meet me outside. Now, Ash.

Slut? What did that make Jessie? But something
was wrong. In the back of her mind, something
wasn't making sense. But her head was foggy, and
Ryan's hands were on her bare breasts. How had he
gotten so far so fast? She looked at the time on her
phone. That couldn't be right. Had they been making
out here against the wall for fifteen minutes?

She knew from experience that the guys at this
party who came for sex weren't easily put off, and her
promise to return wouldn't mean anything to him.

What if Jessie was in trouble? She'd been acting so weird, and calling her Friday morning had been so not like her . . .

Ash.

She'd called her Ash. Short for Ashleigh, her party name.

Jessie knew her real name. "Ashleigh" and "Jenna"— Jessie's party name—were only for show. Maybe she'd called her Ash because she was in her *Party Girl* mode.

While Kirsten had been thinking about Jessie's odd behavior, Ryan had taken his dick out and pulled her dress up. Everything moved in slow motion. It was as if she were watching her body from afar. She knew this feeling, but she hadn't drunk that much. Had she?

"Condom," she whispered.

"Already on, Sugar."

How'd she miss it? She felt him inside her, but didn't remember him entering; her legs were around him, but she didn't remember how they got there.

Then he was done. She didn't know if it took him two minutes or an hour, but they were both sweaty and he had a grin. "Shit, you're hot."

"I have to meet my friend."

"Hurry and we'll go backstage."

"Backstage" was a euphemism for getting horizontal in semiprivate. There were offices off the main warehouse, most empty, but people brought in blankets and mattresses, and there was even some old furniture still inside. If Kirsten were sober she wouldn't even think about it, because the place was filthy.

"Okay." She started for the door. She had her purse

tied around her wrist and felt inside for her phone, but it wasn't there. She looked and saw that the zipper was open; everything had fallen out. She didn't even know what time it was. She looked around the floor but didn't see her phone or money anywhere. She knew she should go back and look for it, but the loud music was making her feel ill again.

She walked outside. The icy air shocked her, but for a minute she felt amazing. And almost instantly sobered, at least enough to feel discomfort from whatever Ryan had done to her against the wall.

What had Jessie wanted her to do? Go out and turn . . . left?

But it had been much longer than ten minutes. Twenty, at least. Maybe more. An hour? She had no concept of time.

Kirsten turned left and walked as straight as she could. She quickly became cold. The body heat of the warehouse, the dancing, and the spotlights someone had brought in had been enough to keep her warm; now she wanted to get back. Or go home. But her train to Virginia didn't leave until tomorrow afternoon. She'd planned on partying, then crashing at a nearby motel. With what she made off the *Party Girl* site, she had plenty of money.

She felt around for her belt and breathed a sigh of relief when she felt her cash in the small zippered pouch. She didn't keep all her money in her purse, only a few bucks, because she didn't want to get stuck in the city flat broke if she lost it. No way was she going to call her mother for help. Maybe Ryan had found her phone and she could call Trey. Trey always said he would help her.

But she didn't want to call her ex-boyfriend. He'd lecture her about her bad behavior and she didn't want to hear it from him, or anyone.

Someone was lying on the ground. At first she thought there were two people screwing, but she was seeing double. She blinked rapidly and realized that only one person was there. A girl in a pink dress.

"Are you okay?" she said at the same time she realized that it was Jessie and she wasn't moving.

Kirsten opened her mouth to scream, but no sound came out. She was paralyzed, couldn't move, couldn't call for help, and Jessie was lying on the ground in an odd position . . .

She could have passed out. Kirsten took a step closer, but somehow she already knew that Jessie was dead. Both her eyes and mouth were open, and one arm was tilted at an unnatural angle.

Kirsten heard movement to the right, then a voice. But the voice sounded a million miles away, faint, as if through a tunnel.

Girls like you . . .

Had someone spoken? Was it in her head? Unsteady on her feet, for a second she feared she'd faint. She turned and walked toward the warehouse, but she couldn't see well. Everything was blurry.

Don't you dare, bitch.

Kirsten bolted at the rough whisper. She ran straight ahead, not knowing where she was going except away from Jessie's body. The voice wasn't real, couldn't be, because she didn't see anyone, only a shadow. Still, she ran as fast as she could. Her heels caught on the cracked cement and she almost fell hard, but she caught herself and took off her shoes and resumed running as fast as she could. Away from the warehouse, away from Jessie.

Jessie had texted her. She'd called her Ash.

Maybe it wasn't Jessie who sent her that message.

Someone had been waiting for *Ashleigh*. Whoever had killed Jessie planned to kill her, too.

Her feet ached, viciously cut on the crumbly asphalt and broken glass. She ran until she saw a small grouping of cars. Maybe she could hide there. Maybe someone had left the keys. She just wanted to go home . . .

She saw someone just sitting in the passenger seat of a small SUV. She didn't know if anyone was really following her, but she quickly glanced over her shoulder. No one. But she'd *heard the voice*! Hadn't she? Oh, God, she couldn't think!

Girls like you . . .

Hearing the voice again, she stumbled and fell, cutting her knees and the palms of her hands. Tears ran down her face.

What was she going to do? Jessie was dead.

Someone was running behind her. Or coming right at her. Kirsten was dizzy and couldn't think. She scrambled to her feet and tried to run again, but the excruciating pain in her feet brought her back down to the cement.

There was no escape.

ONE

As the cold wind whipped around her, FBI agent Suzanne Madeaux lifted the corner of the yellow crime-scene tarp covering the dead girl and swore under her breath.

Jane Doe was somewhere between sixteen and twenty, her blond hair streaked with pink highlights. The teenager's party dress was also pink, and Suzanne absently wondered if she changed her highlights to match her outfit. There was no outward sign of sexual assault or an apparent cause of death. Still, there was no doubt that this was another victim of the killer Suzanne had been tasked to stop.

Jane Doe wore only one shoe.

Dropping the tarp, Suzanne surveyed the scene, trying in vain to keep her long, dark-blond hair out of her face. The relentless wind howled across the cracked, weed-infested parking lot of the abandoned warehouse in Brooklyn. It had also felled a couple of trees nearby; small branches and sticks skittered across the pavement. That wind most likely had destroyed any evidence not inside Jane Doe's body.

Though the corpse didn't appear to be intentionally hidden, waist-high weeds and a small building that had once housed a generator or dumpsters concealed her from any passerby's cursory glance. Suzanne stepped away from the squat structure and looked across the Upper Bay. The tiny Gowanus Bay was to the north, the New Jersey skyline to the west. At night, it would be kind of pretty out here with the city lights across the water, if it weren't so friggin' cold.

A plainclothes NYPD cop approached with a half-smile that Suzanne wouldn't call friendly. "If it ain't Mad Dog Madeaux. We heard this was one of yours."

Suzanne rolled her eyes. Even with her eyes closed, she'd recognize Joey Hicks by his grating, intentionally exaggerated New York accent.

"No secret," she said, making notes to avoid conversation. Hicks wasn't much older than she. Physically fit, he probably thought he was good-looking, considering the swagger. She supposed he had some appeal, but the cocky "all Feds are assholes" attitude he'd displayed the first time they'd met on a murder case had landed him on Suzanne's permanent shit list years ago.

She looked around for his supervisor, but didn't see Vic Panetta. She'd much rather deal with the senior detective, whom she liked. "Who found the body?" Suzanne asked.

"Security guard."

"What's his story?"

"Found her on his morning rounds, about five-thirty."

It was eleven now. "Why hasn't the body been taken to the morgue?"

"No wagon available. Coroner is on the way. Another hour, they say. NYPD doesn't have the resources you Feds got."

She ignored the slight. "What was the guard doing

here last night? Does he patrol more than one building?"

"Yeah." Hicks looked at his notes. Though Suzanne didn't like him, he was a decent cop. "He clocked in at four a.m. for a twelve-hour shift. Rotates between vacant properties throughout Sunset Park and around the bay. Says he doesn't stick to a specific schedule, 'cause vandals watch for that."

"What about the night guard?"

"Night is either Thompson or Bruzzini. According to the day shift, Bruzzini is a slacker."

"I need their contact information." She hesitated. Then—remembering her boss's command to be more collegial to NYPD—she added, "I appreciate your help."

"Did hell freeze over since the last time we worked a case?" Hicks laughed. "I'll get Panetta; I'm sure he'll want to at least make a show of fighting for jurisdiction." He left, still grinning.

Suzanne ignored him. There were no jurisdictional issues—after the third similar murder, an FBI–NYPD task force had been formed. Her supervisor was administratively in charge, and she was the FBI point person on the case. Panetta was the senior ranking NYPD detective.

Tired of her hair flying in her face, Suzanne pulled a N.Y. Mets cap from her pocket and stuffed under it as much of her thick, tangled mess as possible. In her small notepad, she finished writing down her observations and the few facts she knew.

This victim, the fourth, was the first found in Brooklyn. Victim number one, a college freshman, had been killed up in Harlem on a street popular with squatters and the party crowd because every building was boarded up. That had been the eve of Halloween. The second victim had been discovered on the south side of the Bronx, ironically overlooking Rikers Island, on January second. The third victim—the one who brought the attention of the FBI to the serial murders—had been killed in Manhattanville, near Columbia University, eighteen days ago. By the time the task force was put together and evidence shared, for all practical purposes Suzanne had been working the case for less than two weeks.

Besides the one missing shoe and the age of the victims—all adult females under twenty-one—two other commonalities stood out: the victims had been suffocated with a plastic bag that the killer took with him, and they'd each been killed near an abandoned building with evidence of a recent party.

Secret or underground parties were nothing new. Some were relatively innocent, with drinking, dance music, and recreational drugs, while others were far wilder. Raves in the United States had started in Brooklyn in the abandoned underground railroad tunnels, and while they still existed, they'd peaked in popularity a while back. The new fad was sex parties with heavy drinking and hard-core drugs. Music and dancing were precursors to multi-partner anonymous sex. Even before these murders, there had been several drug-related deaths associated with sex parties. If the pattern held true, evidence inside this warehouse would show that this Jane Doe had participated in the latter type of party, which Detective Panetta called "extreme raves."

The press had dubbed the killer the Cinderella

Strangler when someone in the know had leaked the missing-shoe detail to the press. It may not have been a cop who had talked—there were dozens of people working any one crime scene—but most likely it had come from inside the NYPD. The press didn't seem to care that the victims weren't strangled—they were asphyxiated. The Cinderella Asphyxiator just didn't sound as good on the eleven o'clock news.

Suzanne had sent a memo to all private security companies in the five boroughs asking them to be more proactive in shutting down the rampant parties at abandoned sites, but it was like a game of whack-a-mole—when authorities shut down one location, two more sprang up.

Though only two of the first three victims were college students, she'd contacted local colleges and high schools to warn students that there was a killer targeting women at these parties. Unfortunately, Suzanne suspected that getting through the invincible it-won't-happen-to-me mentality of young adults was next to impossible. She could almost hear their reasons. *We won't go out alone. We won't leave with a stranger. We won't drink too much.* Plans for every day of the week, but when it was life or death, Suzanne didn't understand why they couldn't party in the relatively safe dorms and frat houses. Those venues had their own problems, but they probably didn't have a serial killer trolling their halls.

"Suzanne!"

She looked up and waved to Vic Panetta as he strode over. She liked the wiry Italian. He was her exact height, five foot nine, and wore a new wool coat, charcoal gray to match his full head of hair. "Hi, Vic," she said as he approached. "New coat?"

He deadpanned her. "Christmas present from my wife."

"Very nice."

"It cost too much money for a label no one can see," he grumbled. He gestured at the tarp. "We photographed the area, then put the tarp over the body so we don't lose any more evidence."

"Well, the way this wind has been going nonstop for the past couple days, I think we already lost it."

"You take a look?"

"Briefly."

"You noted the missing shoe?"

"Duly."

"Could be under the body."

"You think?"

"Nah." He shook his head, then pulled his phone from his coat pocket and read a message. "Good news, coroner is on the way. ETA ten minutes."

About time, Suzanne thought but didn't say out loud. "Hicks said you were talking to the security guard who found the body?"

"Yeah, he's former NYPD—permanent disability, works three days a week. Takes his job seriously. Got an earful about the night shift."

"Anything I need to know?"

"He suspects Ronald Bruzzini of being bought off. Too much cash in the guy's wallet, but no proof."

"Your guy knew about the parties?"

Panetta shook his head. "Not until after the fact, and he doesn't work nights. He thinks Bruzzini looks the other way. Finds evidence of all kinds of wild parties nearly every week. Hicks and I will follow up on both the night guards, see what shakes out."

"So you think this was one of your extreme raves?" she teased.

He rolled his eyes and let out an exasperated breath. "And then some. They did some cleaning up inside, but left the garbage on the other side of the building. The wind sent it all over kingdom come. The crime scene unit is working inside and out, but contamination is a huge problem. We're printing the place, but getting anything usable—"

"I know. A couple hundred stoned kids, a complete mess, limited resources. If you need our lab, let me know."

"Will do."

NYPD had a decent crime lab, and since it was local Suzanne preferred to keep evidence here. Because Panetta was a well-respected, well-liked twenty-two-year veteran, he worked the system well, and most of the time could get results faster than if Suzanne shipped evidence to the FBI lab at Quantico.

"The press is going to be all over this," Panetta mumbled.

"No comment." She never spoke to the press—not after her diatribe five years ago during a missing-child case. That had landed her on the evening news and in front of the Office of Professional Responsibility. Further, she'd been left with the irritating and unflattering moniker "Mad Dog Madeaux."

"We got a lot of nothing," Panetta said.

There was extensive physical evidence on all of the victims' bodies, but nothing they could use to track the killer. The first three victims had had at least two sex partners within twenty-four hours of their death, but the DNA left behind had either been contaminated or hadn't brought up a match in the system. They had evidence of seven different males total among the first three victims, but none were the same, suggesting that the killer went to extraordinary lengths to avoid leaving DNA on his victims, and possibly didn't have sex with them. Because of the multiple sex partners and the nature of these parties, the coroner could not determine whether the victims had been raped or had had consensual sex.

Not having conclusive evidence as to a killer's motive made profiling him that much harder. A sexual sadist had a different profile than, for example, a man who killed prostitutes because he thought they were whores. Serial killers who raped or tortured their victims would have a different profile than those who didn't sexually molest their victims. The task force couldn't even pinpoint whether this killer was one of the partygoers or whether he waited nearby for a lone female to attack.

Whatever was used to suffocate the victims was taken by the killer—along with one of the victims' shoes—and their bodies weren't moved. They were dead when they fell to the ground.

Panetta said, "By the way, this one didn't die last night."

"I didn't inspect the body that closely."

"The day guard only works Wednesday through Saturday. He doubts that the other day guy does much more than a slapdash inspection of the properties. Our Jane Doe might have been here as early as Saturday night."

"Because?"

"Our ex-cop walked through here on Saturday afternoon and she wasn't here then."

"And you don't think he's the killer?" She was only half joking.

"No, but I'll check him out anyway. I did take a long look at the body, and rigor has come and gone. She's probably been here more than forty-eight hours. The coroner should be able to give us a range."

"I'll leave the forensics in your capable hands. I need her identity ASAP, and in the meantime I'll review the other three victims and reinterview friends. Someone knows something. I'm getting damn pissed at these bratty college kids who zip their lips because they don't want to get in trouble for illegal drugs and parties, but don't seem to care that a killer is hunting on their turf."

TWO

Kirsten Benton had been missing for five days.

Because she'd been dubbed a habitual runaway for her tendency to disappear on the weekends, the Woodbridge, Virginia, police didn't take this episode seriously. Sean Rogan, however, took it very seriously, because Kirsten had broken her pattern.

The other half-dozen times she'd disappeared, she'd returned home by Sunday night. Now it was Wednesday, and her cell phone was going straight to voice mail. Sean had already tried to trace the GPS on her phone but got nowhere. He suspected that she'd either turned it off or the battery was dead.

It could have been an easy case, but now Sean and his partner, Patrick Kincaid, had a lot of legwork—and fingerwork on the computer—ahead to track down the high school senior. Patrick was at the Woodbridge police department talking to the detective in charge of missing persons about Kirsten and retrieving a copy of all the missing-person reports her mother had filed over the past six months. They hoped there was a pattern and they could figure out where she went.

Sean was doing the fingerwork at the Benton household on Kirsten's computer. Teenagers lived for their electronic toys, and between her social networking accounts and emails, he hoped to track her down before the end of the day.

Sitting at Kirsten's desk in her bedroom, he first needed to get rid of Kirsten's hovering mother, Evelyn, who stood behind him as he hacked her daughter's computer password. He ran his hands through his brown hair in frustration but it fell back over his eyes. How was he going to kick a worried mother out?

"Your partner is talking to the police, but I don't know that it's going to do any good."

Evelyn was Sean's distant relative by marriage—well, he couldn't even say that, since she'd divorced his uncle, Tim Benton, who was his mother's stepbrother and not even a blood relative. But Sean's brother Duke took family seriously—no matter how related or estranged or scattered.

Sean said, "If anyone can get the police to take Kirsten's disappearance seriously, it's Patrick. He used to be one of them."

Patrick had joined RCK two years ago when Sean was still living in Sacramento. Three months ago, they had moved to Washington, D.C., and opened RCK East, both hoping to forge their own career paths away from the controlling guidance of their respective older brothers, who were principals in the protective-services company. RCK didn't normally handle missing-person cases—the closest they came were overseas kidnappings—but the Bentons were family.

"Do you want me to call her friends again?" Evelyn asked.

"No, they're in school right now. Did you make the list for me?"

"Yes—"

"Can you go over it again? Make sure you have their phone numbers and any other information you can think of—how much time Kirsten spent with them, any boyfriends or ex-boyfriends. Also, her school schedule and grades. Teachers' emails and phone numbers—we'll want to talk to them to see if Kirsten's behavior has recently changed."

He was trying to give Evelyn something to do, not start a conversation—he and Patrick had listened to her worries for two hours the night before and had all the information they needed to get started—but Evelyn continuted, "She hasn't been herself since I moved here. It was the right thing to do. I couldn't live in L.A. after what Tim did! Right?"

Sean had heard all about her ex-husband's affairs and the nasty divorce and subsequent move three thousand miles away. Her then fourteen-year-old daughter hadn't wanted to move east, but this was where Evelyn had found a job. Evelyn admitted at the beginning that she and Kirsten had had a strained relationship ever since the move to Virginia three years ago. The only reason Sean was here now was because Kirsten had never been gone *this* long, and Tim Benton had hired RCK to find her.

"Let's find Kirsten first, then you two need to have a heart-to-heart, okay?"

"You know she's only looking at colleges in California? She hates me."

He flashed his dimple and blue eyes, and asked her kindly, "Evelyn, can you work on that list for me?"

She finally left the room. Sean felt bad for the

woman, but he couldn't do his job if he had to hold
her hand. Earlier, he'd suggested that Evelyn ask a
friend to come over for the day, but when he and
Patrick had arrived, she'd been alone.

While his laptop ran through a code-breaking program Sean had written, he surveyed Kirsten's sparsely
furnished room. Most teenage girls—if his older sister
had been a good example—had more stuff than
Kirsten Benton. Eden could have opened up a small
department store with all her clothing and makeup,
half of it strewn across the floor. Missing here were a
teenage girl's usual tiny bottles of makeup and per-
fume, along with the stuffed animals and knick-
knacks and general clutter. There weren't even
posters on the walls, save for a single beach scene
above the desk.

He glanced at his program, which still had a few
minutes left to run, then walked around the room
taking a short video with his phone. The only place in
the room with any sign of the girl's personality was
her desk. Almost hidden on a wall that could be
clearly seen only when sitting at her desk was a corkboard filled with photographs of Kirsten and her
friends, movie ticket stubs, and sticky notes with messages like *English essay due MON!!!* and *Movies
Wednesday—team.*

Kirsten's desk had books stacked up against the
wall, and a short bookcase to the left was filled with
the popular teenage books of the day—books about
wizards and vampires and fallen angels. He flipped
through a wall calendar, but it didn't appear that she
used it for anything specific. A friend's birthday was

marked in January, her dad's in May. June 5 had a big red circle around it and a happy face, but he didn't know what that signified since he knew Kirsten would be eighteen in April.

He picked up a stack of thick college brochures. University of San Diego, U.C. Santa Barbara, USC, Pepperdine. All Southern California colleges.

Sean glanced at the beach poster, and the location registered. It was the Malibu pier. He didn't need to be a shrink to figure out that Kirsten Benton was homesick—it was apparent from the barren room, the colleges she'd applied to, and the poster that practically shouted, "I miss my home!"

But the rest of the space was like a hotel room. The bed was plain, with only a white down comforter— no extra pillows or stuffed animals or throw blanket. The nightstand didn't even have a lamp or digital clock—the clock was on her desk. The dresser was uncluttered, the floor bare. He slid back the closet door and noted that the floor was stacked high with stuffed animals and throw pillows. Why weren't they on her bed? Was she compulsively neat?

Three years was a long time to have a room that wasn't lived in.

Sean wished he'd asked Lucy to join him, and not just because he hadn't spent enough time with her lately. She understood teenagers and would know if something was amiss. He emailed her the short video along with a message explaining Kirsten's history.

Evelyn had her own theory: that Kirsten had a new boyfriend, probably in college. She'd confronted her the first time she ran away, but Kirsten had denied it.

According to Evelyn, Kirsten had said she just needed "some space" and refused to tell her mother where she'd gone, even though Evelyn had grounded her and taken away her car.

If something was going on with Kirsten, her friends would be the most likely to know, but none of them had given Evelyn any useful information.

His computer beeped to signal that he'd broken her code. Sean sat down and assessed Kirsten's system. He scanned her files and programs, sorting the files by most recent. Several word-processing documents with titles like ENG_MOCKINGBIRD were dated over the last couple of weeks. She appeared to be a diligent student. To ensure that the files were what they purported to be, he opened them; they were legit. He also noticed that she had several .mov files—videos with numbers for names—but with nothing in them. They appeared to be computer shortcuts, but didn't lead anywhere and had the appearance of temporary files.

Her browsing history was set to delete itself every time she logged off. She'd last logged off on Friday at 4:10 p.m. There were logs he could access and decode to uncover her browsing history, but first he checked her email. Her system password worked for her email as well.

A series of unread emails popped up—she hadn't accessed her email since she logged off on Friday. Someone named Trey Danielson had emailed her eight times in the last three days. The messages were virtually identical, but increased in urgency from *Where are you? You okay?* to the last message from last night:

Call me, text me, anything! I'm worried about you. Your phone is going directly to voice mail. I don't know where you are. I talked to Stacey this morning, but she's being a bitch. Your mom is calling around. Please, K, no questions, just call me.

Sean frowned, logged onto Kirsten's Facebook profile, and noted that several friends had posted comments like:

Missed you in Drama!

Mrs. Robertson is a total bitch! You're so lucky you missed the pop quiz.

Hey, you sick? Hope you can make my party Friday!

Only Trey Danielson seemed truly concerned. He was the best place to start.

Sean responded to the last email Trey had sent to Kirsten:

Trey, I just got home, my mom's at work, she cut off my cell phone. Can you come over ASAP? I need to talk to you.

He hoped the kid took the bait.

Sean was scanning the computer logs when Patrick called. "I'm leaving the police station now," he said. "Evelyn only filed a police report the first time Kirsten disappeared. That's not unusual. Parents of habitual runaways tend to be embarrassed by their kids' behavior, worried that people will think they can't control their kids. However, I got the police interested in this disappearance, enough that they'll bump her to a missing person instead of a runaway. They'll send her photo and vitals to all hospitals and law enforcement in a hundred-mile radius."

"Good."

"I also contacted my friend at NCMEC and he's going to put Kirsten in the system as soon as Woodbridge PD sends him the data, so that's another avenue. They can spread the information far better than any local office."

The National Center for Missing and Exploited Children worked closely with both law enforcement and private investigators in finding minors under all circumstances, runaway or criminal. Having their resources on this case was a big plus.

Sean filled Patrick in on Kirsten's emails as well as on Trey Danielson. "I sent him an email from Kirsten; we'll see if he bites. He's a senior at her school, and based on the pictures of them in his profile it looks like he and Kirsten used to go out. It sounds like he'll be easier to crack than her girlfriends—he's sent her numerous messages."

"Unless it's a CYA."

"CYA?" Sean asked.

"He's covering his ass by sending concerned emails, even if he was the one who had something to do with her disappearance. I've seen it before in domestic cases."

"We'll find out—I asked him to come over ASAP. If he killed her, he might not, but then again if he sent all those worried emails to cover up a crime, he'd come for the same reason, right? Either way, my gut says he'll show."

"You're thinking like a cop now."

Pretending to be insulted, Sean said, "That was low."

Patrick laughed. "Whatever reason he comes, we need to get rid of Evelyn. I think she's too stressed to help right now. I'll think up an errand for her by the time I get there."

"Good idea. I sent Lucy pictures of Kirsten's room and asked her for advice."

Patrick didn't say anything.

"Did I lose you?" Sean prompted.

"Why get Lucy involved?"

Patrick's tone was odd, almost defensive. Sean said, "She's on edge waiting to hear back about her FBI interview. She could use something to distract her. This kind of case is right up her alley, and she might see something we missed." Sean hesitated, then asked, "You got a problem asking Lucy to consult?"

"Of course not," Patrick said and hung up.

Right, Sean thought, *no problem at all.*

Ever since Patrick had found out about Sean's relationship with his sister, he'd been acting weird. Sean understood the overprotective big-brother attitude, but Lucy was twenty-five; it wasn't as if she were a naïve teenager. And she was *good* at this type of work. Lucy was one of the few people Sean knew who not only understood how computer systems and the Internet operated, but understood people as well. She could read a chat transcript and deduce whether the people chatting were predators, victims, or bored kids.

Did Patrick not want Lucy involved with the case because of her relationship with Sean? Or because of her tragic past?

It didn't matter to Sean. As far as he was concerned, Lucy was capable and willing to help, and he'd use all available resources. The added benefit was that they'd be spending more time together. A win–win, as far as Sean was concerned.

THREE

Lucy stepped out of the shower after her late morning run and wrapped her body in a fluffy white robe, a Christmas present two years ago from her sister-in-law Kate. She brushed through her thick black hair, then loosely braided it down her back to keep it out of her way until she had time to dry it. Lucy sat down at her computer and retrieved her email. Lots of birthday wishes. She responded to those from her family, hesitating when she read a message from her sister Carina, who not only wished her a happy birthday but also expressed hopes for Lucy's speedy acceptance into the FBI.

"You and me both, Carina," Lucy mumbled and sent off a quick thank-you.

It could take anywhere from three days to three weeks to hear back from the FBI regarding her interview with the hiring panel, but most applicants who got as far as she did made it to the final stage. Ever since Lucy's internship with the Washington, D.C., Medical Examiner's office ended last week, she'd felt as if she were in limbo.

She just wanted to start her training at Quantico.

Though she hadn't confided in anyone, not her family or even Sean, she'd been nervous about the interview. She'd answered the panel's questions calmly

and honestly, even the hard ones. Like the questions
about her imprisoned former boss Fran Buckley and
Lucy's ex-boyfriend Cody Lorenzo, and what happened that horrific day last month when a paroled ex-
felon nearly killed her and another woman.

And the hardest question of all: What had she been
thinking when she shot and killed her rapist, Adam
Scott, nearly seven years ago?

She'd told them that she believed he would kill her
if he had the chance. When he moved toward her,
she'd shot him.

It was mostly true, but it wasn't the entire truth.

Her stomach tightened uncomfortably. Ever since
her past had come back to bite her in the ass five
weeks ago, she'd been on edge. Nearly seven years . . .
six years, eight months, and two weeks . . . had
passed and she couldn't escape the memories. She'd
managed them just fine for years, but now they were
stuck in her head like a hated song that repeatedly
played in her mind, with no way to make it stop.

A new email popped into her window containing a
large file from Sean. She boxed up her anxiety about
her past and the FBI interview, and clicked on the
message.

> Lucy—
> I'm sending you a video I took of Kirsten's room. Some-
> thing doesn't look right, but I can't figure out exactly what's
> bothering me. Thoughts?
> I know you miss me. ☺ Happy Birthday, don't eat cake
> without me.
> Yours,
> Sean

Lucy smiled, barely suppressing a laugh. Sean always did that for her—lightened her mood. *I know you miss me.* She didn't need to inflate his ego any more by acknowledging the fact. But she was thrilled to have something to occupy her mind.

Sean was unlike most of the guys—rare though they were—she'd dated. It had been unplanned, and she had been entirely unprepared for her strong feelings toward him. She appreciated that he didn't push her. She wanted to spend all her free time with him, but found herself spending less, as if he were an addictive drug that she needed to get out of her system.

Especially after she told Patrick two weeks ago about her and Sean. She'd tried to avoid it as long as she could, though not because Patrick didn't like Sean—they were partners, and had developed a close friendship in the three years they'd worked together for RCK. She really didn't know why she didn't want to tell Patrick. With Dillon and Kate it was different; they'd been around when she and Sean sort of just happened, so it wasn't as though she'd been hiding it. But when Patrick returned from his assignment in California, at first it had seemed too awkward to sit him down and announce the relationship. So she'd finally told him when they were walking back from church in a casual, oh, you know, I like Sean and I think he likes me too kind of way.

"I know," he'd growled.

When he hadn't said anything else, she pushed, friendly; she wanted his blessing. Sean was his partner, she was his sister, and she wanted—*needed*—Patrick's approval.

He just shrugged and said she was a big girl. But

he'd wanted to say something else. What were Patrick's concerns? She knew she shouldn't feel this way, that Sean would tell her Patrick would come around, but Sean didn't understand her close relationship with her brother. Patrick was the one person in her family she was loath to disappoint. She knew it had less to do with the fact that he was her brother, and everything to do with her guilt over the near-fatal injuries he'd sustained on the orders of her attacker, Adam Scott.

Or, maybe, she'd been anticipating Patrick's disapproval.

She kept telling herself that she didn't want an excuse to leave Sean, but she didn't want to fall in love or care about anyone, not now. She hadn't been looking for him, but there he was. Or maybe it was more about how *he* felt about *her*. It wasn't anything he said, it was how he looked at her. How he touched her. He made her feel like she was the only person in the room, special, valuable, *his*. Without verbally staking claim to her, Sean made it clear that he was the man in her life. It was intoxicating and terrifying.

Sean made her forget, at least for a while, that she wasn't normal.

"Stop overanalyzing everything," she mumbled to herself. Right—that was like telling her body to stop breathing.

She clicked on the one-minute video that Sean had sent. It started at the doorway of Kirsten Benton's room and panned around 360 degrees. Bare walls above the plain bed. No personal effects. The dresser, the window—all generic. Only the desk and small bookshelf were cluttered with books and papers, and the only photographs were on a wall where they couldn't be seen by anyone except at a specific angle.

The computer faced the bed.

Heart pounding, she knew what she was looking at, even as she watched the video again in slow motion. She paused the recording when the computer came back into view.

There was a small, round ball on top. A webcam. It faced the bed.

Her face flushed and bile rose in her throat. It took all her willpower not to run to the bathroom and puke. With tight hands, she untwisted the cap on her water bottle and sipped, ridding her mouth of the horrid taste.

She didn't want to respond to Sean. She wanted to pretend that she hadn't seen the video, that she wasn't involved. If she articulated her fears, it would make the truth sound simple, and it was anything but simple.

Maybe she was wrong. There could be another explanation. She always thought the worst; the worst wasn't always the case.

She emailed Sean.

Are there any video files on the computer? They'd be .wmv or .mov or another standard format. Can you access them?

She wasn't surprised when her phone rang less than a minute later.

"Sean," she answered when she saw the caller ID.

"There are dozens of video files," he said. "But they're all shortcuts or temp files—they're empty, nothing attached. I'm running an undelete program. How did you know?"

"I might be wrong." She didn't believe she was. "I *hope* I'm wrong. But there's a webcam facing her bed."

Sean didn't say anything, but the weight of the truth hung between them on the phone. "Shit," he finally said.

"I've seen it many times, particularly on the amateur sex sites. Often, the women don't know they're being recorded. But—"

"But Kirsten did."

"It's her bedroom and her computer," Lucy said.

"I haven't found anything on her computer yet," Sean said. Then he added, "Why would a young, beautiful girl with a bright future take naked pictures of herself and send or post them on the Internet?"

It was more than naked pictures, Lucy suspected, from just what little she already knew about Kirsten's setup and the deleted video files. "Twenty-two percent of teenage girls have posted naked photos of themselves on the Internet," she said, keeping her voice even. The stats had infuriated her when she first learned of them, followed by a deep, numbing sadness. Once those pictures were out on the Web, there was no getting them back. One nude photograph in twenty-four hours would be downloaded on thousands of computers around the world.

"I don't have answers," she said, though she suspected Sean's question had been rhetorical.

"I'll let you know if I find anything." Sean didn't sound like his typical upbeat self. His enthusiasm for everything life had to offer drew Lucy to him, and she hated hearing him so down.

"You can send everything to me," she offered,

though the last thing she wanted to do was go through the teenager's computer files, knowing what she'd most likely discover. "I know what to look for."

He didn't say anything for a moment.

"Sean, I can handle seeing whatever is on her computer."

"I know you can. It's—"

"Don't coddle me. Please." She didn't want to be protected from the evils in the world. It would be her job soon enough, and nothing she saw on Kirsten Benton's computer could compare with what she'd already witnessed firsthand in her life.

"If you have time, I'd appreciate your help. I'll share out her computer and send you a password to access the hard drive."

"I have all the time in the world right now, and I want to help. I wouldn't offer if I didn't."

"It's already done. Check your email."

As he spoke, her email beeped. "You're good," she said.

"I know. Happy birthday, Princess." Sean hung up and Lucy was smiling again.

She logged onto Kirsten's computer and started working her way through the directories one by one.

If her initial instincts were correct, she'd find specific coded headers in the temporary files that were created whenever any program was open on the computer. Most of the data were unreadable, and she wouldn't be able to re-create data that hadn't been specifically saved on Kirsten's computer. However, she could strip the symbols and be able to identify the chat rooms, if any, that Kirsten had entered, including tracking information like the ISP address, time stamps, and similar identifiers.

When she'd volunteered for *Women and Children First!* before it was shut down, she'd learned the ins and outs of how and where sexual predators hunted for their victims. WCF, a victim-rights group that took a proactive role in tracking predators in cyberspace, taught her more about cybercrime than five years of college and postgraduate school. She could discern whether someone was trolling for victims or identify potential victims by how they communicated. It had bemused her that her linguistics skills and fluency in four languages had helped her decipher chat room shorthand, which was a language unto itself.

She created a spreadsheet with the identifiers in Kirsten's temp files. It quickly became clear that Kirsten had frequented a website where she participated in multiple video chats. Similar to the increasingly popular Skype, the primary difference was that the external chat didn't require any additional software over and beyond the webcam attached to the computer. The events weren't recorded on the hard drive, though because of the live streaming, a temp file had been created with start and stop times that helped Lucy catalogue them.

Savvy predators could erase and delete the data within the temp file, but Kirsten wasn't a predator. Yet, based on the extent of the log Lucy was creating, Kirsten didn't appear to be a victim, either. The videos could be innocuous, friends chatting face-to-face over the computer screen. Lucy wanted to believe that, but her mind kept going back to the generic room that Kirsten's webcam would show behind her.

It took her an hour to log all the temp files, and then she created a graphical representation of the data. It was clear that the video chats all originated from the same host. Most of the chats were between ten and twenty minutes, with a few longer than half an hour. Most of them had taken place between four and six in the afternoon, with about 20 percent at night. The afterschool hours were when sexual predators did most of their work—when kids were home without parents and could freely chat on the computer.

Lucy frowned. Kirsten was seventeen, a high school senior. There was no way of knowing whether she was chatting with the same person or different people, because the temp file logged only Kirsten's computer and the server that hosted the chats.

Kirsten might very well have a boyfriend, and maybe they talked nearly every day over webcam. If that were the case, then she most likely ran off to meet him.

Had she been meeting with the same person the past weekends she had disappeared? Had she gone off with someone voluntarily, or was she being held against her will?

Was Kirsten already dead?

Because no matter how careful you thought you were being, whenever you met an online friend in person, you put yourself at risk. Especially in the world in which Kirsten was playing around.

Lucy consciously focused on the task at hand. She wanted to shake sense into Kirsten, but more, she wanted to find and protect her, to shield her from the depravity she'd probably already seen and experienced.

"You can't save the world," Lucy said aloud. Her brother Dillon constantly reminded her that she took things too personally, that she wanted to help everyone, and some people didn't want help.

Lucy put her charts aside and went through the other files. She saw the empty .mov files that Sean had mentioned, and realized they were time stamped to correlate to the chat log files. That was odd, because there shouldn't be two files created with one exchange. But there was definitely no data in them, and no way to re-create the images.

One file stood out because it was in a completely different directory. She downloaded an undelete program to Kirsten's computer, then ran it, watching the computer screen as files were re-created. Many were corrupted or unable to be rebuilt—a common problem if they'd been deleted long ago. Some of those could be recoverable by law enforcement—the FBI had a state-of-the-art recovery process that could re-create more than 90 percent of deleted files, unless the person went to extraordinary lengths to permanently delete the data through a multistep process.

While she waited for her program to finish the laborious process, she wrote up a report for Sean with her ideas as to what the data meant. She was about to send it off when she saw a .mov file undelete. She opened it.

The webcam footage was clearly of Kirsten's room. Kirsten and a male teen were naked on her bed, his mouth on one of her breasts, her hands holding his head.

Lucy stared, stunned. Why was she surprised? Maybe because she had thought that the generic room was for sex chats only—but an amateur sex video was simply one more step down the same dark path.

And while Kirsten and her young companion were definitely amateurs, both teenagers knew the webcam was on, as they moved and adjusted their positions to make sure it caught all the action. It appeared consensual, the two intentionally creating an amateur sex video; Lucy couldn't pretend that Kirsten didn't know.

She couldn't watch anymore. Her hands were shaking when she clicked *stop*, and she got up and paced, her legs weak; she would have puked if she had anything in her stomach.

"What have you been doing, Kirsten?" she whispered to no one.

She couldn't stop shaking. Her fears of being watched by unknown people crawled under her skin like microscopic worms, making the hair rise on the back of her neck. But *she* wasn't being watched. And this wasn't rape; this wasn't a hidden camera. These were two teenagers voluntarily having sex for the world to see.

Lucy became angry, not at herself, but at Kirsten and her boyfriend. What possessed them to do such a thing? Did they even consider the consequences? That once that video was out, it was in cyberspace forever?

They *could* have recorded it just for themselves.

Lucy sat back down and considered how to approach searching for this video online. She didn't want to search the known amateur sex sites—she

knew what would happen to her if she went too deep
into that world. Verbal chats she could manage because they were just words, but images brought back
her nightmares, and with everything that had happened in the last five weeks it was all she could do to
keep those memories at bay. She knew herself well
enough to know that going to the sex sites would be
the tipping point.

Yet what kind of FBI agent would she be if she
couldn't conquer that fear? Because she would likely
have to conduct just this sort of investigation if she
were assigned to cybercrimes, which was her expertise and her dream job. She had to either find a way to
defeat the nightmares and make sure they never returned or learn to live with them.

They'd gone away before; they would go away
again. She had to believe this.

Taking another gulp of water as if to fuel her
courage, Lucy scrolled through Kirsten's browsing
history, which she knew should have a log of all up-
loads. Though Kirsten's history was set to erase every
time she logged off, that didn't mean it couldn't be re-
created. Such a log would be the best bet to find out
where if anywhere Kirsten had uploaded the video,
rather than randomly scanning known amateur sex
sites.

It took Lucy only fifteen minutes to re-create Kris-
ten's browsing history and find a promising site called
Party Girl.

Lucy clicked the link. *Party Girl* was a social networking site obviously aimed at men interested in
online sex. The ads alone promoted live sex cams,
sexting, and pornographic videos. Repugnant to

Lucy, who knew too much of what went on behind the scenes, but all legal—at least on the surface.

Both men and women—ostensibly all over eighteen—had profile pages where they could post their personal videos and photographs. There were links to group chats, private chats, webcam chats, and more.

Kirsten had a profile on the *Party Girl* site, but not under her own name. Her browser led to the Web page of *Ashleigh,* though Ashleigh's pictures were clearly Kirsten's. They were revealing, but not pornographic. Ashleigh's Web profile indicated that she was "into" meeting men online and stated that she was nineteen. Lucy would have to create a membership on the site to access further private information on Ashleigh.

She debated her options. Sean could hack Kirsten's *Party Girl* password, but it would take time. If Lucy registered, she could find out now what *exactly* Kirsten had posted on the Internet. Lucy's computer had extensive firewalls—not only because of her own personal security concerns, but also because Kate taught cybercrime at Quantico. They probably had the best-protected computers outside of the FBI offices.

Creating a profile cost nothing, though if Lucy wanted to view videos or post anything she'd be required to pay a monthly or annual fee. She opted for the free profile and created a false identity, similar to many she'd created in the past while working for WCF. She didn't post a picture, and a pop-up told her that to receive the full benefits of social interaction on *Party Girl,* posting photographs and videos was encouraged. She exited the pop-up and continued with the brief questionnaire.

She became "Amber," a blond nineteen-year-old college student from the East Coast who was interested in friends and relationships. As soon as Lucy received the confirmation email, she logged on.

The site was everything she'd feared. Not only had Kirsten posted part of the video of her having sex, it was clear that she was popular. Ashleigh's page had thousands of hits since going live eight months ago.

Lucy viewed her own page. She had a private *Party Girl* email and the option of having personal messages go to that "blind" email or her personal email. She opted for personal, because she'd created it just for this site and wanted to know if anyone contacted her without having to log onto *Party Girl* every day.

There was also an option to activate "selling," which she almost clicked, then went back to Kirsten's site and scoured it. Sure enough, she had videos that could be purchased individually, or viewed for free—with a paid *Party Girl* membership. Chat rooms were also available, both free and paid.

Sean was going to want to access Kirsten's profile as soon as possible. Lucy sent him the information she'd thus far uncovered and added a message.

I think you'll find the answers you need in Kirsten's profile. I can't tell if her video chats were with the same person, or upward of fifty different people, but you'll definitely want to track down the guy she was having sex with on the video. I saved it on her desktop so you can look at it. I'm going to look into this *Party Girl* site some more. There's nothing illegal with these types of online sex sites; they're akin to 900 numbers. If you get into her profile, see if you can find a log of who she has chatted with. It may be in her private PG email, and also see if there are any message archives. If you're busy, send me her password and I'll go through her profile myself.

She sent Sean the message, then realized she was still in her bathrobe and it was well after noon. She quickly dressed in jeans and a sweater, then jogged down the stairs to make a sandwich. She'd just taken her first bite when she heard the postman drop the mail into the box outside the front door. She retrieved it, sorting through bills and junk mail. In the middle of it all was a letter addressed to Ms. Lucia Kincaid from the Federal Bureau of Investigation.

Heart racing, excited and nervous, she quickly opened it.

Lucy stared at the single page. She didn't blink; she didn't move; she didn't even read it twice. Her eyes were fixed on one phrase in the middle of legalese:

your application is denied

She refolded the single piece of paper, slipped it back into the envelope, and slowly walked up the stairs to her room, each step a small mountain, hands shaking, sandwich forgotten.

She'd failed. The FBI didn't want her.

She fell onto her bed and stared at the ceiling, hope washed away along with her future.

She wasn't going to be an FBI agent. Everything she'd been working toward for nearly seven years, gone. She was twenty-five years old and she had no idea what she was going to do with her life.

It's not fair!

She squeezed back tears. How dare she even think

about fairness! Her life had never been *fair,* but who
in the hell had promised her it would be? Lucy could
blame no one but herself. Kate and her friends and
family had been fully supportive, doing everything
they could to prepare her for the FBI. She'd taken
mock written tests, gone through practice interviews,
used the recommendations of high-ranking FBI agents
to get her in the door—she had more advantages than
most applicants, and she'd still failed.

They'd rejected her.

It was on her, *only* her.

FOUR

Trey Danielson slumped into a kitchen chair in the Bentons' kitchen and glared at Sean and Patrick. "You tricked me," he said.

Sean sat across from Trey, still angry about the video Lucy had uncovered on Kirsten's computer. Lucy should never have had to watch it, but more than his concern about Lucy's sensitivities, Sean was furious that the high school senior had done such a dumbass thing in the first place.

"Where's Kirsten?" he demanded.

Trey shook his head. "I thought she was here! She emailed me—I *thought* she emailed me."

"Kirsten has been missing since Friday afternoon. It's Wednesday."

Trey frowned and looked at the table. Sean wondered whether he was trying to think of a lie or was sincerely worried about his girlfriend.

"You emailed Kirsten several times," Patrick said. "You posted concerned comments to her Web page, wanted her to call you ASAP, and you have no idea where she might have gone?"

"I wish I did. God, I think something's happened to her."

"Why do you think that?" Sean demanded.

Trey didn't answer.

"Trey," Patrick said, "you had a physical relationship with Kirsten. If something happened to her, the police are going to look at you first."

"That's insane!" Trey said. "We broke up months ago! We're *friends*."

"When we show the cops the sex tape you made," Sean said, "you think they're going to believe anything you say?"

Trey's face paled. "What?"

"I saw most of it; don't bother lying." Sean couldn't keep the anger from his voice.

"But—I—" The kid was practically blushing and he looked down at his hands. "You can't show anyone. My parents—shit, they'll kill me. I thought she deleted it!"

"She did," Sean said. "We undeleted it."

Trey looked at him skeptically. "Really?"

"Let's backtrack. When did you and Kirsten start seeing each other?"

"We've been friends since she moved here."

"You know what I mean."

Trey shrugged. "It wasn't like that. I mean, we were friends, and then we went to homecoming last year and started being more than just friends."

"And you broke up when?"

"Right before school started."

"Why?"

"Who the fuck cares why?"

"We do."

Trey scowled. "That has nothing to do with this."

Sean pushed, trying to get the truth out of Trey. "Did you put that sex tape on the Internet? Or pressure Kirsten to do it? Is that why Kirsten broke up with you?"

"*I* broke it off with Kirsten. I didn't want to, but—" He cut himself off.

Sean grew irritated. "Look, Trey, I'm tired of twenty questions, so I'm going to lay it all out for you. I'm a computer security specialist and I'm retrieving every single piece of data off Kirsten's computer, even files she deleted." Sean might not be able to re-create *all* the files, but the kid didn't need to know that. "We know Kirsten has skipped town at least five times since the start of the school year— which, according to you, is right after you broke it off with her. But this time, she didn't come back. Some people think she ran away, possibly with a boyfriend, but her mom and dad deserve to know the truth. And I think you know where she went."

Trey set his mouth in a tight line. He stared at the back of his hands as if counting the hairs.

Patrick picked up where Sean left off. "You made a big show of concern on the Internet—on Kirsten's Web page, in her email. I'll bet if we pulled your phone records it'd show you called her number a dozen times. You know, I used to be a cop, and I worked a case where a guy killed his wife, then made a big show of trying to reach her—calling her friends, calling her cell phone that he'd tossed in the lake along with her dead body—all before filing a police report the next day. But his cleverness tripped him up. The police traced his outgoing cell calls back to the lake where he dumped her body—he made the first so-called worried phone call right after he killed her."

Trey stared, pale. "You think Kirsten's *dead*?"

"The jury's still out," Sean said, "but we're concerned." He considered what Lucy had said about the layout of her room, and bluffed based on the evidence. "We found a log of multiple deleted video files, and considering the layout of her bedroom and the digital recording of you and her getting down and dirty, we don't believe that was a one-time show."

"Did you post the video on the Internet?" Patrick demanded.

"I wouldn't do that! We just did it for fun." He bit his lip.

"You're lying." Patrick slammed his palm on the table. Trey jumped. Even Sean was surprised at his partner's sudden outburst. Patrick was usually the calm, even-tempered Kincaid.

Reluctant, Trey said, "Kirsten posted it. We recorded us, you know, and then she found this website and thought it would be fun to put it up there." Trey's neck reddened. Physical embarrassment was hard to fake. "I told her to take it down, but she didn't. I was so mad I broke it off. We didn't talk for a couple months, but after she and her mom got in this huge fight she came to my house and we just, I guess, made up."

"You mean you had sex?" Patrick said.

"No! Kirsten is really screwed up right now. Her mother was lying to her about a bunch of stuff, and when she ran away the first couple times I thought she'd gone back to California—but she didn't want to be with her dad, either. She couldn't wait until she turned eighteen and could leave."

"What did Kirsten think her mother was lying to her about?"

"It's not my place to say."

"If it factors into why Kirsten ran away and where she might be, spill it," Sean said.

Trey relented, as if relieved to get the information off his chest. "Her mom told her the only good-paying job she could get was here in Virginia. But Kirsten found letters in her mother's desk that proved she'd been offered positions in Los Angeles, but she'd turned them down. Kirsten never wanted to leave L.A., and she confronted Mrs. Benton. I don't know what happened, but I think the first time she ran away was right after that."

Patrick said, "Mrs. Benton hasn't told the police that she and Kirsten had a fight."

"Big surprise. She's all about image. She wanted everyone to think she and Kirsten were so happy, but Kirsten was sick of her mother whining about Mr. Benton cheating on her."

"Do you know where Kirsten went?"

Trey shook his head. "I swear I'd tell you if I knew. I'm worried sick about her. She is so wrapped up in that stupid website, her grades are slipping—she flunked a big test in December. And then she told me she wasn't going to play softball this year. She could get a scholarship, she's that good, but she said she didn't care anymore and was even thinking about not going to college."

Sean frowned. All this information about her changing behavior did not bode well. He barely re-membered his oldest sister, Molly—she was a drug addict by the time she was eighteen, and committed suicide when Sean was five—but from everything Duke had told him about her, she'd run hot and cold and was seriously depressed the three months before she offed herself. Their parents had tried to force Molly into rehab, but she wouldn't go.

They hadn't found evidence of drugs in Kirsten's room, but Sean asked, "Was Kirsten using drugs?"

Trey shrugged. "No. I mean, we smoked pot a couple times, but that's it. But you can't say anything—if my coach found out I'd be cut."

"When was the last time you saw her, or talked to her for any length of time? How did she seem then?"

Trey took a minute to think about it. "Friday in English class, right before lunch. It's the only class we have together. She was all distracted, into her own head, and the teacher called on her a couple times and she didn't know the answer. I asked her if everything was okay, and she said she just had to get away for a while."

Sean asked quietly, "Did she seem depressed? Suicidal?"

"Kirsten wouldn't kill herself, no way."

"If she were doing drugs, that might contribute to depression."

"I don't know." Trey bit his lip.

Patrick asked, "Is there anyone you know outside of the school who Kirsten might go to to 'get away,' as you said?"

Trey shook his head. "Only her dad in California. She missed him a lot, but she also blamed him for her mom being so bitter. But she said that no matter what, when she graduated on June fifth, she was moving back to L.A."

That explained the June 5 circled on her calendar.

Patrick still didn't look satisfied. Sean said to his partner, "What are you thinking?"

He shook his head. "I don't know. This isn't adding up."

Sean disagreed. He felt that he was getting a clear picture of Kirsten Benton. Her parents were split, her mom lied to her, her dad started it by having multiple affairs—he could see her running away. But what didn't make sense was her involvement in the *Party Girl* website. Why post naked pictures? Why post the sex video with Trey? Did her disappearance have anything to do with the website, or was it something completely different?

"I really don't know where Kirsten is!" Trey insisted.

Patrick asked, "Do you know if Kirsten ever hooked up in person with someone she'd met online?"

"No, never," Trey said emphatically.

"Are you sure about that? Because it happens all the time, even with smart girls who should know better."

Sean glanced at Patrick. His face was tight, and Sean knew he was thinking about Lucy. This case was getting to him—a missing high school senior was too close to what had happened to Lucy nearly seven years ago. But it was not the same, though Sean couldn't explain that to Patrick now.

Trey ran his hands through his hair. "Last summer, I'd have said no way would she ever hook up online. Now? I never thought she'd quit softball. I don't know her anymore."

Sean took down Trey's contact information, then gave the kid his card and his cell phone number. "If you hear from Kirsten, call me immediately. If you remember anything else that might help, call me."

After Trey left, Sean turned to Patrick. "What do you think?"

But Patrick was in his own world, staring at the wall. Sean continued, "I believe him, though I think he might know something more, even if he doesn't know it's important. We'll check back with him tomorrow after he thinks more about it."

Patrick said, "We need to spend more time at Kirsten's computer."

"I'm working on breaking her password to the *Party Girl* site, and then we can dig into it."

"We need to find out who she was talking to and if she agreed to meet him in person." His voice vibrated with restrained anger, something Sean had rarely seen in the three years he'd known Patrick.

"That's a given. What's up? What are you thinking?"

Sean didn't like Patrick's aggravated expression. He looked more like his hard-edged military brother Jack. He didn't answer Sean's question, but said instead, "Specifically, we should look for any communication about college and boyfriends."

It was not so much his words as his tone. There was only one topic that could make Patrick this angry.

"You're thinking about Lucy," Sean said.

"It was all about her excitement at going to college," Patrick said quietly, his resentment taking a backseat. "And a predator taking advantage of it."

"We'll cover every possible connection," Sean said, "but this isn't the same situation. Kirsten has a habit of running away. It could be the same guy each time, or different guys. We'll find her and bring her home."

"She knew better," Patrick said.

Sean snapped his head, shocked by what Patrick had said. He couldn't have meant it. "Don't—"

Patrick rubbed his eyes. "Sorry. I have a headache."

"We need to talk." In all the time Sean had known Patrick, this was the first time he'd hinted that Lucy was even partly to blame for her kidnapping nearly seven years ago when she'd agreed to meet someone she'd been talking to online. Lucy had enough blame for herself, especially after Patrick nearly died searching for her. If she suspected that he had unresolved issues, it would shake her to the core. Sean would do anything to protect Lucy, starting with setting Patrick straight.

Patrick stood and paced the Bentons' kitchen. "I didn't mean it like that."

"Bullshit." Sean began to seethe, knowing that Patrick was being unfair. What had happened almost seven years ago was incredibly complex and it remained a volatile issue with all of the Kincaids, but until now Sean had never thought he had to protect Lucy from her own family.

Patrick stared at Sean. The anger was back, a flash, then it disappeared.

"What were you going to say?" Sean asked, his voice low, not wanting a fight but unable to let the conversation stand.

"I need aspirin and food."

"Patrick—"

"And another thing: don't ask Lucy to help on this case."

"She's the one who found the *Party Girl* site and the video. This is right up her alley. Honestly, if we're going to move quickly, we need her expertise."

"How do you think she feels watching shit like that sex tape? Going to sites like *Party Girl*? You let her create a profile!"

"Hold it, I didn't know she'd done it until afterward, but it makes sense, and it's nothing she hasn't done before for WCF."

"Yeah, and look where that's got her,"

"What's the problem here, Patrick?"

"Just keep Lucy out of this. I mean it."

Sean was stunned by Patrick's anger. He'd been on edge since returning from California, leaving his typical calm, reasoned personality on the West Coast. But this venom was so uncharacteristic that Sean didn't know how to respond.

He said, "Lucy knows what she's doing. I wouldn't ask her to do anything she wasn't comfortable with."

"Yes, just like she knew what she was doing when she was setting up those parolees for WCF and the vigilantes?"

"Wait just a minute—"

"Like she knew what she was doing when she got herself kidnapped in front of the church? Or when she nearly died on that island?"

Sean slowly rose from the table, his hands splayed firmly on the oak top to keep them from fisting up.

"Those are different situations," he said through

clenched teeth. "And Lucy is not to blame for either of them."

Patrick blinked, as if he hadn't known what he'd said. "I meant the fire."

"You said the island."

"You know what I meant!"

Unfortunately, Sean knew exactly what Patrick was thinking, and it took all his willpower to control his temper. It was bad enough that Patrick's tone suggested that what had happened five weeks ago when Lucy's stalker pounced was somehow her fault. But the reference to the island where Adam Scott had held her captive nearly seven years ago was unforgivable.

"Let it out, Patrick. Tell me what you're feeling."

"Don't go all Dillon on me," Patrick said, referring to his brother the shrink. "I'm just saying that Lucy gets too involved. She gets in way over her head, and she's not ready for this kind of pressure. Can't you just give her some time to heal? Or is this a way to make her dependent on you?"

"You are way off."

"Just—why her?"

Sean realized Patrick was now talking about his relationship with Lucy, and that the conversation was taking another direction, diverting Sean's attention from Lucy's past. Patrick had clearly been harboring these hostile feelings a long time.

"I care about Lucy," Sean said.

"Like you cared about Ashley? Jessica? Rachel? Emily—both of them? And then there was Shelley—"

Sean listened to Patrick list his ex-girlfriends before cutting him off. "It's not the same thing, and you damn well know it."

Patrick shook his head. "In the three years I've known you, you've had more than two dozen girl-friends, the longest lasting a record-breaking ten weeks."

"You've been keeping track of my relationships?"

"Not until you started sleeping with my sister!"

"You're crazy."

"You're a playboy."

"I may have been, but—"

"So you and Lucy have been together for five weeks? You're halfway to breaking her heart."

"I'm not going to break her heart—"

"Like hell you aren't."

Sean wrestled with his temper, and Patrick pushed.

"Do you think it's healthy for Lucy to help in a case like this? Do you ever think about anyone but your-self?"

Sean came extremely close to decking him. Patrick knew it and stepped forward, almost daring him.

Sean had a sudden thought. He wondered if Lucy's distance from him since Patrick had been back in D.C. was Patrick's doing. "What have you been say-ing to Lucy?" he asked.

"Nothing yet. But I'm watching you, Rogan."

"Don't."

Had they ever been friends? How could he think he'd gotten to know Patrick so well only to realize that he didn't know him at all? If Lucy heard his dia-tribe about Sean's ex-girlfriends, she might be upset. Patrick's approval meant more to her than that of any other member of her family. But if Lucy heard Patrick's comment about the island, she'd be com-pletely devastated.

"I'm going to talk to Kirsten's other friends," Patrick said, signaling that this conversation about Lucy was over. "You finish with her computer. We'll leave at four."

"Agreed." Sean wanted to settle it, but they were at an impasse. If Patrick forced Lucy to choose between her family and Sean, Sean feared that Lucy would pick her family. And even if she did choose Sean, she would be miserable. He couldn't do that to her.

He had to convince Patrick that Lucy was truly the only woman for him. Otherwise . . . no, he had to convince him. There was no alternative.

FIVE

While Sean drove in silence back to D.C., in the passenger seat Patrick received a call on his cell from Kate that Lucy wasn't feeling well. Her birthday dinner was postponed until the weekend.

Sean dropped Patrick off at the town house that housed both the RCK East offices and their separate residences, then drove to the Kincaids. Kate answered the door. "I told Patrick that Lucy isn't feeling well."

"I know. I just wanted to see her."

Kate let him in. "Make it quick. Lucy doesn't get sick often, but when she does she usually overdoes it and makes it worse."

Sean crossed his heart and held up his hand. "Promise."

That elicited a smile from Lucy's sister-in-law. Sean went upstairs and down the long hall to Lucy's room, set back from the rest of the house. He knocked on the door. "It's Sean. Can I come in?"

There was no answer. Sean wondered if she was sleeping. He didn't want to disturb her, but he needed to see her. Partly because he missed her, and partly because he wanted to make sure she was okay with what had happened today with Kirsten Benton and the sex tape. If he had known she'd uncover something like that, he would never have let her help—or would he? Patrick's gut reaction was to shelter Lucy, but Sean knew she'd faced far worse not only with what had happened nearly seven years ago, but during her tenure at WCF.

Still, the *Party Girl* site was offensive, and Lucy was particularly sensitive to the sexual exploitation of young women. He hoped she hadn't canceled her party because she was upset about what she'd seen.

He knocked again. "Luce?"

"I'm not feeling well," came her muffled reply.

He tried the door. It was locked. He couldn't remember her ever locking her door. "Lucy, let me in— I won't stay long."

"I'll call you tomorrow."

Sean frowned. She didn't sound like herself. He hesitated a brief moment before pulling out his lock-pick kit. Ten seconds later, he was inside.

Lucy sat on the far side of the dark room in her oversized chair, the only illumination coming from the streetlight outside.

"I can't believe you picked my lock."

He closed the door behind him. "I was worried about you."

"I'm fine. You can go."

Lucy's face was pale and splotchy, her black hair hung in tangled waves down her back, and she was sitting with her chin on her knees. She was anything but fine.

He crossed the room, then stopped. Her body language was unlike any he'd seen from her. She was truly angry with him.

"You don't know any boundaries, do you?" she snapped.

"Are you upset about the video you found? I'm sorry, Lucy, I didn't know that was there. I should have; I should have thought twice about asking for your help—"

She stared at him and shook her head. "No, I'm not upset about the video."

"Please tell me what's wrong. I didn't do anything, did I?" Maybe he'd hurt her and didn't know it. "Talk to me, please."

She let out a long sigh and closed her eyes. At first he didn't understand what she was doing with her hand, but then he realized she was pointing at her desk.

He went over and saw a notebook full of detailed information in her small, clear block printing. He looked at the pictures of her family, some framed and some loose on the desk. There was a series of four black-and-white pictures of her and Sean from a booth at the mall when he'd taken her window-shopping so he could figure out what she wanted for her birthday without directly asking her. That had been a fun afternoon, and the smile on her face was proof.

And then there was a letter, facedown.

He picked it up. It was from the FBI. He didn't need to read it to know that it contained bad news.

"Lucy—"

"Now you know," she said, cutting him off, "and you can leave."

"No—"

"Sean, can't you just leave me alone? For tonight?

You don't understand. I have nothing left. I need to figure out a bunch of stuff, and I need to do it by myself."

"You're in no condition to make decisions tonight." He walked over to her and knelt in front of her, putting his hands on her shoulders. She was so tense and rigid, her eyes red from her anguish. "I don't know what was going on with that panel, but they're a bunch of incompetent jerks who don't know what the hell they're doing."

She didn't say anything, but her body began shaking.

He kissed her on the top of her head, holding her face against his chest, wishing he could draw all her pain into him. He didn't know what to say or do to fix it. And that hurt nearly as much—that he couldn't solve this.

"We'll work this out," he said.

"This isn't your problem," she whispered.

"Your problems are mine." What did he need to do to prove to her that he was committed to her, through thick and thin, the good and the bad?

"No, Sean."

He ignored her comment. He wasn't going to get into an argument, not when Lucy felt so miserable. "We have a lot of work to do over the next couple days; maybe by the weekend you'll have a different perspective."

She pushed him away. He tried not to take it personally, but it was hard. "I can't help you anymore," she said.

"Of course you can—"

"Don't you get it? I'm done. I'm not going to be an FBI agent. I'm not going to be a cop. I'm not going to be working in cybercrime. It's over."

"I never thought you were a quitter."

"Leave me alone." She turned away.

He stood. "Does your family know?"

She shook her head. "I'll tell them, but not now."

"I won't say anything."

"Thanks," she mumbled without emotion.

He walked toward the door, then stopped in front of her desk. "I need your help on this case. You're smart, you understand these teenagers, and you understand these websites. I could have found all this, but it would have taken me a lot more time because I don't know exactly what to look for. You saved us hours of work, bringing us many steps closer to finding Kirsten."

"And what if I get something wrong?" Lucy countered. "What if I miss something completely?" She shook her head. "I don't want that kind of pressure. I don't know what I'm doing."

"That's a lie, and you damn well know it. Go ahead and feel sorry for yourself tonight." Sean wanted to say something reassuring, but he realized that the last thing Lucy needed right now was someone telling her everything was going to be all right. Self-pity and Lucy didn't go together, and she'd see it herself soon enough. "I'll be here at eight o'clock in the morning and I expect you to come to Woodbridge with me. I need your help or I wouldn't have asked in the first place."

He reached into his pocket and took out the present he'd picked out that night, after they'd taken the pictures in the booth. He had wanted to see Lucy's face when she opened it, but maybe now it was better that she opened it alone.

He put it on top of her notes and left.

Lucy stared at the door. She wanted to be angry at Sean, she *tried* to make herself angry at him, but she wasn't. She was too emotionally drained. The only thing she felt was suffocating waves of despair and failure.

She slowly rose, her limbs stiff from sitting in the chair for hours, and walked to her desk. She picked up the watch-sized box that Sean had left. It was tied with a blue ribbon.

It figured that he would do something like this. She hadn't wanted to open presents today. She hadn't wanted to face anyone and pretend everything was just fine. But she couldn't resist opening it, not knowing what to expect. With Sean, it could be anything.

She untied the ribbon and took off the lid. Inside was a necklace. The pendant was a single daisy made of six amethyst gems, a small diamond in the center. The jewels were set in gold.

She'd never seen anything like it. It was seven stones in a simple design, but the delicacy and complexity of how they were held together was exquisite.

Inside the box was a small card declaring that the necklace was from a local antiques shop she'd been in many times, though she rarely bought anything for herself. A couple of weeks ago they'd gone shopping at the mall, and while walking to a nearby restaurant they'd passed the store. She hadn't seen the daisy, but she had commented to him how she enjoyed browsing and bought most of her Christmas presents there.

Sean had not only remembered, but he'd picked out a piece that she loved, that symbolized his declaration when they first met that he would give her only colorful daisies because they made her smile.

Putting on the necklace, Lucy wept.

Lucy was understandably upset over the idiotic panel's decision, but Sean was downright furious about it and remained so for hours. He continued to work, following up on requests for phone records and ISP information in the Kirsten Benton case. But he couldn't stop thinking about Lucy's denied application.

The FBI had proven to him, yet again, that they had their collective heads up their collective asses. Not so much the investigating agents—he had a grudging respect for them after working a few cases with them in the field—but the mindless bureaucrats who ran the agency. Sean knew there was no other applicant out there better qualified or more dedicated than Lucy.

Sean almost called FBI agent Noah Armstrong, who'd recently befriended the Kincaids when he and Kate worked on a case together, but he stopped himself. He and Noah didn't see eye to eye on most things, and Sean didn't want to ask him for any favors. Instead, he went higher up and called Assistant Director Hans Vigo, whom Sean greatly admired.

"Hans Vigo," the agent answered his cell phone.

"It's Sean Rogan." He glanced at the clock and winced. It was after eleven. "I hope it's not too late to call."

"I was awake."

Sean sat down at his desk. "The FBI denied Lucy's application."

When Hans didn't respond, Sean asked, "Did you know?"

"No, but I thought she might have an uphill battle."

"Uphill? It's *done*. She's out."

"She can appeal."

"Appeal? How?"

"She gets one shot to request a different panel. But Lucy knows that."

Why hadn't she said anything to Sean about appealing? "She's really torn up about this. I don't think she's considered her options."

"Did she tell you anything about the interview? If she felt that someone was unduly biased, or if there were questions that seemed odd to her?"

"No—she thought it went well. She was jazzed afterward. Can you find out who was on the panel? Find out what their problem with her is?"

"I don't know that you, or Lucy, would like the answers."

"What aren't you telling me?"

"Nothing you don't already know. Lucy isn't a typical recruit. The Bureau looks closely at anyone they think may have a hidden agenda."

"They can't blame her for what happened with WCF! Dammit—"

"They can look at anything and everything. WCF is only one factor. There is also the fact that she killed two people."

Sean's blood ran cold. "Was she supposed to die instead?"

"Look at the bigger picture, Sean. They probably assessed that she was too high profile. That's my guess, not because I know anything specific. I don't even know who's on the hiring panel right now, but it's not secret and I'll find out."

Sean latched on to Hans's first statement. "What do you mean Lucy's too 'high profile.' Is it because she was raped? That is just fucked."

"Sean, that's not what I meant," Hans said, his voice calm but firm. "However, it might play a part of the big picture. Not that she was attacked, but everything that happened after that. Any one thing probably wouldn't have alarmed the panel, but she's been involved in several police and FBI investigations from the outside, and she has high-ranking connections."

"That should help her!"

"Sometimes it does. And sometimes connections can hurt a candidate's chances."

That Sean understood. His brother Liam was always a wild card, and had caused their brother Duke and RCK plenty of headaches. And Sean wasn't a Boy Scout, either. He knew he'd cost RCK business in the past, nearly as much as he had gained them.

But Lucy was different, and becoming an FBI agent meant more to her than anything else. Sean didn't want to accept defeat, but listening to Hans it sounded like there were no options.

"Then she's screwed? Why didn't you tell her before she spent the last seven years of her life planning for a career in the FBI?"

"Sean, I understand that you're upset, and I can just imagine how Lucy is feeling about now. But neither of you are naïve. Lucy would be a controversial hire; that's the simple truth."

"Are you going to help or not?"

"Sean, there is no one I know more deserving of a commission from the Bureau than Lucy." Hans sounded irritated. "I personally like and admire her greatly, and know she'd make a top agent. Moreover, we need more people like her. But the FBI is a large government agency, and individuals who stand out *before* they are recruited are red flags. Give me the weekend to find out what I can about the panel. I need to be discreet, because if someone suspects that I'm trying to manipulate the process then Lucy will have even more problems when she appeals. I'll call you next week."

Sean took a deep breath. "I really appreciate this, Hans."

"If it doesn't work out, a talented woman like Lucy still has many options available to her. Naturally, I'll help her in any way I can."

"Thanks, Hans. We both know that, but Lucy wouldn't ask."

"She doesn't have to."

SIX

Girls like you . . .

Kirsten woke up well before dawn Thursday morning, for the first time in days feeling like she wasn't going to die. Still, remnants of a nightmare clawed out from her subconscious. She was still shaking from the bad dream, but she willed herself to stop.

The voice wasn't real. It was your drug-induced imagination.

As much as she wanted to, she didn't believe that.

Sore and weak from being unable to keep anything solid down for three days, she finally felt like eating something more than chicken broth. It still hurt to walk. Who was she kidding? The pain was unbearable, and she crawled to the bathroom. Sitting on the edge of the small tub, she stared at her sorry reflection in the mirror.

Her blond hair was filthy, even though she'd made a feeble attempt to wash it yesterday. She suspected that she didn't get all the shampoo out, because it felt greasy. A faint bruise covered her cheek, light gray against skin already far too pale. She looked like a corpse, and didn't feel much livelier than one.

"You're lucky you're not dead," she whispered. Her mouth was parched and she rose from the tub's edge to reach for the faucet. Excruciating pain shot from her damaged feet up her legs, and she fell to her knees. One of her scabs broke, leaving a bloodstain on the white bathroom carpet.

"Great," she said, then burst into tears.

She pulled herself up and sat back on the edge of the tub. Through the blur of her tears, she looked at the bottoms of her feet. They were bandaged, but blood had seeped through the gauze. She carefully removed it, wincing at the tenderness. Then she took a long look at the damage. It was as if someone had hit her foot repeatedly with a serrated knife. Some cuts were shallow and healing, others deep and bright red. She had only two more pills left in the antibiotic prescription she'd found in the medicine cabinet.

What was she going to do?

She could call her mom. She'd be mad, for sure, but she'd come and get her, and then Kirsten could go home to her own bed.

But she still wouldn't be safe.

What would she tell the police? That Jessie had asked her to come to New York even though it wasn't Kirsten's scheduled weekend to play escort? Right, she was going to admit to her mom that she was an online call girl.

Better to get in trouble for selling sex over the Internet than be dead.

She bit her lip and thought about calling her dad. She had a love/hate relationship with him. Though her mother was a bitter divorcée, her father had started it by having all those affairs. Maybe she should just call him and say, "Well, you like to sleep around. So do I, but at least I get paid for it."

That would go over *so* well. And Kirsten wasn't exactly proud of what she did, though it gave her some control over her life. She finally felt as though she had power, for the first time in three years since she became a pawn in her parents' divorce. When she first joined *Party Girl,* it had been so freeing and exciting she had jumped in with both feet. A part of her knew she did it to get back at her parents, but another part thrilled at being in full command. The power Kirsten had over her clients was intoxicating.

If she'd just stuck with the online sex chats she'd have been fine. But then another *Party Girl,* Jessie, told her about the big blowout bashes in New York, so she started coming up, and was astonished at how invigorating the raves were. Not raves as she'd imagined them, but even more intense.

Somewhere along the way, Kirsten had lost control. She was offered money to go to parties big and small. When she was high, she lost all sense of time and place. Everything began to fall apart, but she hadn't wanted to quit because she felt more alive, more *real,* when she was pretending to be someone else.

But now Jessie was dead! And Jessie had tried to tell her something. She had called her Friday morning begging her to meet her at the party Saturday. And she'd said something else, but Kirsten had been too distracted. Then Jessie wanted to meet outside.

But Jessie didn't send that text. She'd called Kirsten "Ash" instead, her party name.

If Jessie hadn't texted her at the party, who did? Someone who knew what she looked like. Someone who had Jessie's phone. If he had Jessie's phone, he had her phone number, and he might be able to find out where she really lived. Kirsten could call her mother, but would she be safe even back home?

Kirsten was increasingly anxious about the arrangement. She was staying in this amazing apartment. She hadn't left the bedroom and bathroom, but everything was expensive and classy. She'd been so out of it after finding Jessie dead, and then getting sick, she didn't know what she'd agreed to or why the guy had let her stay here in the first place, especially since he himself didn't live here. She couldn't remember what he'd told her about who owned the penthouse or why the owner wasn't here, but she would find out today. Now that she was thinking straight, she would figure out how to make it all right again.

She leaned over and locked the bathroom door, turned on the water in the tub, and pulled off the large T-shirt she wore. Her muscles were stiff from lack of use. She stretched her arms, staring in shock at her naked body, as if it were foreign.

She had small cuts all over her arms and legs, some so deep they would probably scar because they hadn't been stitched. Bruises of all shapes and sizes and colors dotted her limbs, with one large, sickly yellow bruise covering most of her left hip. She touched it and winced. It was tender and painful. She didn't think she'd broken any bones, a miracle considering the state of her body.

She should have gone to the hospital. What must she have looked like when that guy found her running through the parking lot?

You weren't running. You'd fallen, remember?

She didn't remember much, mostly only her feeling. Disconnected when the blond guy was screwing her against the wall. Cold when she was outside. Shock when she found Jessie dead. Fear as she ran because she heard something, thought she was being chased. Was she? She'd heard a voice, but she didn't recognize it. She thought it was Jessie's murderer, but maybe it was help. Or just another partygoer.

She'd never forget her friend's dead eyes.

"What happened to you, Jessie?" she whispered.

Don't you dare, bitch . . .

Kirsten lowered herself slowly into the water. "Ow, ow, ow!" She kept the water only a little warmer than lukewarm, but whatever the temperature, every cut and scrape on her body screamed in protest. Then the sharp pains subsided to a constant, but bearable, ache.

She wanted to believe that Jessie's death had been an accident, but Kirsten knew it wasn't. *Someone* had been lurking around Jessie's body. It was the text message that tipped her off, that someone wanted Jessie *and* her dead. But why? What had she done? And if Kirsten went to the police, what would she tell them? She didn't know anything! She didn't know why Jessie had been scared or even why she had asked Kirsten to come to New York.

Jessie had been involved in *Party Girl* a lot longer than Kirsten, but they didn't talk about their online activities when they met up at the secret parties in New York. They kept an eye out for each other. Kirsten had been thinking of going to Columbia with Jessie next year, had even sent off an application without telling her mother. But her grades had tanked last semester and she didn't think she'd get in.

Maybe quitting softball had been a mistake. She

had an amazing batting average, and last year was the third-ranked pitcher in the state and twenty-ninth in the nation. She still had two weeks before she had to commit to her final high school season.

She stared at her feet. How could she run in two weeks when she couldn't even walk today? How could she think about college when her only true friend was dead? What if they found out about *Party Girl*?

Heart racing, she realized that she'd never considered what anyone would think about her online activities. She almost didn't care if her parents found out, but it wasn't as if she'd announced to everyone at school that she was "Ashleigh." Maybe in the back of her mind she thought no one would recognize her, or she could say, Wow, that girl looks a lot like me. Don't they say everyone has a double?

For the first time since she joined *Party Girl,* she considered her future. It looked bleak.

She washed her hair under the bathtub faucet, which was difficult and cumbersome, but it was too painful to stand in the shower. Her arms shook when she hoisted herself out of the tub. When she'd been conditioning for softball last year, she could bench-press ninety pounds. Now, she didn't think she could lift a ten-pound weight over her head.

She rebandaged her feet and put a large Band-Aid on her knee where the scab had split.

A knock at the door provoked a scream, but she cut it off quickly.

"It's me, Dennis," the voice said.

Dennis? Who was Dennis? She didn't remember

the name of the guy who'd found her. It could have been Dennis. It sounded right.

"Kirsten? Are you okay?"

"Yes," she said, her voice scratchy. "I'm just cleaning up."

"I'm glad you're feeling better. I brought you some clothes. I'll wait in the kitchen."

He walked away. Kirsten had flashes of a boy, not much older than she, carrying her into an elevator that smelled of mint and lavender. There was something off about him, but she had been so sick she couldn't figure it out. He'd brought her water and chicken broth, and she thought he might have even cleaned up when she got sick.

Why was he helping her? Who was he?

She tried taking a step, but the pain was too great and she wondered if there were still rocks and glass embedded in the cuts. Another flash of Dennis cleaning her feet and pulling out a long, jagged piece of glass had her wondering why he hadn't taken her to the hospital.

Kirsten vowed never to take drugs again. She didn't like these dark holes in her memory.

She crawled back to the bedroom and pulled herself onto the bed. Her skin was clammy, and she started to feel feverish again. She wanted to sleep. She rested for a minute, then spotted the shopping bag from Abercrombie & Fitch. She stared at the outrageously expensive clothing inside—all her size. Had she told him, or had he guessed?

The entire chore of bathing and dressing exhausted her and she didn't want to go to the kitchen. She didn't want Dennis to see her crawl, but then again, maybe he already had. All she wanted was to sleep.

Dennis knocked on the bedroom door.

"Come in," she said, her voice raw and scratchy.

Dennis looked sweet, if that was possible for a guy. He was only a few inches taller than Kirsten, but broad-shouldered, as though he worked out. Cute, in a little-kid way, which seemed odd with his build. He looked at her with pale blue eyes through wire-rim glasses.

"I made some soup."

Dennis didn't scare her, but maybe she should be scared. "Why didn't you take me to the hospital?" she asked.

He frowned at her and looked worried. "You told me not to."

"I don't remember that."

"Are you still sick?"

"I don't remember a lot of things. Just bits and pieces. Why didn't I want to go to the hospital?"

"You said someone was going to kill you and you needed a place to hide."

Kirsten definitely didn't remember saying that, though she certainly remembered being terrified that someone was chasing her.

"And you brought me here?"

"My brother is in Europe."

She frowned. Something was wrong. "You said your brother was at the party. Didn't you?" Maybe she was remembering another conversation.

"I have two brothers. Charlie is in Europe, and he always tells me I can stay here whenever I want. I take a class at Columbia." He spoke proudly, and it was his tone that told Kirsten that Dennis was a little slow. Not severely retarded, but not quite normal.

"My brother knows the dean and they said I can audit one class a semester. I'm doing really good."

She didn't know why, but that made her feel better. "Okay. So this is between you and me, right?"

Dennis nodded. "Do you want some soup?"

"Yes, but I can't walk." She frowned at her feet. "It hurts too much."

"I can bring the soup in here."

"Why are you helping me?"

His baffled expression indicated that he didn't understand her question.

"I mean, I must have looked awful the other night. Like I was crazy or something."

"You were scared. Charlie always says we have to help our neighbors."

"I think I'd like Charlie."

Dennis smiled, his eyes lighting up. "I love Charlie. He's nice to me."

"What about your other brother?"

Dennis shrugged. "He's moody. Charlie says he's selfish and won't grow up. But he always takes me to see baseball games. I love baseball."

"I love baseball, too."

Dennis grinned. "And then after the game, if he doesn't have a girlfriend, I get to stay in his apartment and we watch movies, but not scary movies because I don't like them. Last time, we watched *Star Wars,* my favorite."

He really was sweet. Kirsten felt awful for dragging

this kid into her problems. "Thank you for the clothes."

"I looked at the tag in your dress for your size when—" He blushed several shades of red and averted his gaze. "I'm sorry," he mumbled. "It was torn and you weren't talking. I didn't touch you, I promise. Just helped you put on one of Charlie's old shirts."

"It's okay. You took care of me, and I feel a lot better."

"I can take you home, if you want."

She shook her head. "Something strange happened at the warehouse."

"I know. It was in the newspaper."

"What? What was in the newspaper?"

"I didn't read it because it sounded scary, but I saw the picture of the warehouse. I'll bring it in, with your soup. Is it okay if you have soup for breakfast? It's only eight."

"Thank you. And water, please."

A few minutes later, Dennis came in with a tray. It was almost surreal—a fake rose in a bud vase, a bowl of soup, soda crackers, a tall glass of ice water, and the *New York Post* folded neatly. Everything was placed just so.

"It smells great." Though she was starving, the thought of eating made her ill.

He beamed. "I have to go to class. It starts at nine, and I don't want to be late."

"Is it really okay that I'm here?"

He nodded. "Charlie isn't coming back until next week. And he won't mind."

Kirsten wasn't so sure about that, but she didn't argue with Dennis.

"I'll be back after my class." He smiled and waved as he left.

Kirsten opened the newspaper. A headline on the bottom front read:

Cinderella Strangler Strikes Again! P.13

Hands shaking, Kirsten turned to page thirteen.

Fourth victim found at abandoned Brooklyn warehouse

BROOKLYN—Early Wednesday morning the body of an unidentified female was discovered by a private security company in the weed-choked parking lot of the abandoned paper mill near Gowanus Bay.

NYPD lead detective Victor Panetta refused comment, other than to confirm that a female between the ages of 18 and 25 was found at dawn Wednesday and that the investigation was his top priority.

However, sources in the NYPD report that the crime scene matches three previous homicides. The first victim, 19-year-old Columbia University student Alanna Andrews, was discovered at a Haunted House set up in an abandoned apartment building in Harlem in the early morning hours of October 31. Erica Ripley, 21, an employee at a Java Central, was alleged to be the Cinderella Strangler's second victim. She was found on January 2 on the south side of the Bronx, in a field near an abandoned factory. And the third victim was identified as third-year NYU student Heather Garcia, 20, killed on

February 5 at a party in Manhattanville. Her body was discovered next to a dumpster by sanitation workers. All four victims were found after attending an illegal "underground" party at an abandoned site.

The Cinderella Strangler suffocates his victims and takes one of their shoes. Authorities refuse to comment on what the shoe may represent, but psychiatrist Emile DeFelice said the killer may have a foot fetish, or use the shoe in a bizarre sex ritual. Some experts claim that serial killers take personal effects—usually panties or jewelry—from the victim as a so-called souvenir, in order to relive their crime at a later date.

The FBI has created a task force with NYPD and the NY Port Authority, suggesting that they are, in fact, tracking a serial killer.

Those close to the investigation say the task force has no leads. The FBI has sent a communication to all local colleges to raise awareness among students to be extra cautious when attending a rave. Authorities are looking for new ways to put a stop to the illegal parties. Community activists advise caution when attending any event. "Go with someone you know, and leave with someone you know," said a regular partygoer who asked to remain anonymous. "Have fun, but be smart."

Police are asking that anyone with information that may help them in their investigation call the task force hotline number. A $10,000 reward is offered by the FBI for any information leading to the conviction of the killer.

Kirsten pushed the tray aside. Jessie had been murdered by a *serial killer*?

Girls like you . . .

Kirsten didn't know what to do. No one knew where she was.

She looked at the date on the paper. Thursday? It was already *Thursday*? She'd been sick for five days? She had to call her mother, let her know she was okay. The weekends were one thing, but she'd left home Friday night and now her mother must be frantic.

But what could she do? She couldn't crawl around the city. She needed someone she could trust, but she had no one.

Except . . .

Trey would help her, she knew it. Her ex was still furious about the video, but they were talking again, and he'd told her that if she ever needed anything to just ask.

She saw a phone charger in the bedroom, but no phone. What if the owner had only a cell phone?

She crawled out of the bedroom and realized she hadn't been outside the room since she'd arrived. The view of New York City from the picture windows took her breath away. She sat on the floor and looked around.

If she'd thought the bedroom was nice, the living room was gorgeous. Plush gray carpeting; dark-gray leather furniture; glass tables and splashes of blues and greens in paintings and throw rugs. This guy, Dennis's brother, had to be rich.

She saw double doors across the room and made her way over, the effort depleting her energy. She was dizzy and tired.

The double doors led to a den. On the desk was an Apple computer.

"Thank you," she whispered and crawled into the room.

She pulled herself up onto a chair. While she didn't have Charlie's password, she could access the guest account, and was able to get on the Internet.

She logged on to her Facebook page and was about to send Trey a message when she realized she didn't know where she was. She needed to search Charlie's office and find an address, anything, but she could barely see, as if everything on the periphery was black and she saw only what was directly in front of her.

She typed Trey a message and hoped it made sense. She didn't know if she had the strength to crawl back to bed, but she had to try. She needed to sleep.

Don't you dare, bitch . . .

SEVEN

At nine a.m. Thursday, Suzanne met Detective Panetta at the Starbucks around the corner from the apartment of their Jane Doe, identified this morning as Jessica Bell. "Light, no sugar," Panetta said and handed Suzanne her coffee.

She didn't hide her surprise. "After all these years, you remembered?"

He grinned. "My ironclad memory keeps my wife happy."

They walked down West 112th Street, St. John the Divine Cathedral at the far cross street. It was a nice, clean neighborhood lined with apartment buildings of various ages, many filled with college students from nearby Columbia University. The wind had died down, but it had been drizzling on and off all morning.

"Did you see the *Post*?" she asked.

"Couldn't miss it."

"They make us look like idiots."

"You got to ignore them."

"It's hard to ignore a front-page headline."

Suzanne resented the media because they'd fucked up one of her cases a few years back. She pushed aside her frustration and changed the subject.

"So you ID'd the victim fast."

KISS ME, KILL ME

"Had it by last night," Panetta said. "She was reported missing by her roommate Monday morning, so we did a photo ID, then had the university send her prints in for confirmation. The coroner confirms that Jessica Bell was dead at least forty-eight hours before her body was found. It'll be hard to get a specific time of death."

"A range?"

"Not longer than a week, more than forty-eight hours. They're performing some advanced tests that could possibly narrow it further, but those results won't be overnight."

"That's good enough for now; we'll be able to establish when her roommate last saw her and go from there. Chances are that she was at that party and died Saturday night." Suzanne sipped her coffee as she walked. "She didn't go to that party alone."

"You don't know that for a fact."

"College kids may be idiots with their wild parties and drinking and drugs; they may leave with people they don't know. But going *to* the party? Girls don't go alone. Maybe guys do, but not girls. Or they meet up with someone when they get there."

"Point taken."

"So why didn't one of her friends say something? Or look for her? Go to the police department and say, *Hey, I was at a party with my friend Jessica and she disappeared.*" Panetta opened his mouth to respond, but Suzanne answered her own question. "Because they'd be busted. Trespassing. Drunk and disorderly. Vandalism. Underage drinking. Possession of drugs. Whatever it was they were into, it was illegal. But more likely a misdemeanor, and we'd be on the case faster, talk to people faster, track down a witness, and maybe have a fucking clue who this bastard is."

Panetta stopped walking and looked at her feet.

She glanced over her shoulder. "What's wrong?"

"Just looking at the soapbox you're standing on."

She grinned and shook her head. "Okay, I know, it's a sore spot for me." They continued walking. "But you have kids, right?"

"Three daughters."

"What would they do?"

"Call me."

"You sure?"

Panetta nodded. "My oldest has never been in any serious trouble, but the other two have called me several times over the years to pick them up from a party where things got out of hand. I told them they'd rather be grounded than dead, and they agreed." He sighed. "My youngest is graduating from high school in June. She's deciding between Boston U and Georgetown."

"Two great schools," Suzanne said, impressed. "I was a Terrier."

"How'd you like Boston?"

She shrugged. "I like Manhattan more." She'd hated Boston, partly because she'd felt sorely out of place there, a conservative small-town Southern girl going to an urbane, big-city university. It was perhaps ironic, she'd ended up falling in love with New York City after the FBI assigned her here when she graduated from Quantico ten years ago. Now she didn't want to leave. She'd turned down a promotion last year because she would have had to move to Montana. New York was cold enough. She'd have been a supervisory special agent in the Helena regional office—a smaller office, different crimes, and in the middle of nowhere. The incremental increase in pay wasn't enough for her to give up fieldwork, and sitting behind a desk issuing orders wasn't her style.

Besides, she'd grown up in the middle-of-nowhere South; she wasn't working in the middle-of-nowhere North.

They stopped in front of Jessica Bell's seven-story apartment building. At one time, the building had been comprised of large one- and two-bedroom apartments; most had been divided and the place was now more like an off-campus studio dormitory than individual apartments.

Jessica Bell's roommate, Lauren Madrid, appeared shell-shocked when she opened the door and faced Suzanne and Detective Panetta. Lauren was a young, attractive, light-skinned Hispanic—a little on the skinny side maybe, thought Suzanne.

"You're here about Jessie."

"May we come in?" Suzanne asked.

Lauren opened the door wider and Suzanne stepped inside. There were two rooms: a small living area with a kitchen, and a bedroom that they shared. Two twin beds on opposite walls could be seen through the open double doors.

Panetta closed the door when Lauren walked to the worn couch and sat down cross-legged. "She's really dead."

"Yes," Suzanne said, taking a seat next to her. "We have some questions, and for us to catch Jessica's killer, it's critically important that you be completely honest with us."

Lauren looked at her quizzically. "Well, yeah, of course."

"When was the last time you saw your room-mate?"

"She was here Friday morning when I left for my classes. After that I caught a train to Albany, where my parents live. I didn't come home until Sunday night."

"And Jessie wasn't here?"

"No, but I didn't think too much about it, really. I mean, she often stays with her boyfriends."

"Boyfriends? Plural?"

"Well, whoever she's seeing at the time. She didn't like to get attached to anyone. Jessica was kind of wild, but really super nice. My dad has a hard time just paying my tuition, and Jessica took care of November and December rent for me. She didn't take my money when I tried to pay it in January."

"Is Jessica from a wealthy family?" Suzanne asked, though these were hardly luxury accommodations.

Lauren shrugged. "I guess. I don't know."

"Did she have a job?"

"No."

"How long have you known Jessica?"

"Since August. This is my first year, her second. She advertised for a roommate, and we hit it off."

"Did you socialize together?"

"Not really."

Suzanne didn't understand how someone who advertised for a roommate could so easily cover said roommate's rent for two months and not want to be repaid.

Panetta asked, "Do you know Jessica's friends? Does she have a boyfriend? Or an ex-boyfriend?"

"Um," Lauren frowned.

"She had no friends?" Suzanne asked, surprised.

"No, but I don't really know her friends well. She didn't really have a lot of people over here. Oh, there's Josh."

"Boyfriend?"

"Not really, they were more friends with benefits. You know, they had sex but—"

Suzanne cut her off. "I know what friends with benefits means." All too well. "And Josh is a student? Teacher?"

"He's a senior, I think. He lives upstairs, in seven-ten."

After searching Jessica Bell's room and not finding anything useful except an address book and laptop computer—which Suzanne took and gave Lauren a receipt for—they trudged up the three flights to Josh Haynes's apartment.

"Friends with benefits," Panetta grumbled. "I'm not a prude, but to me, sex without love and respect is meaningless."

Maybe, but not always, thought Suzanne. And sometimes, there was affection and respect without love. And why shouldn't she have a guy to expend sexual energy with? She answered her own question. Because there was a double standard, even at the age of thirty-three. Guys could sleep around, but girls—not so much.

After reaching the top-floor hallway, Panetta rapped on Josh Haynes's door. He answered wearing gray sweats and no shirt.

They showed their badges. "We're here about Jessica Bell," Panetta said.

"Is something wrong?"

He seemed concerned, but Suzanne had faced some great criminal actors over the years. Maybe in prison they could brush up on their Shakespeare.

"When was the last time you saw or spoke with Jessica?" Panetta asked.

Josh frowned. "Saturday."

When he didn't offer any more detail, Suzanne prompted, "Did you have a date?"

"We went to a party on Saturday."

"Where was the party?"

"Brooklyn. I went with her because she was nervous about riding the subway at night, but we didn't hang out. She said she had plans."

"I was under the impression you and Jessie were involved," Suzanne said.

"We weren't dating or anything like that."

"Her roommate said you were sleeping together."

"Well, yeah, sometimes, but we weren't exclusive or anything. We just liked hanging together."

"So you went to this party in Brooklyn. At a vacant warehouse?"

"Is that what this is about? The warehouse? It was just a party."

"Jessica is dead." Panetta was blunt.

Josh blanched. "What?"

"Her body was found fifty yards from the main entrance to the warehouse," Suzanne said.

He shook his head. "But—I—don't—" He stopped, confused, and stepped back.

Suzanne took that as an invitation to enter, and Josh didn't stop them.

Panetta's voice was harsh. "You went to a party with your good friend Jessica, didn't leave with her, and didn't bother to check in with her on Sunday? Or Monday morning?"

"We weren't dating—I don't understand. She's not dead."

"We have a positive ID," Suzanne said, closing the door behind her.

Josh sat down heavily on the couch. He lived in a large one-room apartment, about five hundred square feet in the corner of the building, with four, tall narrow windows looking out onto the street. The custom woodwork that may have been original to the building had been well maintained by tenants or landlord.

"I'm just—stunned. Jess."

Panetta said, "We're not here about the illegal party. We're here about a murder."

"She was murdered?" Josh asked, as if that, too, was a revelation.

Suzanne trusted her instincts, and she didn't see Josh as a killer, though most killers didn't look the part.

"Mr. Haynes, we're trying to catch Jessica's killer. We want to talk to anyone she may have seen at the party. Our investigators tell us that at least five hundred people were at the Sunset Park warehouse. You're telling us it was Saturday night, correct?"

Josh nodded. "It was more like eight hundred people at the peak," he added.

"You and Jessica arrived at what time?"

"Just after midnight."

"When was the last time you saw her?"

"Right after we got there. Jess loved to dance. That's why she went to the parties, for the great bands. Everyone can just be themselves. I was doing my own thing."

"Which was?"

He shrugged. "Stuff."

"How did you find out about the party? Did you get an invitation? Read about it on the Internet? I'm a little rusty in this area."

Suzanne suppressed a smile. Vic Panetta knew more than most fifty-year-old detectives about how the college set operated.

Josh was reticent, and Panetta gently pushed. "I understand you're worried because that party was illegal, but I can tell you that unless you killed Jessica Bell, or are covering up for whoever did, I'm not going to arrest you for anything you did at the party. I'm a homicide detective, not a narc. But if you don't help us, I will send your name to the detective in charge of narcotics and gangs and he'll make your life hell."

Josh frowned. "I am kind of involved in organizing some of the parties. But I'm not the only one," he quickly added.

"I'm aware of that."

"We have a website. We don't post the location until two hours before. Only people we know have the password, and they get out the word in their circles, who pass it along. It's mostly college kids and working types who need to blow off steam. Live music, a little drinking and drugs, just fun."

A little drinking and drugs? Suzanne refrained from climbing onto her soapbox again.

"So you don't know everyone who's there?"

"Personally, no, of course not."

Panetta slid over a piece of paper. "These are the other three party locations where a young woman was killed during a secret party. Were any of these your parties?"

Josh looked at the paper. Then he sighed in what sounded like relief. "Only the party in the Bronx, at the factory. My group only has them in warehouses and factories."

"Do you know who organized the other two parties?"

"Manhattanville—the one right near the university. I heard it was a frat party, not very big, maybe two hundred people. Broke up early. The one in Harlem, can't say. But there's one person who knows more about secret parties than anyone in the city. Wade Barnett."

Panetta leaned back, recognition crossing his expression. Suzanne didn't know the guy.

"Did Jessica tell you about any threats she may have received?" Suzanne asked. "Maybe a regular at the parties she attended who paid her too much attention?"

"No. But—" He hesitated.

"Go ahead," Suzanne prompted.

."She seemed kind of jumpy lately. I don't know why, but she didn't say anything to me about it."

"Would she have confided in her roommate?"

"Lauren?" he asked. "No—Lauren didn't approve of the parties, didn't like it when Jess came back wasted."

"Was there anyone Jessica would have confided in?

Maybe a friend, a co-worker, or someone at the college?"

Josh said, "She was close to this girl who was from out of town. Ashleigh. I don't know her last name, only met her once or twice. A month ago, maybe longer, she stayed at Jess's place when Lauren went home to visit her parents."

"Do you know where Ashleigh lives? How we can reach her?"

"No, sorry."

"Was she in town on Saturday?"

Josh thought about it. "Maybe. Jess didn't say she was coming, but like I said, she was jumpy and weird."

Panetta said, "We may have additional questions, so we need your contact information." He handed over his notepad.

Josh wrote everything down and walked them to the door. "I'll ask around to some people I know were there."

"Why don't you give us their names?" Suzanne asked.

"Because they won't talk to you. They'll deny they were there, and then shut me out completely. I want to help, really—Jess and I were good friends. I promise, if I find someone with information, I'll send them to you, okay?"

Suzanne reluctantly agreed. They could get a warrant for the names later if the evidence pointed in that direction.

They left, and she said to Panetta, "We need a full background check on him."

"Consider it done."

She asked Panetta, "Who's Barnett?"

"Twenty years ago this summer, Douglas Barnett was killed in a horrific factory accident outside the city. Five men lost their lives. The company paid out a huge settlement to the families. The oldest Barnett son is a financial whiz kid. Turned a couple million into tens of millions, or more. Runs a foundation and donates a lot of money to charity. Wade is his younger brother. He's always written up on the social pages. Real spoiled-rich-kid type."

"Are you putting him on the suspect list?"

"For what reason? Spoiled nouveau riche kid planning raves? Doesn't make him a killer."

"You don't like him?"

"I don't know him."

"So let's introduce ourselves."

"It might get messy."

"Scared?" she teased.

He deadpanned her. "Politically messy. The Barnetts are connected. We'd better know what we're doing."

"We do."

EIGHT

Lucy didn't talk to Sean the entire drive to Wood-bridge.

She was angry with him, but even angrier with herself. She'd wallowed in misery since getting the letter from the FBI, and that wasn't like her. So she wasn't FBI material. She had to accept it and move on. Deal with it. Grow up.

But anger suppressed the sting of not being good enough.

She had decisions to make, among them whether to stay in D.C. or move back to San Diego. Whether she should go back to school and get her law degree, which several of her professors had encouraged her to do. Or she could follow in Dillon's footsteps and go to medical school to become a psychiatrist.

She hadn't exactly fit in at college, which was why she'd focused so intently and had excelled in her studies. She hadn't been the typical eighteen-year-old college freshman, and she didn't want to return at twenty-five, even if the students in postgraduate school would be similar to her in age.

She'd interned with the Arlington County Sheriff's Department for a year and decided that she didn't want to be a local cop. She was far more interested in the types of crime the FBI investigated than she was in being a beat officer. She'd interned in Congress as well, but she'd never go back there. And the morgue? That had been the most interesting of the three internships, but she didn't want to work with the dead for the rest of her life.

The FBI had been perfect, with a key priority in her area of expertise—cybercrime. She also had a master's in criminal psychology, which would help her working in any of the FBI squads.

If Lucy had been in limbo waiting for the FBI letter, she felt even more unsettled now.

She was also ready to move out of her brother's house.

She'd lived with Dillon and his wife Kate for more than six years, ever since she'd moved to D.C. to attend Georgetown. She'd never lived on campus; that first year it had been difficult to just go out alone. The week she'd graduated high school, she'd been raped and grossly humiliated when her attack had been aired live on the Internet. Though she'd put on a brave face for her family, it had taken Lucy a lot longer to compartmentalize the pain than she'd let on. Moving in with Dillon and Kate had saved her from the watchful eye of her family, and the distance had helped her piece together her life and dreams.

She didn't honestly know whether she was still living with them because of her publicly stated reason that after Quantico she would go wherever the FBI sent her and get her own place then (so why spend the money now on her own apartment?) or because she was too scared to live on her own.

The fact that her nightmares had returned five weeks ago had been weighing heavily on her. She'd been spending less time with Sean because she didn't want him to know. She'd dealt with bad dreams before, on her own. She'd do it again.

But everything was crashing down *now*, and it was easier to be angry with Sean for pushing her into helping than to address her future.

And if she were really being honest, she wanted to feel sorry for herself. She replayed the FBI interview over and over in her head, trying to figure out what she'd done wrong. Driving to the Virginia suburbs outside D.C. with Sean, focusing on another girl's problems instead of her own, annoyed her, distracted her from her self-pity. Selfish? *Yes.* If she'd had the energy to argue with Sean, she would be home right now, in bed, trying to sleep, since it had eluded her all night. Yet she thought that she might make the difference in tracking the whereabouts of Kirsten Benton, she hadn't tried to get out of it when Sean picked her up.

Sean turned off I-95 into the Woodbridge suburb. With fifty thousand residents, planned developments, and strategically placed parks and schools, Woodbridge was a great place to raise kids, but Lucy could imagine how teenagers might easily go stir-crazy. Especially a teenager who had been transplanted three thousand miles from her friends and family by a mother who couldn't see beyond her own pain and feelings of betrayal.

Several houses in the Bentons' neighborhood had "for sale" or "bank owned" signs posted in the yard, an all-too-familiar sight across the country, particularly in the halted growth of suburbia. Sean stopped in front of a split-level house more than twenty years old, standard fare for this part of Virginia. The neighborhood was pleasant but unremarkable, the houses on wide lots with bare trees including thinned-out pines separating them from their neighbors. Quiet, not particularly quaint, and now empty, which Lucy suspected had more to do with commuters than the foul weather.

What kind of home did Kirsten have before her father betrayed her mother and her mother ran away with Kirsten? What did Kirsten see when she came home from school every day—or, more important, what *didn't* she see? She was four months from graduating, her future bright, colleges wanting her, yet she sought something she couldn't get from her family, couldn't get from her new friends, something that took her away again and again . . .

Lucy's stomach clenched as she realized that it was four months before graduation when she first started talking to the man she believed was nineteen-year-old Georgetown freshman Trevor Conrad. Someone who seemed to know and understand her better than her friends did, better than her family did. What Lucy had not known until it was too late was that he'd researched her long before he contacted her. Knew her favorite bands. Her favorite movies. Her favorite books. All because of places she'd visited and made comments about on the World Wide Web. He knew she was the youngest of seven, came from a family of cops and military heroes. He understood—even though she never said it in so many words—that she wanted to get away from home because of the deep sadness that had permeated her family after the mur-

der of her nephew Justin when she and Justin were
only seven.

"Trevor Conrad" had known more about her than
anyone else, and she'd walked right into his trap.

Had Kirsten made similar mistakes?

"Lucy, what's wrong?" Sean asked.

She shook her head, realizing that she was staring
into space and Sean had been trying to talk to her
about Kirsten and her mother. "What isn't wrong?"
she countered, not able to discuss her thoughts right
now. "I'm ready, though you hardly need me."

"We need to talk to Kirsten's friends, and you've
worked with teens. You know their in-speak, so to
speak." He smiled at his humor.

"And you don't?" she said. "I'm here, so let's get
on with it."

He took her hand and kissed it. "You're not really
mad at me."

She raised her eyebrows. "Yes, I am." But she
wasn't, not at Sean. Not anymore.

He reached out and lifted the amethyst daisy pendant off her chest. "No, you're not."

"I'm not going to take my anger out on a beautiful
piece of jewelry just because the gift-giver picked the
lock on my bedroom door."

He kissed her. "I'll try not to do it again."

"Try?"

"I'm not going to make any promises I'm not sure
I can keep."

Lucy supposed that honesty was better than false
promises, but she cherished her privacy, and Sean was
going to have to learn that sometimes she needed to
be alone.

They walked up to the front door. Sean had a key and let them in. "Evelyn had to work today, but that's just as well because I work better without someone asking a million questions."

"She's worried."

Sean closed the door behind them. "I don't like that Kirsten hasn't contacted anyone, not her mother or a friend."

"Unless one of her friends is keeping a secret."

"That's what I was thinking." He walked down the hall to the kitchen. "First I'm going to check Kirsten's cell phone records. Evelyn told me she left them on the kitchen table."

He motioned up the stairs. "Kirsten's room is at the top on the right. Patrick and I searched it yesterday, didn't notice anything odd other than what I told you. But maybe you'll see something different."

"Because I'm a girl?"

"Exactly." He kissed her again. "I'm going to set up down here and go through the phone records."

Sean watched as Lucy went upstairs. He hadn't been sure she'd like the daisy necklace because she rarely wore jewelry. He was pleased to see the pendant around her neck.

Sean sat at the table and pulled out his spreadsheet of Kirsten's friends and their phone numbers. He compared that list to the cell phone log. Nothing looked unusual. Next, he looked at the phone numbers on the log that didn't match up to Kirsten's known friends.

There was one number in the 917 area code that kept coming up. Sean searched the prefix. It was retained for cell phones in New York City. Who did

Kirsten know in New York? Sean looked at last Friday's phone calls and noted that the same number called Kirsten in the morning and they spoke for eight minutes.

He dialed the number. It went straight to voice mail, a generic computer voice telling him to leave a message at the tone.

He emailed Patrick to run a reverse telephone directory search on that number while he continued to go through the rest of the current calls.

The last call Kirsten made was at 1:07 Sunday morning, to that same 917 number. It lasted one minute.

The records didn't identify where text messages were sent or at what time, and there was no way of getting those messages unless Sean had the physical phone.

Kirsten called two 212 phone numbers on Saturday, in addition to short calls to the original number. Sean dialed them. One was a restaurant. He asked for their hours and location. Manhattan? He quickly pulled the address up on a map and noted that it was only three blocks from Penn Station.

Amtrak had service from Union Station in D.C. to Penn Station in New York. If Kirsten paid cash, there was no way to trace it. That's why she didn't take her car when she left home; she had taken a train to New York. From Woodbridge, there was both train and bus service direct to Union Station.

He called the second number.

"Clover Motel, Brooklyn."

Brooklyn? That wasn't near Penn Station. "I'm looking for a guest, Kirsten Benton."

"Room number?"

"I don't have it. She would have checked in Friday night."

"Just a sec."

Sean heard the phone placed on a desk and television noise in the background. He Googled the motel for the address. The motel didn't look too bad, though it wasn't a place Sean would stay. Had Kirsten reserved a room, or was she calling a guest?

"Sorry," the clerk came back on the line. "We have no guest by that name."

"What about Ashleigh Benton?"

The clerk sighed. A moment later he said, "No. No Benton. No Kirsten. No Ashleigh. Anything else?" the clerk asked.

"Did you work last Friday night?"

"Who are you?"

"I'm a private investigator looking for a missing teenager."

"How do I know you're not some crazy asshole? You want information, you come down with proper ID, and I'll tell you. I can spot a fake, so don't be pulling any shit with me." The clerk hung up.

Sean didn't much want to go to New York just to talk to a motel clerk when he didn't know for certain that Kirsten had been there.

Lucy shouted from upstairs, "Sean!"

He took the stairs two at a time and almost ran right into Lucy as she stood in the doorway.

"I wasn't sure you heard me," she said.

"What happened?"

"Kirsten emailed Trey." She strode over to the computer. "And he responded."

Facebook threaded messages so you could see the original message and every response chronologically. Kirsten had sent Trey a message at 7:58 a.m.

Trey,

I don't know where to start. I've been sick. I didn't even know it was Thursday until I woke up this morning. I'm better, but I sort of can't walk right now.

It's a long story, but I have no way of getting home. I lost my phone. Tell my mom that I'm OK. I have plenty of money and so, yeah.

I don't know what to do! I'm too scared to go home but scared to stay, too. Isn't that silly? Jessie's message was all wrong! And who would hurt her? I think they know me but maybe not. But don't tell anyone where I am! Please please please. My head is foggy and I can't think. But it's all weird here and the news in the paper doesn't explain anything. I already miss her maybe it was my fault I don't know anything.

Can you pick me up in New York when I figure out where I am? I'm somewhere very nice. It's pretty and there's a big bridge.

So sorry everything you were right I was stupid about everything I want to play softball but now I can't I want to

Several of her sentences were incomplete, and her message ended there, unsigned. Trey had responded at 8:10 a.m. from his mobile phone:

Kirsten, are you still there? What's wrong? I'm leaving for New York right now. Email or call me as soon as you get this message. Are you in the city? Which bridge? It'll take me at least five hours to get there. I'll let you know as soon as I arrive. T.

"He's going to New York?" Sean was furious. "He promised he would call me if she contacted him!"

"I'm worried about her," Lucy said.

"Because she was sick?"

"Read her message carefully. There's a lot of information there, but she must have a fever or maybe she's drugged." Lucy frowned. "She left on Friday?"

Sean nodded. "Did you save that message?"

"Yes, I have a screen capture and I emailed it to myself."

"She has a friend in New York, but when I tried the number it went straight to a generic voice mail. Patrick is running it now. She received a call from that cell number on Friday morning, and left Friday afternoon. She made several calls to the same number after she presumably arrived in New York."

"Where is she staying?" Lucy asked, more to herself.

"She called a motel when she arrived in New York, but the clerk said he didn't have her registered, under Kirsten or Ashleigh."

"Did you describe her?"

"Didn't get the chance. He hung up on me. I don't think the motel has earned even one star."

Lucy said, "Did you see this? *Who would hurt her?* You need to ask her mother if she has a friend or relative in New York."

"As soon as I talk to Trey." Sean dialed his number. The phone rang four times before bouncing to voice mail.

"Trey, I saw the message Kirsten sent you. Don't be an idiot. Call me."

Sean hung up. "Can we send Kirsten a message? A strange guy might scare her, but you—"

Lucy nodded. "I understand." Lucy logged onto her own account and sent Kirsten a message with her contact information as well as some advice.

Call the police as soon as you can and tell them you need to be put in protective custody.

NINE

Suzanne and Detective Panetta had been sitting in the waiting room of CJB Investments for twenty minutes, watching the bustling staff. In the adjoining suite, the Barnett Family Trust offered grants and scholarships to young people for college or the arts.

Suzanne spoke in a low voice, reading information off her BlackBerry. "Wade Barnett is twenty-five, works for his brother, graduated from NYU two years ago. No federal record. You?"

"Two DWIs, that's it. License suspended for a year. Some other stuff. Nothing official, but my boss said he's been pulled in a couple times. Charges dropped."

"On what?"

"Illegal gambling, drunk and disorderly at a nightclub when he was underage. A lot of spoiled rich kids get their hands slapped and sent on their way. The DWIs were more serious; they definitely stuck."

"Where does he live?"

"Upper West Side."

Suzanne said, "On the business side, the investment company is doing well. I put an inquiry into our White Collar Crimes Unit, and it looks like CJB is pretty clean. Ditto the charitable trust. According to my analyst, their last tax filing showed just over fourteen million in scholarships, with an operating budget of less than ten percent."

"Good management. I don't think it's Wade Barnett."

"CJ Barnett is the principal," Suzanne said.

"We tread lightly, Suzanne," Panetta reminded her. "The Barnett Trust is well respected."

"I'm not looking to tarnish anyone's reputation. Just want the truth."

An attractive young female came out to the lobby. "Mr. Barnett is available now. May I bring you anything to drink? Water? Coffee? A glass of wine?"

Suzanne shook her head and Panetta just grinned. They walked into Barnett's large corner office, which seemed incongruous with the rest of the office they'd seen. The expansive view of lower Manhattan was the first thing that struck Suzanne, followed by the opulent office space, which was bigger than her East Village apartment. The steel-gray carpets were soft and plush, the art trendy and local, and an entire wall a shrine to the New York Yankees. Being a Yankees fan scored Barnett points with Panetta. Suzanne preferred the Mets.

Wade Barnett was lounging on his couch talking on the phone. His feet were bare, and he wore simple khakis and an oxford-style shirt with a tie, sleeves rolled up. His brown hair was thick and shaggy, in one of those styles where he could step out of the shower looking good. His poise and style suggested he knew he was attractive.

"Gotta go, Jimmy. But we're on for the Knicks tonight, right? I'll swing by and pick you up at the bar in an hour."

He hung up. "It's not baseball, but it'll pass the time until April," he said.

Even Wade Barnett's welcoming smile was charming, in an arrogant and privileged way.

"I'm Special Agent Suzanne Madeaux with the FBI. This is NYPD Detective Vic Panetta. Thank you for taking the time to meet with us. We hope you'll be able to help with a case we're working."

"Shoot." He sat up straight and grabbed a baseball off the table, tossing it between his hands. "Sit, please. What can I do?"

Suzanne and Panetta sat in leather chairs across from Barnett. Panetta said, "We came to you because we heard you were familiar with underground parties in the city."

Barnett frowned. "I don't care to talk about that."

Suzanne knew they would lose him quickly if they were too rigid. She said, "We're not here about the parties specifically, we're here about a murder. And because you're in the know about the parties. I don't really care at this point if you're the one setting them up. What I *do* care about are four dead young women."

Barnett leaned forward. "Is this about the Cinderella Strangler?"

Suzanne cringed at the moniker, but nodded. "We need to know who set up those parties and how the guests found out about them. Whether they were open or closed. If there's a formal invite list. Who's in charge. Their families deserve to know what happened."

"I'd love to help, really—I feel rotten about those

girls. But you should know the parties aren't exactly formal. No one calls me to set them up; there's no invite list, really nothing in writing. When someone sets up a party, word gets out and people show up."

"How do people hear about the parties?" Suzanne asked. Though Josh Haynes had explained how information spread, she wanted Barnett's version.

"Mostly online or text messages. Those who go know what to do, it sort of feeds on itself, they bring friends, and so on."

"Is there a specific website?"

"No, not for all the parties. Different groups might have their own sites, you know, like a club or a fraternity or whatever. But there's no central website for every party in the city."

"We were led to believe that there wasn't an underground party in New York that you didn't sanction."

"*Whoa!* I wouldn't say that." Barnett's expression changed from helpful to wary. "Do I need a lawyer? My brother is a stickler about this kind of stuff. I got in trouble once for mouthing off to a cop, and I don't want to be in trouble."

"And I want to stop a psychopath before he kills another young woman," said Suzanne. "I'd think you'd want the same thing. If word gets out that a serial killer is targeting your parties, attendance might drop way down."

"Serial killer?" He looked troubled, but she didn't know if it was an act. "I really can't help. They're not *my* parties. I just hear about most of them. Not all, certainly, but people tell me things. You know how it is." He shrugged as if to say *because I'm me*.

Suzanne bit back a snarky comment and instead

said, "You keep your finger on the pulse of the parties, so to speak."

He nodded.

"How many are there?"

"A night? A week? A year? It varies. There are so many fascinating abandoned structures that are perfectly safe, left to rot by bankrupt companies or absentee owners. I've been buying some as I can, fixing them up, reselling or leasing them. I love the old architecture, the original designs, the fascinating history of some of these places."

Suzanne made a note to check on Barnett's financials. He talked a good game, but Panetta had said that big brother CJ ran the show.

"It would be helpful to us if we knew the extent of the parties. If we want to stop this killer, we need to know when and where he might strike again."

"There are secret parties every night, most relatively small. There's a variety of party types—the raves, the frat parties, the drug parties, the sex parties. Sometimes a combination, but then there're also the people who go. Some are all black, some all white, some race isn't an issue. The big parties—over maybe two hundred people—are usually on the weekends. I wouldn't say *every* weekend, but close to it. There's something for everyone—not all of the parties are drugs and drinking and dancing. There's a large black Christian church that has a huge revival-type party once a year, gospel rock, amazing food, and totally dry. They don't have the money to lease a place big enough, so they find a building that fits their needs."

Every weekend? They had four dead girls in four

months, but no specific pattern in location or date—
only that they were killed late on a Saturday night,
and the time between murders was getting shorter.

Suzanne slid across the glass coffee table a list with
the locations of the bodies and the estimated day the
victim was killed. "We need to know who organized
these parties. We think we know who put on the parties in the Bronx and Brooklyn, but the frat party
here, and then the Harlem party, we need more info.
Any ideas?"

Barnett looked at the list. "The frat party is a college thing; I don't know much about that. You should
talk to Alpha Gamma Pi—they're not the biggest frat
at Columbia, but they're on the ball."

Suzanne made a note, though she was pretty confident that she'd read in Panetta's reports that he'd can-
vassed all the frats and didn't get anything useful.

Panetta opened a file and showed Barnett the photographs of the four dead women. They weren't the
morgue photos, but pictures provided by their families or the DMV.

"Do you know any of these young women? Maybe
you met them at a party, or through business or college?"

Barnett stared at the pictures. His face was blank,
almost impassive, but Suzanne noticed he swallowed
several times.

He shook his head. "No," he said. He cleared his
throat. "Sorry."

Suzanne would bet her pension that he knew at
least one of the girls. Maybe all of them. Maybe she
was facing a killer.

Panetta also picked up the strange vibes. He

glanced at her and gave a brief shake of his head, and she concurred. They needed more information, and then they'd bring him in for a formal interview at the station.

Suzanne stood and said, "Thank you for your time, Mr. Barnett. If you think of anything else, or hear something that might help us narrow down which parties this murderer may be targeting, please call either myself or Detective Panetta. You have our cards."

Outside the door, Suzanne lowered her voice. "Something's going on. He knows at least one of these victims."

"Absolutely. And either he's surprised that some-one's dead or he's surprised that we're on to him."

"Either way, he's a person of interest."

Suzanne talked Panetta into grabbing a drink at a bar to discuss the case. He agreed, provided it was near his subway stop. He called his wife and said he'd be an hour late. By the time he'd disconnected, there were two beers in front of them.

They toasted. "To catch a killer," Panetta said.

Suzanne sipped her bottled Samuel Adams, a fa-vorite of hers since college. Panetta drank Coors Light on tap. "Barnett," she said.

"Ballsy. Arrogant. Until he saw the pictures."

"Guilty?"

"Of something. But murder? He doesn't seem the kind of guy who'd kill a girl with a plastic bag over her head."

"He doesn't seem like the kind of guy who'd beat them to a pulp, either. Did you notice his hands?"

Panetta laughed. "Manicured."

"Soft. No hard labor. He's more the type of dude who'd push a girl off a bridge in a moment of rage."

"Really?" Panetta looked at her as if she were an alien.

She shrugged. "I know, sometimes you can't tell who's a killer by looking at them, but I assess people by how they'd kill—if they were driven to it. He doesn't appear to have the personality of a serial killer. But I'm going to run him up the flagpole, get a full background and psych profile on him based on what we know. Ted Bundy didn't look like a serial killer on the surface."

"Do you think he was feeding us a line about the fraternity? Trying to steer us away?"

She sipped her beer as she thought. "Maybe, but we need to follow up anyway. You talked to the frats, right?"

"Hicks and three officers spoke to the president of each fraternity at Columbia, and all denied that they'd organized the party. But three of the four victims were college students, two at Columbia."

"It was the second victim who wasn't a student, right?"

"Erica Ripley. She was twenty-one, worked at a coffeehouse."

"Still, three of the four—"

"Underground parties are a favorite of the college crowd."

"With how many colleges and universities there are in New York City, two of the victims were at Columbia?"

"I can assure you that we followed up with what

we had," Panetta said, slightly defensive. "But we had shit. No one came forward. Of those we spoke to afterward, they were either surprised the victim was at the party, or they said they'd warned the victim that the parties were dangerous and to be careful. We have little physical evidence."

"I wasn't second-guessing your investigation." Suzanne hoped she hadn't come off as overly critical. "Just thinking out loud."

After a moment, Panetta said, "I agree, we should take another walk through the frats."

"We can split them up."

"I'll get the list from Hicks."

"What happened to the roommate of the first victim?" Suzanne asked. "Did you say she dropped out and moved back home?"

"Jill Reeves," Panetta said.

"You remember her?"

"It was the first interview of the case. She took it hard. She and the victim had been best friends since they were kids."

Suzanne hadn't been involved in the investigation at that point. "I'd like to talk to her, if you don't mind. Now that we know more, maybe she'll have additional information that didn't seem important at the time." The first victim, Alanna Andrews, had been killed the last week of October. The other three were all killed since the beginning of the year.

The murders themselves stuck out because of the lack of violence. No rape, no blood at all. All the victims had sex prior to their murders, but not with the same men. It was theoretically possible for the killer to have used a condom and not left his DNA on the

victims, but even with protection there would likely
be hair and other trace evidence to match up. But
until they had a suspect, getting any of those results
was impossible.

"Have the victims been tested for the standard date
rape drugs?" she asked. "It might explain lack of
physical evidence of rape."

"I don't recall. I think not, because there didn't
seem to be a sexual component to the crimes. With
the budget being so tight, the lab is being careful with
what we order, but they'd preserve blood and tissue
for future testing. If they were intentionally drugged,
would that change anything?"

"It might change the profile of the killer."

"Do you have a profile?"

"Not officially." When she first got the case she
talked to Quantico, but they didn't have enough information to develop a working profile. She should
send the new information and physical evidence to
them and see what they could come up with psycho-
logically. "Would you mind if I contact the NYPD lab
and have them send blood and tissue samples to
Quantico to run a pattern of drug tests?"

"Be my guest."

It might not yield any valuable information, but it
was definitely worth a shot.

"The girls were definitely high," Panetta pointed
out. "They did a standard tox and drug screen, and
they were all legally drunk and had narcotics in their
system."

"The same type of drugs?"

"No, not that I recall. Two on speed, one had high-
end cocaine—there were still crystals in her nasal cav-

ities. One had not only been smoking pot, but there was a nice little stash in her purse."

"This last victim didn't have a purse on her."

"Neither did the second," Panetta pointed out. "She had an ankle band with fifty dollars in it."

"I'm familiar—I used to go to a lot of rock concerts. You don't want to carry around a purse."

Something connected these victims, other than their age. Two blondes, a redhead, a brunette. Heights ranged from five foot three to five foot six. Three college students, one not. Three Caucasian, one Hispanic. No defensive wounds, which made sense because they were drunk and drugged. But Suzanne suspected that there was a date rape drug in there, even if the killer hadn't raped the victims. Mixed with alcohol, those drugs often caused the victims to become lethargic or unconscious. It would make it that much easier to put a plastic bag over their head and suffocate them without any fuss.

"I had been thinking that the killer had to be strong to hold the girls up while they died," Suzanne said, "but he wouldn't have to be particularly strong if they were under the influence."

"Hmm, maybe."

"You disagree?"

"I've seen guys drunker than a skunk fight back hard. Maybe our vics were unable to get out of the guy's grip—they hadn't seen the bag or whatever he used—because they were too stoned to know what was happening at first. But they'd know pretty quick." Panetta finished his beer. "I asked the coroner to send lung samples to your lab at Quantico. He

can't pinpoint what type of plastic was used to suffocate the victims, and with the workload—"

"No explanation necessary. I'll light a fire under
their asses and hopefully we'll get something that
helps." She wasn't holding her breath. If she were
going to suffocate someone, she'd use a common
plastic garbage bag, something not easily traceable.
But she was a trained cop. A common killer—even an
uncommon psychopath—might not be so smart. She
could hope. "The fact that none of our victims fought
back lends credence to the theory that they were
dosed with GHB or something."

"Hate to tell you, but at these parties I've heard
that both the boys and girls take the drugs voluntarily. Maybe the girls weren't slipped the drugs, but it
was part of the overall party experience."

Suzanne didn't understand that. She enjoyed sex—
quite a lot—and she'd never needed drugs or alcohol
to loosen her up. She liked her beer after work, and
that was it.

She nodded toward his beer. "Another?"

Panetta shook his head. "Thanks, but I need to get
home."

He took out his wallet.

"I got this one." She gestured to the bartender for
a second Sam Adams.

"Thanks, kid."

"I'm going to talk to Haynes again, and I'm thinking if we talk to Barnett when he doesn't expect it, we
can rattle him. I'd like to find something specific to
rattle him with."

"If you go for Barnett, ring me. I don't trust that
brat as far as I can throw him."

"You think he's the killer."

"I think he's a spoiled rich kid who doesn't know boundaries. He could kill, if provoked. But I don't know if he's who we're looking for."

Suzanne watched Panetta walk away with a wave to the other off-duty cops in the bar.

The bartender put her second bottle in front of her and took her empty away.

Barnett was capable of murder, perhaps, but Suzanne didn't think he was smart enough to kill four women and not leave any evidence or witnesses. If he killed, it would be out of rage or passion. Like at a girlfriend who dumped him. When women end up dead, cops look at the men in their lives. Stranger murders are much rarer.

She wasn't going to second-guess Panetta—and after the third murder, when she was brought on board, she'd already bought into the theory that they were dealing with a serial killer. But that didn't mean that the killer hadn't been involved with at least one of the victims. Statistically, most serial killers knew one or more of their victims personally—whether they were friendly with the person or it was someone they saw regularly.

Like a college student.

Or the barista at a coffeehouse.

Alanna Andrews was the first victim. Erica Ripley, the second, was the only victim who didn't attend college. Suzanne would start with them.

Satisfied that she had a place to begin first thing in the morning, she focused on the big-screen TV.

Seven p.m. The Knicks were playing at Madison Square Garden. She didn't care either way about basketball, and she could go home and review her notes and plan her interviews with the people in Andrews's and Ripley's lives. But she'd been reviewing the files every night since she landed on the task force, and nothing had changed except her focus. Suzanne needed a break, just to unwind, so she could come in fresh in the morning.

She pulled out her cell phone and dialed her closest friend in the city. "Mac, it's Suz. Have plans tonight?"

"Just getting off duty."

"I'm sitting at Uglies with my Sam Adams watching the Knicks game."

"I'll be there in fifteen minutes."

Suzanne hung up and sipped her beer. She had friends with benefits, too, some of which were quite impressive.

TEN

Sean sat at his desk in his second-floor office. Lucy was sitting across from him, typing away on her laptop. The rain that had started when they left Woodbridge was a deluge by the time they'd pulled into his driveway. The steady downpour continued to drum against the windows.

The narrow, three-story, hundred-year-old house was both Sean's business and residence. He and Patrick had done most of the renovation work themselves in December when they established RCK East. The living room downstairs had been converted into the main office, the library into Patrick's office, and the formal parlor would someday be their assistant's workspace—that is, when they had enough business to justify hiring an administrator. In the back, cut off from their work area by double doors, was the kitchen and living area. An enclosed sunporch led to a postage-stamp backyard dominated by two towering old trees.

Sean hoped the trees survived the storm. The winds were fierce.

Originally, combining their business and residences had seemed a smart move to save money while they built the business. Sean and Patrick had no problems living together because each had his own space. How-

ever, that was before Sean started sleeping with
Patrick's sister. Now, Sean wished he had his own
apartment. Lucy had been uncomfortable sleeping
with Sean under her older brother's roof, and Sean
certainly wasn't going to ask her to stay with him
now that Patrick was back in town. At least not until
Patrick got over his problems with their relationship.
Sean didn't want to do anything to put his new relationship with Lucy in jeopardy.

He wanted to spend his time with her lying around
in bed, talking, making love, watching her sleep. He
missed the wonderful week they'd had before Patrick
returned from his last job, when Lucy had spent every
night in his bed.

"Do I have a zit on my nose or something?" Lucy
asked.

He shook his head. "Sorry, I was thinking."

"You were staring at me."

"I was staring into space and you're in the way."
He grinned and leaned forward. "You're much prettier than empty space."

"I think there's a compliment in there somewhere,"
Lucy said.

His computer beeped. He pulled up a message from
Jayne Morgan, the computer magician at RCK. She
could pull information out of thin air, or so it seemed.

He read the note and smiled. "Jayne came through.
We got the name on that 917 number Kirsten has
been calling. Jessica Bell."

"Any idea who she is?"

"No, just the name and her address."

"That's a plus. New York City?"

"Yes." He typed it into his computer. Up popped a map. "Three blocks from Columbia University."

"Is she a student?" Lucy asked. "Maybe Kirsten was talking to her about going to school there."

"She was only applying to California colleges," Sean said.

"How do you know?"

"Her mother had a copy of all her applications. And I saw the brochures in her room."

"Have you been able to retrieve her deleted emails?"

"Not yet. The program is still running, but the older they are the less likely I'll be able to get them. I'm going to run a search on Jessica Bell at this address and see if I can learn anything more. Maybe Kirsten went to New York to visit this Jessica Bell, and got sick."

"And didn't have Jessica call her mother?" Lucy shook her head.

"Their relationship was rocky. Kirsten emailed Trey, not her mother, to let them know she was okay."

"She was anything but okay."

Sean caught Lucy's eye. "She could have been high when she wrote that."

"At eight in the morning?"

"Maybe left over from the night before."

"I've been analyzing the message she sent," Lucy said. "Sick can mean any number of things—being hungover, food poisoning, the flu—but she also says that she can't walk."

"You think she broke her leg?"

"If that's the case, wouldn't your search of the hospitals have come up with something?"

"Not if she refused to give her name, or used a false identity."

"If she didn't give her name, wouldn't they have recognized her from the photo on the missing persons flyer?"

"I got this case yesterday morning. Less than forty-eight hours ago. I don't think the hospitals have someone sitting on the emails and fax machines twenty-four/seven getting ready to distribute photos to all staff. Besides, we only sent out beyond a hundred miles when I found out about New York."

Lucy glanced down.

"I didn't mean to sound like that," Sean said. "It's just that in my experience missing teenagers are a lower priority. They probably posted her photo on a board and if someone recognizes her, they'll contact the Woodbridge Police Department, or RCK. But she's been missing since Friday, and the last time she used her phone was late Saturday night. Let's assume she got hurt, broke her leg or something. Went to the hospital. If she tried to use her insurance, her name would be in the system, and as a minor they would have contacted her mother, or protective services."

"You're right."

Lucy didn't say anything more, and Sean mentally hit himself. She had been so defeated this morning, thinking she wasn't good enough for the FBI, and here he'd shot down one of her theories.

He let it sit for a minute, then said, "What if she didn't go to the hospital?"

Lucy either didn't hear him or was ignoring him.

"Lucy, what is it?"

"It's not important. You're right, she was probably high."

"Stop."

She glared at him. "What?"

"You're doing it again. I want to know what you're thinking."

"Why? It's really just a way-out-there idea. You should probably talk to Kate. I bet she'll have a reasonable theory."

"If I wanted to bring Kate into the investigation, I would have done it already, but right now this isn't a federal case, and she can't help me."

Lucy was torn, he could see it. He'd jabbed her where it hurt, because she didn't want to feel like a failure. He needed her on her game, focused on finding Kirsten, and the only way to get there was to push her hard enough for her to realize that without her, they'd be two steps behind.

"I think she's in hiding," Lucy finally said. "I think she's sick—either from drugs or the flu—but she's hiding from someone. See?" She slid over a handwritten sheet where she'd copied down phrases from Kirsten's email, rewording a couple but keeping them in context, removing all the extra words and unintelligible thoughts, and reorganizing the main ideas into groups under two headings.

<u>Personal Facts</u>
I've been sick
I can't walk right now
No way of getting home
Lost my phone

Plenty of money
In New York (view of bridge?)
Want to play softball, now can't

Friend
Her message was wrong
Who would hurt her?
They might know me
Scared (to stay or go)
I already miss her
The paper doesn't explain

Sean read the list twice, and saw exactly what Lucy did. "Her friend is dead."

She nodded. "Could it be Jessica Bell?"

Sean narrowed his search to media sites. "If it was her, her death hasn't been reported, at least not with her name."

"Or maybe her body hasn't been found. What if Kirsten saw something? Or she went to meet her friend and she was already dead? We don't even know why she was going to New York. Unless—"

Lucy turned to her laptop and started typing rapidly.

"What are you looking for?"

"Just checking something."

Sean resisted the urge to get up and look over her shoulder. He continued to narrow his search parameters on Jessica Bell by including Columbia University in the mix. He quickly confirmed that she was a student.

"That's it," Lucy said. "Look." She turned her laptop to face him.

Lucy had brought up Kirsten's page on Facebook, and showed all her "friends."

Jessica Bell was among them.

"See her?" Lucy said.

Sean nodded and reached over to click on Jessica's profile, to get a clearer image of the blonde, but Lucy slapped his hand. "Wait a minute, there's more." She switched tabs, and there was Kirsten's *Party Girl* page. "Do you see her network of friends at the bottom?"

"Yes."

"Now click on the girl named 'Jenna.' "

Sean did as Lucy said, and a larger picture came up. "It's Jessica."

"Exactly. That's why Kirsten went to New York—to visit Jessica—and I suspect it had something to do with activities related to the *Party Girl* site. It's no coincidence."

Sean looked at Lucy's list of Kirsten's key phrases. "She's scared because something happened to Jessica, and she's hiding. Or maybe she's hiding out with Jessica. If the two of them are in trouble, they might think it's better to lay low for a while."

"Especially if they were injured or attacked. But, from the message, it seems that Jessica is the one who's missing. And if that's the case, who's Kirsten staying with?"

"Maybe at Jessica's apartment."

"Could be. She's scared, but sounds like she doesn't want to leave. She says it's pretty and there's a view of a bridge. Is there a bridge near Jessica's apartment?"

"There are lots of bridges in New York," he said. "That's what Google Earth is for." He zeroed in on

Jessica's address. "She wouldn't be able to see any bridge from that location. So if Kirsten's not at Jessica's, who's helping her?"

"Maybe someone else on her friend list." Lucy pulled out a sheet where she'd noted all the friends on Kirsten's Facebook and *Party Girl* profiles.

"That's a lot of people to go through, but we can get started tonight. Before we go to New York."

"You're going to New York?"

"*We* are going to New York," Sean said. "You and me. That's where Kirsten is, and Trey is likely there by now if he didn't drown in this storm."

"You really want me to go?"

"I won't go without you," he said.

"Let's get back to work." Lucy stretched her back, then turned the laptop back to face herself. Sean rose and walked behind her chair. He put his hands on her shoulders and used his thumbs on her muscles. "You're really tense. You've been working too long without a break." He switched to his palms and wondered how much of her tightness was from the FBI letter and how much was from their work today.

"Umm," she moaned and closed her eyes, her head tilting back as she relaxed, revealing her long, elegant, smooth neck. "Don't stop."

Lucy had no idea how sexy she looked in this position. Her lips parted a fraction, and he swallowed. He wanted to make love to her right here, right now, on his desk. Or the floor. Or he'd carry her to his bed— he didn't really care where they were.

He leaned over and kissed her, upside down. Then he continued rubbing her upper back and arms.

"What was that for?"

"I was compelled to kiss you. You must have cast a spell over me. I'm completely enchanted, Princess."

"That's right," she teased with a sly smile, "so keep working on those muscles, Prince Charming, and I might share another kiss."

"All right, if you insist." Her hair hung down the back of the chair in black waves. Her cheeks were high and well formed, her nose long and narrow, her skin with just a hint of brown, a light blend of her Irish-Cuban heritage. He stared at the daisy that rested in the dip of her neck and was taken aback at the powerful emotions hitting him. He'd known Lucy was special from the beginning, but at this moment, he felt something else: a complex need to love and protect her, to support her now and later, to give her everything he could—not material objects, but his real self.

He was far from perfect. Smart? Oh, yeah, he was a damn genius, if anyone looked at his IQ. Sometimes too smart, and he had a past that someone who liked him might charitably call "colorful." But Sean was still the same person he'd always been, the one with the overwhelming need to right wrongs, even if that meant breaking the law. He was no vigilante, not by a long shot, but he could not tolerate bullies. They made him see red, and that had gotten him into hot water many times.

Lucy needed to know everything about him, but it wasn't as if he could just sit her down and give her a chronological history of his life, the good, the bad, and the illegal. His big brother Duke had gotten him out of trouble more times than he could count, but Duke didn't know everything. And even now, Sean didn't regret his past. If he hadn't turned the tables on that pedophile professor at Stanford, how many other little girls would the man have molested before he was caught?

Sometimes, you had to do the right thing even when it got you in trouble.

Lucy looked peaceful, an expression he hadn't seen on her much lately. He loved that he was able to give her that momentary peace, that she could relax with him, that he made her laugh and smile.

He kissed her again; he couldn't resist.

"Your hands are amazing," she said, obviously enjoying the shoulder massage.

"I know."

"The Rogan ego speaks."

"Yes, ma'am." He turned her chair to face him.

She opened her eyes and raised an eyebrow. "Done so soon?"

"I haven't gotten started yet." Putting his hands on the armrests on either side of her, he leaned over and kissed her, drawing her bottom lip into his mouth. Her hands went up to the back of his neck, her long fingers in his hair.

I've missed you.

"What?" she murmured faintly.

Had he spoken out loud? Maybe he had. He pulled his lips reluctantly from hers. "I've missed being with you. I was spoiled when you stayed here. Ten days. I liked sliding between the sheets and smelling you even after you went back home, but even Rogans have to wash their sheets."

It was a joke, at least the last part, but she didn't smile.

"What?" He kissed her. "Did I say something?"

She shook her head and pulled his lips back to hers. He couldn't read Lucy the way he read other people, yet her depth and complexity had drawn him in from the beginning.

"Excuse me," a voice came from the doorway.

Lucy jumped, her body instantly tense, and Sean stood, taking one of Lucy's hands into his.

Patrick stood in the doorway, a dark cloud over his face. Lucy saw it, and she looked embarrassed.

That angered Sean. He wasn't angry at Lucy, but he was furious with Patrick for sounding so self-righteous in his tone, for making Lucy uncomfortable. What he and Lucy shared should make her happy, but Patrick was doing everything he could to put a wedge between them, however subtle. Their conversation yesterday had revealed the ugly truth, and if Patrick thought Sean was backing down he was an idiot.

"I have the preliminary background checks done on Trey Danielson and his family, and the server host information from the *Party Girl* website."

"Anything interesting?" Sean asked. Lucy tried to extract her hand, but he wouldn't let her go.

"Danielson's father is a high-ranking consultant for the Congressional House Committee on Appropriations. His mother works for the Library of Congress. They've been married for twenty-six years. Danielson has an older brother, career Army, deployed in Afghanistan, rank first lieutenant. Twenty-four years, went through the ROTC program at University of Virginia. Nothing pops on any of them, but with the dad's position I need to be cautious so I don't trip any invisible wires the FBI might have on him. So far I haven't found anything on the kids, either, at least in official records. Trey has a 2005 Ford Ranger registered in his name. I sent you the license, make, and model."

Patrick continued. "As far as the server that hosts the *Party Girl* site, it's routed through several different servers, but I traced it to New York City. There's a duplicate site in Europe."

"New York?" Yet another connection. "Do you have an address?"

"Just the provider, but that means nothing. It's just an office. I don't know where the servers are, and the site itself has full privacy protections, using the provider as the contact and address."

"That's all I need," Sean said. "Once I know the host I can track down who pays the bills."

"Don't you dare hack into the database," Patrick said.

Sean didn't like Patrick's tone. "I have no intention of hacking into any place. I have plenty of legal ways to get the information we need, especially since Lucy and I are going to New York in the morning."

Patrick looked at Lucy, then said to Sean, "You're bringing my sister? I'm your partner."

Sean realized he'd handled this poorly, but Patrick had overstepped with the hacking comment.

"Kirsten is a teenager who may need help when we find her. We don't know what's been going on with her, but she's more apt to trust Lucy than a strange man."

"Sounds good," Patrick said sarcastically.

"What's your problem?"

"I thought we were equal partners. But if you're calling the shots, fine. I'll hold down the fort here."

Lucy stood. "It's not like that, Patrick."

"It's not like what?"

"Hold it," Sean said. He needed to defuse the situation. "You want to go to New York, go right ahead, but Lucy is the one who figured out that Kirsten and Jessica Bell—the 917 number she had been calling for several months and the last call she made—are both on the *Party Girl* site. She understands how these things work better than either of us. And Kirsten is in serious trouble."

"Then you should bring in the police."

"I will, when we have more than a cryptic message to go on. What can the police do?"

"Put out a BOLO? Talk to their informants? Work the case?"

"For a teenager who has been branded a habitual runaway?" Sean shook his head. "When I have something to turn over, I will. I'm not a maverick."

"Really?"

Lucy said, "Patrick, I think that Kirsten got into something she can't get out of, and she's confused and scared and doesn't have anyone to turn to. When we find her, we'll have the answers. And get her the necessary help. She's only seventeen. I doubt she considered the repercussions of what she was doing on the *Party Girl* site."

"It was pretty clear from the photographs," he snapped.

"You think that because she made a bad decision she deserves what she gets?" Sean asked.

"That's not what I meant."

"Then what did you mean?"

Patrick didn't answer, but he looked torn. Sean wasn't about to cut him any slack, however.

"What time are we leaving tomorrow?" Lucy asked Sean.

"Early. I'd fly, but in this weather it's probably best we drive." He looked at Patrick. "Unless you want to go."

Patrick shook his head.

"I'll pick you up at seven," Sean told Lucy. "I should take you home now; it's getting late."

Lucy nodded. "Thanks, but I'd like Patrick to drive me." She gave Sean a look that he thought held something secret, but he couldn't figure it out. "Okay, Patrick?"

Her big brother shrugged. "I'll get my keys." He left.

"Luce, what's wrong? Did I do or say something—"

She cut Sean off. "No, of course not." She kissed him. It was a peck, nothing more, as if she were afraid Patrick would walk in again. "I want to talk to my brother, and it's better if it's just him and me."

Sean frowned and grabbed her hands. "Why are you so tense when Patrick is around?"

"I'm not."

"You act like he caught us doing something wrong."

"No, I just feel funny—he hasn't really come around to us seeing each other."

"And what if he doesn't?"

"He will."

She kissed him again, and this time Sean didn't let her back off. He held the back of her head, and kissed her long enough for her to feel it all the way home. "We're going on vacation," he said. "You, me, no one else." They'd been planning to go after she'd recuperated from the attack five weeks ago, but then she'd needed to prepare for her FBI interview, and he knew she'd be too preoccupied waiting for the results to enjoy a long weekend away. Now? As soon as they found Kirsten, he was taking her away.

She smiled. "I'm looking forward to it."

Three or four days, time to be together without any work, without stress, and without her overprotective brother.

Patrick pulled into the narrow driveway behind Dillon's Lexus but kept the engine running. The heat had just started to warm the car when they reached the Kincaid house.

"You wanted to talk?" he asked.

"What's wrong?" Lucy asked from the passenger seat.

"Nothing's wrong."

She shook her head. "Right. Nothing. You obviously don't like me being involved with Sean. But he's your friend and partner. You trust him. You like him."

"In business, yes." Patrick glared at her. "Not sleeping with my sister."

"Okay, just get over it; you're acting silly." Lucy was trying to make the conversation light because she couldn't bear for Patrick not to approve. *That*

sounded silly, too—she'd never sought his approval
for any previous boyfriend, but with Sean it was different because of the complexity of their personal and
business lives. "You should be happy that I'm involved with someone you like and respect."

"And you should respect my feelings and trust
me."

Lucy really didn't understand why Patrick was
being so negative about Sean. She pushed. "Patrick,
you need to trust *me*. I'm twenty-five, I can pick my
own boyfriends. Sean has been wonderful for me.
He's teaching me how to have fun, something I've
missed for a long time. He makes me *laugh*. If you're
worried that if things fall apart it'll impact you and
your business, don't. I'm mature enough to know that
relationships don't always succeed."

"Why do you care what I think anyway?"

"Because you're my brother and I love you."

Patrick rubbed his eyes. "Luce, I'm sorry I've been
a wet blanket. I don't want to be." He looked at her
with the love and kindness she'd always associated
with him. "Your happiness means more to me than
anything. But I know Sean. Business? He's honestly
the smartest person I know. He's a lot smarter than he
acts sometimes, truly brilliant, and not just with computers. Also, he really cares about people, and he
never gives up. He has a lot going for him.

"But with women," Patrick continued, his tone
going from admiring to disdainful, "time and again,
he's been shallow and self-indulgent. He has a past
I'm sure he hasn't shared with you, and I don't think
you're going to like it very much. He doesn't stick,

not in relationships. He doesn't even see it in himself. In the short time I've known him, he's had dozens of girlfriends. Models and actresses and trust-fund bimbos. Most of them as self-indulgent as he is. He grew tired of them, because that's the way he is. You deserve someone who will love you, who will stick by you, forever. In good times and bad, that kind of commitment. *You* need to come first."

Lucy didn't like this conversation, and almost regretted having started it, but at least she knew exactly where Patrick stood. "I understand what you're saying, but I don't think you know Sean as well as you think."

"Maybe *you* don't."

"Just let me work my way through this. Sean isn't perfect, and neither am I. But you need to have faith in me, even if I make a mistake. No matter what happens, I'll be okay."

He shrugged. "I can't change the way I feel. I'm sure you'll be fine—you always seem to bounce back. I've always supported your decisions because I understood them, but you need to be honest with yourself. Your decisions about men have never been good, and I don't see them changing now."

Nothing Patrick could have said would have stunned Lucy more. She got out of the car, stepping into the rain, and walked to the front door without looking back.

Maybe she had it wrong. Maybe he was talking about her ex-boyfriend Cody, or the one disaster of a relationship in college. Not what happened nearly seven years ago when she was eighteen.

She pushed it aside and walked through the door. Patrick couldn't have been thinking about what had happened with Adam Scott, or how she'd been foolish and stupid.

Dillon and Kate were in the family room watching a movie. She called out to them that she was setting the alarm, then went straight upstairs, not wanting to talk to anyone.

Patrick wasn't thinking about her ill-fated online chats with the man she thought was college student Trevor Conrad. She'd never rid herself of the guilt she still harbored over her stupidity back then. She'd thought she was so smart, so safe. She had been anything but. Maybe it was that lack of common sense that had kept her out of the FBI.

"No, he didn't mean that." Lucy pushed it from her mind.

But Patrick's other words came back.

He grew tired of them, because that's the way he is.

She'd believed Sean when he'd told her that he liked her because she wasn't like his other girlfriends, but maybe it was just a novelty. Maybe he'd grow tired of her—she was certainly not the fun and exciting, drop-everything-let's-go-to-Hawaii type. He'd been talking about going away with her for the weekend practically since they met—and he was getting irritated that they hadn't yet done it, she could tell.

She didn't know why it bothered her so much. She'd told him she wanted to go slow, take things one day at a time. Could she really blame him if he decided she was too boring and serious for him?

Tears stung her eyes as if he'd already dumped her. She cared about Sean so much . . . she couldn't change that even if she wanted to. She was surprised at how close they'd gotten so quickly. Maybe Patrick had a point that she needed to take a step back emotionally.

If she could.

ELEVEN

Suzanne drove nearly two hours to meet Jill Reeves, the roommate of the first Cinderella Strangler victim.

Jill, who'd been a freshman, dropped out of college after the murder of her roommate and moved back home to Hamden, Connecticut, outside of New Haven. Suzanne had read Vic Panetta's notes from his interview of her, and while Suzanne didn't think that the senior detective had missed anything, it didn't hurt to have another sit-down. Because of the long drive, she called Reeves's mother first to confirm that her daughter would be home.

She called Panetta as she was waiting for a pool car at FBI headquarters. "I'm leaving in two minutes for Hamden. Sure you don't want to come?"

"Knock yourself out, kid. I have another case I'm in the middle of. Should be able to wrap it up today. Plus, I have a stack of paperwork I want to finish before sundown. I'll let you know if I learn anything from our lab."

"Maybe we should work on a more effective deterrent to homicide: *Save a tree, don't murder anyone.*"

She hung up and maneuvered her way through Manhattan traffic. She'd left at the tail end of the morning commute, and once she was off the island, highway traffic moved at a steady clip.

Jill Reeves and Alanna Andrews had been best friends growing up; they'd even gone to Columbia together. Two months after they got there, Alanna was murdered. Jill, heartbroken, dropped out at the end of the semester and went home. Suzanne, normally suspicious, had wondered if Panetta had followed up with the girl—until there was a second murder, there had been no reason to believe that a serial killer was responsible for Alanna's death. In fact, he had—he'd even driven to Hamden for Alanna's funeral and talked to her parents, trying to assess whether someone from her hometown had taken advantage of her relocation to kill her. But the facts stayed the same; Alanna had disappeared from a party that the two girls had attended. Jill had gotten drunk and went home with a guy, believing that Alanna was fine—or Jill had been too drunk to care. The next morning, her roommate didn't show up and didn't answer her cell phone. Jill called the police.

This fall would mark Suzanne's ten-year anniversary with the FBI. She'd seen a lot of crap on the Violent Crimes Squad, and knew that there were always some cases that were never solved. She didn't want this to be one of them.

Hamden was a sleepy and quaint town; small, but still bigger than the teeny Louisiana town Suzanne had grown up in before moving to Baton Rouge as a teenager. The Reeveses lived in a well-maintained and renovated older house near the downtown area. It was kind of cute, but after living in New York for nearly ten years, Suzanne would go crazy in a town this small.

Mrs. Reeves answered almost as soon as Suzanne knocked. "I saw you drive up. Jill is in the living room."

"Lovely home," Suzanne said.

"Thank you." Mrs. Reeves beamed as she closed the door. "It's been in my family for more than a hundred years. My husband and I are trying to bring it back to its original glory."

"You're doing a terrific job."

Jill Reeves sat on an antique couch, her back rigid.

"Honey, this is the FBI agent who called. Suzanne Madden."

"Madeaux," Suzanne corrected.

Mrs. Reeves frowned, then said, "Ma*deaux*. French?"

"Cajun." She smiled at Jill. "Thank you for agreeing to talk to me."

Mrs. Reeves said, "We're still in shock. Alanna was always such a good girl. I don't know what possessed her to go to such a party."

Suzanne looked at Jill. She didn't say anything.

Suzanne said, "Most college students go to a party or two. It's part of the experience."

Mrs. Reeves sat down. "Not Jill. She knows the dangers."

Right. Suzanne wasn't going to get anything out of Jill with the mother in the room. "Mrs. Reeves, would you mind stepping out? I need to speak to Jill in private."

She frowned. "But shouldn't I be here to protect her rights? She already told me everything, anyway."

Hardly. "Jill isn't a suspect; she's not in any trouble. I just want to ask her some follow-up questions."

"Then why can't I stay? I'm worried about her. She doesn't want to go back to college."

"Mom," Jill said with an exasperated sigh, "just leave, okay?"

Mrs. Reeves pursed her lips, rose from the chair, and left. Suzanne crossed the room and closed the double doors.

"Thanks for not saying anything," Jill said to Suzanne.

"You lied to your parents, even after your best friend was killed?" Suzanne wasn't going to coddle the young woman. She sat in the chair across from Jill.

"You don't understand," Jill said.

"Try me."

She shrugged. "It's not important anymore. It's just—my parents are older. They're old enough to be *your* parents," she said as if Suzanne were ancient. "They were forty when they adopted me. They don't get *anything*. I could tell them I was going to a rave and they'd say, 'Oh, that sounds like fun!'" She shook her head.

"Okay, let's get one thing straight between us. Don't lie to me. If I find out you're lying to me about anything, I'll send your parents a copy of the police report."

"You can't do that!"

"It's public record. I can and will do it." She took out her copy of the report to reiterate her point. "I'm assuming you were honest with Detective Panetta."

She nodded. "I didn't lie to my parents, either. They

just assumed I didn't go to the party—they didn't even ask me—I just didn't correct them. I'm not doing any of that stuff; that's why I left college. It was getting out of hand, and I don't want to be that person anymore. I was just accepted to a small college in Pennsylvania for the fall, but I haven't told them yet."

"Why not?"

She shrugged. "I just don't know what I want anymore."

"Hey, I understand that." Until she'd been recruited by the FBI while at Boston College, Suzanne didn't know what she wanted to do with her life. She didn't even declare her major until junior year because she kept changing her mind.

"I haven't done any drugs or drinking since, I swear to God. If I hadn't been so wasted when Alanna was killed, maybe I would have noticed she wasn't around. Maybe I could have stopped her from going off with the wrong guy. I don't know." Tears filled her eyes and she looked down at her hands. "We've been friends since kindergarten. I still want to call her every night before bed, like I used to. I often pick up the phone and then remember she's dead."

Suzanne reached out and squeezed her hand. "If you can help me, maybe I can find Alanna's killer and put him in prison. That's justice. It's why I'm a cop."

Jill nodded. "I promise, the entire truth. But—" She hesitated.

"No buts, Jill. The truth."

She nodded.

"Have you heard about the other murders?"

Jill nodded, wiping a stray tear from her face. "The news. The Cinderella Strangler. That's him, right?"

"Yes. There are four victims now. He targets the types of parties where you and Alanna went on October thirtieth. We don't know how he picks his victims. Three of the victims were college students—Alanna; Heather Garcia, who was a junior at NYU; and the most recent victim, Jessica Bell, a sophomore at Columbia. Did you know Jessica Bell?"

Jill shook her head. "The name isn't familiar. But I left after a few months. It's a big school."

"That's okay." Suzanne looked at her notes and Panetta's report. "You told Detective Panetta that this was the first party of this type that you'd gone to. Is that correct?"

Jill looked sheepish. "Well, no, but that's not what he asked. He asked if Alanna or I had gone to any other underground parties since arriving at Columbia. I didn't lie—it was the first we'd been to since we started college."

"But you understood the question, obviously."

"Yes. But . . . I didn't want him to think that we were sluts or anything. Even though . . . " She hesitated.

"You need to tell me the truth or more girls are going to die. You understand that, right? Four murders—that's well past the textbook criteria for a serial killer. I need to figure out how and why he's targeting these victims, because that will lead us to him." She knew that, as the first victim, Alanna had the highest chance of having a personal connection to the killer. Serial killers rarely begin by killing random strangers.

The first victim was usually personal, or had a personal significance to the killer.

But Jill didn't need to know that, not yet.

Suzanne said, "Something happened that night with Alanna that set him off. Something that maybe you saw or heard without recognizing its importance. First—how many of these types of parties have you been to in your lifetime?"

"That was my second, I swear. The first time we were seniors in high school. But Alanna had been to a bunch of them."

"Here in Hamden?"

"No. We took the train to the city. It was harder for me to disappear for the weekend, but Alanna's parents didn't really care what she did as long as her grades were good. That first time, I convinced my parents that I was somewhere else, and had a million excuses ready if they checked up on me. Alanna had talked about how much fun they were, and begged me to go with her."

"Was that party similar to the one you went to this past October?"

"I—" She looked down again, her face reddening. "I had broken up with my boyfriend when I went to that first party. I was so angry—I just wanted to find a guy and have sex, as if that would have punished Gary or something. I'd smoked pot a couple times before, but I'd never done real drugs—I was so wired. It was like my mind and my body were two different things. It just got out of hand. I didn't want to do it again, but after a while I think I just pushed aside the bad parts and remembered the great music and the fun stuff, so when Alanna told me about the Haunted House, it sounded okay."

"How did she hear about it?"

"Alanna knew about all of them. She wanted to get her grades on solid ground so her parents wouldn't pull her from college, so she worked hard for the first two months. But after she aced her midterms, she said she needed to go wild."

"What about the party when you were a senior?"

"Alanna went to stay with her cousin in New York for a month the summer before our senior year. She told me all about it—I was shocked. I guess I was a little more sheltered back then. Alanna was like a trendsetter, always the first to try new things."

"Before you went, what did she tell you it was going to be like?"

"Just that there would be a live band and lots of dancing and drinking—" She hesitated.

"Tell me, Jill."

"She said when she went to the party in New York, she'd had sex with three different guys. Didn't even know their names. It stunned me—I mean, she'd lost her virginity before me, I don't know why I was so surprised, except that, well, I was. She said it was empowering."

Suzanne made a note. Maybe Alanna had other secrets she hadn't shared with Jill. Her cousin in New York might know more, especially if that's where Alanna's partying lifestyle began.

"Back to the party in October, the Haunted House. Alanna heard about the party, you went with her, and according to your statement, the last time you saw her was when she was dancing around one a.m.?"

Jill nodded. "I don't know the exact time, but we didn't even get there until after eleven. I didn't want to do any drugs, but I made a mistake and drank something I shouldn't have and felt all weirded out. When I found Alanna, I told her I was sick, but she said she was having fun and didn't want to leave. She gave me a pill. I don't know what it was, but it did make me feel a little better.

"The rest of the night was a bit foggy," Jill continued. "I hooked up with this guy—I don't even know his name." Tears started again. "I can't believe I did that, just anonymous sex, and I didn't know him. We went back to his apartment and did things I barely remember. I felt sick for days, but Alanna was dead."

"Was there anyone at these parties who you knew? By name?"

"Not really—I mean, I might have known names that night, but I don't remember."

"What about someone who Alanna talked about who you didn't know?"

"I don't understand."

"Someone Alanna mentioned as inviting her to the parties?"

She shook her head.

"What about her cousin?"

"Whitney."

"Whitney Andrews?"

"I don't know, she has a different last name. I only met her a couple times."

Suzanne made note and asked, "What about a boyfriend? You'd told the detective that Alanna wasn't seeing anyone specific. Was that true?"

"She didn't have a boyfriend."

"What about someone who showed her more interest than she wanted?"

"Alanna liked it when guys flirted with her. I know it makes it sound like she was a slut, and maybe she was kind of, but you didn't know her, and I don't want people thinking bad things about her."

"I don't think anything bad about Alanna or any of the other victims. My job is to find out who killed her and put him in prison for the rest of his life. Who Alanna was or what she did is not important to me beyond relevance in this case. What about an ex-boyfriend?"

"She had one guy in high school, Zach Correli, who was a year older than us. He went to college in Maine. When they broke up, I don't think she was heartbroken, and neither was he."

But it was something Suzanne needed to look into. If Correli wasn't in New York when Alanna was killed, it should be easy to prove.

"One more thing," Suzanne said. "Did Alanna have a job? Someplace where she might have met someone you didn't? Maybe volunteer work, or part-time. Detective Panetta didn't have anything listed except that she was a full-time student."

"She didn't have a job while in college. I worked part-time on campus for my scholarship. Her parents had a college fund for her. She's never really been broke."

"Last thing. This might be a little hard, but I'd like to show you the pictures of the other three victims, to see if you know them."

She showed the photos to Jill one by one. There

was no recognition until she saw Jessica Bell. "She looks familiar. She's dead?"

"Last weekend."

"Oh, God."

"Do you know who she is?"

Jill shook her head. "She just looks familiar. Maybe I had a class with her, or I saw her somewhere."

"Maybe at the Halloween party?"

"Maybe." Jill frowned. "I honestly don't know."

"That's okay. You did great, and I really appreciate your honesty." Suzanne put the photographs back in the folder, then took Jill's hands and squeezed them. "Don't live in the past. I know you harbor a lot of regret and guilt. But I can tell you that it'll eat you up if you let it. I think you should go to that Pennsylvania college. Alanna wouldn't want you stuck in limbo."

Suzanne handed Jill her card. "If you remember anything else, or just want to talk, call me."

She left, and because she was in Hamden she stopped by the Andrewses' house two blocks from where Jill lived. At first she thought no one was home, then a woman in her seventies answered the door. "Yes?"

"Hello, I'm Special Agent Madeaux from New York. I'm sorry to bother you, but I was in town and had a question."

The woman's face clouded. "About Alanna?"

"Yes, ma'am. Actually about her cousin, Whitney."

"Whitney." The woman sighed. "Is she in trouble?"

"No, not that I know of. But I was told that she and Alanna were close and I haven't spoken to her yet regarding Alanna's murder. Do you have her current address and phone number?"

"Yes. Wait here, please." She closed the door. Several moments later she returned with a piece of paper with shaky writing. Whitney Morrissey, Brooklyn, and a number. "I don't have her address, but her mother told me she was living in Brooklyn now. She's an artist, very good, too. Goes to art shows all the time. But it's a hard way to make a living."

"Thank you for this."

"I know what they said about my granddaughter—but I'm not going to remember that. Alanna was a sweet girl. She never hurt anyone. Never. She played cards with me every Sunday night." Tears welled in the lady's eyes. "I have fourteen grandchildren, and Alanna is the only one who always remembered my birthday." She looked sharply at Suzanne. "You don't know who hurt my granddaughter, do you?"

"Not yet, ma'am, but finding out is my number one priority."

TWELVE

When Sean and Lucy left Washington at seven in the morning it was raining steadily. As they drove north, the rain slacked off, and by the time they hit the New Jersey border it was nothing but scattered showers and occasional gusts of wind. They were on 495 heading east toward Manhattan and Lucy couldn't help but stare at the approaching landscape of skyscrapers.

"Don't tell me you haven't been to New York City," Sean said.

She shook her head, awestruck.

"And how long have you lived in D.C.?"

"Six years. But I've been busy."

"I wish the weather had been better so I could fly you in. It's even better from the sky."

Lucy felt she already knew New York from movies and television, but the sheer vastness of concrete and roads and buildings leading up to the city was overwhelming. The closer she got to Manhattan, the more she marveled at the ingenuity. She also felt apprehension about the population. "Aren't there eight million people here?"

"That's in the entire city, and I think it's about 8.5 million now. Manhattan is under two million, but has the highest density."

"And you know this off the top of your head."

"Useless trivia," Sean said.

Though D.C. was dense, it didn't have miles of towering buildings, a seemingly never-ending concrete city. The architecture of New York intrigued Lucy: Some buildings were simple and bland, others old and ornate. New and old, big and small, all pushed together into something that should have been ugly but was surprisingly beautiful.

"This isn't our weekend away," Sean said.

She glanced at him. "I know."

"Just want to make that clear. Though we'll probably be here all weekend, it's business, not pleasure."

Lucy didn't say anything because they were entering a tunnel. She grabbed Sean's thigh.

"What?"

"I don't like tunnels."

"You take the D.C. Metro all the time."

"It's not the same."

She didn't tell him why. She didn't want to remember being chained in the hull of a ship, not knowing where she was going, not being in control. Being raped had been only the worst part of the trauma of those two days. Fears she'd never imagined had planted themselves in the hours before the vicious attack, growing exponentially until she thought she'd lose her mind before she died. Now, while she kept her emotions under tight control, the fears sat dormant until times like this, when she was trapped in a long tunnel deep under the Hudson River.

"This is the Lincoln Tunnel," Sean said, putting a hand over one of hers. "Truly a feat of engineering.

Three tunnels servicing around 120,000 vehicles a day."

"I know what you're trying to do. I'll be okay." She swallowed. "I would appreciate it if you'd keep both hands on the steering wheel."

Sean turned on the stereo and pressed one of the six numbers. A CD slipped into place and Led Zeppelin burst through the speakers.

"It's been a long time since I rock and rolled," Sean bellowed with Robert Plant.

A car braked suddenly in front of them and Lucy bit back a yelp. Sean downshifted so quickly she didn't see him take his hand off the steering wheel. She thought she heard him mutter, *"Asshole,"* but with the loud music she wasn't sure.

Three minutes later they emerged from the tunnel into traffic. Sean maneuvered as if he had been a New York City cab driver in a previous life.

Lucy had learned in the short time she'd been involved with Sean that his car was an extension of himself, and she resisted the urge to ask him if he knew where they were going. He had customized his GPS, which he trusted as if it could drive the car without him.

Lucy had been impressed with the architecture from their approach, but now she was truly in awe, tilting her head to see as much as possible. It took them fifteen minutes to reach the Upper West Side, where Columbia University was located. Sean pulled over in a loading zone outside a huge church. Lucy stared. "I've heard of this place—that's St. John the Divine."

"If we're here on Sunday, maybe you'll want to go to church there."

"It's Episcopal, not Catholic, but I've heard it's exquisite. They recently renovated it."

"How about this—when you're done talking to Jessica, I'll meet you here. I hope to be back from Brooklyn before the rush hour, but if not, this place looks big enough to keep you entertained."

Lucy glanced at the alarming mass of traffic around them. "You mean this isn't rush hour?"

Sean grinned, then kissed her. "Be careful, Luce. We don't know exactly what's going on. Let me know what you find out."

Driving to New York, they'd agreed that Lucy would go to Jessica's apartment, talk to her if possible, or if she wasn't there, talk to her neighbors. She also planned to show Kirsten's photo around and find out if anyone had seen her this past week. Sean would head to Brooklyn and check out the Clover Motel, since Kirsten had called there the day she disappeared. Both would be on the lookout for Trey. Sean had enhanced and printed a photo of Trey off the high school website so Lucy was familiar with his appearance.

"I plan to return in less than three hours, but if something comes up and I'm following a lead, stay here," Sean told her.

"I'll be just fine. I'm not helpless."

"Helpless? Hardly." He kissed her. "Just be careful."

"You, too. Even Rogans aren't invincible."

Sean put one hand to his chest in mock disgust. "That's a nasty rumor to spread."

She smiled and put her hand on the door.

"One more thing." He reached into his pocket and took out a leather business card holder.

"What's this?" She opened it. Inside were Rogan-Caruso-Kincaid business cards with the gold embossed logo of a sword and shield in the corner. Her name and phone number were printed in the center. "What? How?"

"My computer. I had a few sheets of blank cards printed when Patrick and I had our cards made. I thought if you need to hand them out, it would look more official. You'd be amazed what people tell private investigators."

"Thanks." She didn't know what to think. She didn't work for RCK, but seeing the makeshift cards was a visual reminder that she hadn't gotten into the FBI and had no real identity.

"Hey, they're supposed to be a good thing, not make you sad."

She smiled. "They're great. Thanks." She put them in her satchel and put the strap over her neck and across her chest. "Three hours, meet here at the cathedral. Check."

Lucy got out and watched Sean pull into traffic.

Weather permitting, D.C. was a walking town, but New York was D.C. times a hundred. More people, more buildings, more traffic. Lucy looked at her phone and the map she'd retrieved of the three square blocks immediately around her. Jessica's apartment was on the right, a block and a half straight ahead down West 112th Street. Lucy wished she had more time to enjoy her first trip to New York City, but maybe after they found Kirsten and got her home, she and Sean could come back for a weekend.

It wasn't as if she had anything else to do.

"Stop it," she muttered. She took a deep breath and resolved not to feel sorry for herself. She hadn't been an FBI agent when she'd helped trap pedophiles for WCF or when she'd analyzed cold cases for the Arlington Sheriff's Department. She could help Sean and Patrick find a runaway now, because nothing had changed in her.

She kept telling herself that, because deep down she didn't believe it.

Jessica's seven-story apartment building had a fire escape going up the side like in the movies, and Lucy spent a few minutes looking up and wondering what the view would be from the roof. While Lucy had a fear of confining places, she had no fear of heights.

But figuring out how to get to the roof wasn't in the cards now. She suspected that, for security reasons, the fire escape could be lowered only from above, and even if she stood on a parked car she couldn't reach the bottom rung of the ladder.

The building had a small entry with mailboxes and call buttons. She couldn't go upstairs without having a key or being let in by a tenant. Of course, if Sean were here, he could probably bypass the electrical system, but Lucy preferred more clearly legal methods. If Jessica wasn't here, she might be able to get in through a neighbor.

She pressed 406, Jessica's apartment. When she didn't think anyone was going to answer and was about to try another bell, a breathless female voice said, "Hello?"

"Jessica?"

The girl didn't say anything, but the door buzzed and Lucy entered and walked upstairs.

A petite brunette stood in the doorway of apartment 406. She wasn't Jessica Bell, unless Jessica used a completely different photo for her *Party Girl* profile.

"Hi, I'm Lauren, Jessie's roommate." The girl bit her lip, then said, "I'm sorry you haven't heard, but Jessie's dead."

Lucy must have looked like she was in shock, because Lauren invited her in. "Can I get you some water?"

"No, thank you," Lucy said. "I'm Lucy Kincaid, and—"

"I've had so many people calling, now that the police released her name. I'm sorry you had to hear it like this. Were you in a class with her?"

"No, I don't know Jessica personally," Lucy said.

Lauren frowned, so Lucy pushed on. She handed Lauren one of her RCK cards and said, "I'm looking for a runaway who was friends with Jessica. I was hoping that Jessica would know where she is."

"A runaway?" Lauren asked, skeptical.

"Yes." Lucy took out a paper that Sean had printed with two photographs of Kirsten, her senior portrait and a more glamorous picture of her from the *Party Girl* site, though it wasn't risqué. "Have you seen her in the last week or so?"

"Ashleigh," Lauren said. "She stayed here a couple of times when I went home to visit my parents."

The excitement of being right gave Lucy a thrill. "What about last weekend?"

Lauren shook her head. "Jessica was killed by the

Cinderella Strangler last weekend. At least, that's what the police think. It's awful."

"The Cinderella Strangler?"

"You had to have heard, it's been in the papers for months. The killer takes a shoe. It's weird, and I didn't really think about it, but now that Jessie's dead, it's so real, and much scarier."

"I'm from Washington," Lucy said, tapping the address on the business card. "What did the police say?"

"They don't know anything, at least that's what the newspapers said. No leads, nothing."

Lucy had a hundred questions about the murders, but Lauren wasn't the right person to ask. Instead, she said, "Do you have a paper I can see?"

"No, I read it online. The *Post* had a big thing on the murders yesterday."

"Was Jessie supposed to meet Ashleigh last weekend?"

"I don't know. I don't have classes on Friday and usually leave by noon to go home. I'm not really into the weekend scene here. Jessie was more into the parties and stuff. But Jessie's friend Josh knows Ashleigh. He told me the police talked to him about Jessie, because Josh sometimes goes out with her. They weren't really dating, but he's been so upset about what happened he hasn't left his apartment since Wednesday. I made him a tray of tamales. I was going to bring them up, but I feel kind of weird."

"I can do it for you," Lucy said. "I need to talk to him. Ashleigh might be in trouble, and I need all the information I can get to find her."

"Was she out with Jessie Saturday night?"

"We think so, or they were supposed to meet."

"Oh, God, that's awful."

Lauren handed Lucy the tamales, and directed her to Josh Haynes's apartment on the top floor. She walked up the stairs while pondering what could have happened last Saturday. What if Kirsten had seen her friend murdered? Her message could have been so odd because she was still in shock. Or if she'd been drugged, she might not know what she had seen. But if the killer saw her, he might be looking for her.

She had to talk to Sean, but first she needed to get up to speed on the murders and talk to Jessica's boyfriend. She stood in the hallway outside Josh's apartment and used her phone to search for the article Lauren had mentioned. She read it carefully, committing the details to memory.

Four young women, two of whom had been students at Columbia University, appeared to have been killed by the "Cinderella Strangler," who suffocated them and took one of their shoes. There was no mention of sexual assault, but the paper also didn't state that the victims *hadn't* been sexually assaulted. The police traditionally held back key details from the media and public in order to prevent copycats and help them know if they had the real killer when they found a suspect. Lucy was surprised the detail about the missing shoe had been released. She would have held that back. Perhaps the sexual assault wasn't revealed because of the manner of death or specific violence done to the body.

The first murder was on October 30, nearly four months ago. Four deaths in four months. Serial killer? The FBI was involved, an Agent Suzanne Madeaux. Lucy wondered if she should call Noah and ask whether he could get her more information about the case. Or maybe just an intro to the field agent in charge, so Lucy could give her the information about the *Party Girl* website and Kirsten and Jessica's connection.

Lauren had been right. The *Post*'s article was incredibly detailed and gave a time line of each crime, the location, and a victim profile. Each had been killed at an underground, or "secret," party at an abandoned building. Each victim was under twenty-two. And each had been suffocated.

Lucy needed more information, because what was revealed by the press wasn't enough to create a profile of the killer.

What was she thinking? That the New York FBI office was incompetent? Of course they had the information they needed for a profile. Why would they need her, when they probably had their own in-house profiler, considering the size of the regional office? Or they could call upon Dr. Hans Vigo, the legendary profiler now assigned to Quantico. They didn't need Lucy's inexperienced opinion, and there was no reason Agent Madeaux would share any case information with her.

Her job was to find Kirsten Benton, and she'd share what she knew of Jessica's double life on the *Party Girl* website if the FBI didn't already know about it.

First things first. Deliver these tamales to Josh Haynes and find out what he knew about Kirsten, aka Ashleigh.

She knocked on his door.

It took Josh several minutes to answer. Wearing pajama bottoms and a torn T-shirt, he looked as if he'd just rolled out of bed.

"Yeah?"

"Lauren asked me to bring these tamales up for you."

Josh sighed and opened the door. "She thinks food is going to make everything better."

Lucy walked in and put the tray on his small counter. The kitchen was not bigger than her bathroom—which was tiny—just a small alcove with a narrow stove, small refrigerator, and sink. The tray took up half the available counter space. The rest of the apartment was nice. Though not spacious, it had high ceilings and tall, narrow windows.

"She means well," Lucy said.

"Yeah." He stared out the window.

"You cared for Jessica."

He didn't say anything. "Are you Lauren's friend or Jessie's?"

"Neither. I'm Lucy Kincaid. I'm trying to find a friend of Jessica's, Ashleigh."

"Why?"

"She's missing."

"God, this is so fucked. You think something happened to her, too?"

"I don't know, but I think Ashleigh was supposed to go to a party with Jessica the weekend she was killed."

"*I* took Jess to that party." Josh sat heavily on one of the two kitchen chairs. "She was acting weird that night. I should have stayed with her. She would still be alive."

"Josh, you don't know that. You don't know what

might have happened. What do you mean Jess was acting weird?"

"Just, I don't know, skittish. Stressed. I thought it was because of her classes; she was taking a tough schedule. She couldn't relax. And then she asked if I'd take her to the party, and I thought it was her way of making up, but then she was all weird about that, too. She didn't talk on the subway, and I was mad because she wouldn't tell me what was going on. Why wouldn't she talk to me? Am I that big of a jerk?"

Lucy touched his arm lightly. "She asked you to take her to the party. That says something, don't you think?"

"Then why didn't she ask me to stay with her? If she was scared of something, why didn't she want me to protect her? And why go to the party in the first place?"

An excellent question. Lucy suspected the answer also had to do with why Kirsten went to the party. Maybe it wasn't that Jessie was scared for herself— maybe she wanted to tell Kirsten to be careful.

"Josh," she said, sliding over one of her new cards, "here's my number. If Ashleigh contacts you, would you please let me know? It's important. If she's in trouble, we can help. And if she knows anything about who killed Jessica, we can protect her."

He stared at the card.

"Do you think Wade Barnett killed her?" Josh asked.

Lucy hesitated. She didn't want to admit that she didn't know who Wade Barnett was, but at the same time, she wanted to know why Josh had asked the question.

She replied, "I can't honestly say; I'm not investigating her murder. Did he know Ashleigh or Jessica?"

"I think Jess met him, here at one of my parties."

"One of the underground parties?"

"No, right here." He waved his arm around his space. "I have five neighbors on the floor, and they're cool with it. My friend across the hall opens up his apartment and we take over the floor. A couple times a year."

"Was Ashleigh at any of those parties?"

"Maybe. I don't remember. She always disappeared when I was sober, and really, I just wanted to be with Jess. I should have told her how I felt about her; I just thought—I don't know, we're both in college, we both like to have fun." He shrugged, his eyes red.

"Did the police mention Wade Barnett as a suspect?" she asked, surprised.

"No, I told the cops about him. They were asking about the underground parties and I said they should talk to him because he keeps tabs on the best parties."

"Did you see him at the party where Jessica died?"

"No," Josh admitted, "but there were hundreds of people there."

"I'm sure the police talked to him, and they know what they're doing. Let them do their job. I need to do mine. Remember, if you hear from Ashleigh—or even talk to someone who heard from her—call me. It's important."

Sean wasn't entirely comfortable leaving Lucy on her own the first time she was in New York City, but she wasn't reckless and he wanted her to rebuild her shattered confidence. He'd left her a block from Jessica's apartment, and the cathedral would provide a distraction if she was done early. Still, he wanted to get his trip to Brooklyn over with as quickly as possible.

The three-story, U-shaped Clover Motel looked much better online. Situated in a desolate neighborhood, with faded blue paint, peeling in more places than not, its weather-damaged doors might have once been green but now looked puce. The entire structure and grounds were in dire need of repair. There didn't seem to be much of anything in the area except a few businesses and several boarded-up buildings.

Sean parked where he could see his GT from the office. The room was small, and the clerk sat behind a thick sheet of Plexiglas.

"Sixty-four dollars a night single room, or three hundred for the week, paid up front."

Sean said, "I'm a P.I. looking for a missing girl."

The clerk looked at him with disinterest. He was chewing tobacco, his lips stained, a bit of snuff caught in his greasy black mustache. "So?"

Sean held up the picture of Kirsten. "She called the motel a week ago, on Friday, about eleven p.m."

"Like I'm going to remember a call."

"Do you recognize her?"

He shrugged, but Sean saw him looking closely while pretending to be nonchalant.

Sean slid him a twenty through the narrow slot in the window. "Well?"

"She rented a room for two nights. Paid cash."

"Was she with anyone?"

"Not that I saw."

"When did she check out?"

"She didn't. People don't check out all the time, they just leave the key. I didn't think anything of it until the maid got there Monday to change the sheets and found her suitcase."

"Did you call her?"

The clerk sighed and spat a wad of chaw into the cup. "Nope."

"Where's her suitcase now?"

"In the back."

Sean tempered his anger at the drawn-out questions and answers. The clerk knew what he wanted.

He slid another twenty through the slot. "Can I see it?"

The clerk palmed the twenty and slowly stood and sauntered across his small space. He reached under a table and pulled out a small black suitcase with wheels, the kind seen en masse at any airport. Bright pink duct tape had been wrapped around the handle.

The clerk opened the door and handed Sean the suitcase. "It's all yours; just sign a receipt. I'm keeping her deposit, because she didn't leave the key—it wasn't in the room. You know how much it costs to rekey the locks in this place?"

The clerk wrote out a sloppy note, and Sean scribbled a signature.

"When did you last see her?"

"I checked her in late Friday, but I don't work weekends."

"Had she stayed here before?"

"I'd never checked her in. I'd remember that hot blonde in a heartbeat."

Sean stared at the old pervert with distaste,

couldn't summon a thank-you at that point, and left with Kirsten's suitcase.

He put the suitcase in his trunk and opened it. Clothes. Toiletries, shoes. Enough for two or three days. Inside the zippered front pocket was a canceled Amtrak ticket from D.C. to New York, plus an unused return ticket for last Sunday at 3:10 p.m. A hundred dollars in twenties was tucked away in the same pocket.

He closed her suitcase and the trunk and sat in the driver's seat.

Had he found the suitcase but not the message Kirsten had sent to Trey, Sean would think she was dead. But something had happened over the weekend that had left her disoriented, and possibly injured, and she was in hiding.

He pulled out his phone and saw that Lucy had sent him an email.

Jessica Bell is dead. She was murdered last weekend at a warehouse party in Brooklyn. Maybe you can check it out if you're still there? An article about four identical murders is attached.

Both Jessica's roommate and her boyfriend recognized Kirsten as "Ashleigh," and the boyfriend saw her a few weeks ago. I'm going to talk to a couple neighbors to get a better idea of the last time they remember Kirsten visiting. What if the other three victims were also on the *Party Girl* site? I'm going to check into it before meeting you at the church.

Sean read the article Lucy had found. Nowhere in it did it mention *Party Girl* or Jessica's alter ego "Jenna." Had the police made the connection but were keeping it quiet? Lucy was smart; she'd discover if there was a connection. If there was, maybe Kirsten had a legitimate reason to go into hiding.

Sean understood people, but he understood computers and networks better. He might not be able to trace Kirsten's steps after she checked into the Clover Motel, but he *could* retrace her steps on the *Party Girl* site; namely, all her contacts. Like Jessica Bell, there were probably others Kirsten trusted, people she could turn to if she was in trouble.

Or, he thought, someone who *was* trouble. If *Party Girl* was the connection to the four murders, then a psycho was targeting girls from the site. Sean would have to turn that information over to the police, but first he wanted to check out the abandoned warehouse where Jessica had been murdered. He didn't expect to find any clues to Kirsten's disappearance, but it would help for him to know where she had been, and where her friend had died.

He plugged the location identified in the newspaper into his GPS. The abandoned warehouse, a former printing supply chain, was only a few blocks from the Clover Motel.

THIRTEEN

Suzanne risked Friday afternoon traffic and drove directly to Whitney Morrissey's place from Hamden. The twenty-four-year-old lived in Brooklyn, in a warehouse that had been converted into artist studios, with two businesses on the ground floor: an insurance agency and a rental company.

She buzzed 3A, Whitney's apartment, and waited. Then buzzed again. She had tried calling when she was driving, but there had been no answer. She hadn't left a message.

"Yeah?" A scratchy voice came through the intercom.

"Whitney Morrissey?"

"That's me."

"I'm Special Agent Suzanne Madeaux with the FBI and I have some questions regarding your cousin, Alanna Andrews."

Dead silence. A good thirty seconds later, the door buzzed open and Suzanne entered. She walked up two flights of stairs to the third floor. Whitney stood in her doorway. She wore an oversized NYU T-shirt and had long bare legs. Thick blond hair fell halfway down her back in a tangle of wild curls.

"FBI?" Whitney asked.

Suzanne handed her a business card. "I have questions about the month your cousin lived here."

"Here?" Whitney glanced behind her. Suzanne couldn't see what or who she was looking at.

"Is that a problem?"

"I have a friend over." She bit her lip.

"I also have questions about the party in October where Alanna was murdered."

"Can we talk later?"

"No, we can't."

If the woman played hardball, Suzanne would have to get a warrant, and that took time and paperwork.

Suzanne despised paperwork.

Whitney sighed and shut her door, closing off her apartment. "You don't mind talking out here?"

Suzanne shook her head. Whitney would be more forthcoming without an audience. "How many of the underground parties did you take Alanna to when she stayed with you that summer?"

"Two or three."

"And did she meet anyone?"

Whitney looked at her as if she were an idiot. "They were big parties. I'm sure she met lots of people."

Suzanne didn't like this girl. "I should clarify. Did she meet anyone at any of the parties who she continued to see afterward?"

"I don't know. She didn't tell me about anyone."

"Were you at the October thirtieth party in Harlem? The Haunted House?"

She hesitated.

"I'd like to state that this is an active police investi-

gation and if I find out you've lied to me, I'll keep dig-
ging until I hit the truth."

Whitney curled her lip. "I showed up for a while,
but left early."

"How early?"

"Two."

Two in the morning was early? "Did you see
Alanna there?"

"Yeah. For just a minute. She was with a guy."

"Anyone you know?"

She shook her head. "I'd seen him around, but I
don't know his name."

"Were you at the Brooklyn party last weekend?"

"The one near the docks? I heard about it, but I
didn't go. I had an art show that weekend and needed
to sleep."

It had the ring of truth, but Suzanne made a note to
follow up on it. "What kind of art?"

"Charcoal drawings, mostly. Some watercolors."

"Would you mind showing me something?"

She looked skeptical. "Why?"

Suzanne shrugged. "Just curious."

Whitney opened the door and walked away but
didn't let Suzanne in. Through the narrow opening
she saw one large room with a wall of small-paned
warehouse windows left over from the original building. The far wall had an intricate painting directly on
the wall in black and greens that looked like a mosaic
of the New York skyline. She couldn't see anything
on the right except for a closed door. The place
smelled like paint cleaner with a faint undercurrent of
marijuana. Now Suzanne understood why Whitney
didn't want her inside.

Whitney came back with a sketchbook and handed it to Suzanne, along with a postcard. "This was from my show. It was in Central Park."

"I remember," said Suzanne, surprised. "I was jogging through the park when they were setting up on Saturday morning."

She glanced through the sketchbook, not really interested, just wanting something tangible to confirm that Whitney wasn't making up the art show alibi. She couldn't help but notice that Whitney had talent. Most of the drawings were faces, a few buildings, and New York landmarks.

"You're really good."

Whitney smiled sheepishly as she took the sketchbook back. "Thanks. But it's hard to make money with these sketches. And the last thing I want to do is go into commercial art."

"Sometimes you have to make a living doing what you don't particularly like so you have the time and money to do what you love to do."

"Exactly!" Whitney said. "Alanna and I weren't really close, but I liked her and I feel bad about what happened. You don't have any idea who killed her?"

Suzanne didn't answer the question, but asked, "You're an artist and have a good eye for detail. Would you mind looking at three pictures and telling me if you remember seeing any of these women?"

"You're talking about the other victims."

"Yes."

Whitney nodded, but bit her lip.

"Did you see their photos in the paper?"

"Yeah—"

Suzanne took out the folder and showed her the

pictures one by one. Whitney recognized them, Suzanne was certain of it, but she didn't say anything right away.

"I may have seen them before, but I don't know when or where. All three look kind of familiar, but I didn't know them, like their names or anything. I'm sorry."

"I have a favor to ask," said Suzanne.

Whitney eyed her suspiciously.

"The guy you saw Alanna with the night she died, would you be able to draw him?"

"You think he killed her?"

"I don't know, but I'd like to talk to him."

Whitney closed her eyes. A moment later she opened them and said, "Yeah, I think I can."

"Call me when you're done and I'll pick it up. It's important—the sooner you can do it, the better."

Suzanne left Whitney's apartment and called her office as she turned the car around. She verified that the autopsy report from Jessica Bell was on her desk, and that the blood and tissue samples had been sealed and sent via courier from the coroner to the FBI lab. If anything came from them, the chain of evidence had to be preserved or the court would throw all the material out. Everything was moving quickly on her end, but anytime they were dealing with lab work, speed wasn't really an option, regardless of what the movies and television touted.

She was talking to her squad's chief analyst when Vic Panetta called. "I'll call you back," she told Chris. She clicked over to Panetta. "Got a lead on a witness. A guy the first vic's cousin saw with Andrews the night she was killed. We're working on a sketch."

"Good, but we have another problem. The security company overseeing the old printing warehouse in Brooklyn just called me about a prowler. Caucasian, six foot one to six foot two, dark hair, wearing jeans and a black jacket."

"I'm still in Brooklyn; I'll check it out."

"The security guard, our ex-cop Rich Berenz, is on scene but he's sitting back and watching. He'll detain if the trespasser tries to leave."

"Call him back and tell him my ETA is six minutes."

She turned around again and headed straight for the warehouse.

Killers often returned to the scene of the crime to relive their sick thrills, and Suzanne hoped that was the case this time.

FOURTEEN

Lucy methodically went to every apartment in Jessica Bell's building looking for information on Kirsten. More than half the apartments didn't have anyone home, but it soon became clear that among the college-age crowd, most knew Jessica and "Ashleigh" from a wild party on the top floor New Year's Eve.

She couldn't help but think about Wade Barnett and his connection to both Josh Haynes and the underground parties. Coincidence? The police were looking into him, and Lucy trusted them to do their job. Later, she would turn over whatever information she found, but she believed exactly what she'd told Jessica's boyfriend: The police would catch the killer; Lucy needed to focus on finding Kirsten.

She walked two short blocks to a Starbucks on Broadway and booted up her laptop while sipping her mocha. She logged onto her fake profile on the *Party Girl* site and looked through Kirsten's friends to see if she recognized the other three victims.

There were so many beautiful young women endangering themselves, Lucy had to consciously close off her emotions to review each profile impartially. She saved a photo of each friend into a separate file, along with the person's online name, to review more closely later.

Almost immediately, she found the second victim, Erica Ripley. She was a pretty, short-haired redhead with big green eyes. She smiled seductively in the photo, pixie-like and coy.

Lucy saved her profile and information, and continued her search. Ten minutes later, she found Heather Garcia, a light-skinned Latina, who posted on her profile that she was studying to be a teacher.

Not anymore. They were both dead.

These two victims were friends with both "Ashleigh" and "Jenna."

Lucy doubted the police had uncovered this thread. Otherwise why would they have kept the profiles up there? Unless they were using them to lure a killer, so he didn't know the police suspected how he trolled for his victims.

Still, she was disturbed to see three of the four Cinderella Strangler victims on the *Party Girl* site. She searched the site more broadly for the first victim, Alanna Andrews, but couldn't find her. Maybe her profile had been removed, or she'd never had one.

Three out of four of the Cinderella Strangler's victims—and Kirsten, who was in hiding—were part of an online sex group. Their photographs and videos were there for anyone to see, and sexual predators fed on explicit images. Even though the girls had used false identities, they weren't protected. Lucy's sister, a detective in San Diego, had had a case years ago where a young man learned that a girl he had a crush on had an anonymous online sex diary. He killed her and two others before he was stopped.

Lucy logged into Kirsten's email, but there were no

new messages from Kirsten or Trey. She checked the "sent" box, then went to the deleted files. Nothing.

She created a chronological sequence of events, and incorporated the *Party Girl* profiles, the dates of the four murders, and the weekends Kirsten had left home.

Though the spreadsheet created a clear time line, there was no clear connection between Kirsten and the four victims. The first victim, Alanna Andrews, didn't have a *Party Girl* profile, but Lucy added a question mark in case she'd had a profile that was taken down. Kirsten was in New York when the last two college students were killed, but not the first two. Lucy searched Kirsten's email for any messages from any of the victims. She found only Jessica Bell in her address book. After reading a few of the messages, Lucy realized they had become close friends and Kirsten was thinking of going to Columbia. They also had a lot in common—parents who'd gone through a nasty divorce and changing high schools in the middle of the year were two of the big similarities.

Lucy felt for Kirsten and Jessica. She appreciated the close bond the girls had. There was no doubt in her mind that if Jessica was in trouble, Kirsten would drop everything and come to New York to help her.

Lucy would do the same for her family, but she had no close friends. The friends she'd made in high school didn't know how to respond to Lucy's very public attack nearly seven years ago. Instead of staying in contact, they'd gone off to college, never emailing, never calling. At the time, Lucy didn't much think about it because she'd been so wrapped up in Patrick's coma and her own guilt and pain. It wasn't until she was in her second year of college that Lucy realized how alone she truly was. By that time, she found it difficult to maintain more than superficial friendships. Her one boyfriend in college had told her she was emotionally cold and hard to get close to. He was right. She couldn't warm up to anyone. She wasn't skittish, but she was wary.

Which made what was happening between her and Sean unusual and daunting and wonderful, all at the same time.

Lucy logged out of Kirsten's email and Googled Wade Barnett to see what popped up. She was surprised by the hundreds of results.

Skimming the first ten links, she realized that Wade Barnett was a wealthy twenty-five-year-old investor. He worked for his brother, CJ Barnett, and had graduated from NYU. Both were die-hard Yankee fans.

The third victim had been a student at NYU.

Wade Barnett had thousands of mentions in social and sports articles. He'd majored in finance, but seemed to be drawn to architecture and real estate. He was in charge of real-estate investments for CJB Investments, and had bought several abandoned buildings in the city. Additionally, he'd donated a large chunk of money to a historical preservation society to restore several decaying landmarks.

Barnett's photo showed an attractive guy with an engaging smile. He obviously played to the camera. The police had talked about him with Josh Haynes, but based on what Josh said, he'd been the one who'd brought up Barnett's name.

Wade likely had met both Jessica and Kirsten at Josh's party. Did he know the other girls personally through the parties in New York? If the first victim's profile had been deleted from *Party Girl*, he could have known all of them through the site.

Lucy logged back onto her own *Party Girl* profile. She searched the site for males, under thirty, in New York. One thousand profiles popped up, the limit that the site would allow for a search. She went back to Kirsten's profile and looked at the profiles of all the men following her. She didn't see any of the Barnett brothers, but half the profiles didn't have photographs.

She thought she was onto something, but would need to spend more time on it than she had right now.

She went back to her Google search and narrowed it to Barnett images. Maybe she could find a screen name he used, or an email address, that she could plug into the *Party Girl* site to find him.

She didn't expect to find a photograph of him with the first victim.

It was early October, taken at a Yankees playoff game. The caption:

Wade Barnett, real estate investor, celebrating Yankee win with latest girlfriend.

Though only the young woman's profile was in the picture, there was no doubt in Lucy's mind that the girl embracing Wade Barnett was Alanna Andrews. The picture had been taken four weeks before Alanna was murdered.

Lucy's heart raced. The pieces of the puzzle were falling into place, and she felt on the cusp of an important discovery. Maybe the police already knew about Barnett and Andrews. Maybe they were investigating him or following up on his alibis. But until the killer was publicly identified and in jail, Lucy feared Kirsten would stay in hiding.

Sean needed to know about the *Party Girl* connection between the last three victims and Kirsten, and Wade Barnett's connection to the first victim and possible connection to Jessica Bell and Kirsten. Lucy called him, but his phone went to voice mail after five rings.

"Sean, it's Lucy. I found something. Three of the four Strangler victims are *Party Girl* members. Wade Barnett, who was at the same New Year's Eve party as Kirsten and Jessica, dated the first victim. I'm sending you a spreadsheet of everything I found. We need to call the FBI."

Sean couldn't reach for his vibrating phone because a security guard old enough to be his grandfather had a gun pointed at him. The guy already had a shaky trigger finger, so no way was Sean going to startle him. He was standing thirty feet away. He probably wouldn't miss if he fired.

Keeping his hands up, Sean said, "Sir, my name is Sean Rogan and I'm a private investigator."

"Just shut up, the NYPD is on their way."

"Great," Sean said. *Dammit.* He wanted to talk to the cops on his terms, not as a trespasser. They were more apt to take him seriously, as well as keep him in the loop, if he went to them with his facts and theories.

The guard didn't seem like an amateur. Instead, his squinting and shaking indicated that the man's eyesight was poor. He was scared of screwing up, Sean realized. "What's your name?" he asked.

"Just stand there. Don't move."

"I'm not moving," Sean said. He hated having a gun pointed at him. He'd been shot once before, but had been wearing a bulletproof vest at the time. Still, it had hurt like hell and given him a bruise that had lasted for weeks. His brother Duke told him he was lucky not to have a cracked rib. Sean didn't want to compare the difference between being shot with and without the vest.

A few raindrops blew at him from a gust of wind strong enough to make him sway and to push the tall weeds flat to the ground. The guard stepped to the side. "Don't move," he repeated louder, to be heard over the howl of the wind.

"I'm from Washington looking for a runaway."

"Save it."

Sean's charm wasn't winning this old man over. And the fact that he carried a gun—illegal in New York City—was going to get him into trouble. He had two options when the cops arrived: tell them about the weapon, or risk being searched and having them find it. Duke always told him to be straightforward and honest when dealing with law enforcement, but in Sean's experience that didn't always turn out so well.

A white sedan turned off the road and came toward them. It was obviously law enforcement, lights in the grille, a tall antenna attached to the trunk. Federal? This just got better and better.

A tall blonde got out of the car, her hair a mess from the weather even though she had it pulled back.

Her eyes were on Sean, but she approached the security guard. "Panetta said you were just watching."

"The detective told me not to let him leave."

"Okay, thanks. Why don't you put the gun down?" She had her eyes on the gun, but Sean knew if he made any sudden moves, she'd draw on him. She had that look about her, as if she could see ten things at once and react to a single threat accurately and without hesitation.

The guard still frowned and lowered his weapon, though he still had it in hand.

The cop said, "I'm FBI Special Agent Suzanne Madeaux. And you are?"

"Sean Rogan, private investigator."

"Rogan?"

"Rogan-Caruso-Kincaid. Heard of us?"

"No. Do you have identification?"

"Yes. May I put my hands down?" He gestured to his front pocket.

She nodded. "Slowly."

He complied, and held out his wallet.

Suzanne approached and took it, but stepped out of reach while she looked through it. She glanced at the back of his GT. "California plates?"

"I opened an office in D.C. in December. Haven't gotten my new plates yet."

"What are you doing out here this afternoon, Mr. Rogan?"

"I was hired to find a runaway. In the course of my investigation I traced her here, and connected her with one of your Cinderella Strangler victims."

Suzanne frowned. "She's one of the victims? I've talked to all the families."

"She was friends with Jessica Bell, the fourth victim. In fact, my partner and I found some evidence that may help in your investigation."

"Where's your partner now?" Suzanne glanced around quickly but methodically, her posture alert.

Sean wasn't going to tell the Fed that Lucy was talking to Jessica's friends. "Trying to trace her location." Close enough, not exactly a lie.

"Why are you here?"

"Kirsten Benton is a seventeen-year-old habitual runaway who always came home after a couple of days, until now. I started working the case on Wednesday."

"That doesn't answer my question," the fed said. "Why are you at the crime scene?"

"Kirsten called the Clover Motel on Friday night, paid cash for two nights, but she left without her suitcase or return train ticket. My partner learned that Kirsten's friend Jessica was murdered last Saturday, and I came out here to get a sense of Kirsten's mindset. I think she was here the night Jessica was killed. And, I think she saw something." The rain came down harder and Sean was practically shouting over the wind. "I have a lot more, and I'd be happy to tell you everything while we stand here and get wet, but maybe we can get coffee or something?"

"How about this? You follow me to FBI headquarters. If everything checks out, you're free to go." She pocketed Sean's ID. "I'll keep this as collateral." She looked pointedly at Sean. "Do you have a weapon on your person?"

"Holstered, on my belt."

Suzanne's glare narrowed and darkened. She disarmed him and said, "You should have informed me immediately. Strike one, Mr. Rogan." She walked toward her car. "Call your partner and have her meet us."

FIFTEEN

Kirsten woke up to two men arguing.

She opened her eyes, but her vision was blurry. The harder she focused on seeing, the more her head hurt.

Hiding from Jessie's killer didn't seem so important anymore. She was still terrified that even if she went home she wouldn't be safe, but she wanted to go home. She was so lonely, so scared. She wished she could remember what she'd heard and saw when she'd found Jessie, but it was all a blur. Every time she tried to think back to that night, her heart raced and she began to panic once again.

Dennis had been so sweet to her, so kind and gentle. He'd found her on the floor of the den after she emailed Trey and carried her to the bedroom. He fed her soup and made sure she drank juice. But she wasn't feeling any better. In fact, she felt worse.

She was dying.

"Don't yell at me!" she heard Dennis say.

The bedroom door was open only a crack.

"Dammit, Dennis, this is my life we're talking about! If I want to yell, I'm going to yell! I've been looking all over for you since yesterday. You haven't answered your phone, and then I find out you're staying here?"

"Charlie says I can stay here whenever I want."

"Well goody-goody, my life is fucked and you're staying in Charlie's penthouse while he's screwing women all over Europe."

"Charlie isn't like that."

The visitor barked out a laugh. "He has everyone fooled, but he's a red-blooded American just like everyone else."

"Why have you been looking for me?" Dennis said. "I thought you were still mad at me for leaving Saturday."

"I am, but we have more important things to deal with right now."

While Kirsten recognized the voice, she didn't know from where. She tried to sit up but couldn't. She lay back and closed her eyes, focusing on listening, though now the words were coming from even farther away. Like a tunnel. She needed to sleep. But all she'd done was sleep.

Dennis said something she couldn't quite make out, then his brother said, "It's complicated. I think I have it under control, but I could have used your help. Okay, listen to me. This is important, Dennis."

"I'm listening! I'm slow, not stupid."

"Dennis, I know you're not stupid. Just please pay attention; this is important."

"Okay." Dennis sounded like he was sulking.

"If the police come by and ask you any questions about me—anything, no matter what—play dumb. You don't know anything about my social life and nothing about my girlfriends."

Kirsten whimpered. She knew who Dennis's brother was.

Wade.

She'd had cybersex with him, then met him in person at a New Year's Eve party. Kirsten had walked in on him and Jessie having sex. Jessie had really liked him.

Oh, God, had Wade killed Jessica? Had it been his whispered voice she'd heard?

"But why?" Dennis said.

"Trust me on this, okay, Dennis? I've always looked out for you; this is your opportunity to look out for me. Okay?"

"But I don't understand."

"You don't have to. All you need to know is *nothing*. If Charlie finds out about this, he's going to cut me off. I'll just have the pathetic settlement money. Dammit, this is so fucked!"

Dennis said slowly, "This has something to do with that girl who got killed at the party."

Kirsten bit her lip to keep from crying out, and tried to swallow a cough. It came out weakly.

Please, don't let him hear me.

"Don't be such a dumb shit, of course it does!"

"Don't call me names. I don't like it when you say I'm stupid."

"I didn't! Geez, Dennis, I'm coming to you for help. I never said you were stupid. You're my little brother, right?"

"I'm sorry."

"It's going to be okay. Really. It doesn't mean anything. So what if I knew the victims? I know a lot of people. It's just a coincidence. But you know how the police are. They'd love to take down a Barnett."

"You didn't hurt anyone?"

"No!"

"But you were there. You made me sit in the car for hours."

"And you left me! The cab was taking fucking forever so I got a ride home from some skank. I was lucky she didn't get us killed. That's why I have you come along, to be my driver. But I wasn't there, right?"

"Of course you were. I took you."

"No! You didn't. You didn't take me to that party. Okay? Got that? I don't know what's going on, but someone has it in for me. It's going to be fine, it is, as long as you don't know anything."

"You want me to lie?"

"I want you to act stupid. Just act more retarded or something."

Kirsten wanted to run away, but she couldn't run or walk or even stand. What was Dennis going to do? Lie for his brother? Her head spun, even though she was lying down.

Wade said, "Denny, I'm sorry—I didn't mean it like that." His voice was soft and sounded sincere. But he wanted Dennis to lie.

"It's okay."

"No, it's not. I'm just under a lot of stress right now."

Dennis said, "I don't like any of this."

"I didn't hurt anyone. I swear to you, I didn't."

Kirsten didn't believe Wade. He'd been at the party! Was it his voice she'd heard? It had been so far away, she didn't know or couldn't remember. As far away as the voices sounded now. Down a long, dark tunnel.

Dennis said, "I believe you."

No, Dennis! Kirsten wanted to scream.

But she didn't. She couldn't. She was spiraling down, into blackness.

Her chest ached. Was she coughing?

"Oh, my God, Dennis, what have you done?"

The voice was so far away.

"Kirsten? What's wrong?"

Someone touched her head. She couldn't talk.

"What happened?" Wade demanded. "What did you do to her?"

He saved my life!

"I found her," Dennis said.

"Oh no. No. I know her. We have to get her out of here! Damn, she's blazing hot."

If Kirsten had the energy, she'd laugh. She was anything but hot. Her body was icy cold. So cold.

"She's sick. I'm taking care of her."

"Sick? She's more than sick, Dennis. We have to get her to the hospital. Call 911—no. No. I can't. You can't."

"What do you mean?"

"Don't you see? They'll take our names. If they know about my website, they might know about her. I can't risk that."

"We can't just leave her somewhere."

"We have to. What if she brings the police here?"

"No!"

"Shit. Okay, I have an idea. Get her stuff. Everything. Now."

Kirsten faded away. She didn't hear what Wade's plan was. For all she knew, he was going to kill her.

Somehow, dying didn't scare her as much as she had thought it would.

SIXTEEN

Watching Sean pace the FBI interview room was exhausting. "If that woman doesn't come back in five minutes," he said, "I'm leaving. We've been in here for over an hour." He looked at his watch and frowned. "One hour and twenty minutes."

"You don't like waiting much, do you?" Lucy asked.

"Without my phone, without my laptop, without even a piece of paper?"

She put her hand on her chest in mock insult. "What about me? I'm here."

He stopped walking and sat across from her. He held her hands and kissed them both. "And *you* are amazing. You totally blew Agent Madeaux away with your time line."

"So you've told me. *Twice*." But Lucy was very pleased that she'd found something valuable to the Cinderella Strangler investigation. She only hoped it led them to Kirsten. "I hope it helps."

"They hadn't made the *Party Girl* connection, and didn't know that Barnett knew the first victim."

"I suspect Wade Barnett knew all of the victims before he killed them."

"And you're concluding all of this because he dated the first victim?"

"It's logical. And suffocation is intimate. He'd have to hold his victims close, restrain them in some way. I wish I could see the crime scene reports. The information in the newspaper was vague."

Lucy backtracked a bit. "I should say that Barnett's the most *likely* to have killed these women. We know he knew the first and fourth victim, as well as Kirsten."

"But your gut tells you he's guilty."

"I need to see the evidence. But if I were running this investigation, I would bring him in for some intensive questioning."

Sean grinned. "I'd like to see you in action."

Lucy couldn't hide her smile, though she reddened at his attention. She said, "It's interesting that they didn't report that the victims were sexually assaulted."

The door opened and Suzanne Madeaux said, "We can't prove sexual assault. The coroner believes that sex was consensual, but the evidence is inconclusive."

An older cop with Italian features, NYPD badge clipped to his slacks, followed her. "Detective Vic Panetta," Suzanne said by way of introduction, "Sean Rogan, Lucy Kincaid. Sorry to keep you two waiting. Vic and I are heading the task force on these murders and I needed to call him in and get him up to speed before I could get back here."

Suzanne sat down with a file folder. Detective Panetta sat across from her and shook both Sean and Lucy's hands.

"Agent Armstrong vouched for both of you," Suzanne said. "But we have a problem." She looked at Lucy. "The *Party Girl* website doesn't exist."

Lucy's stomach dropped. "It must be down. I have

printouts of the profile pages, as well as screen captures."

"I'll need to see those, but I'm telling you, the site has vanished. The URL is available for purchase."

"That's not possible," Lucy said. "I was on the site this afternoon."

Sean said, "It's a pain in the ass, takes a day or two, but you can surrender your URL."

Suzanne said, "I need to know everyone you spoke to since you became involved in this case. You must have said or done something that tipped someone off, and they pulled down our only evidence that connects the four victims."

"Hold it," Sean said. "You didn't even know about the *Party Girl* website. It wasn't *your* evidence until we handed it to you on a silver platter."

"Three victims," Lucy said. "The first victim wasn't on the *Party Girl* site."

"You may have missed her," Suzanne said dismissively. "But now we have no way of knowing because the site has disappeared. Look, I'm not here to get into an argument; I need information. I have a killer out there targeting young women, and our only good lead is gone."

"It's not gone," Sean said. "We have the intel you need. And nothing Lucy or I did caused it to disappear. I told you it takes at least twenty-four hours to cancel a URL. Ownership is traceable, but whoever owned *Party Girl* did it through a blind company. I have my staff in California working on it."

Suzanne rubbed her eyes. "Mr. Rogan, I'll have to ask you to refrain from any investigation into that website. It's now our domain, and I'm sending everything to our cybercrimes lab at Quantico."

Lucy glanced at Sean. He looked down at the table, biting back a smile. She didn't think it was important for Suzanne to know—at this point—that Lucy's sister-in-law Kate Donovan was one of the point people for cybercrime at Quantico.

"Ms. Kincaid," Suzanne continued, "whom did you speak to today?"

"Where is my laptop?" Lucy asked.

"Why?"

"I've kept a log of everything I've done since Sean brought me in Wednesday morning, including a report of everyone I spoke to, what they said and my impressions. It would be easier to give you a copy than sit here for an hour."

Suzanne wasn't expecting that answer. Lucy didn't take pleasure in her diligence; had she said or done something that had tipped off the killer? Sean would know how a URL could be surrendered, but they'd been working on the case for three days. Maybe it was the fake profile she'd created. Or the email she sent to Kirsten yesterday. What if she'd screwed up the entire investigation? If another young woman died because Lucy had been too bold or asked the wrong question or didn't see a clue, she wouldn't be able to live with herself.

Suzanne said, "I don't like bringing civilians into the middle of an ongoing investigation. Normally, I wouldn't allow you in the conference room except that Agent Armstrong was sure that you could be of help. And you didn't tell me, Ms. Kincaid, that you're an applicant for the Bureau."

Lucy's face reddened and her stomach churned. She should tell Agent Madeaux that she'd been rejected. It felt deceptive to pretend to be something she wasn't, and she was no longer an applicant.

Sean spoke before she could. "Lucy aced her written test. Highest in her group. I understand that your case is confidential. My job is to find Kirsten Benton. Yours is to catch a killer. We'll share everything we have, and I hope you'll be looking for Kirsten if your investigation takes you down that path."

"Follow me," Suzanne said as she stood.

Lucy glanced at Sean and frowned. He shook his head almost imperceptibly, and she looked away. She didn't like Suzanne thinking she was on her way to the FBI Academy, because when the Fed found out the truth she'd lose all respect for her.

Her apprehension faded when she stepped into the small, windowless conference room that had become the repository of all things related to the Cinderella Strangler investigation.

The table could seat six, but the two end chairs had been removed to make more room to walk around the periphery. The wall to the right had an oversized magnetic whiteboard with photos of the victims and crime scenes, plus handwritten notes. Lucy saw that her time line had been printed out and someone had made notes along the margin.

Suzanne gestured toward a chair. "Make yourself comfortable," she said. She slid over Lucy's laptop.

Feeling like she was onstage, Lucy booted up her computer and retrieved her report. Suzanne handed Lucy the end of a long cord. "This printer is ancient, no wireless."

Lucy plugged it in and sent her document to print four copies. Suzanne retrieved and distributed them.

Detective Panetta and Suzanne read in silence. Lucy, antsy, walked over to the magnetic board.

Four victims, one missing teenager. If Wade Barnett was the killer and had had consensual sex with the victims, why kill them?

They were all killed near a large party. That told Lucy the killer was bold, arrogant, confident that he wouldn't be caught. Yet the murders themselves were intimate. Unhurried. Almost patient.

"Ms. Kincaid," the detective said, "those photos can be hard to take."

"I worked at the morgue for a year," she said. "I've seen worse."

She reviewed an autopsy report. It concluded that the murder weapon had been a plastic bag.

"Was the plastic bag used to suffocate the victims recovered at any of the crime scenes?" Lucy asked almost without realizing that she'd spoken.

When no one said anything, Lucy looked at an irritated Suzanne. The Fed didn't hide her emotions. "We're trying to keep information from the press, and it hasn't helped that someone leaked the information about the missing shoe."

"I'm not going to talk to the press. I'm just curious. Why would the killer take the plastic bag? It would be more efficient to leave it with the body, or not even remove it from her face. The killer wasn't concerned about getting caught. When you cut off someone's air supply, it takes three to seven minutes to render them unconscious, and another minute or two before they're brain-dead. Why not just tie the plastic bag around the victim's head and leave her? Get away from the scene as soon as possible—there were hundreds of people in the area; someone could easily have spotted the attack. Yet the killer stayed with the victim long enough to ensure that she was dead, then removed the plastic bag and left with it." She looked at the one bare foot on the last victim. "I wonder if he put the shoe in the plastic bag? Why?"

Suzanne cleared her throat. "We've sent a copy of the reports to Quantico for a profile of the killer."

"You don't have enough here to create a viable profile," Lucy said.

"With all due respect, Ms. Kincaid, our Behavioral Science Unit knows what they're doing."

"Of course they do, but not knowing if the victims were sexually assaulted is a crucial piece of the puzzle."

"Maybe the guy can't perform," Panetta said. "Blamed the girl."

"That's a crime of anger and passion," Lucy said. "If he attempted sex and couldn't finish, he'd most likely have hit her first, strangled her, beaten her, or stabbed her. Statistically, sex-related crimes have violent deaths. This isn't violent. It's premeditated—the killer brought the plastic bag and took it with him. Why? It's almost like . . ." Something was eluding her and she wished she could spend more time with the files.

Lucy asked, "Who goes to these parties?"

Panetta said, "Mostly the under-thirty crowd, a lot of college students blowing off steam on the weekends. Teenagers. Some are headbangers; most are into the alternative music scene; some parties are exclusive to the Yuppie types—work on Wall Street during the day, and party at night. Instead of pot and mesc and beer they snort coke and drink gin."

"Wade Barnett has a history of playing in the party scene," Lucy said. "If Wade Barnett is the killer—"

Suzanne cut her off and leaned forward. "Whoa, stop right there. Now you're jumping to conclusions."

"He knew the first and fourth victims. He's the most viable suspect."

"*If* Barnett is a suspect, he's *my* suspect. Last I checked, I still have a badge and you don't. Understand?"

Lucy nodded and turned back to the crime board. Suzanne was right. She'd overstepped.

Lucy tapped an index card on the board with Wade Barnett's name on it. "You already had him on your suspect list, didn't you?"

"We interviewed him. His name came up in the investigation. We're following up on things he said, and we'll follow up on what you uncovered."

Suzanne stood up and stretched. "It's late. I appreciate your insight. I'll be in touch if I hear anything about your missing teenager."

Sean leaned back in his chair, making no sign of leaving. "You should listen to Lucy. She has a master's in criminal psychology."

Lucy blushed. She didn't want Sean pushing this. "Agent Madeaux is right," Lucy said.

Suzanne sighed. "Let me sleep on it, okay? It's been a long couple days. If you think of anything else that might be helpful for me to know, give me a ring."

"Thank you," Lucy said. "You might want to ask Dr. Vigo to look at this case. I'm sure he'll take it, though he doesn't run the department anymore. I, um, think there's a complexity here that is uncommon."

"Why?"

She shrugged. "Just, I don't know, I can't really explain it without knowing more about each crime scene and victim. If you have any questions about my report, call me. I'm happy to help."

Sean said, "I need my pistol back."

Suzanne said, "You understand that you're not allowed to bring a firearm into the City of New York. Will you be leaving tomorrow?"

"We'll be leaving when we find Kirsten."

The silence made Lucy uncomfortable. Sean didn't always play nice with law enforcement.

Suzanne picked up the phone and pressed three buttons. "This is Agent Madeaux. Would you please retrieve Mr. Rogan's weapon and escort him and Ms. Kincaid to their vehicle? Thank you."

Once Rogan and Kincaid were gone, Suzanne stared at the whiteboard trying to see what Lucy Kincaid had seen.

"What are we missing?" she asked Panetta.

"*Are* we missing something?" he countered. "Lucy Kincaid writes a terrific report, and someday the kid will make a great cop, but she's still a twenty-five-year-old FBI recruit. She has no practical experience in criminal investigations."

"I don't know if that's true. Noah Armstrong—the agent down in Washington—said something that had me thinking he's worked with her in the past. I'll pull her file tomorrow and see what's up."

You don't have enough here to create a viable profile.

That was what Quantico had told Suzanne at the beginning. Except they had more now than two weeks ago. And there was more here than they'd had in other cases where the profile had been right on the money.

Cops had been solving crimes for years, long before psychological criminal profiling became an official FBI squad, back in the seventies. Good cops didn't need a shrink to tell them that someone was a sociopath or had a drunk for a father or that rape was a crime of anger. Most crimes were solved with lots of legwork, logic, and common sense.

Suzanne had watched Lucy closely while she looked at the board. She wondered why she had been so interested in the autopsy report. Suzanne had read Jessica Bell's report, the one posted on the board, and nothing had stood out. It read just like the other three—except the coroner stated that intercourse in the immediate time prior to death was inconclusive. He speculated—not on the report—that the victim didn't have sex, consensual or otherwise, the night she died.

Maybe Panetta was onto something, that the guy couldn't get it up. If there was no sexual assault, did that really change the profile much? Maybe Suzanne should take Lucy's suggestion and call Dr. Vigo. That was going around protocol—her boss wouldn't like it. But over the years she'd done a lot of things her boss hadn't liked.

She said to Panetta, "Are you planning on taking off tomorrow?"

"It *is* Saturday." He sighed. "I guess not."

"We need to reinterview Wade Barnett. Formally this time. And each victim was killed on a Saturday; it's the only other commonality. Let's see if we can keep him in prison overnight."

"He'll lawyer up."

"Fine. He said he didn't know any of the victims, yet we have a witness who connects him with Jessica Bell, and a photo that puts him with Alanna Andrews. Lying to a federal officer is a crime. I can get a warrant on that fact alone."

Panetta shook his head. "I always thought there was something wrong in that you can lie to street cops but not federal agents."

SEVENTEEN

Earlier, Sean had made reservations at the Park Central Hotel in midtown, near both Central Park and Times Square. Lucy was tired and didn't talk as he drove them, wrapped up in the case notes she'd read and trying to figure out what was so strange about the crime scenes. Sean had his hands full maneuvering the car through the hordes of people in the theater district.

She appreciated Sean's faith in her, but truly didn't want him to continue pushing her credentials. It made her uneasy, and reminded her that her credentials weren't good enough for the FBI. She needed to put that behind her and decide what was next.

It was after eleven at night when they finally checked into their room. Lucy walked in and saw a table set with covered dishes and wine. She dropped her bag, walked over, and lifted the covers from the plates. There were sandwiches, cheese and crackers, and chocolate mousse stored on ice. There was even a bottle of chardonnay in a wine bucket.

"You ordered all this?" she asked.

"I knew you wouldn't want to sit at a restaurant after the day we've had, and we missed dinner. It's just sandwiches and stuff, but I for one can't sleep if I'm hungry."

All her frustrations disappeared. Sean truly thought of everything—she would have thought about food after she went to bed and would have slept on an empty stomach.

"Hey, Luce, what's wrong? You were so quiet in the car."

She shook her head and smiled. "I was upset with you. Now, it doesn't seem important."

"It is important, because it mattered to you. What did I do?"

"It's nothing—I just—I'm not going to be in the FBI. You made it hard for me to explain that, so now I feel like I am lying to Agent Madeaux. After all your praise about my test scores and my master's, I couldn't very well say, 'Oh, but I wasn't accepted after all.' "

"Noah didn't tell her—"

"Noah doesn't know. *No one* does, except you."

Sean cleared his throat. "I, uh, meant to tell you earlier, but then there wasn't a good time, and I convinced myself that I'd wait until he had answers."

"You told Noah?"

"No. I talked to Hans Vigo."

Lucy sat heavily on the edge of the bed, feeling hollow again, not wanting to believe Sean had discussed the matter with Hans. "Why?"

He sat next to her and made her look at him. "Because something's not right about your application denial, and Hans is the best person to find out what happened."

"I wish you hadn't done that. I don't want anybody's help. If I can't get in on my own, I don't want to be an agent."

"Hans is not going to get you in, but you will want to appeal this decision."

"Don't tell me what I want!"

"Lucy, you need to know what this is all about."

"No," she said quietly. "I don't want to know."

"Why the hell not?"

"Because it changes nothing. And it will simply confirm what I already do know: that my past will never go away. I don't want to be told that I'm damaged or emotionally unstable."

"You are neither, Lucy," Sean said emphatically. "Don't even say it."

"It doesn't matter if I am or not. That's how people see me."

"No they don't. Hans said—" He stopped.

Lucy looked him in the eye, trying to keep her face calm, but her heart was pounding. She didn't like people manipulating her, even if they did it for all the right reasons.

Sean simply said, "You may be considered too controversial."

Lucy started laughing. "Controversial?"

"Am I missing something?"

She smiled and put a hand to her mouth to hold back another laugh. "I guess I had never considered that. I've been sure since I got the letter that they thought I was damaged goods."

"No one sees you as a victim, Lucy."

She continued. "Or that I killed my rapist and showed no remorse."

Sean frowned. "I don't understand."

But she didn't elaborate. "Or maybe they thought I was flighty because I had three vastly different internships over three years, but no real job. For about five minutes I cast blame on Kate, because if anyone was controversial in the FBI during the last decade, it was my sister-in-law.

"But Sean, *why* doesn't matter. I can find a hundred reasons to justify the panel's decision. It's still binding."

"You should appeal."

"I didn't think you really wanted me to be an FBI agent."

Sean wanted to explain himself, but didn't know how he could without sounding sappy or stupid. "You're right that I'm not a big fan of the FBI, but there are a few good agents out there. I'd much rather you come work for me, because you're good."

Lucy shook her head. "Sean, I'm not working for you and Patrick."

"Your name's already on the door," he said, hopeful.

She smiled and continued to shake her head.

"I thought it was a long shot. But seriously, you should appeal because *you* want it. You shouldn't have to settle for anything less than your dream."

Lucy threw her arms around Sean in a rare initiation of physical affection. It startled him, and they fell backward onto the bed. She kissed him. "You win."

He wrapped his arms around her waist. "I like my prize."

"I'll think more about appealing. But if Hans calls you back, I want to talk to him. I understand why you called him. You have an overwhelming need to fix things."

"I can't stand unfairness."

"Life isn't fair."

"That's why when I *can* do something, I do it. I never intended to go behind your back, but I'd never seen you so defeated. It broke my heart."

Lucy put her hand on Sean's chest, her touch making his pulse quicken. He loved this woman so much, but she would bolt if he told her. He knew she loved him, too; she just hadn't admitted it to him, or to herself.

One day at a time, Sean.

Lucy would give her all to save the innocent. But in her quest for justice, would she keep anything for herself?

Maybe that's where he came in. When she had nothing left, she could fill up on him. Sean wanted so desperately for Lucy to see that she needed him, not because he was a big, strong male and she was a weak female who needed a man—far from it. She needed him because he could be her anchor; he needed her because she gave him purpose and meaning he'd never had before.

He held her face in his hands. "You give to everyone, and you need to take sometimes. Take from me. Anything you need, anything you want, is yours."

She kissed him. It wasn't the tentative kiss he'd learned to expect from her. He didn't need to coax out her hidden passions; this kiss was bold and seductive. A full-body kiss, her chest pressed against his, one of her legs between his, her hands on his head, his face, her touch setting him on fire.

She planted her knees on the bed and sat up, pulling off her sweater, revealing her round breasts barely contained in a sexy, black lace demi-cup bra.

He pulled off his T-shirt and stretched up to kiss her between her breasts. She smelled both spicy and flowery, and he breathed in her skin, intoxicated. His hands moved over her smooth back. He unclasped her bra with one hand, then slowly eased it down.

She was gorgeous. And all his.

Lucy gasped when the cool air hit her breasts, and then Sean's mouth claimed one and his hand sought out the other. She closed her eyes, her body responding to the conflicting sensations—wet and dry; soft and rough; hot and hotter.

Sean was passionate in everything he did—from driving to work to play. He did nothing halfway, and that included making love. His intensity and physical awareness—of both his own body and hers—was exhilarating and irresistible. But also terrifying. She'd never been so completely explored, as if Sean needed to memorize every cell in her body.

Sean rose from the bed, and she wrapped her arms around his neck to keep from sliding to the floor. He kissed her, his mouth hot and greedy, as if she were his lifeline. He turned them around and dropped her to the bed, her legs hanging off the edge. "You're beautiful."

He smiled and knelt on the floor. He kissed her stomach while he slowly unzipped her jeans. Then he rolled them off her hips and pulled them down to the floor while his mouth followed, placing kisses one by one down the outside of her thigh. He kissed her feet, and Lucy was startled at the jolt of lust she felt when he licked her ankles. It was the anticipation, his slow-moving mouth, his hands moving up and down her legs, never stopping.

She hadn't realized until that moment that she'd missed him. They'd had ten days alone, almost like a honeymoon, and then the last month had spent little time together. And even when they had been together, they had not been alone. This intimacy was new to her, this need for physical contact. She hadn't known this was what she'd been missing, but she'd never before craved a man the way she did Sean.

As if sensing the shift inside her, from romance to passion, Sean kissed the inside of her thighs, her legs spreading on their own. His hands reached under her and held her butt, his fingers kneading. She was capable of no conscious thought, eager to explore Sean as he explored her. Her hands fisted in the comforter when Sean blew kisses over the flesh he'd just licked. When his tongue flickered over her sweet spot, she drew in her breath. She couldn't exhale, couldn't breathe, couldn't *think*.

She went from simmer to boil so fast she didn't have time to bite back a cry as her orgasm exploded.

Sean nibbled her inner thighs, but his kisses were hotter, his hands moving up her sides as his mouth covered her stomach, kissing her ribs, her breasts, her neck, and suddenly he devoured her mouth again, hot and focused. His rock-hard body pressed against her, quivering with restraint, and his hands reached behind her neck, his fingers entwined with her long, thick hair.

Her hands grabbed his shoulders to steady herself.

"Luce," he whispered on a hot breath. "I can't get enough of you. I've missed you this week. God, I've missed you." He kissed her jawline, then her neck, his tongue and mouth claiming every inch of her flesh as they edged their way to the nape of her neck. He licked the tender hollow spot at her throat, sending another jolt of electric-charged desire through her body. He chuckled softly.

"You sound pleased with yourself," she said, her voice sounding nothing like her.

"I am. With me. With you. Us." He drew her earlobe into his mouth and nibbled. He touched her everywhere, his talented fingers knowing exactly which muscle to massage hard, which to skim, which to kiss.

She wanted to explore Sean, but his skin was hot and flushed and he already had his pants off. When had that happened? She couldn't remember. She felt drunk, even without drinking any wine.

He reached down to the floor and it wasn't until he pulled his wallet out of his jeans that she realized what he was doing. She had never paid much attention when he'd put on a condom in the past. It had embarrassed her a bit; she didn't know why, didn't want to think about it. Now she found herself watching, intrigued, and feeling playful. She reached out and put her hands on his as he rolled the condom on.

Why was he shaking? He was always so confident in bed, so positive he could make her happy, and he did. Was he nervous?

Sean had made her more comfortable with sex than the two partners who had come before him. She was emboldened as she pushed his hands away and finished putting on the condom. She ran her fingers lightly over the base of his quivering penis, so solid, but covered in soft, warm skin.

She surprised herself again when she sat up and kissed the tip.

"You do that and I'm going to completely lose it," he said through clenched teeth.

He urged her back down on the bed, his mouth open and seeking hers. He kissed her as if it were the last time. His penis touched her at just the right spot, as if it had a mind of its own. He thrust into her quickly and she gasped from the sudden invasion. He held himself still, his hands clasped in hers, a bead of sweat dripping from his chest to hers.

She'd always been on top, more comfortable when she was in control. She hesitated, just a fraction, but Sean was so in tune with her body and emotions that he knew what she had thought.

He whispered in her ear, "Just say the word, Luce. I'm yours, any way you want."

She kissed him hard, his understanding and faith in her overwhelming and so appreciated.

"Just like this," she managed to say.

As he started to move within her, slowly at first, the wonderful wave Lucy was becoming familiar with every time she and Sean were together grew quickly. They developed a rhythm that was both new and familiar; they were still exploring, but amazingly perceptive as they each anticipated the changes within the other.

Sean knew he wasn't going to last. Not with Lucy beneath him for the first time, the trust and faith she'd placed in him as overpowering as the sexual combustibility burning between them. She didn't know or understand what her touch, her scent, her body did to him. He could never get enough of her, never wanted to get enough. He could make love to her daily and enjoy it each and every time. She was becoming bolder; he pictured her lips on his cock and he couldn't hold back. Didn't want to.

"Lucy," he breathed into her neck, then he stretched up and stared at her glowing face, her eyes closed, her mouth open, her skin flushed as her body kept pace with his increased tempo. He groaned as his orgasm hit, wishing he could have held off until Lucy was done, but she had completely undone him. He rocked against her, bringing her to her peak, watching as her chest rose and her back arched. Her hands squeezed his ass so hard it would have hurt if it didn't feel so extraordinarily good.

Her body froze and she let out a quiet cry as her pleasure poured through her. Then, simultaneously, every one of her muscles relaxed.

Sean collapsed onto his back, pulling her with him, holding her for a long minute as she basked in her femininity and power.

"You are amazing," he said before realizing the words were out of his mouth.

"So are you," she said with a smile.

He kissed her. Then again. He could make love to her all night. He wanted to.

"We need to eat. And sleep."

"We do," she agreed, but made no move to get up.

He kissed her again. "Stay."

"I couldn't move if I wanted."

He smiled and reluctantly rose from the bed. He walked to the bathroom and stared at his reflection in the mirror.

"Sean Rogan, you are hopelessly, irrevocably, in love."

He wanted to tell her. But he didn't want to scare her. Lucy wanted slow and steady. He would be slow and steady.

For now.

He finished in the bathroom, and returned to find Lucy sitting on the edge of the bed in his T-shirt eating one of the sandwiches.

"I thought I said don't move."

"I worked up an appetite."

Sean found his boxers on the floor and stepped into them, then sat next to Lucy and grabbed a sandwich.

"This doesn't count as our weekend away," Sean said, reiterating what he'd told her last night.

"It doesn't?" Lucy feigned ignorance.

"Nope. We'll call this a prequel."

She sipped her wine with a smile. "Fine by me."

EIGHTEEN

Wade Barnett sat in the interview room with his lawyer, James Thorpe. Suzanne hadn't dealt with Thorpe before, but Panetta knew him. "Five hundred dollars an hour," he'd grumbled to her before they walked into the room. "Attorney for the rich and infamous."

"I gather you're not a fan of his?"

"So perceptive, for a Fed."

She rolled her eyes and opened the door. "Mr. Barnett, thank you for coming down here this morning."

"I didn't have a choice," Wade grumbled.

"You always have a choice," Suzanne said.

"Then I'm leaving."

"Well, of course, you're not under arrest, but I can fix that since you lied to me Thursday. Did you know that lying to a federal law enforcement agent is a crime? Now, if I hadn't joined Detective Panetta, we wouldn't be able to arrest you right now. But, because you lied to me—a *federal* agent—I came up with a damn good reason to get a warrant for your apartment and your office."

"You can't—"

Thorpe put a hand on Barnett's forearm. "Hear them out."

Suzanne was having fun with the interrogation. This was her favorite part of the job.

"Thank you," Suzanne said, filling her tone with sincerity. Barnett was wary. He was squirming. He was acting so guilty she expected him to make a full confession this morning before lunch.

She'd go out and celebrate. With champagne.

Panetta said, "Mr. Barnett, you told us on Thursday that you didn't recognize any of these young women." He spread the four photos in front of Barnett.

Barnett didn't say anything. Suzanne took out the *New York Post* photo of Barnett and Alanna Andrews kissing in the Barnett box at Yankee Stadium.

"Do you remember this?"

No response.

"Mr. Barnett," Suzanne said, "please answer the question. Do you remember taking Alanna Andrews to this Yankees game? That is you, correct? And Ms. Andrews?"

Again, he didn't answer. He stared at the pictures.

Suzanne could play this game all day.

"Mr. Thorpe," she said, "your client can answer questions now, or he can answer them from Rikers. Jurisdiction can go either way. New York doesn't have a death penalty. The United States does."

Thorpe leaned over and whispered in Barnett's ear.

It still took Barnett a full minute before he replied. "Yes."

"Yes, this is you and Ms. Andrews kissing?"

He nodded.

"That wasn't too difficult, was it?"

Thorpe said, "Agent Madeaux, with all due respect, cut to the chase. Of what do you accuse my client?"

"I haven't accused him of anything except lying to a federal officer about knowing these women."

Thorpe said, "When you approached him in his office, he was in shock. He didn't understand what you meant."

"He didn't understand, 'Do you recognize any of these women?'" Suzanne shook her head. "I have a witness who says that you met this young lady," she tapped Jessica Bell's photograph, "at a New Year's Eve party. Less than a mile from where this college student"—she pointed to Heather Garcia's image—"was murdered."

Barnett was slowly shaking his head. Suzanne continued. "I have solid proof that you knew two of the victims but lied to me about it. When we search your home and office, I'm pretty confident that we'll find evidence that you killed them."

"No. No, I didn't kill anyone."

"I'll tell you my theory," she said. "I think you have some problems, sexually speaking."

Barnett laughed. "I have no problems in bed."

"Let me just play this out a bit. There was this website—it's not there anymore, but fortunately, we have an archive of it. It's called *Party Girl*. Are you familiar with it?"

Barnett didn't say anything, but he was no longer laughing.

"Mr. Barnett, answer the question."

Thorpe and Barnett consulted, then Barnett said, "I'm not certain."

"You're not certain of what? Whether you have

sexual problems or that you visited the *Party Girl* website in order to have online mutual masturbation parties?"

Thorpe cleared his throat. "That's uncalled-for."

"On the contrary," Panetta said, "we have four dead women; two of whom we know your client associated with."

Barnett said, "I dated Alanna for a while. We broke up about a week after the Yankees game."

"Why?"

"She found out I was cheating on her."

"With whom?"

He didn't say anything.

"Please answer," Suzanne snapped.

Barnett closed his eyes. "With Erica."

Suzanne avoided the overwhelming urge to give Vic Panetta a high five.

"Erica Ripley?" Suzanne gave the name of the Cinderella Strangler's second victim.

"Yes," he confirmed.

Instead of celebrating, she slid over Kirsten Benton's senior portrait. "Do you know this girl?"

Barnett was shaking. "Yes," he whispered.

"How?"

"She's a friend of Jessica's."

"Where is she?"

He stared at her and looked surprised. "What do you mean?"

"She came to New York last weekend to stay with Jessica Bell. Jessica is dead; Kirsten is missing."

"She told me her name was Ashleigh."

Suzanne glanced at her notes—they were Lucy Kincaid's meticulous notes that she'd brought into the interrogation—and sure enough, Kirsten's *Party Girl* screen name was Ashleigh. Why would Barnett deny he knew who she really was? Maybe because he didn't know—he knew the girls by their screen names. Except he had known Jessica's and Erica's real names. Suzanne put aside the discrepancy to ponder later, and asked, "Where is Kirsten Benton?"

"I don't know."

"You'd better figure it out."

Thorpe said, "My client said he doesn't know where the girl is. It sounds to me like you're fishing."

"Hardly," Suzanne snapped. "We have proof that he personally knew three of the four Cinderella Strangler victims." She slapped her hand on Heather Garcia's photo. "Did you know Heather?"

Barnett nodded.

"Sleep with her?"

He hesitated, then nodded.

"Did you kill these women?"

"No. No. No. I did *not* kill anyone. I swear on my father's grave, I didn't kill anyone!"

When Suzanne and Panetta walked out of the interview room fifteen minutes later, Barnett was on his way to arraignment for lying to a federal officer—Suzanne's way of making sure he didn't flee before she had hard proof he was guilty of murder.

"Good job," Panetta said.

"I feel like I should take that Lucy Kincaid out to celebrate. I can't believe I missed the connection between Alanna Andrews and Wade Barnett."

"His name didn't come up until this week," Panetta said. "And it's me who should be beating myself up. You didn't even get the case until after New Year's."

"We got him now. It's just a matter of crossing the t's and dotting the i's."

Her boss, SSA Steven Blackford, walked down her cubicle row. "Good work, Suzanne, Detective." Blackford shook Panetta's hand. "But it's not over yet. I have a warrant here that you'll probably want to execute personally."

She smiled. Life was good. She'd stopped a killer.

Really, it seemed a sin to have this much fun putting away the bad guys.

NINETEEN

Sean's cell phone rang when he stepped out of the shower. He grabbed it, not recognizing the number.

"Rogan."

"This is Trey Danielson."

Sean quickly dried off as he said, "Where the hell have you been? I called you half a dozen times and told you to get your ass back to Woodbridge."

"I got the messages, but you don't understand."

"Explain yourself."

Sean wasn't in the mood to listen to Trey's excuses, but he didn't want the kid wandering around New York causing problems for him while he searched for Kirsten.

"I should have stopped her last summer. I knew what she was doing, and I was more angry than anything, and hurt, and I said things I shouldn't have. I turned my back on her, and now she's in trouble—"

Sean cut him off. He forced his voice to be calm. "I understand what you're saying, Trey, but consider that you are the only person Kirsten has contacted since she disappeared. She trusts you. I'm in New York and I'm not leaving until I find her."

"Neither am I."

"Trey, there are a lot of things going on that you

don't know about. I can't have you getting in the middle of it."

"But I found something. That's why I'm calling you."

Sean slipped on his jeans and left the bathroom. "What did you find?"

"Her phone."

Sean caught Lucy's eye and mouthed *Trey*.

"You found Kirsten's phone. How?"

"Some guy called me. Said he was working his way through her speed dials. I was number three."

Sean didn't know what to think. "What's his name?"

"Ryan."

"Ryan what?"

"I don't know."

"I want his address."

"I'm in this for the long haul, Sean. I need to find her."

"Give me his address."

"I'll meet you there."

"You don't know who he is or if he knows something about her disappearance."

"I called you, didn't I? I'll admit, I'm nervous, okay? Her message freaked me out. It's not like her! But if I have to talk to him myself, I will."

Sean hit the hotel-room desk with his palm. "I'm on my way," he said through clenched teeth. "Where?"

"I'm at a Starbucks near his apartment. Third and Sixty-first."

"Don't move. I'll be there in less than thirty minutes."

Sean hung up and told Lucy, "Someone found Kirsten's phone and called Trey because he was on speed dial."

He finished dressing and said, "Do you want to come?"

She shook her head. "While you were in the shower, Suzanne called and said they'd arrested Wade Barnett and she was about to go out with a search warrant. He admitted to knowing Kirsten by her screen name Ashleigh, but denied knowing anything about the *Party Girl* site."

"He's lying."

"Probably. He's now admitted knowing all four of the Cinderella Strangler victims, but denied killing them, and says he hasn't seen Kirsten in two months."

Sean sensed that Lucy's mind was elsewhere. "What's bothering you? Something is on your mind."

"I want to know more about him. I read all the newspaper articles yesterday, about his background, and his efforts to preserve some of the historical buildings—"

"Lucy, some bad guys aren't one hundred percent evil. It doesn't mean he isn't a killer."

She frowned and pursed her mouth. "I know that. And if he was using the *Party Girl* site for cybersex or real sex, then he's a jerk. And he could be a killer. But, well, I don't know that he'll fit the profile."

"Hold it—you told Suzanne yesterday that there wasn't enough information to come up with a profile."

"There wasn't because they didn't know whether it was sexually motivated or not."

"Why does that make a difference?"

"On Jessica Bell's autopsy report it stated that she hadn't had sex for several hours, or longer, before she was killed."

"Maybe he was interrupted."

"None of the girls had torn clothing or any indication that they fought off an attack."

"How do you know that?"

"It was all up on the board in the office."

"I didn't catch that."

"It helps that I'm used to reading police reports."

"Well," Sean said, playing devil's advocate, "Wade knew the victims. They may not have thought they were in danger."

"But *why*? Maybe that's what's messing me up. They all had sex with him, at least online—"

"Maybe they were fine when it was online, but not when it was physical, and he snapped."

"Maybe."

"I'm sorry. I didn't mean to cut you off."

"It's okay. I'm just thinking out loud. You need to go and meet Trey. I'm calling Hans, and maybe he'll see where my thinking is wrong."

Sean stepped forward and kissed her. "Lucy, don't assume that you're wrong."

"I don't know what I think, but Suzanne is now positive Wade is guilty." Yesterday, Lucy was as well. But the more she thought about the method of murder, the more she felt that she'd jumped to a faulty conclusion.

"I thought he was innocent until proven guilty?"

"That's the courts. Cops don't arrest you unless they believe you're guilty. She's probably right."

Sean kissed her again. "Trust your instincts, Lucy.

Talk to Hans. Tell him I said hi. I'll let you know what I learn from the guy who found Kirsten's phone."

Lucy called Hans, but it went to voice mail. She and Sean had gone to the hotel's gym first thing in the morning, so she couldn't run again. She didn't want to be in the hotel all day. Maybe she should have gone with Sean.

But something was bothering her about the murders.

"This isn't your case," she mumbled to herself. And Suzanne Madeaux seemed to be sharp. Lucy liked her; Suzanne reminded her of her sister-in-law Kate. Straightforward, confident, smart. Maybe a little rough around the edges, like a tomboy who hadn't accepted that she'd grown into an attractive woman. When Suzanne had called earlier, she'd invited Lucy and Sean out for dinner to celebrate Wade Barnett's arrest. And maybe they would go, but Lucy didn't feel right celebrating anything while Kirsten was still missing. Or while she had doubts.

Her cell phone rang, and she saw that it was a private 202 number. "Hello," she answered.

"Lucy, it's Hans Vigo."

"Thanks for calling me back so quickly."

"Of course. What can I do for you?"

"I'm in New York with Sean—"

"Noah clued me in on the runaway you're looking for."

"Good." She thought it was odd that Hans and Noah were talking about the case—they didn't even work in the same office—but she didn't say anything. And now that she was talking to Hans, she didn't know exactly how to bring up her concerns. "There's a related investigation, the Cinderella Strangler who suffocated four young women, and I suggested that the agent in charge of the case contact you directly for a profile."

"Of course, but the BSU staff is more than capable. I vouch for all of them." Hans had been one of the early agents involved with the Behavioral Science Unit.

"Well, I don't know anyone else but you," Lucy said. "Sorry, I know you're really busy."

"There had to be a reason you thought of me. What is it?"

"It's probably not even important anymore. Agent Madeaux arrested a suspect this morning and already got a search warrant."

"Yet you called."

Lucy sat at the hotel-room desk and stared at her notes from the past week without really seeing them. She felt like an idiot. What was she doing second-guessing a smart, seasoned agent like Suzanne? Wade Barnett had lied to the police about knowing those women. Someone had taken down the *Party Girl* site—and according to Suzanne, they'd spoken with Barnett Thursday morning. Sean said it would take at least twenty-four hours if Barnett wasn't serving the site himself. "Never mind."

"It's always good to hear from you, Lucy."

He was going to hang up. She blurted out, "Sean told me he talked to you about my application. I haven't told my family."

Hans said, "Neither have I, Lucy."

"I would never have asked you to look into it. I know why I failed."

"You do?"

"You told Sean I might be too controversial. I don't think that's it. I think—" She hesitated, then said, "I wanted it too much."

"What do you mean?"

"I've been thinking about this since I got the letter. One of the questions they asked was why I hadn't settled on a career. I knew that the FBI had become a place for second careers—so few people are recruited out of college anymore, unless they have a special skill. But I said that I had always wanted to work in the Bureau, that everything I did was self-training— working in the morgue, working for the sheriff's department. But the female panelist commented that I didn't have a passion for anything."

Lucy continued, her words tumbling out. "I kept talking because I was worried that they thought I was too cold or hardened or something. I rambled about my passions—for stopping sexual predators and working in cybercrime and everything I wanted to do to protect the innocent, and I said too much. Either they thought I was playing them, or that I was radical."

"Lucy, don't overanalyze—"

She interrupted, "The rest of the interview went so smoothly! Nothing stood out. Except—if it wasn't wanting it so badly that I panicked, then it's only because of one other thing."

"Adam Scott."

She said, "I killed an unarmed man."

"There were extenuating circumstances."

"I shot him six times. And I would do it again. And those two facts are in my record, and there's nothing I can do to change it."

Hans didn't say anything.

Lucy said, "I wouldn't blame anyone for thinking I could end up just like Fran Buckley."

Fran, a retired FBI agent, had been her mentor at WCF, the victim's rights advocacy group Lucy had volunteered with for three years. But Fran's illegal activities had shut WCF down and caused the FBI untold problems from which Lucy was certain they were still reeling.

"The Bureau likes to believe they always make the right hiring decisions," Hans said. "But in any business, government or private, there are always rotten eggs. I had one who worked for me and I didn't see how psychopathic she was. No one did, until she shot her partner and left her for dead.

"You may be right," Hans continued, "on either theory. I don't know. I told Sean I would discreetly look into your application, but if you want me to pull back, I will. Whatever you want me to do, I hope you'll still appeal the decision."

"I haven't decided. I wasn't going to, but—"

"You still want it."

"Yes."

"You'll have to fight for it. But you're more than capable."

"Thank you."

"Now what did you really call me about?"

Lucy said, "It's how these girls were killed. The killer either didn't have sex with the victims or it was consensual. The last victim hadn't had sex recently. No sign of physical trauma, no defensive wounds on any of the victims, and they were all suffocated with some sort of plastic bags—which were then removed and taken by the killer. Their bodies weren't moved after they died—the killer suffocated and dropped them right there. No postmortem abuse, either. The killer took one shoe—hence the moniker 'Cinderella Strangler.' "

"Did the killer tie the bag around the victim, or hold it in place?"

Lucy thought back to the autopsy report she'd read. "There were no ligature marks or anything to indicate rope or tape was used to hold the plastic in place. There was some bruising, but not in a strangulation pattern. I didn't see photos of bruising, but the coroner wrote 'inconsistent with strangulation.'"

"Bruises likely left from how the killer held the bag."

"The victims weren't restrained, but they were drugged. And because they were all at raves, the drugs were most likely taken voluntarily by the victims. All the victims left the party and no one has come forward to say they saw anyone in duress. There aren't a lot of witnesses—though my missing teenager may have seen something when the last victim was killed. She wrote something to that effect in a convoluted message she sent her ex-boyfriend."

"But you said the FBI made an arrest?"

"Yes. Wade Barnett. I haven't met him, and maybe if I do these doubts won't linger—"

"They had good cause to arrest him?"

"He lied about knowing the victims; he lied about

having a physical or online sexual relationship with the victims. He then admitted it, but of course denies killing them."

"It sounds like sex was consensual?"

"Yes, it appears so. Of course there are many cases where a killer has a relationship and, in anger or because the victim cuts it off, he stalks or kills her. But *four* times? And then there's the method. This killer is cold. He or she puts plastic over the heads of their victims, who are so drugged they hardly fight back, and then waits. Five to seven minutes before the victim is dead. That's a long time to watch someone die. More than that—there are no premortem injuries consistent with the victims being on the ground *while* they were dying. I was looking for cuts from glass or rocks that might have indicated the victim fighting from a prone position. But if the killer didn't use a rope to tie the bag—"

"He used his hands."

"Right. To hold the bag in place."

"Which suggests that the victims were upright and the killer held them while they died. That's a very intimate way to kill."

"That's what I said!" Lucy exclaimed, excited that Hans saw the crime the same way she did.

"Which could in its own way be a sexual murder, even if the killer didn't attempt intercourse."

"I hadn't thought of it like that."

"Did you realize what you said before?"

"That I didn't think about it as a sexual crime?"

"No. You said *he or she* in reference to the killer."

"I didn't notice. Considering the victim profiles and

the intimate aspect of the crimes, of course the killer would be male."

"I think I know what has been bothering you about the murders," Hans said. "It's that the victims were suffocated. Suffocation is traditionally a more feminine method of murder. Along with poisoning, it is more common among female killers than male killers."

"Wade Barnett is a good suspect," Lucy said, weighing Hans's comments. She hadn't considered a female killer; why was that? But the manner of death had caught her attention and wouldn't let go.

"Is there any physical evidence connecting him to the murders?"

"Not that I know about. But the investigation isn't over. The FBI has a search warrant, and lying about knowing the victims is a big red flag."

"People lie for many different reasons."

Lucy asked, "Do you really think that a woman could hold someone for the seven minutes it takes for them to die? Then coldly remove the bag, drop the body to the ground, remove one shoe, and walk away?"

"Yes," Hans said without hesitation. "Female killers can be just as cold-blooded and merciless as their male counterparts. Was there any bruising on the torso?"

"I don't know. I only saw the one autopsy report."

"If you consider that the victims were, in a sense, poisoned with drugs—even if they took the drugs willingly—which made them compliant, then were suffocated, without any sexual component, that makes it even more likely to be a female killer. I wouldn't rule out the current suspect, of course, but I'd hesitate to bring the case to the U.S. Attorney without solid physical evidence tying him to the murders."

"Suzanne Madeaux is a smart agent," Lucy said. "I shouldn't have said anything."

"But it's been on your mind. I'm glad you called. How long are you staying in New York?"

"I don't know. Sean said until we find Kirsten. And maybe when we do, she'll be the eyewitness we need to indict Wade Barnett."

Or point them in a completely different direction.

TWENTY

Suzanne and Vic Panetta split the search warrant— she took Barnett's residence, Panetta took his office.

Barnett lived in a secured high-rise in the upper nineties off Central Park West. The tall building with views of Central Park from the higher floors was bordered by older four-story town houses, some single residences and some converted into apartments. Suzanne preferred her flat on the Lower East Side to the opulence of Barnett's apartment building, but she admitted that she coveted one of the brownstones.

Not in the cards on a government salary.

She flashed her badge and warrant to the doorman, who rang the manager on duty. Ten minutes later, she was let into Barnett's nineteenth-floor five-room apartment.

It was a larger version of his office. Cool gray carpeting; white leather furniture; lots of steel and glass. Yankees posters—framed and signed; an eclectic version of art on the walls from realistic charcoal drawings to flashy, bright paintings that didn't appear to be anything specific. But the framed artwork that caught Suzanne's eye were photographs of abandoned warehouses. She recognized the printing supply house where Jessica Bell had been killed.

"Where do you want us to start?" asked Andie Swann, from the Evidence Response Team.

"Photograph everything, then dedicate someone to the computer and any electronics. Our warrant covers everything in his apartment and any storage, in addition to his car. And can you also get someone to pull down those photographs?"

"Of the buildings?"

"Yes. I want to know who took them and when and ID every site." She didn't immediately see photographs of the first three crime scenes, but that didn't mean they weren't around.

She turned to the manager. "Does Mr. Barnett have a vehicle stored on the property? Any storage unit?"

"We have an underground garage where he has a slot, number 103. We have storage units, but he doesn't rent one."

She said to Andie, "Send someone down to the garage to check on the status of the car and arrange for transport."

The manager said, "Oh, no, he never drives it. It's a classic."

"What good is a car you can't drive?"

"I suppose he might take it out on occasion, but I haven't seen it missing in months. It doesn't have a roof."

"You mean it's a convertible?"

"No, it doesn't have a roof. He bought it at auction, and the roof was damaged. He only drives it on nice days if he's going out of town."

Suzanne looked at Andie and Andie nodded. She would check it out. "Prints, fibers, and trace," Suzanne called after her.

"Mr. Barnett is a good tenant," the manager said. "We've never had any problems with him. No complaints."

"Good to know," she said in dismissal. "You're welcome to stay and observe, but I ask that you stay in the hall. Let my people do their job."

"No, go ahead; just please let me know when you're leaving so I can lock up."

"I'll be putting a police seal on the door," she said.

Suzanne slipped on latex gloves and walked through the apartment. A large living area, a separate dining area, a kitchen that was bigger than her entire one-bedroom apartment. And the view of Central Park was nice. But the best thing about the place was the light—lots of windows, lots of open space. Two bedrooms, two bathrooms, and an office. Large space for a bachelor. Had to be at least 2,000 square feet. Maybe more. For a New York City apartment with a view, that was rare and pricey.

Suzanne walked through the apartment slowly, taking in the atmosphere, imagining Wade Barnett living here. Killers came in all shapes and sizes and economic classes. Psychopaths weren't rich or poor; black or white; men or women. Suzanne believed any human being had the capacity to kill, given the right motivation. But while most people killed only when they were in immediate jeopardy, psychopaths killed for pleasure. Whether it was a gangbanger who had no regard for human life or a serial killer with a sick, twisted view of women, they could come from any socioeconomic background.

She wouldn't allow Wade Barnett to get away with murder because he was rich.

While Andie was down in the garage and her team methodically worked through the apartment, Suzanne went to Barnett's office, which was more cluttered than the living areas. The computer tech was already at work, and Suzanne focused on the contents of the desk. They were already working on getting Barnett's financials, but because he was paid by a trust it was tricky. She'd leave those details to the accountants and lawyers.

Nothing jumped out at her. Baseball, architecture, and the historical society. His bookshelves were lined with books on those same three subjects, with few exceptions. He had three Yankee game balls, all signed by the player who'd hit a home run. They were displayed under lights, behind glass. An award from a local preservation society was prominently displayed on the wall, next to a picture of the former mayor handing a teenage Wade Barnett a plaque.

On the surface, Barnett appeared to be an all-around good guy. Arrogant, but a longtime advocate of things he cared about. What turned a guy like this into a serial killer?

Andie Swann walked into the office. "Car's clean. No way he drove that out to Brooklyn on Saturday, not with the weather. The interior is immaculate, no water damage, nothing to indicate that he's used it recently. I asked security to prepare the logs for every time he took the car out from October first through today, and one of my team is vacuuming for trace, but I don't expect anything."

Andie asked the computer tech, "When are you going to be done in here?"

"He recently wiped histories and deleted a bunch

of files, but it's a surface job. I can put it all back together at the office. It'll take me thirty minutes to
label, log, and box everything up."

Suzanne hoped the computer yielded hard evidence
because there was no way any more serious charges
would stick to Barnett just because he'd lied about
knowing the victims. DNA or finding the victims'
shoes would be ideal. Even if she could prove that he
was at all four parties and knew all four victims, she
wouldn't be able to get the U.S. Attorney to bite unless there was physical evidence tying him to at least
one of the murders.

One of Andie's people stepped into the office. "We
found this letter in the nightstand drawer of the main
bedroom," he said to Suzanne and Andie. The letter
had been sealed in a plastic bag and tagged.

The tech continued. "There was a stack of writing
paper. We also bagged it because of impressions on
the bottom sheets. We might be able to get something
from those. This was at the bottom of the pile, and
folded."

"Thanks." Suzanne took the undated letter. It had
an angled crease and was only partially written.
Suzanne often did that when she was writing to her
eighty-nine-year-old grandmother, who refused to get
a computer, if she misspelled a word or decided not to
tell her something. She'd written Gram her first year
of college and received the letter back, her grammar
and misspellings corrected, a week later.

> Dear Alanna,
>   I'm a jerk. My brother says I don't know a good thing

*when I have it, and he's right. You were my good thing
and I blew it. I miss you.*

*I'd love to promise I won't screw up again, but I
know I will. And you don't deserve that. I'd say I can't
help myself, but we both know it's not true. I'm too selfish to make a commitment.*

But it hurts when I see you, and so I'm trying to avoid

The last incomplete sentence was scribbled out, but
Suzanne could easily read it.

"Who writes letters anymore?" Andie asked.

Suzanne didn't want to admit that she thought it
was sweet—not the apology for the fact that Barnett
obviously did something unforgivable to Alanna—
before he killed her—but that in this day and age, a
handwritten letter seemed more sincere than sending
an email or text message.

Another tech looked through the doorway. "Suzanne, there's a guy here says he's Barnett's brother."

"I'll talk to him," she said and walked out.

The young man—hardly older than a teenager—
stood just inside the door biting his thumbnail. His
hair was too long in the front, partly covering his
eyes, but overall he was a clean-cut kid.

"Mr. Barnett?" Suzanne said as she approached.

He looked startled, almost mousy, then nodded.
"Dennis Barnett."

"Nice to meet you, Dennis. Do you live here with
your brother?"

He shook his head. "I live in Staten Island with my
mother. But sometimes I stay with my brother. My
other brother, Charlie."

"Charlie? Is that CJ Barnett?"

Dennis nodded. "He says CJ is his business name, but I still call him Charlie." Dennis was mildly retarded, Suzanne realized as she spoke to him, but didn't seem to be impaired. "Is Wade in trouble?"

"Yes, he is. I'm sorry to have to tell you that." She showed him her badge and ID. "My name is Suzanne Madeaux. I'm a special agent with the FBI."

He looked around. "Where's Wade?"

"I'm sorry, Dennis, but he's in jail right now."

Dennis's eyes widened. "W-why?"

"Well, it's a bit complicated." Suzanne didn't want to upset the kid; she felt sorry for him. She opted to start with the sanitized version. "He lied to me, and it's a crime to lie to a federal law enforcement agent. Did you know that?"

He shook his head.

"I asked Wade if he knew some young women. I showed him their pictures. He told me he didn't, but then I found out that he knew them really well."

"Wade knows a lot of girls."

"Does he date a lot?"

"Oh, yes. He likes to have sex."

"With the same woman or different women?"

"Different. Sometimes he has a girlfriend, but he always screws it up."

"Is that what he told you?"

"No. Charlie says that. Because Wade can't be man-ag-a-mis."

"Do you mean *monogamous*? Meaning, staying faithful to one person?"

Dennis smiled. "Yes. Monogamous."

"Do you know any of his girlfriends?"

He shrugged. "Some."

"Like Alanna?"

He smiled. "I liked Alanna."

"She was nice?"

He said in a low voice, "Some of Wade's girlfriends were mean to me. I know I'm not too smart. My mom says it's the way God made me and I'm perfect the way I am, but moms got to say that. But I don't think as fast as normal people. Wade didn't like it when his girlfriends said mean things, like I was too stupid to understand."

"But Alanna didn't do that."

"No, never! She even got mad at Wade once when I accidentally knocked over a statue he had over there"—he pointed to the credenza in the dining room—"and it broke into a million pieces and then he yelled at me. I cried, I was really sorry, and Alanna helped me pick up every single piece. And Wade said he was sorry. He never says sorry unless he really means it, so I know he meant it."

Suzanne was having a hard time putting Wade Barnett as his younger brother described him into the role of a killer. But most killers weren't pure evil S.O.B.s. Maybe Wade put himself in the investigation spotlight because he wanted to be stopped. Maybe killing his ex-girlfriend was an accident, and he killed the others . . . why? Or maybe she was off about the whole motive and the guy was just a psycho who was nice to his little brother.

"Why did Wade and Alanna break up?"

Dennis rolled his eyes. "Because he's a big jerk."

Suzanne's ears pricked up. "Why do you say that?"

"Because that's what Wade said. He said he was a big jerk and Alanna wouldn't forgive him."

"Did he tell you why?"

"I thought it was 'cause he slept with another girl, but I don't know for sure."

Suzanne needed a long conversation with her suspect.

"If I showed you some pictures, could you tell me if you recognize any of them?"

He nodded, then he stopped. "Why?"

"I'm trying to—" she almost said help his brother, but she couldn't do it to this kid. He'd believe her, and when he found out she'd lied to prove his brother was a killer, he'd be devastated. She decided to go for the straightforward approach.

"Dennis, you're an adult, so I'm going to be honest with you, okay?"

He nodded.

"Four young women your brother knew are dead. That's what he lied to us about. He told me he didn't know the girls, but we learned that he did. That's part of my job, finding out when people are lying. People lie so they don't get in trouble. I think your brother might have lied because he hurt those girls."

Dennis's bottom lip was trembling. "Wade wouldn't."

"You know, I was walking around here thinking that Wade seems like a good guy. He likes the Yankees. I like baseball, too."

"He *loves* the Yankees."

Suzanne smiled. "And he has these awards for preserving historic property; he obviously cares a lot about the city. I can see why you like him a lot. You probably admire him, too."

Dennis gave a half-shrug, half-nod.

"Is he a good brother?"

"Yeah. He didn't like how Mom made him watch me all the time, even when I got bigger. He said I was a dork. But he didn't like it if someone else ever called me a dork."

Having brothers and sisters herself, Suzanne understood.

Suzanne switched the line of questioning. "Have you been to any of the underground parties your brother likes to go to?"

"I don't like them."

"But you've gone."

"I went once. Much too loud. It hurt my ears and I hated it. I stay in the car now."

Suzanne's instincts vibrated in her gut. "Why do you go?"

"Wade lost his license for drunk driving. I have to drive him."

"So you were at the party in Brooklyn last Saturday?"

"I—" He stopped talking and frowned. He started biting his thumbnail again and didn't look at her. "You're making me confused."

"It's an easy question," she said. "You're a smart kid; I think you know why I'm asking."

"No. No." He wouldn't look at her.

Suzanne couldn't figure out if this was an act or self-preservation. Dennis didn't want to think about his brother being a cold-blooded killer, so he just shut down when he figured out where she was going with the questioning.

Either way, she was onto something, and she'd get

Dennis to tell the truth. It was just a matter of time and patience.

She had all the time in the world.

Until James Thorpe walked into the apartment a minute later and put an end to her questioning of Dennis Barnett.

TWENTY-ONE

Ryan lived in a nondescript, run-down, brown, eight-story apartment building with at least one hundred units in the Fifties near Third. Whereas the Upper West Side near Columbia was a mix of quaint old and new, this section had a mix of office buildings circa the 1950s and a hodgepodge of apartment housing.

Sean appreciated New York, he liked visiting, but seeing so many people packed together reminded him that he was a bit homesick for California and the elbow room he'd enjoyed.

"Keep your mouth shut," Sean told Trey when he buzzed Ryan's apartment.

"But—"

Sean shot him a stern look and Trey scowled, but didn't talk back.

"Yup," a voice said in the speaker.

"You called about a phone."

"Come on up."

The door buzzed and Sean led the way to the third-floor apartment. The hallways were so narrow he and Trey had to walk single file. The entire building smelled of stale food from poor ventilation, but it wasn't a tenement.

When Ryan opened the door, he seemed apprehensive at the sight of Sean and Trey. Ryan was of average height, gaunt but clean-cut enough that he might still be considered attractive to the opposite sex.

Sean handed him his card. "The phone you found belongs to a runaway. I need to ask you a few questions."

"You're a private eye?" Ryan asked, skeptical.

"I was hired by her parents to find her. I know she was supposed to be at a party in Sunset Park. Can we come in?"

Sean took Ryan's moment of hesitation to enter the apartment. Trey was right behind him.

The place looked like a typical, sloppy college student's studio apartment. Bed in the corner that doubled as a couch; large-screen television that dwarfed the room; a couple of chairs; desk with computer, books, and papers; and a small lopsided table. Dirty clothes were heaped in one corner. Two posters were tacked to the beige walls—one showing a sleek red Lamborghini with a naked blonde on the hood, the other commemorating the Pittsburgh Steelers' Super Bowl XLIII victory.

"I just found the phone." Ryan stood next to the open door as if he would bolt at the first sign of trouble.

Sean spotted Kirsten's smart phone next to the computer. He picked it up. It had a crack on the front of the screen, but he didn't know whether the damage was old or new. It was on, with only one battery bar.

"You just now found the phone? I couldn't get a GPS lock on it, but it has one bar."

"I mean, I found it Saturday night, but I forgot. I

was pretty wasted, didn't know I had it in my pocket. I was doing laundry this morning and found it. It was totally dead, but I had an old charger that fit and, um, I liked the girl who dropped it, thought we could go out if I gave her the phone."

Trey stepped forward and opened his mouth to talk, but Sean cut him off. He showed Ryan Kirsten's photo.

"Is this the girl who dropped the phone?"

Ryan grinned. "Yeah. Ashleigh. She's hot." Then he looked nervous and said to Trey, "You're not her brother, are you?"

"Boyfriend," Trey said.

"I doubt that," Ryan snorted.

Sean said, "Trey, do you need to step out?"

"No," he grumbled.

To Ryan: "Tell me what happened Saturday night."

"Is she really missing?"

"Yes."

"It was a rave. Seven hundred people, maybe more. I lost track of her."

"When did you find the phone? I know she used it late Saturday night."

"Um, no. I was, um, dancing with her. We had a little action, she said she had to meet a friend but would be back. She took off, then I saw her phone on the floor."

Sean kept his face neutral, but he knew what Ryan meant with his euphemisms. He wanted to pound sense into the jerk, but that wouldn't get them any closer to finding Kirsten.

"How did you know it was hers?"

"Saw her with it. She said she was coming back. But she didn't, and I pocketed her phone, got another drink. Forgot all about it until I found it this morning and remembered how she—" He cut himself off with a glance at Trey.

Trey burst out, "And you didn't go look for her? You weren't worried that something might have happened?"

"Hey! It was a big party. I figured she hooked up with someone else. She was dressed for it."

Trey stepped forward aggressively, and Sean had to put his hand on his chest to physically hold him back. Ryan backed up, obviously not wanting a confrontation. He was definitely not the stand-up-and-defend-your-girl kind of guy. Trey, however, was, and Sean needed to defuse the situation.

Sean showed Ryan Wade Barnett's photograph. "Know him?"

"Sure. Wade."

"Was he at the party?"

"Oh, yeah. He knows how to have fun."

"Do you remember what time he arrived? When he left?"

Ryan shook his head and leaned against the door-jamb. "Have no idea when he showed up, but he made a stink as the party was winding down that his ride had left."

"Did he call a car service? Do you know how he got home?"

"He left with some girl, but he didn't look too happy about it."

"Can I take your charger? You said it was an old one."

"Well—"

Sean put a twenty-dollar bill on the desk and picked up the charger. "Thanks for your help." He walked out, Trey on his heels.

Before Ryan had even closed the door, Trey said, "Do you believe that guy? Kirsten would never go out with a loser like that."

"At least he tried to get her phone back to her. This is going to help."

"He didn't even know her name!" Trey said, shaking his head.

"And you have to let it drop. He's a witness; don't tell him anything he doesn't already know, got it?" Sean was already scrolling through the text messages on Kirsten's phone. He skipped the messages that had been sent Sunday and Monday before the phone died—they were from her mother, Trey, and a few friends at her school—and looked at the messages during the time frame of the party.

At 1:13 a.m., a message from "Jessie" came in:

Don't be such a slut and meet me outside. Now, Ash.

Twenty-three minutes before that last message from Jessie, she had sent another:

Plz, K, need 2 talk 2 u. I'm freezing.

And eight minutes before that, at 12:42 a.m., Jessie had texted:

i see u with that guy. we need 2 talk now. im getting worried. outside 10 min.

Sean frowned. There were other messages between Jessie and Kirsten, but the battery was flashing low. He saw that there were nineteen voice mail messages, but didn't know if the phone would last until he could retrieve them all. He pocketed the phone. He'd go back to the hotel, charge the phone, and download everything. He'd listen to the voice mail while Lucy put together the text message threads chronologically.

"What did it say?" Trey asked.

"I'm trying to create a time line before she lost her phone. I need to download the text messages and retrieve her voice mails. Go home, Trey."

"No."

Sean stopped walking. "I appreciate you calling me. You did the right thing, and I have information that may lead me to where she's hiding out. But it's going to take all my time and concentration, and I can't worry about you getting into trouble."

"I'm not!"

"Don't tell me you didn't think about going back to talk to that guy."

"No," he said, averting his eyes.

"Trey, you're eighteen, you can do what you want, but I'm telling you to stay out of it."

Trey glared at him.

"You're not going to listen to me, are you? What are your plans? How are you going to find her? You don't know anything about her life as Ashleigh, and you damn well better not go back to Ryan's apartment."

"I have to do something!"

Sean sympathized with the love-struck teen. If it

were him, he would have gotten into far more trouble if he were looking for his missing ex-girlfriend.

"Do you have a picture of Kirsten?"

"The same one you have, but wallet size."

"Good. Get a list of all the hospitals and clinics in Manhattan and Brooklyn. Show her picture to several staff members; see if anyone has seen her."

"The police sent out a notice to all hospitals," he said.

"Yes, and so did I. But some of these places get busy; they might not have made the connection. And in her message, she said she couldn't walk. She might have broken her leg or sprained her ankle, which means she may have gone to a clinic to get it looked at."

"There have to be hundreds of those places—it would take all week to go to all of them."

"Start in Brooklyn closest to Sunset Park. That's where the party was. Work your way out from there."

"She said she could see a bridge," Trey said.

Smart. "Good point. Find clinics near the bridges leading out of Brooklyn. She also said it was a nice place, so the neighborhood may be a bit upscale."

Trey nodded. "Okay, I can do that. Do you really think it'll help find her?"

"Yes, it gives us one more avenue." He got out his wallet and handed Trey all but a few of his business cards. "Give these out. Tell people to call me if they remember anything after you leave, got it?"

"Got it."

Sean waited across from Ryan's apartment to make

sure that Trey didn't circle around and go back. Sean considered going up himself—he didn't think Ryan knew anything more, but he needed a lesson in how to treat women. Trey hadn't quite figured out what "a little action" at a rave meant, but Sean knew exactly what Ryan was doing. Had he been the one to drug her? Would he do it again to another girl?

Sean crossed the street and went back up to Ryan's apartment. He didn't need to be buzzed in—the buzzer was a standard electronic gadget that Sean easily bypassed.

Ryan was leaving with a basket of laundry. "Hey," he said, nervous.

Sean grabbed the basket and dropped it to the floor. He got in Ryan's face until Ryan backed up against the wall.

"I don't like you," Sean said. "You use women without a thought."

"I-I d-didn't," Ryan stuttered. "Sh-sh-she was willing. I swear."

"Did you drug her?"

"No!"

"I know she was high on something."

"Everyone was. The drinks were spiked. It was a really wild party, but I swear, I didn't give her anything. I wouldn't do that! P-p-please believe me."

Ryan tried to squirm away and Sean put his forearm across the skinny kid's chest and held him there.

"You may not have given her a mickey, but you sure took advantage of it."

"I'm s-sorry!"

"I have a lot of friends. I'm putting the word out on

you. If you ever show up at another rave and take advantage of another girl, and I find out, you won't have a dick left to screw around with."

Sean turned and walked away, confident that the kid believed everything he'd said.

TWENTY-TWO

Suzanne was in a fantastic mood after the morning interrogation of Wade Barnett, serving the warrants, and a late working lunch with Vic Panetta to compare notes. She had the computer from Barnett's apartment with deleted files her cybercrimes team was confident they could rebuild; and at Barnett's office, Panetta had found a coffee mug with a picture of Wade and Alanna Andrews smiling with a heart.

The only little tickle of doubt that crept into her mind was why Barnett would delete his home computer files but not destroy the mug that proved he'd had a relationship with the first victim, or the half-written apology. They also hadn't found the victims' shoes in either place.

Panetta walked back to FBI headquarters with Suzanne from the deli where they'd eaten, and said, "We have a viable suspect; we just need to seal the deal."

"We're arraigning him on perjury Monday morning," Suzanne told Panetta. "He'll make bail, unless we find hard physical evidence in the next thirty-six hours and change the charge to four counts murder."

"Looks like I'll be missing dinner with my family tonight."

"Sorry," Suzanne said without meaning it. Late

nights and weekends were the nature of the business, and every cop who ever had a case take ahold of him knew it.

"Time for a lot of legwork. I'll send Hicks and a team out to start interviewing co-workers, friends, and family."

"You take Barnett's side, we'll work the victims' friends on my end. Except Thorpe, Barnett's lawyer, put the quash on talking to Dennis Barnett, the nineteen-year-old brother."

"Why?"

"He stated that the kid was mentally incapacitated. I don't buy it. He's slow, but not severely handicapped. And get this: he told me that he drove his brother to these parties after Wade lost his license for those two DWIs."

"Did he take Wade to the parties in question?"

"I was working him until the damn lawyer walked in. I can get a warrant to interview him. I'll probably need a shrink in the room to testify that he wasn't under duress, was competent to answer questions. Dennis Barnett is our single best witness, but he doesn't want to get his brother in trouble."

"You don't think they were working together?" Panetta asked.

"I sat with Dennis for nearly twenty minutes. I don't think the kid can lie; at least, he won't be able to keep it up. He never answered my question about the Sunset Park party, only asked me if his brother was in trouble. If little brother is involved, it won't take long to break him. But the Barnett attorney took him home, and now his mother is freaked out, and I have to find a way to get him back in here while not risking having his testimony tossed. But the important thing is that Wade Barnett is in jail, and he's not getting out until Monday at the earliest."

Panetta headed to his precinct station and Suzanne entered the large federal complex. The only thing that had been enticing about the position she'd been offered in Montana was that the Helena office was so small, she'd likely be on a first-name basis with everyone from the special agent in charge down to the janitor. Here, she considered herself lucky to see a familiar face before she reached her squad.

She'd been assigned to Violent Crimes before 9/11, but after world terrorism breached American shores with such violence, priorities had been shifted to counterterrorism and counterintelligence. When she'd received her commission, there had been well over two hundred agents in New York's Violent Crime Squad, not including the five resident agency field offices. She'd watched as her colleagues were reassigned to other squads, until now there were only thirty-two dedicated VCMT agents at headquarters and a handful of support staff. She'd joked with her cop friend Mac that either she was so bad at her job that they didn't want her anywhere else, or she was so good that they didn't dare take her away from Violent Crimes.

Her messages and emails had stacked up, typical of any day but more so in the middle of a joint task force investigation like the Cinderella Strangler case. She quickly prioritized the messages, responded to the emails that needed immediate answers, and then focused on contacting friends of the victims. She preferred to talk to people in person, because body language often said more than words. She couldn't justify another trip to New Haven to talk to Alanna Andrews's roommate, but Alanna was the girl Barnett seemed to have publicly dated. She could talk to the cousin again—Whitney Morrissey had possibly seen a witness, or the killer, with her cousin that night. Had she finished the sketch? Suzanne made a note to follow up on that. If she had an eyewitness, that would go a long way with the U.S. Attorney.

For the other locals, she split the list between those she wanted to talk to in person—such as the staff at the coffeehouse where Erica Ripley, the second victim, had worked—and those she was comfortable calling, such as Jessica Bell's roommate. She planned to talk to Josh Haynes again in person. He was the one who'd first mentioned Wade Barnett—but only in connection with the parties, not Barnett's relationship with Jessica Bell. Had he known? Lucy Kincaid thought he'd acted distraught over Jessica's death; had he been in love with her? A "friend with benefits" who got too close? If he had found out that Wade Barnett was sleeping with her, would he have killed her?

That didn't explain the first three victims. But according to Lucy, Wade had met Jessica at Josh Haynes's party.

The rest of the weekend promised to be as busy as her morning, but Suzanne was invigorated. This was the part of the job she liked the best: building a mountain of evidence to convict a killer. She planned on turning over an airtight case to the U.S. Attorney as soon as possible.

She called Alanna's roommate Jill Reeves first, glad

she'd gotten her cell phone number so she didn't have to maneuver her way around her hovering mother.

"Hi, Jill. It's Special Agent Suzanne Madeaux from New York. Can I ask you a few more questions?"

"Sure."

"During our investigation, we've been looking into the past relationships of each victim, to see if there is any connection. You indicated that Alanna didn't have a boyfriend, or anyone who made her uncomfortable, when she was killed, correct?"

"Yes."

"What about a past boyfriend?"

"I told the detective that none of her boyfriends were mad at her or anything."

"Were you aware of Alanna's relationship with Wade Barnett?"

"Yeah, but why? You don't think he killed her? Wade?" She sounded skeptical.

"When did they first start seeing each other?"

"I don't know for sure," she said slowly. "Is it important?"

"Yes."

"Well, I think they met that summer Alanna stayed with her cousin. Alanna was really secretive about it, probably because he was so much older."

Suzanne counted back. Alanna would have been seventeen, Barnett twenty-three.

Jill continued. "I know they were really serious when we first moved to New York, about a week before classes started. Like for two months they were inseparable."

"Do you know why they broke up?"

"No."

"You were her best friend."

"She wouldn't talk about it."

"A witness told me he cheated on her."

"Well, cheated how?"

"Had sex with another woman?"

"That wouldn't bother her."

Suzanne didn't believe it. "Her rich, handsome, older boyfriend cheating on her wouldn't have fazed her?"

"They had a sort of open relationship."

"You're going to have to explain that."

"Well, an open relationship means—"

"I know what an open relationship is. Why did you qualify it with 'sort of'?"

"At the parties they went to, people had sex with strangers. It was just the thing, and Alanna and Wade used to play these sex games. It's like they were both addicted to it, but they still loved each other. But they had an agreement that it was open only at the raves."

"So if he had sex outside of a rave then that was cheating."

"Yeah. But Alanna never gave me a reason for the breakup specifically. I think she was hurt, whatever it was, then she convinced me to go to the Haunted House. And that's—" Jill's throat hitched. "But Wade sent her this letter and apologized for being a jerk."

"You read the letter?"

"No, just a couple lines."

"Do you have it? Is it with Alanna's things?"

"She tore it up. Oh! She said something when she threw the pieces away. She said she could tolerate a lot, but not lying."

"That helps, thank you."

Suzanne wrapped up that call, then talked to Jessica Bell's roommate. Lauren had heard Jessica mention she knew Wade Barnett, but she'd never met him and didn't think that Jessica was involved with him.

She tried Alanna's cousin Whitney Morrissey, but her voice mail came on. Suzanne left a message, giving her cell phone number since she planned to be in the field, and looked at the clock. It was already after four and she had a hundred things to do. She saw a text message on her cell phone from Sean Rogan. Damn, he'd called her while she was eating lunch and she'd said she'd call him back. That was two hours ago.

We'll meet you at your office.

She dialed his number.

"Rogan."

"It's Suzanne Madeaux. Sorry, I'm about to leave— I should have called you back. I have interviews all day; just tell me over—"

He interrupted. "Lucy and I will be there in ten minutes. You'll want to see what we found."

Irritation flared, but she tried to keep it out of her tone. "Sean, I appreciate your help, but unless it's directly related to the Strangler investigation, it's going to have to wait."

"It is. See you in a few minutes."

He hung up. She stared at the phone, then slammed it down in the cradle.

"If you break another phone, Facilities is going to charge you," the squad secretary said as she approached Suzanne's desk.

"It's justified," she said.

"You have a call from Washington on line four. It sounded important."

"Thanks. Oh, call down to security and tell them to escort Sean Rogan and Lucy Kincaid up when they get here. They're apparently coming by with information they won't tell me on the phone." Her phone rang and she picked up the receiver again, looking at it carefully to make sure she hadn't cracked it. "Agent Madeaux, Violent Crimes."

"Agent Madeaux, this is Assistant Director Hans Vigo from D.C. I hope this isn't a bad time?"

Suzanne automatically said, "No, of course not," while her mind raced through all the reasons why an assistant director would be calling her, and why the name Hans Vigo sounded familiar. She had evidence at the lab on not only her current case, but several others; she had a case going to trial in three weeks and was awaiting expert testimony confirmation; then there was . . . Hans Vigo. Profiler. Lucy Kincaid had mentioned him yesterday.

All that ran through her mind in less than five seconds.

Vigo said, "I've been reading about your serial killer investigation and wanted to offer my assistance if you require it."

"Um, great, thanks." She was flustered by the call, but recovered quickly. "We have a suspect in custody, and I'm confident that BSU can handle any psych profile we might need for trial."

"Of course, we have a terrific team down at Quantico. They told me you'd requested a profile a few weeks ago."

"Yes, but I didn't have lot of my evidence at that time."

"Lee told me there wasn't enough information for a good profile, but if you have additional evidence now, please send it down."

"Dr. Vigo, may I ask why you have an interest in this case?"

"I had a call this morning about it, and it's unusual enough that it intrigued me."

Suzanne moved from simmering to boiling anger, but tried to keep it out of her voice. "Would that call have been from Lucy Kincaid?"

She must not have done a good enough job, because Vigo's tone changed slightly from friendly to formal. "Ms. Kincaid called about another matter, and told me she was in New York."

Just how connected was this young wannabe FBI agent? "And talked about my case? With all due respect, Dr. Vigo, I have ten years' experience working cases just like this one, and I have one of the highest clearance rates in the Bureau." She didn't want to sound defensive, but she did. She backtracked a bit and added, "I appreciate your insight, and Ms. Kincaid seems like a smart woman, but if I fly off in ten different directions at once I'll never be able to logically put this case together."

"I agree," he said. "I've looked at some of your cases, and your methodical approach to serial murders is outstanding. I certainly prefer such a straightforward method of investigation. Nine times out of ten it gets you exactly where you need to be to close the case."

"Thank you, sir." She didn't have to wait long for

the *but* she expected—even though he didn't use the word.

"Occam's razor—specifically, the principle of parsimony—suggests that the simplest explanation is more often the correct one. In crime analysis, we've seen this proven time and time again—and it's why we look first to the husband when a wife is murdered, or to a male relative when a child is molested, for example.

"Behavioral science—profiling—works because we have a long history of crime and punishment in this country," Vigo said. "We can look at what has occurred in the past and why, and coupled with our knowledge of human psychology determine—with amazing accuracy—the most likely victim type, or killer, in violent crimes, particularly serial crimes.

"In some cases, a killer defies conventional wisdom," Vigo continued. "We focus on the obvious because in our training, the obvious is usually correct. When a woman is raped, we look to male offenders. When black women are killed, we look to a black offender. When four young women are killed at a party, we look to a male offender who knew all of them."

Suzanne responded slowly. "Are you suggesting that I'm wrong about my primary suspect?"

"No, of course not. Clearly, Wade Barnett had the means and opportunity, and because he knew all four women he likely has motive, even if it's unclear without more evidence or a confession what that might be. I'd just suggest that while you're continuing to put together your case against him, you also continue working with the assumption that he's innocent."

Suzanne didn't quite know what to say. "Dr. Vigo, my methods have never been questioned by headquarters. Perhaps you should be talking to my supervisor."

"I'm so sorry, Agent Madeaux, I didn't mean to sound critical. And sometimes I'm a bit tactless—I should have considered that we haven't worked together before, and calling you up out of the blue must seem like I'm taking over the case. I'm still getting used to my title—titles make me nervous."

"Do you think I have the wrong guy?" she asked bluntly.

"Yes," he said simply.

Suzanne's mood turned dark. "I'll send you everything I have, Dr. Vigo."

"Thank you, Agent Madeaux."

"I guess I should thank *you*."

"I've been wrong before."

He didn't sound like he was wrong often. "I'm not releasing him." She didn't think she was wrong about Wade Barnett, but one thing Vigo said had stuck with her.

We look to a male offender who knew all of them.

Offender. There was nothing in Wade Barnett's background that showed violence against women. Not one accusation of rape or abuse, or a dismissed case. He was known to be a ladies' man, a different woman on his arm all the time. Yet Suzanne couldn't forget the photo mug of Barnett and Alanna Andrews that he kept in his drawer.

On the other hand, why didn't he come forward?

He had to have known the girl he had once cared about was dead.

"Of course not," Hans said. "Keep him where he is. He may be guilty."

"But you don't think so."

"I appreciate your taking my call, Suzanne. If anything jumps out at me when I receive the reports, I'll call you."

She gave him her cell phone number and hung up.

Suzanne didn't know what to make of the conversation, and didn't have time to think about it because security buzzed her to say that Rogan and Kincaid were here and where would she like to put them?

Her ego wanted to tell the guard to lock them up, but instead she said, "Conference 22C."

TWENTY-THREE

As soon as Lucy stepped into the conference room, she knew something had happened to change Suzanne's attitude. She was cool and off-putting, and Lucy wished she knew why. Was it because Sean hadn't asked if they could come by? Lucy didn't think that was a good enough reason, considering that when they'd called earlier, Suzanne had promised to call back in thirty minutes.

Still, this was a complex case and she was busy, and if Lucy understood anything about cops after living in a family full of them, it was that they didn't like to be bossed around. And Sean could be bossy.

So Lucy started the conversation off by saying, "We're sorry to drop in like this, but we think the information we found might help."

Suzanne nodded. "By all means. I'm yours."

Her easygoing tone contradicted her physical tension. Sean noticed; it was a subtle shift in his own posture that Lucy didn't think Suzanne noticed. Suddenly, Lucy felt that she was in the middle of a silent battle.

Sean said, "A Hunter College student found Kirsten Benton's cell phone at the abandoned warehouse during the party. He forgot about it and found it this morning. I retrieved it, and I talked to him about Kirsten. In the course of our conversation, I asked if he knew who Wade Barnett was. He did, and confirmed that he was at the Sunset Park warehouse the night Jessica died. He left around three a.m. with an unknown woman."

Suzanne nodded. "So I understand that you interviewed a witness about my primary suspect in a capital murder case."

Lucy's stomach flipped.

Sean said, "You could say that, but it was ancillary to my search for a missing minor." He slid over a copy of Kirsten's text messages from the thirty-six-hour period before Jessica was killed. "I downloaded her text messages and put them in chronological order along with other facts, including phone calls she'd made. Read the last two pages."

Suzanne picked up the packet, skimmed the opening pages, then read where Sean indicated.

SATURDAY

Time	From	To	Message
1026	Kirsten	Jessica	U there?
1045	Jessica	Kirsten	r u in ny?
1046	Kirsten	Jessica	yes-why didn't u call me back?
1046	Jessica	Kirsten	i had stuff. u could have come ovr.
1047	Kirsten	Jessica	Your roommate hates me.
1047	Jessica	Kirsten	haha shes just jealous u have tits & she doesnt.
1049	Kirsten	Jessica	Can I come over now?
1050	Jessica	Kirsten	no, im not home. sorry. ill give u a key later. cant wait til u move hr 4 good.
1050	Kirsten	Jessica	Call me!!!!!
1051	Jessica	Kirsten	1-sec
1109			*12 minute cell phone conversation, Kirsten & Jessica*
2143	Jessica	Kirsten	youll be there?

2146	Kirsten	Jessica	Yes, u sure?
2147	Jessica	Kirsten	we have 2 know
2151	Kirsten	Jessica	Don't be late, Jess!
2152	Jessica	Kirsten	i wont-se corner.
2347	Kirsten	Jessica	ok I'm here. It's packed.
2355			*1 min call Kirsten to Jessica. Possible voice mail.*
2359	Jessica	Kirsten	im late. 30 min.
0002	Kirsten	Jessica	ok. 30.
0035	Kirsten	Jessica	I'm freezing my ass off. I'm going inside. Now you're scaring me. Text me when you get here.
0042	Jessica	Kirsten	i see u with that guy. we need 2 talk now. im getting worried. outside 10 min.
0044	Kirsten	Jessica	K
0050	Jessica	Kirsten	Plz, k, need 2 talk 2 u. i'm freezing.
0113	Jessica	Kirsten	Don't be such a slut and meet me outside. Now, Ash.

Suzanne frowned. "Is this accurate?"

"You noticed the change in messaging."

"It's obvious."

Sean nodded. "Someone else sent Kirsten that last message. And that person only knew her by her *Party Girl* name."

Lucy said, "We know she used the name whenever she came to New York—both Josh Haynes and Lauren Madrid knew her only as Ashleigh. But Jessica knew her real name."

"Maybe they were in their roles?" Suzanne said, though by her tone she didn't believe it.

"I think it's clear that this gives you a good window for time of death," Sean said.

Suzanne didn't say anything, but made a few notes on the packet.

Lucy said, "In Kirsten's message to her ex-boyfriend on Thursday, she said that there was something about the text that was wrong, and I think even through the haze of whatever drugs she was on, she noticed that Jessica called her 'Ash,' that it wasn't written in their usual shorthand."

"Thank you," Suzanne said. "Is that it?"

Lucy nodded, but she was antsy. She thought that Suzanne and she had gotten off to a good start yesterday, and then this morning she was talking about dinner. "We're sorry to take up so much of your time. You're obviously busy, so if we need to cancel dinner to pitch in and help, we'd be glad to."

Suzanne looked confused for a moment, then said, "Look, I appreciated your help yesterday. We're working two different cases that happen to overlap. I can't tell you to stop looking for Kirsten Benton, but apparently you have enough clout to bring in the brass over my head."

"I don't know what you're talking about," Sean said.

Suzanne stared at Lucy. "She does."

It came clear to Lucy. "You called Hans and he told you I discussed the case with him. I wasn't second-guessing—"

"I didn't call Washington. When I arrested Barnett this morning, getting a profile of a killer I had in jail was the last thing on my mind. But now I have to. I have dozens of potential witnesses to interview, but when an assistant director at national headquarters calls and asks for something, however nicely he does it, I have to spend my time putting it together."

"I'm really sorry. I didn't know Hans would call."

"Hans? Really? You're on a first-name basis. You

could have clued me in earlier that you have connections."

"Any connections I might have aren't important. I didn't try to pull one over on you. I'm not even an agent."

"Yeah, but you act like one. I'd love to have your help because obviously, you two know what you're doing. But I got blindsided today and feel like a damn rookie again."

"Please believe me, Suzanne, I didn't know Hans was going to call. I wish he hadn't."

Suzanne let out a long, pent-up sigh. "I'm glad he did," she said, though she didn't sound happy about it. "I don't think I'm wrong about Wade Barnett, but—I'm not one hundred percent convinced he's a killer. I have thirty-six hours to get convinced, because he's going to be arraigned on Monday, and *if* he's guilty, I have to convince the U.S. Attorney to remand him into custody. No judge is going to let him sit in prison for lying to me. We could push and get a conviction, but he's not going to do time for it. If he's guilty, I don't want him on the streets. But if he's not guilty, I need to find the killer before someone else dies."

Sean said, "I've served as a civilian consultant in the past. I have clearance; you can contact Washington."

Suzanne considered his offer. She said to Lucy, "Do you know what Dr. Vigo needs for a profile?"

She nodded. "Absolutely."

"I need to make a call. Stay here." Suzanne walked out.

Sean turned to Lucy. "You didn't tell me you talked to Hans about this case."

"Something was bothering me about it, and Hans knew exactly what it was after I explained everything."

"What?"

"That suffocation is a feminine way to kill."

"Which means what exactly? That a woman is the killer?"

"Maybe. Maybe not. Hans agreed that while the murders were intimate, they weren't sexual. There was no violence."

"No violence?" Sean questioned.

"No *excessive* violence. The victims were weak, compliant. The killer held them while they died. And that's the other big red flag."

"Why?"

"Because whoever killed those women watched them die. Suffocation isn't quick."

"Shit, that's sadistic."

Suzanne returned with a dark, curly-haired female in her late thirties. "This is Andie Swann, the best of the best on our Evidence Response Team."

Andie rolled her eyes. "I pay Suzanne for compliments."

"What? In beer?" Suzanne laughed. She tossed Sean and Lucy two badges. No photo, but their names were printed on the cards. "Now if you need to take a leak, you don't have to call in security to escort you. Andie is going to babysit you, however, because I'm responsible for these files. She's also smart and has been my evidence coordinator from the beginning of the joint task force, so pick her brain."

Lucy asked, "What do you want us to do?"

"You know what Dr. Vigo needs. Give it to him."

Sean wasn't happy. "You want us to do your paper-work?"

"You created it."

Lucy was elated. "I'm happy to do it."

Sean glanced at her and frowned. She ignored him. Sean was all action, but Lucy loved picking through reports for the gold nuggets that solved puzzles.

Suzanne said, "This isn't a punishment. Dr. Vigo asked me to do this, and I'm trusting that you know what you're doing. Otherwise I'll be the one who looks bad."

"I promise, you'll look good." Lucy hesitated, then said, "Sean might be more use to you outside the building."

"That's okay," Sean said. "I'll help you."

"No, you'll hinder me. I know what I'm doing."

Suzanne said, "I don't need a partner."

Sean grinned. "You got one." He winked at Lucy and mouthed *thank you*.

After Suzanne and Sean left, Andie asked, "Are you related to Dr. Dillon Kincaid?"

"He's my brother."

"I worked on a case with him years ago when I was in the L.A. office. He's probably the best forensic psychiatrist I ever worked with."

"He's good."

"Tell him I said hi. Is he still in San Diego?"

"Washington. He's married now, to an agent, has a private consulting practice but works mostly for the Bureau of Prisons." Lucy walked over to the whiteboard. "This is Jessica Bell's autopsy report. I need all four. Do you know where they are?"

"Certainly. Suzanne might seem disorganized, but she's logical, if you know the way she thinks."

"And you do."

"I've been here seven years, and if I were murdered, she's the one I'd want investigating the crime."

Sean gave Suzanne some space. Even though she'd accepted their assistance—almost seemed to appreciate and want the help—she was irritated that the case was getting out of her control. Sean understood that feeling.

She parked near the coffeehouse where Erica Ripley had worked and wrapped up a phone conversation. "If you can stay there for another hour, I'll be there." She hung up. "That was the cousin of the first victim. She works at an art gallery near Central Park."

"Erica Ripley was the second victim, correct?"

Suzanne nodded. "The only victim who didn't attend college."

"But she was on the *Party Girl* site," Sean reminded her.

Suzanne shot him a glance. "Right, the website I can't access."

"I'm working on that."

"How?"

"My partner, Patrick Kincaid, used to run the San Diego P.D. e-crimes division, before cybercrime was as big as it is. He's rebuilding the site from the cache on my computer in D.C., and through Google, which usually retains cache information only seventy-two hours, but if you know what you're doing you can pull out older data. We might not get everything, but it'll be good enough for court."

"I don't know—the defense could argue that the data was manipulated when it was rebuilt."

"Patrick is an expert witness. He has clearance up the wazoo; I'm not worried about the defense."

"Kincaid, huh?"

"Lucy's brother."

"She *is* well connected. You are, too. I checked your file. You have high clearance."

"I have to. I've been hired by federal agencies to hack their security. I break in; my brother Duke plugs the holes."

Suzanne was obviously surprised. "What are you doing looking for a missing teenager?"

"Long story. But Kirsten's my cousin."

"Why didn't you tell me?"

"She's a cousin by marriage. I haven't seen her since she was little, but Duke is very loyal to family, even family that we don't talk to. Kirsten's dad called, we jumped."

"And you don't want to?"

"Of course I do. It's not what RCK usually works on, so I'm stumbling a bit in the dark."

"Could have fooled me."

Suzanne went up to the counter and spoke to the manager, then motioned for Sean to sit down near the back. "The manager is sending over the two people closest to Erica."

Less than a minute later, a petite girl with short, dyed red hair and a skinny guy, both in their early twenties, came over.

Suzanne glanced at their name tags. "Jordan, Ken, thank you. I'm sorry about your friend."

Jordan nodded soberly. "It's just so awful."

"I still miss her," Ken said. "Erica was always happy."

Jordan agreed. "Our manager said you needed to talk to us?"

"I just have a few follow-up questions. You told Detective Panetta that Erica didn't have a regular boyfriend."

"Right."

"What about past boyfriends?"

The two looked at each other and shrugged. Jordan said, "Erica really wasn't into the dating scene. I mean, she saw a few guys, but nothing that was remotely serious."

Suzanne put out a picture of Wade Barnett. "Do you recognize this man?"

"No," Jordan said.

Ken looked longer at the picture. "Yeah, I think so. He came in once near closing to see Erica. Erica was surprised to see him, but happy, too. I asked her about it and she said they'd had a one-night stand the week before and he wanted to go out again."

Jordan added, "Erica was way casual about sex. She used to be really overweight, but lost it all and was in totally great shape—worked out all the time. Kind of an obsession." She looked at Ken for confirmation.

"Every day," he said. "I think she liked the attention she was getting."

Suzanne showed the two the pictures of the other victims. They didn't recognize them.

Sean asked, "In the days before Erica was killed, did she express any concern that she was being watched? Maybe followed?"

Ken shook his head, but Jordan piped up. "Yeah, she did. I didn't think about it, but for two years she rode the subway here from Brooklyn. Then she started asking me to walk with her. At first she said she just wanted to talk, but then I asked her if she was worried about something. She said she thought someone was following her, but wasn't totally serious, you know? Like she thought she was being stupid."

Suzanne wrapped up the interview and they left. "We have time to swing by Jessica's building."

On the way there, Suzanne got a call. She didn't say much, but Sean knew immediately that she was livid about something. She said, "Make sure Panetta knows," then hung up.

"Bad news?"

"The fucking press released the news that Wade Barnett is our suspect. No one knew!" She glanced at Sean.

"Not me."

She shook her head. "I'll bet a million bucks it was the manager at Barnett's apartment building. Mousey little bastard. Just makes my life more difficult. My idea of hell is standing in the middle of a sea of reporters shoving cameras and microphones in my face, wielding little stubby yellow pencils like swords, and all of them shouting questions at me."

Neither Lauren nor Josh was at home, so Suzanne drove around the top of Central Park and down the east side to their next destination: an artsy dessert place. She explained, "Whitney Morrissey is the

cousin of the first victim. According to Alanna Andrews's closest friend, Whitney is the one who introduced Alanna to underground parties when she was
seventeen."

Suzanne approached a leggy blonde with enough
curly hair for three women, dressed impeccably in a
stylish blue suit that matched her eyes. "Thank you
for waiting for us," she said to the attractive woman.
"This is Sean Rogan; he's a private consultant helping
on my case."

Whitney nodded and gave him a half-smile. She
seemed preoccupied to Sean, but she had been waiting for them quite a while.

"You work at a gallery?" he asked her as he and
Suzanne sat.

"The contemporary art museum across the street. I
give tours on the weekends, unless I have an art
show."

Suzanne said, "I've been reexamining each victim's
background, specifically men they were involved with
in the weeks or months before they were murdered.
Do you know if your cousin was seeing anyone in
particular?"

Whitney shook her head. "You should talk to her
friend Jill. Alanna and I weren't all that close."

"But she stayed with you for half a summer."

"And I liked her, but I'm twenty-four, she was nineteen. We didn't have a lot in common."

"Other than the raves?" Suzanne said.

"We went to a few together."

"Do you know if your cousin was romantically involved with a real-estate investor named Wade Barnett?"

Whitney was noticeably surprised.

"You know him?" Suzanne asked.

"Of course. The Barnetts are major benefactors of the arts. They give away numerous art grants every year. I'd be stunned if Alanna was dating a Barnett."

Suzanne said, "I have proof they were involved; I'm just trying to figure out when and why they split."

"I wouldn't know," she said. "But—I think I might have introduced them. It was a long time ago. Probably the first party I took Alanna to. But I didn't know they kept in touch."

"That helps," Suzanne said. "Confirms what we already know."

"I worked on that drawing you asked for," Whitney said. She reached into her wide purse and handed Suzanne a manila file folder. "I finished it last night, but have been tweaking it on my breaks. It's not perfect, but it's close."

Suzanne opened the folder and Sean leaned over to take a look. Whitney was talented. The pencil drawing was as good as those of any FBI sketch artist. "You could have a career doing this," Sean told her.

"Thank you," Whitney said.

The man seen with Alanna the night she died was a young, attractive Caucasian roughly the same age as the victims. "I gather you don't know what his eye color is?"

She shook her head. "He had brown hair. I made the shading about right in terms of color density. Not dark, not light."

There was something familiar about the picture, but Whitney hadn't drawn a full-on head shot. The

man's face was turned partly away, as if to kiss someone.

It definitely wasn't Wade Barnett.

Of course, that didn't mean Wade Barnett was innocent.

"Did this guy kill my cousin?" asked Whitney.

"I don't know," said Suzanne. "All I know is what
you told me—you saw him with her the night she
died. No one has come forward from those parties
to say they've seen anything, and that's the crux of
our problem. I'd bet if I could talk to six people who
were there, I could piece together what happened to
Alanna. People observe things they might not necessarily realize are important. But—that was four
months ago. Memories fade." She leaned forward.
"The party last Saturday in Sunset Park. Were you
there?"

"I told you I wasn't."

"Do you know anyone who was?"

She shrugged. "I might, I don't know. I can ask
around, see if I can get anyone to talk to you."

"I'd appreciate it."

Sean followed Suzanne out. "I can't believe it took
that woman four months to come forward with that
sketch," Sean said. "And that you didn't call her on
the carpet for it."

Suzanne walked briskly toward her car. "What can
I do about it? No one talked to her after the murder,
no one knew to ask her if she'd seen anything."

"But she was at the same party where her cousin was
murdered, but didn't go to the police on her own."

"I can't tell you how many cases I've worked where
someone doesn't cooperate because they think they're

going to get into trouble for a minor crime. The party was illegal, there were illicit drugs, some people think they'll be culpable. Murder trumps trespassing, but people can be damn selfish. Only think about their own situation."

That was certainly true in many situations, but Sean had great disdain for such selfishness. He'd gotten his hand slapped any number of times when he'd admitted to breaking the law to expose a greater crime.

"Where to now?" Sean asked.

"Back to headquarters. It's time to call it a night."

TWENTY-FOUR

The three-story redbrick building stood alone in a vast cement field. It was silently guarded by construction equipment that twenty-one-year-old Sierra Hinkle doubted was operational. She stood on the top floor, where each window had been broken, leaving only empty holes looking out on the Upper Bay that was laid out before her like a black pit. The rain that had threatened all day now gushed from the sky in endless sheets of water. She stood at one of the openings, her long curly brown hair damp from the weather and her own sweat from hours of dancing.

Holding the wall for support, she looked down. It seemed too far. Would she die if she fell? Three stories? No, but she might break something. Sierra was so stoned she wouldn't feel it, and then she might die from the cold. Would anyone even see her tumble off the ledge? Would they even find her body, or would she float away in the bay? Would anyone care?

Pounding music from below shook the building, but there was no one except the four hundred of them to hear. She smiled at the illogic. But it was true; to the north was open space, then another abandoned building; to the south was open space, then a road that led to a shipyard in Gowanus Bay. At least, she *thought* that's where she was. She hadn't come to the party alone.

Sierra enjoyed the peace up here on the third floor, though it was so much colder without hordes of frenetic bodies moving to the music. Still, she'd nearly passed out from the heat and sweat and wet dog smell as people ran inside to get out of the rain. Even an umbrella couldn't keep anyone dry. While downstairs the windowless walls protected the dancers from the rain, up here, the wind pushed the rain through the broken windows.

She laughed out loud, stoned, but she could still think. She didn't remember what she had taken. Pot and some pills—something that made her see colors and rainbows and slowed down time. And a delicious drink someone handed her, even though she knew better than to drink anything but bottled water.

Up here on the third floor, people got a little privacy. Here they could do anything. Sierra laughed again. Privacy in this large, open room with forty people here and there? A guy and girl were fucking in the center, as if they were onstage, and some people watched. In the corner a group of seven was sitting in a circle holding hands and passing around a pipe. Off to one side another group was dancing completely naked, eyes closed, moving to the music that came up from two stories below. She watched them and considered joining. Naked and free.

She wanted to escape.

Downstairs, where it was wild, she'd screwed two guys. She'd never done that before, not two in one night. She'd enjoyed the physical sensations that had been enhanced by whatever drugs she'd consumed, the freedom of being someone she wasn't. But in the back of her mind, the deep inside part she pretended didn't exist, she chastised herself for her reckless behavior.

You're letting him hurt you when you do things like this.

And she lied to her inner voice, told it that though her stepfather had hurt her and stolen her innocence, *she* was now in control. She could fuck who she wanted and when. He no longer had power over her.

Why was it, then, that she always thought about him when she was partying? Did he still have such control over her that even though she'd escaped, she lived wild to punish him? Wasn't it she who was being punished?

Self-hate flowed through her veins.

I hate you I hate you I hate you!

Maybe she should jump.

She held her arm out the opening and let the rain pummel her flesh. It felt wonderful. Suddenly, the need to be clean overpowered her. She didn't want to jump, she didn't want to die; she wanted the rain to cleanse her, to make her whole and complete and fully alive again.

Sierra jumped off the ledge and skipped across the floor, down two flights of stairs, bumping into people but no one cared and neither did she. She ran out the back exit, toward the open field that led to the bay she'd seen from the window. The rain soaked her before she'd gone twenty feet.

She laughed and spun around. She didn't know how long she danced alone, drenched but giddy. All she knew was that *this* was true freedom, standing in the rain in the middle of nowhere, black all around, no sound but water hitting the broken ground.

She tripped, caught herself, then stopped and looked around. She didn't hear the music anymore; the lights were way far away. And she was freezing.

How long had she been standing in the rain? Her short hair was plastered to her head and she was shaking so violently her teeth chattered.

Her vision blurred, but she stared at the lights until the building came more into focus. Wow, she'd run a long way! Hugging herself, she headed back and hoped Becca hadn't left. She wouldn't do that to her, would she? Make her walk to the subway alone?

Now she heard it. The party was still going full blast. She had sobered up some, and had a headache and a nasty taste in her mouth. She was starving. She hoped she could find Becca and they could head back to their apartment in Brooklyn, hitting an all-night diner on the way.

She passed a bulldozer that had been stripped of everything but the metal body. The music got louder; she was close. How foolish she'd been to run outside, alone, in the rain! What drugs had she taken? Her mouth was so parched, all she wanted was to drain an entire water bottle. She stopped walking and tilted her head up, opening her mouth to quench her thirst.

Sierra felt something on her forehead and put her hand up thinking it was a bird, but that was silly in this weather. Then the rain stopped, because no more water was falling into her mouth. Something was on her face, and she realized with panic that a plastic bag had been pulled over her head.

She stumbled back, trying to grab the bag that was

wrapped around her neck. She bumped up against someone and opened her mouth to scream. She stayed silent; she had no air. Hands flailing, she tried again to grab the plastic around her neck, but it was slick and wet and smooth and she couldn't get a grip. She scratched herself, then thought, *break the plastic!*

She clawed at it, but it would not break. Her eyes were open, but she couldn't see. Was she already dead? So dark, no air, she reached behind her and touched a raincoat, tried to pull it, but her fingers couldn't hold on to anything so slick. She was cold and hot at the same time, and she couldn't breathe.

Someone was standing right behind her! Touching her. Holding her. Holding the plastic over her head.

You're going to die.

Her chest burned as her heart raced, faster, faster, using the last of the oxygen in her body. The carbon dioxide her body created couldn't be expelled, and it poisoned her. Her blood burned. She'd been so cold before; now she was combustible.

In her panic, she had one clear thought. *Play dead.*

Against all instincts, she fell to her knees and relaxed her body.

"Good try, but I know that game," a harsh voice whispered in her ear, distorted through the plastic.

The bag pulled tighter. Sierra fought, adrenaline surging even as her consciousness began to fade. She tried to turn around, to face her attacker, to push back, anything to loosen the hold on her. Her neck rubbed painfully against the edge of the plastic, but that was minor compared to the pain in her chest as carbon dioxide filled her lungs and flowed through her bloodstream. She half turned, fighting for her life, knowing this was her last chance. She pushed, and kicked and hit something while she tumbled down, arms reaching out for someone to save her. She grabbed on to something and pulled; her attacker grunted.

"Fucking bitch!"

A sharp pain stabbed her head as she hit the ground; then she was numb; then she felt nothing.

A full two minutes later, the killer yanked off the plastic bag, removed one of Sierra's shoes, and slowly walked away.

TWENTY-FIVE

Sean heard Lucy cry out at the same time something hit his chest. Waking instantly, he reached for his gun on the nightstand, but quickly realized there was no intruder.

Lucy was writhing next to him, her hands swatting the air in front of her, eyes squeezed closed. She hit him again, and he switched on the hotel room's light. His heart raced, but he spoke calmly. "Lucy. Lucy, wake up."

Was he not supposed to wake someone in a nightmare? He didn't know, but he couldn't let her remain in this terrified state. Sweat coated her face, but her skin was ice cold. Every muscle was coiled; she was in full panic.

"Lucy! It's Sean! I'm right here." He spoke right in her face, hoping she would hear him through whatever torment she was suffering. He desperately needed to break her out of her dream.

Suddenly, she jumped out of the bed and backed against the wall, eyes wild, clearly not remembering where she was.

He leapt over the bed and stood in front of her, palms up, wanting to hold her but fearing that if he touched her she'd scream. "Lucy, it's me. It's Sean. You're safe."

At first, she didn't see him. The fear in her eyes was as real as if she were at that moment facing an attacker. Then her eyes widened in recognition and her lips trembled. She threw her arms around his neck, tears running down her cheeks as her body shook in silent sobs.

He picked her up and carried her to the couch on the other side of the suite. He sat with her in his lap and she gripped him tightly. "Don't let go. Don't let go," she repeated.

"Never." He rocked her until at last her body began to relax. Her heart was beating so hard he thought he could hear it. Or was that his? He kissed the top of her head. "I'm right here, Lucy. You're safe. You're safe," he repeated, as much for himself as for her.

Her breathing evened out as he held her. He didn't know how long he sat with Lucy cradled in his lap, holding her, stroking her hair, still damp from her panic, rubbing her back, not thinking. He couldn't think about anything. He just needed to touch Lucy. Every nerve in his body was raw with grief-coated anger from seeing the raw terror on Lucy's face in the moment between sleep and waking.

He thought she might have fallen back to sleep, but when he shifted position, she sighed and nuzzled his chest, her knees drawing up. He kissed her forehead and realized she was cold.

He started to get up but she said, "Don't go."

"I'm not going anywhere. You're freezing; I want to get you warm."

Sean carried her to bed, then lay down next to her and pulled the blankets around her. He reached over and turned off the light, hoping he could hold her until her heart rate returned to normal, until she fell into a dreamless sleep in his arms. He would cling to her the rest of the night, protecting her from her fears. His heart still pounded.

"I'm sorry," she whispered.

"You have nothing to be sorry for." He continued to touch her, as if to assure himself that she was safe. Her face burrowed into his neck, and he kissed her forehead. "How long?"

She didn't say anything and he thought she wasn't going to answer.

"Lucy?"

"They went away for a long time. But the last couple weeks . . ." Her voice trailed off.

Sean bit back a profanity that Lucy didn't need to hear right now. Five weeks ago, her past had confronted her again when her rapist had been found shot to death only miles from her house. Why didn't he see that she was in pain, even now?

"It's not every night," she added.

"Even once is too often." He kissed her forehead again, and adjusted her into the nook of his arm. Her body curved against his. Her feet were cold. He pulled one of them between his calves to warm it.

Sean wanted to sleep in Lucy's bed every night. He wanted to protect her from dangers real and imagined and remembered. He wanted to hold her close, to make love to her, or just listen to her breathe in peaceful sleep. He wanted to make her smile and hear her laugh every single day of his life. He wanted to show Lucy how much he loved her. He dreaded returning to Washington knowing they'd be going back to their separate homes.

"Sometimes," she whispered, "I feel so empty. Like there's nothing left inside and I'm alone."

"Oh, sweetheart, don't." He found her lips and kissed her. "You're never going to be alone. I'm here." He kissed her again. "I love you, Lucy. I'm not going anywhere."

I love you.

Lucy's breath hitched when she tried to tell Sean she loved him. She couldn't get the words out. She wanted to, but fear stopped her, fear of losing Sean, fear of losing herself. Fear that she would never be normal, no matter how much she pretended that everything was all right. The nightmares, her past, her future—or what was left of it. She wanted to love Sean, she wanted to stay here with him, to forget that anyone else existed, to forget pain and sorrow so deep that if she thought about it she'd break into a million pieces and no one would be able to help her. She didn't want Sean to suffer her burden. It wasn't fair to him.

She was teetering on the brink. Her cool façade was just that, an act, a hard shell she'd erected not only to stop pain from coming in, but to prevent her emotions from leaking out. Sometimes she felt blank, without the capacity to love or hate, able only to exist. And sometimes the deep-seated fear and hate and regret and endless sorrow that simmered in her core threatened to boil over until she wanted to scream. How could she cultivate the ability to love someone, to hope for a bright future, when she didn't even know if she had love to give?

She couldn't speak, but she could give Sean a small piece of herself, show him that she needed him.

Lucy felt for his unshaven face and held it between her hands, then kissed him. She kissed him until she felt as warm inside as she was outside, wrapped in his arms. His body temperature was always raised; he could wear shorts in winter and be hot to the touch. She kissed him until all remnants of the nightmare memories that had been plaguing her for weeks faded far away into the dark corners of her mind. She kissed him as if she were dying and he was her only hope for survival. And maybe he was. Maybe he could save her from shattering.

It was a fine line between commitment and obsession, a narrow path separating sanity from lunacy. She walked it every day, an acrobat on a tightrope, fearing she'd fall straight down and there would be no safety net, personally or professionally. Lucy knew she could lose herself in her past just as easily as she could lose herself in her future. She felt close to being a whole, normal person only when she was pursuing justice, focused on helping others.

Except now. Except with Sean.

Her hands were on his bare chest, and she pushed him onto his back, rolling on top of him, never letting his lips leave hers. His biceps flexed around her body as she straddled him. She felt a groan deep in his chest. She had no words, no thoughts, just a deep, extreme physical need.

Never had she been so forward, so urgent, in lovemaking. Sean's hands were on her back, holding her tight, as if afraid to let her go and lose this unspoken, overwhelming desire. She tossed her T-shirt and panties across the room and pushed down Sean's boxers, without breaking contact for more than a fraction of a second. She needed his hands, his arms, his entire body wrapped around her, inside her, filling her emptiness, completing her as only he could.

She gasped as she controlled Sean's entry, but slid down smoothly, firmly, without hesitation. She broke the kiss as her back arched up, sweat coating her body and his. She held still for a long moment, savoring this instant flash of pleasure so natural, so real, so primal. A wave of heat washed over her and she pushed the blankets off impatiently.

Sean pulled her back to his chest, his lips on hers, as their bodies moved in unison, jumping from first gear to overdrive. Lucy gasped each time he went deep, his hands pulling her onto him as he pushed himself into her. Their lovemaking was perfectly timed, as if they joined together like this every night and had for years, though it was all still new and fresh and exploratory.

Sean said something but Lucy couldn't hear over her rushing blood, as every muscle in her body tightened simultaneously, then released in a flood of ecstasy that surprised her so much she exclaimed Sean's name in a voice that sounded nothing like her.

Sean thrust in a final time and held her tightly against him, their bodies hot and thoroughly pleasured. He didn't let go when he was done, his hands moving from her butt to her back to her hair. He grabbed it in his fists and pulled her face to his and kissed her again, just as passionate and heated as before.

"Lucy," he murmured into her mouth.

Lucy felt languid and so relaxed she didn't think she could move. Sean sensed the shift inside her, and adjusted their position so she returned to the crook of his arm, but her head tilted so he could kiss her. She sighed contentedly, feeling like a lazy cat must when stretched out under a sunbeam.

"You're smiling," Sean said.

"I am." And like a lazy cat, she was satiated and tired. She sank into a blissfully dreamless sleep.

TWENTY-SIX

The rain that had fallen in buckets half the night was now a light but steady trickle at seven o'clock Sunday morning. Suzanne had worn thick socks and rain boots, but her feet were the only part of her body that was dry.

The fifth victim of the Cinderella Strangler had been found outside an abandoned storage facility in Red Hook, where once again an underground party had been raging through the night. Jessica Bell had died practically a stone's throw away in Sunset Park just one week ago.

Because her primary suspect was locked up on Rikers Island, Suzanne wanted to believe Sierra Hinkle had been killed by a copycat. But she'd stayed up half the night reading the report Lucy Kincaid had prepared for Hans Vigo, and she now believed she'd been wrong.

Suzanne had half expected the name, address, and phone number of the killer at the end of Lucy's detailed analysis, but of course it wasn't there. And while Lucy had stopped short of providing a psychological profile of the killer, Suzanne read between the lines. Lucy damn well had a psych analysis in mind, but she hadn't included it, whether out of deference

to the assistant director or because she didn't want to
go out on a limb.

Lucy had provided statistics regarding similar serial murders that gave information, but no conclusions. She'd taken Suzanne's methodical time line and
added in the victims' *Party Girl* information, which
Suzanne hadn't had before Friday, plus she'd incorporated the missing girl Kirsten Benton as a potential
witness.

Lucy had seen one thing in the autopsy reports
that Suzanne hadn't, and the discrepancy had kept
Suzanne from sleeping more than an hour. Because all
she could think about was that if she'd caught the difference when she first got the case, she might have understood the significance in time to save the lives of
Jessica Bell and Sierra Hinkle.

*The lungs of victim #1 had traces of an ultrafine black
powder that was sent to the NYPD lab. No lab report is
attached to the autopsy report, or filed with other docu-
mentation. The other three victims had no black substance in their lungs. Per coroner, substance had been
recently introduced to victim's lungs and was possibly
remnants of something that had been carried in the plastic
bag used to asphyxiate the victim. The other three victims
were likely suffocated with a plastic bag that had never
been used—brought specifically for the purpose. Which
suggests that killing the first victim had been spontaneous,
using a bag that the killer had on him or her or found at
the scene, but the other killings were premeditated.*

Suzanne remembered reading the note about the
black powder, but had assumed that the lab couldn't

identify it, or was backed up, or *something*. Because she'd completely missed the subtle difference in the autopsy reports, she hadn't followed up on the lab report or had Quantico take over the testing.

She'd noted the various crimes' similarities: isolated location, victim's age, intoxication level, and recent sexual activity. She hadn't noticed that the first victim was most likely killed spontaneously, and the others systematically stalked and murdered.

Why?

Which was why Suzanne had called Sean Rogan and asked him to bring Lucy to the latest crime scene. Lucy may have held back her psychological profile in the report to Hans Vigo, but Suzanne would damn well get her to share her theory. Because if they couldn't find the killer in the next six days, Suzanne feared that come next Sunday morning she'd be standing over another dead girl in the middle of another deserted lot next to one more abandoned building. And there were so many in the five boroughs of New York City, there was no freakin' way the NYPD and the FBI could stake out every single one.

She was missing something, but damn if she could figure out what it was.

Vic Panetta looked as tired as she felt. "The group who found the body is sitting it out inside the building," he said when he approached her.

"Where was the body found?" she asked.

He gestured to a temporary bright-orange shelter. "Though she was found quickly—we're guessing less than an hour after she was killed—the storm saturated the area. There is an apparent head injury, like she hit her head on the bulldozer over by where she died, or a rock on the ground. Responding officers quickly put up a tarp and the crime scene team set up a larger tent.

"We also have several potential witnesses. Because of the weather, there were only about half as many people at this rave as at the last crime scene, and many were still here when officers arrived. We have thirty names, prints, and phone numbers to follow up on, but we let them leave."

"Prints?"

"We had everyone sign a roster and assigned a different pen for each person, bagged and tagged them."

"Smart—the pen isn't too small to get a viable print?"

Panetta held up an example. It was a large, smooth plastic pen, like one that might be found in a souvenir shop. These were dark blue, with *New York Police Department* in white.

Suzanne smiled. "And who found the body?"

"They're inside. Three of them. The girl is the roommate of the victim, identified her as Sierra Hinkle, nineteen. Name is Becca Johansen. She and Sierra both work as waitresses in Brooklyn, three subway stops away. One guy said he was with Becca for most of the night; the other guy stayed, he says, because he'd met the victim earlier in the evening. My guess? They had sex and he's worried his DNA will be all over her and doesn't want us to think he killed her."

"He said that?"

"Just the hinky way he was acting."

"Vic," Suzanne said, keeping her voice low so none of the other cops could overhear, "I asked Lucy Kincaid to come out and walk through the scene. I'm going to walk through with her."

"Fine by me. Any reason why?"

She handed him a copy of Lucy's report. "She put together information for an FBI profile that I read last night and sent off to headquarters first thing this morning."

"It's pretty obvious that Wade Barnett isn't our killer," said Panetta, "unless she identified the likelihood of a partner. Which I'm not ruling out."

"No partner. Lucy didn't make any conclusions, but I did. The most important thing is that she kept referring to the killer as 'he or she.'"

"A female killer?"

"It's not out of the realm of possibility. She quoted statistics of suffocation in murder cases, and far more women choose that method than men."

"Yeah, maybe—in mercy killings and child murders, maybe. But this is violent." He gestured toward the orange tent.

"It's something we should keep in mind as a possibility."

"I'd look first at Barnett's younger brother."

Suzanne was surprised. "Why?"

"You said yourself that Dennis drove Barnett to the parties. He stayed in the car. He would have seen if someone wandered off. Took the opportunity to kill them, get back in the car, and wait for his brother."

"Why?"

"Don't know. Maybe that's a question for your profiler, or Ms. Kincaid."

Suzanne thought about Dennis Barnett as a murderer. She didn't see it. Truth was, she'd let her emotions get involved during her interview with him. She liked him, thought he was genuine. She'd had a mentally retarded next-door neighbor in Eunice—if you could call three acres over "next door." Bobby was her age and had been teased and bullied because he was slow; other kids called him Forrest Gump. So Suzanne had bought a video of the movie, using every dime she had, and watched it with Bobby. Told him that Forrest Gump was a hero, that he met two presidents of the United States, and was a championship runner.

Bobby never got out of the small town, and worked as a busboy in a diner. Probably still teased and bullied, but Suzanne hadn't gone back.

Dennis reminded her of Bobby. She didn't want him to be guilty, but she couldn't discount the possibility.

She saw Sean Rogan drive up in his black GT. "That's them," she told Panetta. "Can you tell your guys to let them through?"

Panetta got on the radio and cleared them.

Suzanne watched the two approach. Sean had his arm around Lucy's shoulder. It seemed casual, but protective at the same time. She'd thought something was going on between the two of them, but it was certainly obvious now.

Lucy was pale and wore no makeup, and her wavy hair was down and tucked behind her ears, making her look younger than she had last night. Sean held a large umbrella over both of them.

Sean spotted Suzanne and gave her a look that surprised her—he was angry.

She met them halfway. "Thank you for coming out."

"You called at six in the morning."

"Right after I got the call. Sorry to wake you up."

"I was awake," Sean said.

"It's fine," Lucy said. "Really, thank you for including us."

"I stayed up late to read your report," Suzanne said. "But you didn't give a psych profile."

"I'm not a profiler. I thought you wanted me to compile the evidence and statements for you to send to Hans."

"Yes, but I guess I expected a conclusion. I have the wrong guy in prison. I missed something, and I need to find out what before someone else dies."

"Same M.O.?"

"Appears so," Suzanne said, leading the way to the tent. "I haven't seen the body yet; the coroner just arrived. Nineteen, waitress here in Brooklyn, has no affiliation at all with Columbia University, either as an employee or as a student. Neither does her roommate, who found the body."

Lucy followed Suzanne, listening to the facts of the case. She already suspected why Sierra Hinkle was murdered, she just didn't know who killed her. But she'd keep her ideas to herself for now, because she needed facts. All she had was a theory.

"Who knew you had arrested Wade Barnett?" she asked.

"Everyone in the world," Suzanne said sarcastically. "The *Post* reported that we had a suspect in custody early on, and then the six o'clock news broke the fact that the FBI had arrested Wade Barnett. Our statement that Barnett had not been arrested for murder didn't mean squat to the press, who'd already found the same photo of Barnett and Alanna Andrews that you found. If they'd had that much interest in the dead girl, maybe we could have put the connection together earlier, but they didn't care about her when she died. Not until a high-profile, wealthy real-estate investor was arrested."

Suzanne was a hothead, Lucy realized. She'd seen a bit of it yesterday, but now it clearly showed. Suzanne reminded Lucy of her brother, Connor, a former cop who had a temper that had gotten him in trouble many times. It had taken marriage to calm him down some.

Suzanne entered the tent. "What do you have for me?" she asked the coroner.

Lucy and Sean were about to step inside, but the coroner barked out, "Two at a time only! This place is already too crowded."

Sean squeezed her shoulder. "You okay?"

She nodded. "Thanks."

"I'll wait right here."

Following Suzanne in, Lucy stood to the side, assessing the immediate area. There was a bulldozer just outside the tent, about eight feet from where the victim had died. The ground was soaked, concrete and mud and weeds. Several beer bottles and a broken whiskey bottle were near the victim, but they appeared to have been there for much longer than the girl's body.

The coroner said, "Rigor has just begun, and I have her body temperature. Factoring in the temperature last night and this morning, I can state with a high degree of certainty that she died between one and three in the morning."

Detective Panetta was standing outside the tent with Sean. "Her roommate last saw her at approximately one-thirty."

"That gives us ninety minutes," Suzanne said.

Lucy watched as the coroner finished his visual inspection. She noticed that the girl had a cut on her head. Right next to her head was a jagged rock about five inches across, a fresh scrape on the surface. "Suzanne," she said, "I think she hit her head on that rock. That scrape looks about the same diameter as the cut on her head."

The coroner glared at her. He was older, small and wiry, with gray hair and thick glasses sitting low on his nose. "I saw that. I haven't let the crime techs in yet. Who are you?"

Lucy swallowed uneasily. Suzanne responded, "She's with me."

"Trainee?" he grunted.

"Something like that," Suzanne said.

Sierra Hinkle was a brunette, wearing a red sweaterdress so short that when she fell, it had bunched up, exposing one bare buttock and her thong panties. Lucy desperately wanted to cover her, but knew the coroner needed to inspect the body before he could move it. At least the tent gave Sierra privacy from onlookers.

Lucy looked at the victim's feet. She wore one silver shoe. It was glittery, but flat. She assessed the victim's height—she was tall, probably five foot ten. Much taller than the other victims.

There was another key difference. Her neck was swollen and red. "Suzanne," Lucy said quietly, not wanting the coroner to overhear her assessment. "Look at her neck."

Suzanne did. "You're right, it's cut up." Suzanne wasn't as discreet as Lucy was trying to be.

The coroner snapped at Lucy, "You want my job?"

Lucy changed her tactic with the coroner. She really wanted to see something else on the body.

"Actually," she said, "I worked at the D.C. morgue for the last year." She glanced at Suzanne and mouthed, *"Gloves?"*

Suzanne reached into her back pocket and pulled out an extra pair of latex gloves. Lucy put them on and squatted across from the coroner.

"You have a different opinion on time of death?" he asked.

"No, I think you're right."

"You haven't felt the body."

He was daring her. Most cops were squeamish about touching the dead. Lucy wasn't one of them. She pressed her hands into the victim's stomach. "Organs still soft, pliable." She moved her hands out from the center.

The coroner had the best time of death because he'd taken a rectal temperature and extrapolated from that. But the fact that rigor mortis had just begun—a process that starts about three hours after death—gave them a good guess at when she'd died. Still more important at this point was that full lividity—when the blood settled at the lowest point in the body, usually five to six hours after death—hadn't been achieved. In fact, it appeared to have just begun, Lucy surmised.

"Are you ready to turn the body?" she asked the coroner, looking him straight in the eye.

"You want to?"

"Not particularly, but I will. We need a plastic sheet here."

Suzanne handed her a folded tarp. Lucy spread it out next to the body. The coroner hid a smile behind his thick mustache.

Lucy said, "I'll pull her, you push."

The coroner nodded and together they turned the body from her side, as she'd been, to her stomach. Lucy discreetly pulled down her skirt so her bottom was covered. "Lividity started, but is certainly not complete," she said.

"Which confirms my time of death."

"I wasn't questioning time of death," she said. "What I wanted to see was her neck. Can you grab the tarp and pull it under the rest of her body? I'll hold her."

The coroner reached and started to pull the folded edge of the tarp under the body, then stopped.

"Photographer!" he called out.

A moment later, an NYPD crime scene investigator came in.

Lucy looked at what the coroner saw. A large dark-green button. There were still threads in the button's holes, as if it had been ripped out.

The photographer took several pictures. The coroner picked the button up with tweezers and put it in an evidence bag.

Lucy asked, "Do you think they can get prints off that?"

"Probably not, but it's worth a try," the coroner said. His attitude had completely changed, and Lucy hid her grin. "It might not be from the killer."

The coroner finished pulling the plastic under the body, then they rolled her back to her original position.

"Why do you want to see her neck?"

"She's taller than the other victims. I think her killer was shorter than her."

Suzanne asked, "How can you tell?"

"The autopsy reports on the other victims had the bruising in a fairly straight pattern on the neck. These cuts are angled down, from her chin toward her shoulders, as if the killer were holding the plastic bag over her head and pulling down at an angle. I also think she fought back more than the other victims. There's a rawness to her wound that I didn't see in the others."

Suzanne said, "Hey, are those nails real or fake?"

"Fake," Lucy and the coroner said at the same time. "Four are broken off," the coroner added.

"Her index and middle fingers," Lucy said.

The coroner bagged her hands. "There are threads and possible fabric in her palm. I don't want to take them out here. We could lose trace evidence. I'll bag them at the morgue."

Suzanne said, "I don't have to tell you it's a rush."

"No, Special Agent Madeaux, you don't have to tell me."

Lucy stood. "Thank you for letting me help."

"You a Fed?" the coroner asked with distaste.

"No."

"You're not NYPD."

"No."

"Want a job?"

She smiled. "Maybe."

"Let me know."

Lucy stepped out from under the tarp. Suzanne followed. "Carl Brewer is an ass. He doesn't like anyone, except obviously you."

"He reminds me of someone I know," Lucy said. "It's all about appreciating his expertise and being smart at the same time."

Suzanne shook her head and led the way to the abandoned building. "We're going to talk to the victim's roommate and two other potential witnesses." She stepped over a broken bottle. "The killer got sloppy. We never had physical evidence before."

"She should never have gone after a girl taller than her," said Lucy.

"She?" Suzanne and Panetta said simultaneously. Suzanne added, "Your report didn't indicate male or female."

Lucy frowned. "It has to do with the motive."

"What motive?" Suzanne asked.

"I don't want to say right now."

Suzanne stopped walking. "I don't care what you want; let's hear your theory."

"I'm still working on it."

"Work faster."

Suzanne stood staring at her. Lucy looked up at Sean. "I don't think this is a good idea. It's reckless to form a theory without enough information."

Sean said, "It gives the cops one direction, but doesn't close off all the other avenues."

Lucy wanted Sean to support her, but he didn't.

"Lucy," he said, "tell Suzanne what you told me in the car."

"Yes, tell me," Suzanne said.

"I think this girl was killed because you arrested Wade Barnett and the killer doesn't want him in jail. The only way to prove that he isn't the Cinderella Strangler is to kill again. I think this victim was picked randomly—because she was outside, alone."

"Or she left with the killer."

"Possibly," Lucy said, though she didn't think so. Too great a chance to be seen.

"Is she one of the girls on the *Party Girl* website?" Suzanne asked.

Sean answered. "I don't know, but with your permission I'll send her photo to my partner in Washington. He's nearly done rebuilding the site; he can go through looking for her."

"I'll have her ID emailed to him."

Suzanne started walking again. "So the question is: Does Wade Barnett have a partner? If yes, who? If no, why would the killer want him out of prison?"

"We know Wade had sex with at least three of the victims," Lucy began. She was about to share the rest of her theory, the one she still hadn't quite worked through, taking a huge risk of being wrong. But Detective Panetta interrupted her.

"Dennis Barnett."

They turned and looked at him. Suzanne's face fell, and Lucy said, "The younger brother?"

"According to Suzanne's report, he's protective of

his older brother. He stated that he was Wade Barnett's driver for the last six months when Barnett lost his license after two DWIs. He sat in the parking lot while his brother partied and had sex with whomever. Maybe it ate away at him. Or he can't get it up, or he's jealous of his big bro, or just a sociopath. So he kills the stray girl."

"I don't know," Suzanne said slowly. "Dennis told me that Alanna Andrews was kind to him and that she had defended him when Wade got frustrated with him."

"Maybe little brother wanted her for himself," Panetta said, "and she said no. The first victim usually goes to the heart of the serial murderer, isn't that generally true?"

The cop looked at Lucy. She nodded and said, "The first victim usually has a personal significance for the killer."

Suzanne frowned. "Dennis is five foot nine, according to his driver's license." She turned to Lucy. "What do you think?"

Lucy didn't want to be at center stage. She didn't know what to think—her theory was all shot to hell if Dennis Barnett was the Cinderella Strangler. She'd been thinking last night, and seemed to have it confirmed when another victim died, that the killer was an ex-girlfriend of Wade Barnett's. Someone whom he'd cheated on, most likely with the first victim, Alanna Andrews. That her death had been spontaneous because the killer had just found out about the affair.

She had hoped to go with Suzanne to interview Wade Barnett and ask him questions about his ex-girlfriends, particularly any with a history of violence. A girl who might have broken things when she was mad. Someone impulsive. Someone who had not expected him to break up with her, and who had let him know that with anger rather than tears.

She'd wanted to confirm her theory that Wade Barnett had also slept with Heather Garcia, the third victim, and more important, Lucy wanted to know if he'd had a sexual relationship with Kirsten Benton. If so, it meant Kirsten was in even greater danger.

But a younger brother? One who had already stated that he was not only at each crime scene but alone? A younger brother who might have had a difficult time finding women to date him because of mild mental retardation.

Suzanne said, "Dennis Barnett is enrolled to audit classes at Columbia University. He's only in one class, but he's been attending for the last year and a half."

"Two of the victims were from Columbia. Erica Ripley worked not far away, also in Manhattan," Panetta said.

"It's logical," Lucy said, because it was.

But she didn't think it was right. She bit her lip. Sean said, "What about your other theory?"

Suzanne said, "Right now, I need to bring in Dennis Barnett. I need a psychologist, since his attorney has brought up the fact that I first interviewed him without full knowledge of his emotional and mental state."

"I'm a psychologist," Lucy said.

"I need a criminal psychologist," Suzanne said.

Panetta said, "I can call in the shrink the department uses."

Sean said, "Lucy is a criminal psychologist, unless you don't accept those with a master's degree from Georgetown."

Suzanne rubbed her eyes. "You're already up to speed," she said. "Will you do it?"

"Of course," Lucy said.

"Let's go, then."

Sean asked Suzanne, "Can Lucy ride with you? I have a few things to look into on my missing person case."

"Of course. I'll get her back to your hotel when we're done."

Lucy said quietly to Sean, "Did something happen?"

"Trey has been calling me. He's in Brooklyn. I told him I would meet him. You okay with this?"

She nodded.

He leaned in and kissed her lightly, then whispered in her ear, "You don't think Dennis Barnett is the killer, do you?"

"I don't know."

He looked at her, and seemed disappointed. "I trust your instincts, Lucy. You need to trust them as well."

Sean walked away, and Lucy wished she had as much faith in herself as Sean did.

TWENTY-SEVEN

Trey had rented a motel room in Brooklyn at a place a half-star more upscale than the Clover Motel where Kirsten had stayed. Sean called him as he pulled into the parking lot. "I'm here."

"I'm coming."

"What room—" but Trey had already hung up.

While waiting for Trey, Sean sent Patrick a message about the *Party Girl* website and latest victim. Patrick responded:

I have it 90% rebuilt. I hosted it on the RCK intranet so you can access it.

Sean grinned. Patrick was as methodical as Lucy. He couldn't have picked a better partner than Patrick, or a better woman to fall in love with than Lucy.

He wished she'd told Suzanne her theory, even if it wasn't completely formulated. She had stood up to the coroner because she had hands-on experience with the dead. And after Suzanne had Lucy prepare the report for Hans Vigo, Sean thought her confidence had returned. She might not have the years of experience that Hans had, but she had the right instincts and would someday be the go-to person in the

FBI for criminal profiling. Sean was certain of it—if she appealed their wrongheaded decision.

But he wondered if her work last night analyzing the four murder cases had contributed to the terrifying nightmare she'd had. Or had she told the truth, that the bad dreams had returned after one of her rapists had been killed, propelling her attack to the forefront of her carefully rebuilt life?

He shifted in his seat, antsy, waiting for Trey. He'd been thinking about last night—the nightmare, Lucy's confession of feeling alone and empty, his declaration of love. He did love her; there was no doubt in his mind. Lucy loved him, too; she just didn't know it yet. But when she made love to him, she showed it. The intensity of her response, the urgency, had intoxicated him. He'd remembered at the last second that he hadn't put on a condom, and he thought he'd said something to her, but then he'd pushed thoughts of protection aside. She sent him over the edge, and he didn't want to hold back.

So many problems could come from forgetting to wear a condom, pregnancy at the top of that list. It was his responsibility, he'd always believed that, and Duke had pounded it into his head from the minute he'd found out that Sean was having sex in high school.

Sean would be thirty this year. Lucy was twenty-five. They were certainly old enough to get married and have a family, but Sean wasn't ready, and he doubted Lucy was, either. For him, it was the whole family dynamic. He hadn't had the same kind of close-knit family that Lucy had. He was afraid he wouldn't make a good father. But marriage? He'd never considered it an option before he met Lucy, yet he'd marry her in a heartbeat.

But he wanted her to marry him because she loved him, when she could tell him that she loved him with words as well as actions. Not because she was pregnant. Not because she thought they had to get married.

He had to talk to her about their slipup. He couldn't ignore it. Surely she'd noticed as well. And knowing Lucy, she'd convince herself that not only would she not marry him because she was pregnant, but that she *couldn't* even though she knew he loved her. She'd think up some logical reason, but love wasn't logical. Love was beyond reason, and there was no way he'd let Lucy raise their child by herself, family support or not. He'd somehow figure out how to be a good father.

But truly, the chances were against her getting pregnant from one slipup. He'd be extremely diligent from now on, not let himself get carried away again. He had known what was going on, he should have found a way to reach his wallet, but he didn't want to stop Lucy for fear of severing the overwhelming physical and emotional passion between them.

A knock on the window startled Sean, and he glanced over. Trey peered in, and Sean unlocked the door. The cold air that rushed in cleared his thoughts so he could focus wholly on the present.

"I found Kirsten," Trey said.

"Where?" Sean started the car.

"Manhattan Catholic Hospital."

Sean typed it into his GPS. "Manhattan?"

"I started in Brooklyn like you said, spent all yesterday going from hospital to hospital, and only got through a fraction of my list. When it started raining, I started calling. I had my spiel down, went through the entire list. There were two unknown females in hospitals in Brooklyn that fit Kirsten's description. I went to see both, and they weren't her.

"So this morning I started in Manhattan. There are so many hospitals and clinics, so I focused on public hospitals thinking that if someone didn't have a name or insurance, that's where they'd end up. MCH has her. I know it. I talked to the head nurse, who was super nice, and I told her Kirsten had an oval-shaped mole on her upper right thigh." Trey cleared his throat. "You can see it when she wears a bathing suit."

"And the nurse confirmed it."

"Yes. I didn't want to call Mrs. Benton, not until I know for sure."

"Good idea." Sean frowned. He should have been calling the hospitals. He'd thought that between the police bulletin and the RCK memo, any hospital would have contacted one of them. Would they have found her sooner? Been able to talk to her, find out if she'd seen who killed her friend Jessie before Sierra Hinkle died?

Trey continued talking. "She was found unconscious in a church Friday night."

"A church?"

"The priest was locking up at midnight and found her lying on a pew. He brought her to MCH. They wouldn't tell me anything else on the phone, only confirmed her description."

"Evelyn gave me power of attorney so I can find

out more at the hospital about Kirsten's condition," Sean said.

It took less than ten minutes in light Sunday-morning traffic to reach MCH once Sean was on the Brooklyn Bridge. The emergency room was near full, so Sean went to the main entrance. "Whom did you speak to?" he asked Trey.

"A nurse. Jeanne McMahon."

Sean asked for the nurse, and several minutes later an older nurse dressed in colorful red scrubs with a neon-green stethoscope around her neck stepped off the elevator. She looked suspiciously like Mrs. Santa Claus.

"Did you call about the poor blond girl?"

"Yes. I'm Trey Danielson."

"Sean Rogan," Sean said and handed her his card along with Evelyn's power of attorney and Kirsten's photo. "Is this her?"

Jeanne nodded. "Looks like her. She hasn't regained consciousness since she was admitted." Jeanne led them to one set of elevators. "We have her in ICU. She's one sick little girl."

"I need to confirm that it's Kirsten, then contact her mother and the police."

"The police? She didn't do anything, did she?"

"She may be a witness to a crime. We think she's been in hiding."

"If she was hiding, someone had to be helping her."

"Why do you think so?"

"She wouldn't have been able to walk. Her feet are severely cut up and infected. We've done everything we can to bring down her fever. She seems to have stabilized, but hasn't responded to antibiotics. The doctor is going to assess her shortly and probably change her medication. She needs surgery, but her system is too weak to tolerate it."

"Do you know how she ended up at the church?"

"I have no idea, and Father Frisco is so upset about it. He's been here several times a day since he brought her in. He's in and out of the church in the evenings. He thinks she may have been left while he had a late supper about eight, but he didn't find her until midnight when he checked the pews."

Jeanne led them out of the elevator and down several corridors. "In fact, Father Frisco came to visit shortly after Trey called, and I told him someone inquired about the girl, and he found someone to cover his masses so he could talk to you."

They turned into the waiting area for ICU. "I need to ask that you both put on masks before entering ICU, and after you confirm that she's your missing girl, only one of you can stay with her."

Trey glanced at Sean, eyes wide. Sean nodded. Trey could stay. He needed to call Evelyn and then look at Kirsten's records and personal effects to see if there was any clue as to where she'd been since last Saturday night.

The blonde in the bed was sickly thin, her skin almost translucent. Her hair was limp, but clean. She had an IV in her arm and monitors registering her heart rate and her body temperature.

"Kirsten," Trey said, his voice hitching.

"It's her," Sean confirmed to the nurse.

The priest, Father Frisco, sat in the corner praying with a rosary. He was younger than Sean expected—closer to Duke's age, around forty. He supposed he had a stereotypical view of Catholic priests being old, gray, and from Ireland or Mexico. Father Frisco was a tall, dark-haired Italian.

"What happened to her?" Trey demanded. "Why is she so skinny?"

"Shh," the nurse admonished.

Sean said, "Stay with her. I'll find answers."

Father Frisco rose and shook Trey's hand, holding it while he spoke. "Talk to her. She's not responding, but maybe a familiar voice will draw her back."

Tears in his eyes, Trey sat down and tentatively reached for Kirsten's hand.

Sean walked back out to Jeanne at the nurses' station, with Father Frisco right behind him.

"Father, Jeanne explained how you found Kirsten. Why do you think she didn't walk in on her own?"

"Her feet were bandaged, and they were clean. If she walked even a short distance, they would have been dirty."

"And," Jeanne added, "when we inspected her injuries, we determined that she wouldn't have been able to walk. The tendon in her right foot is severed, but began to heal improperly. Walking on it would have been impossible. We can do surgery to correct the worst damage, but first we need to stabilize her and beat the infection."

"We sent a notice around to all hospitals on Wednesday," Sean said. "Did you see it?"

"We post current notices, and keep older missing persons in a book. But there are so many from all over the country. When we get a Jane Doe we go through the book again, but it's been a busy weekend. We would have identified her eventually. And the ad-

ministration filed a police report on Friday when we
admitted her. But these things take time to work
through the system."

"Do you know what caused the damage to her
feet?"

Jeanne nodded. "Someone had cleaned her feet,
but not well enough. There were small pieces of
gravel deep in cuts that had started to heal, but because of the infection they weren't healing properly.
We also found a piece of colored glass, probably from
a beer bottle, under her skin."

"Someone cleaned and bandaged her feet?"

"Probably daily. The bandages on her feet were
clean with little discharge, except pus from the infection and a small amount of blood. We ran blood tests
and had some odd results, so sent them and hair samples to an outside lab for testing."

"Hair samples?"

"Primarily for illegal drugs and certain poisons
that may be out of her blood system, but show up in
hair for months afterward."

"When do you think she sustained the injuries?"

Jeanne pulled her file. "The doctor said they were
five to seven days old when she was admitted on Friday."

That put her injuries most likely the night that Jessica was killed.

Sean turned to Father Frisco. "Are there any security cameras at your church?"

He shook his head.

"Why do you think she was brought to your
church and not any other?" Sean asked.

"Are you suggesting this might be one of my

parishioners?" From the weary tone it was obvious that the priest, too, had considered the possibility. "Why not take her to a hospital?"

"Security," Sean said. "Whoever left her in the church didn't want to be seen with her." Someone who has a lot to lose. The person also cared about her enough to leave her indoors where she would get help. And because she was left in a Catholic church, either someone lives in the area around the church or is Catholic. He changed the subject. "How was she dressed? May I see her personal effects?"

Father Frisco said, "She was dressed warmly in new clothes and had a blanket on her."

Jeanne said, "The shirt still had a tag on it; I thought she might have shoplifted the item, except that there was a return sticker on the back that some of the stores put on."

That might tell Sean when she bought it, or if someone else bought it for her. "I need her clothing, the blanket, everything she had with her."

"I'll get them." Jeanne strode down the hall.

Father Frisco stated more than asked, "The people who left her, they didn't want her to die."

"I think whoever it was wanted to help her, but her condition worsened and he panicked."

"Who?"

Sean had an idea, but he needed to do some research before he called Suzanne Madeaux.

First, he had an important call to make.

"Excuse me, Father, but I need to tell Kirsten's mother that we found her daughter."

TWENTY-EIGHT

Lucy prepared Suzanne and Detective Panetta for the interview. She first convinced Suzanne to interview Dennis Barnett at NYPD headquarters, because the bustling atmosphere with uniforms and guns screamed authority and Lucy believed Dennis Barnett would be unusually obedient to authority.

She then cautioned the cops against leading or browbeating him in any way. "Any competent defense attorney will get a confession thrown out."

Panetta said, "His IQ isn't low enough to qualify for medical deficiency, and even if it were, the D.A. would still prosecute. There's enough precedent."

"It's low enough that counsel could argue his natural obedience to authority led him to say whatever he thought you wanted to hear."

"How many interviews have you conducted, Ms. Kincaid?" Panetta asked.

Lucy couldn't respond. The detective was right; she wasn't a cop. Her experience hadn't prepared her for this; what was she even thinking agreeing to act as psychologist? She had a master's degree, that was it. No experience other than what life had handed her.

Suzanne said, "We're not going to browbeat anyone. But I want to nail him, and I want it airtight. How do we get a confession?"

Lucy said, "He wants to please, and you have to convince him that only the complete truth will make you happy."

"How do you know that?" she asked.

"I read his statement to you, when you talked to him in his brother's apartment. He wants to be good and do the right thing, but because of his relationship with his brothers, I think he'll respond better to the detective." She glanced at Panetta and encountered his disbelieving frown. She straightened her spine and continued.

"His entire life he has looked up to CJ and Wade," she said. "He parrots what they say, as you can tell if you read his statement closely. CJ's disapproval over Wade's lifestyle came through clearly, though Dennis doesn't feel the same. He sees Wade as both his corrector and defender. Wade wants Dennis to be normal because he wants a brother, so he takes him to the parties and to shows and other places. But Dennis is slow and clumsy, and Wade gets frustrated. Dennis will do anything to please Wade, and Wade will say anything to protect Dennis. If Wade is innocent, and believes Dennis is guilty, he'll confess."

"If he's innocent?" Panetta shook his head. "Only in the movies. I get people confessing to everything under the sun mostly for attention, but I've never had anyone confess to protect someone unless they were threatened."

"He *is* threatened," Lucy said. "If Dennis goes to jail for murder, the guilt will eat him up. He'll blame himself for not seeing it, or not stopping it."

"Or Wade will be in prison, too, if they did it together," Suzanne said, "Probably on death row."

"He'll consider himself a failure because he couldn't raise his brother."

"He's only five years older."

"Their mother abdicated the responsibility for raising Dennis to CJ and Wade. CJ became the father, a financial genius who turned their settlement into a fortune, and Wade became the mother, the playmate."

Lucy was losing them. She wasn't good at this; she'd always had Hans or her brother Dillon to bounce her ideas off of first.

"I've read every interview and statement, and all articles I could find on the brothers. It's clear that when their father was killed in the workplace accident, CJ became the male father figure—he was fourteen. He pressured Wade to grow up, which is why Wade is both responsible outwardly—historic preservation, philanthropy, civic responsibility—and extremely childish. He sleeps around with numerous women, he's obsessed with baseball, and he's jealous of Dennis."

"Why?"

"Because Dennis gets to be a kid forever. Wade was forced by his father's death and his older brother's disapproval to grow up before he was ready."

"So is Dennis guilty?" Suzanne asked. "Or were they a team?"

"If Dennis is guilty, he'll confess. He'll tell the truth, whether Wade was involved or knew about it. He's scared of getting in trouble. I can't be certain without seeing Dennis with his mother, but his brief statement, and the fact that he didn't ask for his mother or want her with him, makes me think he doesn't have a strong bond with her, which also supports my theory that the brothers raised him. I can speculate why, but I honestly don't know without interviewing her or seeing them together."

Hicks stuck his head into the interview room. "Barnett and his lawyer are here."

"Put him next door," Panetta said.

Hicks handed Panetta a file. "This came in from the lab last night. The FBI called Friday to find out where it was." He shot Suzanne a look.

"I didn't call about a lab report," Suzanne said.

Lucy cleared her throat. "I did. It was the residue test from the first victim. The report wasn't attached to the autopsy, and I didn't know if it had gotten lost or they hadn't gotten to it."

Hicks said, "They ran it yesterday, put it at the top of the pile." He winked. "Must be your sexy voice."

"Get our suspect," Panetta ordered and opened the report. He skimmed it. "The black powder is ninety-eight percent ultrafine charcoal and two percent gum."

"Gum?" Lucy questioned. "Could she have aspirated a piece of gum when she was being suffocated?"

Panetta handed her the report. She read it, but didn't understand it—except it wasn't chewing gum.

"As you pointed out," Suzanne said, "the first murder was spontaneous. You were at the crime scene this morning; those abandoned buildings are neither clean nor sanitary. The killer could have grabbed whatever was handy."

"Maybe our suspect had charcoal in a bag to go home and barbecue after he killed her," Panetta reasoned.

Lucy gathered up her files. Panetta wasn't serious. She thought this report was important simply because it was an anomaly, but she needed to think it through, and right now both Panetta and Suzanne were itching to talk to Dennis Barnett.

"In your first conversation, Suzanne, he talked about Wade's girlfriends who were mean to him," Lucy said. "Find out how they were mean. What they did, how that made him feel, what his actions were. Did he ever defend himself and how? Was it always Wade standing up for him? And you'll have to ask about his mother, his childhood."

"So he has mommy issues," Panetta said, obviously irritated.

"Everyone has mommy issues," Lucy countered. "I didn't say it was an excuse to kill."

They left the small conference room and went next door. A one-way mirror showed Dennis Barnett with his attorney. Dennis was wide-eyed and curious. Maybe a bit scared, but more interested in the room. His attorney was older and dressed in a suit. He didn't look happy.

Lucy focused on Dennis. He was broad-shouldered and muscular. He had blue eyes and an inquisitive childlike gaze. He also fidgeted.

He turned around to look behind him, at the blank wall, and Lucy had a flash of recognition. She stopped Panetta from opening the door.

The detective looked at her, irritated. He hadn't liked her assessment, he was old-school—the "psychobabble" wouldn't appeal to his investigative approach.

"Suzanne, where's the witness drawing?" Without

waiting for her response, Lucy riffled through her file folders until she found a copy.

"It's him. His profile."

Suzanne looked at the drawing, then at Dennis Barnett. "I didn't see it at first, but I think you're right."

Panetta walked over and frowned. "I didn't see it either, but it's the profile. But everything is a bit exaggerated in the picture."

Lucy agreed. "He looks mean in the drawing, but not sitting in the room. He appears harmless now."

"It was done from an older memory," Suzanne said. "Unless the witness views a lineup and identifies him, I don't think we'll be able to use it."

Until now, Lucy hadn't believed that Dennis Barnett was guilty. She was certain that the killer was obsessed with Wade Barnett, either an ex-girlfriend or someone who knew him well, such as a secretary.

She was wrong. How many other things had she been wrong about? Why was she even here in the first place?

She sent Sean a message.

I was wrong. The man the witness drew with Alanna Andrews the night she was killed is Dennis Barnett.

Sean considered breaking into Charles Barnett's Brooklyn Heights penthouse apartment a challenge. It was a secure building with state-of-the-art locks, a doorman, and a security camera. But it was still just a place, and Sean had never yet been defeated by a building, or a computer system.

It took less than ten minutes to assess the best ap-

proach to breaching the twelve-story building, then
one minute to bypass the electronic lock that led to
the parking garage under the building.

He smiled as he drove his GT into the structure and
parked in 12A, Charles Barnett's empty slot. He was
in Europe, Wade Barnett was still at Rikers, and by
now, the FBI would be interviewing Dennis Barnett.
The apartment should be empty.

Once he was upstairs, Sean picked the lock of Barnett's apartment and slipped inside, quietly closing
the door behind him. He had left his gun in his
trunk—on the off chance that someone was living in
Barnett's apartment, Sean might be able to talk himself out of an arrest for breaking and entering, but not
if he was armed. Still, if his hunch was right, no one
would be there.

He listened for any hint that someone was in the
apartment, but it was dead silent. The place was tidy
but not immaculate. There were a few glasses on the
counter in the kitchen, the kitchen chairs weren't
pushed in, and the cushions on the couch weren't
aligned. It didn't necessarily mean anything.

But even through the steady drizzle, Sean could see
the Brooklyn Bridge outside the picture windows.

There were three bedrooms. One was small and appeared unused. The second had a hastily made bed,
the dresser littered with coins and crumpled dollars.
Sean went through the items and found a receipt from
Abercrombie & Fitch for $310.07. The credit card
was in the name of Dennis Barnett.

He'd brought the tag from Kirsten's shirt with him.
It, too, was from Abercrombie & Fitch, and he compared the item number to the receipt.

Match.

Dennis had bought her two pairs of sweatpants, a sweater, two shirts, and four pairs of underwear. Sean searched the bedroom and found no other clothing from the receipt.

He then went to the master bedroom and knew this was where Kirsten had stayed for five days.

The bed had been stripped and made, but the dirty bloodstained sheets were in the hamper. Bloody bandages were in the bathroom garbage, and supplies from a local pharmacy were spread out on the nightstand: gauze, bandage tape, topical antibiotics, pain relievers.

Sean went to the den and booted up the computer. He looked through the browser history and saw that Kirsten had definitely sent the message from this computer on Thursday morning.

He stared out the window as he put together the final pieces of the puzzle. Dennis Barnett had been caring for Kirsten here in this apartment. Why had he not taken her to the hospital when it was clear that she was very sick? Had she convinced him that someone was trying to kill her? Or had she gradually gotten worse, leaving him with no choice?

Did Wade Barnett know? And if he did, why hadn't he gone to the police or the hospital? What was he trying to hide?

Sean didn't have all the answers, but if Dennis Barnett had gone out of his way to bring Kirsten home from the party, nurse her, then leave her at the church when he couldn't care for her any longer, he didn't see how he could coldly kill five other young women.

He sent Lucy a message detailing what he'd found, letting her reach her own conclusions.

He saw her message about the man in the drawing being Dennis Barnett. What had the artist said? That she'd seen someone with Alanna the night she died. Dennis Barnett already admitted to being a driver to the parties that his brother attended; it didn't mean he'd killed Alanna.

Sean sat back down at Charles Barnett's computer and logged on to the secure RCK East server to access the *Party Girl* website that Patrick rebuilt. But Patrick had taken it one step further: He'd created an index of all content, including all registered users.

He scanned the list of registered users for any name that might be Wade Barnett. Most people used something familiar to them, something that was part of their personal identity. He clicked through a couple of promising names; neither of them was Wade Barnett.

Then he found what he was looking for near the end of the alphabetical list.

YankeeFan00

He clicked through and smiled. While it didn't have Wade Barnett's photograph, it had two important pointers:

He'd posted that he was a twenty-six-year-old preservationist from New York.

And among his friends were Erica Ripley, Heather Garcia, Jessica Bell, and Kirsten Benton, all under false names, but all with their real images.

He sent the data to Lucy and Suzanne, logged off

the RCK site, and wiped memory of the visit from the computer while leaving all else intact, then left.

In his car, he called FBI agent Noah Armstrong. He and Noah didn't see eye to eye on everything, but Noah had vouched for him with Suzanne Madeaux.

He needed someone with the clout to get him into Rikers Island.

TWENTY-NINE

After fifteen minutes of relatively softball questions, Dennis Barnett was becoming confused and agitated. Lucy didn't think it was because of guilt. Dennis had been eager to help at the beginning, but he didn't understand why the questions were about him.

Suzanne asked for the third time, "And how did that make you feel when Wade's girlfriend called you a dumbass?"

Dennis frowned. "I'm slow, not stupid. You asked me that."

"I'm trying to understand your feelings."

"No you're not. You're trying to make me feel bad."

Panetta said, "Why would we want to make you feel bad? Unless you have something to feel bad about?"

Dennis looked at his lawyer. "You said we were coming here to help Wade."

"We *are* here to help Wade," the lawyer said. "That's why you need to tell these officers the truth."

Lucy's instincts started buzzing. The lawyer had to know that Dennis was a suspect; had he not told him? Or had Dennis not understood?

Suzanne noticed the same thing and said, "Dennis, another young woman was killed last night."

He frowned.

"I'd like to show you her picture. It would help if you tell us if you know her or have seen her anywhere."

He nodded.

Suzanne showed him Sierra Hinkle's driver's-license photo. Lucy watched his face closely. It was completely blank, except for his forehead, which was crinkled in concentration.

"I don't know her."

Suzanne then showed him Jessica Bell.

He stared and bit his thumbnail. "If I saw her, is that going to get Wade in trouble?"

"If you lie, Wade will get in trouble," Lucy said. She'd been quiet most of the interview, but she sensed a turn in Dennis's demeanor.

The lawyer broke the moment. "I don't understand this line of questioning."

Suzanne said, "And I don't understand who you're working for, Dennis, or someone else."

Lucy focused on Dennis and said, "Dennis, do you know why Wade is in jail right now?"

"Because she"—he looked at Suzanne with a childish expression of anger—"thinks he hurt Alanna."

"Actually," Lucy said, "we don't know who hurt Alanna." She felt Panetta turn his gaze to her. He was not happy. "Wade is in jail because he lied to Agent Madeaux. Did you know that lying to the FBI is a crime?"

He nodded. "She told me."

"It's true. If you lie and we can prove it, then you

will have to go to jail, too. I like you, Dennis. I don't want you to go to jail."

"I don't want to go to jail." He looked at Jessica's picture. "That's Jenna."

"Jenna?" Suzanne said. "How do you know her?"

"I stay with Wade sometimes. She was talking on his computer."

"Talking?" Suzanne prompted.

Dennis turned bright red and whispered, "She was naked. Wade didn't see me come in at first. Then he got mad and yelled at me."

Panetta steered the conversation away from that angle and asked, "Were you mad at Jenna?"

"No, I—"

"Because I would be," Panetta said.

Lucy wanted to shut the detective down. Dennis was getting agitated again, and it was because he was embarrassed, not because he killed her.

"I wasn't mad at anyone. Wade told me to knock from then on, and I said the door was open, and then he just turned off the computer. That was a long time ago. Last summer."

Suzanne put the pictures of Erica Ripley and Heather Garcia in front of Dennis. "What about these two? Do you know them?"

He pointed to Heather. "I don't know her. But that's Erica. She works at the Java Central coffee-house. She came with us to a party once, but—" He frowned, thinking.

"What party?"

"It was real hot. Labor Day weekend and I wanted to go to Martha's Vineyard with Charlie, but Wade wanted me to drive him to a party. He just lost his license because he was drinking. He said I was the only one he trusted. So we went. He made me come in because it was too hot to sit in the car. I did *not* like it. It was so loud my head hurt. And Wade was drinking, and he gets stupid when he drinks."

"Who says that?" Lucy asked him.

"Charlie. It's why Wade lost his license. Charlie said, 'You deserve it, you get stupid when you drink.'"

"What stupid thing did Wade do that night?" Suzanne asked.

"Lots of them. He wanted me to have sex with a girl I never met before and I didn't want to. Alanna was mad at him about that. Then he hurt Alanna's feelings because he brought Erica to the party. She said, 'I don't care if you fuck around here, but don't bring it home.'"

Lucy wondered if Dennis had an eidetic memory, or at least an enhanced auditory memory.

Suzanne prompted, "You told me earlier that Wade and Alanna broke up. But they went to a Yankees game together after that party."

"They broke up, then Wade said he was sorry and gave her the tickets. She said, 'This is your last chance.' Charlie said it would never work out because they had an open relationship."

"Do you know what an open relationship is?" Lucy asked.

"When you have a girlfriend but still have sex with other girls."

"And after the Yankees game?" Suzanne asked.

"I don't know what happened. But Wade was real upset about it and said he fucked up again."

Panetta asked, "Were you mad at Alanna?"

Dennis shook his head. "She was nice to me."

"Was Erica nice to you?" Lucy asked.

Dennis shrugged. "Sometimes."

"What about Jessica?"

"Who?"

Suzanne touched the photo. "Her name is Jessica."

He shook his head. "Her name is *Jenna*."

"She only pretended her name was Jenna."

He brightened. "Oh, I get it."

Lucy glanced at her phone, then opened Sean's message.

Found Kirsten. She's in the hospital sick with an infection.
Dennis was taking care of her at his brother Charles's apartment in Brooklyn Heights. I have proof. More in a sec.

Lucy opened her files and pulled out a picture of Kirsten. "Do you know this girl?"

His lip trembled. "What happened?"

"Can you tell me?"

He looked panicked. "You're only showing me pictures of dead girls! Did she die?"

"No," Lucy said. Suzanne narrowed her gaze at Lucy, telling her to back off. Lucy swallowed. She was certain her first instinct was right, that Dennis didn't kill those girls, and neither did Wade. "She's fine. She's in the hospital."

He breathed easier. "Okay, good. Wade told me—" He stopped talking and looked at his hands folded on the table.

Suzanne said, "You need to tell the truth."

He wrestled with it for about thirty seconds. "If I

tell you the truth, promise me you won't get mad at Wade and make him stay in jail."

Suzanne said, "If Wade didn't kill these girls, I promise he won't stay in jail."

Lucy knew that Suzanne couldn't promise any such thing. Already, Wade was in serious trouble for compromising an investigation and for attempting to destroy evidence.

Dennis believed her. "Okay, I found Kirsten last weekend and she was real scared and hurt and I wanted to take her to the doctor, but she was crying and said no. Wade told me I shouldn't have kept her at Charlie's because she was real sick, and then she wouldn't wake up. Wade thought I hurt her, but I told him I didn't, and he believed me but said it looked bad because he knew her."

"Wade knows Kirsten?" Suzanne said.

"He said he did. He said something weird was going on and that he would figure it out, but he told me—remember you promised he won't get in trouble." He was looking at Suzanne for an answer.

"Yes I did."

He accepted the nonanswer and said, "He told me he knew all the women who were killed by the Cinderella Strangler. He was really scared."

"Because he killed them and didn't want to go to jail?" Panetta asked.

"No!" Dennis slapped his hand on the table in his first physical burst of anger. "No, no, no! He didn't kill anyone."

Suzanne said, "Wade is in jail because he told me he didn't know the four girls who were killed. That he

knew them, had sex with them, and lied about it—
that looks very bad."

"But he didn't! I know it."

"Did you kill those girls?" Panetta demanded.

Dennis's eyes widened and he shook his head.

Suzanne prompted, "Maybe you were upset because Wade was spending more time with them than
with you."

He continued to shake his head.

"He embarrassed you at that party," Panetta said.
"Told you to have sex with someone you didn't like.
Did the girls laugh at you? Or did they want Wade
but not you? Did you love Alanna? Is that why you
killed her—because she loved your brother, who
didn't deserve her?"

Dennis was crying. "I didn't kill Alanna. I didn't. I
didn't." He put his head down. "I want to see Wade.
Please."

The lawyer said, "This conversation is over."

"One more question," Lucy said. She reached out
and touched Dennis on the arm. He was trembling.
He looked at her when she said his name softly.

"Dennis. You have a good memory. I want you to
think back to when you found Kirsten running."

He sniffed. "She wasn't running. She fell down.
That's when I got out of my car and picked her up."

"What did she say to you?"

"She said, 'Don't let her get me.'"

Noah came through.

Sean arrived at Rikers Island just before two on
Sunday afternoon, hauling ass the entire way because
of a mandatory two p.m. registration deadline that

even Noah couldn't get the Department of Corrections to waive. But after being cleared and given a visitor's pass, Sean was approached by a guy in a suit. "Mr. Rogan, Special Agent Steven Plunkett, the FBI liaison for Rikers."

Sean shook his extended hand and followed him down a series of corridors. At several junctions, they stopped and waited for the guard to release the lock and allow them to pass.

Sean supposed that he should have gone through Suzanne Madeaux, but they were in the middle of interviewing Dennis Barnett, and Sean was concerned about Kirsten's safety. If the killer found out that Kirsten was in the hospital, she was in jeopardy.

Lucy hadn't had enough faith in her analysis to follow up on her theory, but Sean didn't doubt it. Lucy thought the killer was a woman.

And Sean suspected Wade Barnett knew who it was.

Plunkett ran through the rules with Sean about prisoner interaction, but Sean was only half listening. By the time they reached a private room—the type where lawyers met with their clients—Sean had his game plan set. He wasn't surprised that Plunkett stayed in the room.

Wade Barnett didn't smile when Sean entered. "Who are you?" he demanded.

"Sean Rogan, private investigator. Kirsten Benton is my cousin."

There was partial recognition in Barnett's eyes, and Sean added, "You know her as Ashleigh."

Barnett closed his eyes. "I didn't know Dennis was keeping her."

"I believe you."

Barnett looked at him. "Why? No one has believed a word I've said."

"That happens when you lie to the cops. If they find out, they don't believe anything else you say." Sean had some experience with that principle. "I'm going to tell you what I think. You correct me. I need answers, and I need them now—because Kirsten is in danger."

He seemed surprised. "But—"

"Yes, a priest found her and took her to the hospital, and I found your brother's apartment and know she was well taken care of. Except that she has a serious infection and is still unconscious."

"I took her in as soon as I found out, believe me—"

"You didn't take her to the hospital, but I'm going to overlook that. I think, when the FBI and NYPD came to talk to you about the murders of four women you had sex with, you panicked. You knew Alanna had been killed. But I don't think you put the others together. There wasn't much press on Erica Ripley's murder, and it wasn't until after New Year's that the press dubbed the killer the Cinderella Strangler.

"You ran the *Party Girl* website through an off-shore company that hosted it for you. When the police talked to you Thursday morning, you finally put the murders together. But it wasn't just because you had sex with those four women. It was because you thought you'd be liable for their deaths because they were all members of the *Party Girl* website. You thought someone was using your site to target their victims. So you paid to have the site taken down.

"Fortunately, my partner and I are smarter than you, and we retrieved cached data and rebuilt the whole enchilada." Sean watched Barnett's face register complete surprise.

Sean continued. "You probably started thinking Thursday night that you personally knew these victims. There were nine hundred sixty-one female profiles on *Party Girl*. What are the odds that four who live in New York would be killed? What are the odds that you would have slept with all four women?"

Sean leaned forward. "That's when you tracked down your brother Dennis. I don't know if you thought he was killing them, or—"

"Stay away from my brother," Wade said. "He wouldn't hurt anyone."

"That's what my girlfriend said. But the police are interviewing him right now. You want to know why?"

"Dennis would not survive in prison. How could they? He didn't kill anyone!"

"And neither did you. A fifth victim turned up last night."

"Wade's entire body sagged. "What?"

"Sierra Hinkle. And my partner already checked—she wasn't on the *Party Girl* site under any name. Did you know her?"

"No."

"She was a waitress in Brooklyn."

"I didn't know her."

Sean took Sierra Hinkle's picture out of his pocket and showed Barnett, just to be certain.

"I've never seen her."

"Do you want to know why she was killed?"

"You're going to tell me either way."

"Because you're in prison. That's not what your ex-girlfriend wanted."

"You're insane. Alanna's dead."

"She wasn't your only girlfriend. Think back. A woman you dated who didn't take it well when you broke it off. Someone who has been in and out of your life, probably for many years." Sean thought back to what Lucy had said about Dennis and Wade's relationship, and how Wade protected his younger brother. "She didn't like Dennis, was probably mean to him, but never around you because she knew you wouldn't put up with it. Dennis would not have liked her."

"Dennis liked all my girlfriends," Wade said. But he was thinking.

Sean tried a different tactic. "You lost your license, but this is New York. Why have Dennis drive you to all the parties?"

"I live on the Upper West Side. Most of the parties aren't walking distance. I don't take the subway, and I don't care to walk to Brooklyn. Cabs are unreliable."

Sean hesitated. "Did Dennis take you to all the parties? Was he at the Haunted House where Alanna was killed?"

Wade thought about it. "No. He wasn't. That was the night before Halloween. Dennis gets scared easily."

Sean knew exactly who the Cinderella Strangler was.

Lucy stared at the photocopy of the drawing that portrayed a mean-looking Dennis Barnett with

Alanna the night she was killed. Suzanne and Panetta had pushed, but he never looked like this. But it was *him;* there was no doubt.

Suzanne said, "I don't know what to think."

"He could be lying. We need to push him on the last murder," Panetta said. "He could have killed Hinkle to get his brother out of prison. Did it the same way because he'd watched his brother kill four other girls."

"No," Lucy said. "Dennis didn't kill anyone."

Panetta rubbed the back of his neck. "Ms. Kincaid, I appreciate your help, but all the evidence points to Wade Barnett and Dennis Barnett working together."

Suzanne said, "It seems so, but there's really only one way to know for certain. We interview Kirsten Benton."

"She's still unconscious," Lucy said.

"What did the doctor say about her prognosis?"

"They're changing her medication and he's optimistic."

Panetta said, "We keep both of them in lockup until we can talk to her."

"We have no reason to hold Dennis," Suzanne said.

"We have a witness."

"We'll need her to view a lineup."

Lucy only half listened to the conversation. "Suzanne, do you have the original drawing?"

"It's in the evidence room at my headquarters."

"Was it done in pencil?"

"Um, charcoal is pencil, right?"

"Charcoal was in the lungs of the first victim. Charcoal and gum." Lucy pulled out her phone and did a quick search. Suzanne rose from her chair and paced, her hands rubbing the back of her neck. "Gum is a component of charcoal pencils used for drawings."

"That's it," Suzanne said. "That's the personal connection. I didn't see it before, but it makes complete sense. The final piece of the puzzle."

"What is?" Panetta asked.

"That drawing—the artist is Whitney Morrissey. She was at the Haunted House party in Harlem. She's Alanna Andrews's cousin."

"Hold it," Panetta said. "Are you saying a woman killed these girls?"

Lucy nodded. "It fits everything I said before."

"But what you said also fits Dennis Barnett."

"Yes, but he wasn't jealous of Wade's girlfriends. He cared about Alanna in particular, and he saved Kirsten. Go ask him about Whitney."

Suzanne walked into holding and saw Dennis Barnett in the corner, terrified. She told the guard to get him out.

He leaned toward her and said, "I don't like it here."

"I have one more question. Do you know Whitney Morrissey?"

Dennis wrinkled his nose. "Yes."

"How?"

"She's one of Wade's girlfriends. She doesn't like me."

"Is your brother still dating her?"

"No. Wade heard her say mean things about me. He broke up with her. Then he met Alanna and was happy."

"Did Whitney do anything to Wade? Threaten him?"

Dennis shook his head. "She told him she was going to kill herself. But she didn't. She called him all the time. He changed his number. Then she came to Charlie's apartment for Wade's birthday in September and made Charlie so mad that he took away the CJB grant he'd given her."

"Grant?"

"For art. Charlie says 'cause we have a lot of money we need to give a lot of it away. I never knew our dad because I was a baby when he died, but he loved art so Charlie gives money to artists."

Dennis glanced back at the holding cell. "Please don't make me go back in there."

"You don't have to. I'm going to have a police officer take you home. But Dennis, no matter what, don't leave your house until you hear from me, okay?"

He crossed his heart with his index finger. "I promise."

THIRTY

"Tell your boyfriend to stay far away from me," Suzanne said to Lucy as they pulled up in front of Whitney Morrissey's Brooklyn apartment.

Suzanne had wanted to throttle Sean for talking to Wade Barnett, but then she'd have to take on a battle with the Washington Field Office and her liaison with Rikers. That her suspect wasn't guilty meant squat—Sean had interfered with a federal murder investigation and was still in hot water with her.

"He's at the hospital with Kirsten and her mother," Lucy said.

"Tell me you didn't know what he was up to," Suzanne growled.

"I didn't."

"I'll call you up when we secure the apartment."

Suzanne met Panetta outside the building. He said, "She's either not in the apartment or not answering the door. I have officers at each exit."

"I'm ready."

Two NYPD officers followed Suzanne and Panetta up the stairs to Whitney Morrissey's loft apartment. Suzanne knocked on the door. "Whitney, it's Suzanne Madeaux with the FBI. Remember me? We need to talk." She waited. "Whitney, open the door."

There were no sounds of movement, but they proceeded with caution. Panetta nodded to the officer to unlock the door with the master key they'd retrieved from the property manager. It worked one lock, but not the other.

"She has to make this difficult," Panetta mumbled and called the locksmith waiting downstairs.

Five minutes later, they were inside Whitney's apartment.

The officers searched the two-room apartment and quickly ascertained that Whitney wasn't inside.

The living area was as Suzanne remembered it: bright, airy, with art everywhere. She put on gloves and walked through, not seeing anything that struck her as odd. Whitney's art was truly exceptional. She stopped in front of a large, incredibly detailed charcoal drawing of a street scene: a row of town houses on a tree-lined street, people walking, a hot-dog vendor on the corner.

What had been the tipping point in her obsession with Wade Barnett, turning her from stalker to killer? That he was sleeping with other women? That his brother had pulled her art grant? Or that Barnett was sleeping with her cousin, Alanna?

"Suzanne." Panetta motioned for her to come into the bedroom.

She stopped in the doorway. She couldn't speak. She'd never seen anything like this—no level of obsession came even close.

One wall was covered with corkboard on which hundreds of drawings were pinned. But it was the subject matter that was so disturbing: image after image of Wade Barnett and Whitney Morrissey.

Most of the drawings were of Wade. Some were

just his face; others looked almost like photographs, with Wade sitting in a coffee shop by the window, the perspective from across the street. Or Wade at Yankee Stadium cheering. Or Wade at a party. There were other people in the pictures as well, but they were indistinct compared to Wade, who seemed to have a light shining on him.

Then there were the drawings of Wade and Whitney, most of them highly erotic. Suzanne would have admired the level of attention and detail if the whole scene weren't so deeply disturbing.

His face was everywhere, in all sizes. On every wall and surface. She looked around the room, and noticed something painted on the ceiling. She walked over to the bed and looked up. Whitney had painted a portrait of Wade Barnett over her bed.

Calling Whitney Morrissey sick seemed both obvious and a gross understatement.

"We need to call in my ERT unit," Suzanne said. "They're waiting outside."

"And you should probably call in Ms. Kincaid," Panetta said, looking at Whitney's slanted art desk. He'd turned on the small lamp that cast a bright light over the surface.

A sketchbook was open to the first page: a familiar image, not just because it was Wade, but because it was Wade and Alanna at the Yankees game, the same photo that had been published in the newspaper. Except for one stark difference.

Alanna's features had been exaggerated to the point of being monstrous. Her large eyes were made larger and off-center; her long nose had been drawn longer, with a hook at the end; the hand that had rested on Wade's shoulder had grown warts and hairs. Her hair, which had been blown out by the wind, was now snakes, all looking to attack Wade. Every detail was so perfect, yet grotesquely twisted.

"There's more," Panetta said, turning the page. It was Erica Ripley, behind the counter where she worked, talking to Wade. Out of her mouth flowed bile that dripped onto the counter.

Suzanne had seen a lot of tragedy in the ten years she'd been an FBI agent. She'd even seen a dead body when she was a kid, something that had had a lasting impact on her. But somehow, the twisted art of Whitney Morrissey disturbed her on a far deeper level. Blood, violence, murder—Suzanne understood the basic dark side of human nature. But the vicious mind of an obsessed killer who used her talent to distort reality into something so perverse it became a scene from a horror movie? Suzanne was unusually shaken.

She and Panetta stepped out of Whitney's bedroom and already she breathed easier. She called Andie, her head ERT. "We're ready for your team, and Lucy Kincaid."

Sean talked to the NYPD guard at length before he was comfortable enough to leave Kirsten under his watch.

Evelyn and Trey were taking turns sitting with her. She'd responded to the new antibiotics, awakening for the first time since she'd been admitted right after Evelyn arrived. Now the doctors were scheduling surgery to repair the damage to her feet and remove glass and rocks that had become embedded under her skin. Kirsten would be moving to a private room tonight.

Sean stepped into the room and told Evelyn he was leaving, but that the guard would be on the door until Whitney Morrissey was arrested.

Evelyn rose, tears in her eyes, and hugged him. "Thank you, Sean."

"You should thank Trey. He's the one who went from hospital to hospital until he found her."

"I'm just so happy to have her back. I'm going to take her back to California. New start. Go to college. Try and get my life together so Kirsten can have her own life, too."

"I'm glad."

Sean was about to leave when he saw Trey sitting in a plastic chair in the hall, his head in his hands. Sean sat next to him, put a hand on one shoulder. "You're tired. Maybe you should go back to the motel and sleep a couple hours."

He shook his head. "I just don't know what to do now. I love her. I don't want to go back to the way it was."

"It'll never be the way it was." Sean wasn't one to be giving advice—until Lucy, he'd never gotten past the superficial stage in any relationship. But if he had learned anything in the six weeks he and Lucy had been together, it was that he'd become a better person. He needed Lucy, and he'd do whatever it took to make her happy.

"We've all made mistakes, but what matters is who you are inside. You're a good man, Trey."

Evelyn stepped out and waved to Trey. "She's awake again and wants to see you."

Trey rubbed his wet eyes and smiled. "Thank you, Sean." He followed Evelyn back into Kirsten's room.

Sean wished he could be more elated at the good news that Kirsten was alive and would survive her ordeal, but he knew she was going to have a long, tough road ahead of her. Physically, she'd heal. But the emotional and psychological damage of her online activities, coupled with finding her friend dead and being the target of a serial killer—those would take much longer to fade.

But Kirsten *was* safe, and Sean took heart in that.

He left the hospital and drove to Whitney Morrissey's Brooklyn apartment, where the police were serving their warrant. Lucy had sent him a message thirty minutes ago that Whitney was gone, but that there was ample evidence of her guilt.

He pulled up behind an NYPD police car and parked. He was stopped by a patrolman as he tried to walk down the sidewalk, and waved to Suzanne, who was standing in front of Morrissey's building. She pretended to ignore him.

Sean knew she was furious with him for talking to Wade Barnett, but they'd saved time in getting the information, and he hadn't screwed up her investigation. However, he decided not to mention that to her because it would probably irritate her even more.

He didn't see Lucy. "Officer, I'm expected," he said.

The cop didn't budge. "Sure."

"Agent Madeaux and Detective Panetta."

The officer looked over his shoulder. "They're in conference. You can wait."

Fortunately, it had stopped raining, but it was cold and everything was wet.

He walked a few feet away and called Suzanne with his cell. He watched her look at her phone, then across the street at him, then pocket it.

He hung up and dialed again. On the third try, she answered, her eyes on him.

"I'm sorry," he said.

"No you're not."

"Okay, I'm not sorry. But let me through anyway."

"I don't know how Lucy puts up with you. You're really annoying."

"And handsome and charming and I drive a cool car."

He saw her smile, but she quickly hid it. "You owe me big-time for not slapping you with a misdemeanor."

"The paperwork wouldn't be worth it."

She hung up on him. For a moment he thought she really wasn't going to let him through, but then a detective approached and said, "Mad Dog said you can go upstairs if you wear gloves, don't touch anything, and stay out of her way."

"Mad Dog?" Sean took the latex gloves the cop handed him.

The detective grinned. "She's something else. Google her when you get home."

Sean walked up the stairs to the third-floor apartment. He found Lucy in the bedroom with Andie Swann, the head ERT. They were cataloguing drawings.

Lucy had emailed him a heads-up about the shrine to Wade Barnett in Whitney's bedroom, but he wasn't quite prepared for the sheer volume of drawings, or the painting on the ceiling.

"A psychotic Michelangelo?" he said.

Lucy glanced over her shoulder. She was in her cool, professional mode. Her face was blank and serious, her eyes dark, intelligent, and observant. He'd seen her like this before. She closed off her emotions so completely she was almost like an android. He didn't like it, even though he knew it was for self-preservation. He much preferred the Lucy who'd made love to him with heart and passion last night.

It was a sudden revelation, striking him as if God himself had put the knowledge in his head with the force of lightning. Lucy needed him to save her from herself. She wanted this life fighting the bad guys and saving the innocent, and she was so good at it, Sean would never expect her to walk away. But the violence, the intensity of the work, the inhumanity of the psychopaths she understood in ways even Hans Vigo couldn't, would kill her spirit until she wasn't able to shed the robotic shell she erected when she was working. He'd seen her shields go up in a fraction of a second, and it took hours—sometimes days—to bring them down.

In some ways, Lucy was a lot like his oldest brother. Sean barely knew Kane. A lifelong soldier, he'd been a mercenary in South America for at least the last fifteen years. He was hard as a rock, cold, and calculating. Sean never remembered him smiling or relaxing. He was always on alert, always at attention. He'd taken it upon himself and his team of dedicated men to rescue Americans kidnapped for ransom out of the country; he fought human trafficking in the

trenches, sometimes as brutally as those who bought
and sold human beings. If Kane had any humanity
left, Sean hadn't seen it, except in the cause he was
fighting.

Lucy had that same capacity: to close herself off so
completely, to shut down her own emotions, in order
to do a job few people wanted and few people did
well. Like Kane, she was a mercenary, but instead of
doing it for money or a political cause, she did it for
justice. She didn't have to be in this killer's obscene
bedroom helping the FBI gather evidence that they
hoped would lead to Whitney Morrissey's capture.
But Lucy was here because she could help. She
wanted justice for the victims as much as she wanted
Morrissey stopped simply because it was the right
thing to do, and she had the skills to do it. And maybe
deep down, she had to do it to give her past, and her
future, purpose.

Sean had to provide her a wall of protection so she
could let down her shields and be truly happy, truly
free, when she wasn't working. She needed to feel safe
and loved every day, every night, so she could work
these hard cases and not lose her empathy, or her humanity.

He walked behind her, touched her lightly on her
back, kissed her hair. He looked at the sketchbook
Andie and Lucy were going through. On the page was
Wade Barnett, naked, being pulled by ugly witches
with warts on their faces and boils on their backs.

"Well, and here I thought Whitney loved him in a
sicko kind of way."

Lucy shot him a glance. "Look at the faces."

He did, repulsed by the realism; then he saw what Lucy meant. "That's Jessica. And Kirsten. And Alanna—who are the others? There are nine."

"When we show this to Wade Barnett, he'll confirm that he slept with or had an online sexual relationship with all these women through the *Party Girl* site."

"How long has she been stalking him?" Sean asked.

Andie said, "The first entry in her journal is dated two and a half years ago."

"Whitney transferred from a small college in Connecticut to NYU," Lucy said. "Her first day on campus she bumped into Wade coming out of her advisor's office. She dropped her purse and he helped her pick everything up. She fixated on him."

"Because he acted like a gentleman?"

"I need to go through her journal in more depth," Lucy said, "but from what I read, she learned everything she could about him and his family. I don't know when they actually started dating, but it was months, maybe a year, after that initial meeting. I doubt Wade even remembers it."

"Why start killing these women now?"

"Before Alanna, Whitney didn't personally know any of Wade's girlfriends," Lucy said, slipping into her psychoanalytic role so smoothly that it disturbed Sean. "Before Wade started sleeping with Whitney, she considered other women her competition. She would be prettier, more talented, kinder, not as clingy, more attentive—whatever it was she thought Wade wanted. Wade played around; he wasn't serious about any of the women he slept with."

Sean was distinctly uncomfortable, but he didn't

think Lucy noticed. He hoped she didn't. Before he'd met her, he was a lot like Wade. Not the wild parties or drugs or cybersex, but Sean had a different girlfriend every couple of months. He broke the relationships off smoothly; in fact he was the master of easy splits. He didn't want to look at that fact too closely; Lucy's brother Patrick was right about his lack of commitment.

Lucy went on. "But after Wade became involved with Whitney, everything changed. Now it was her responsibility to make him happy. I'm sure Wade would agree with my assessment—Whitney was the perfect girlfriend at first. *Too* perfect. She would do anything he wanted, but because she is at her core insecure, she would need constant reassurance that he wanted to be with her. She wouldn't trust him, so she would follow him. She would have caused at least one scene between Wade and another woman, and that's likely when he realized she was obsessed. *He* wouldn't have called her obsessed. He would have said she was clingy or demanding, but there would have been some public scene that had him breaking it off."

"And she still followed him?"

"Yes. I don't think there have been many days she hasn't at least caught a brief glimpse of Wade. At some point, I'm betting while he was drunk, he slept with her again, giving her hope, convincing her that he truly loved her, but all the other women in his life were the problem. It was the faceless women that kept Wade from committing to her."

"But Alanna was her cousin," Andie said.

"And that was the stressor. I suspect that Whitney

knew about the *Party Girl* website. She stalked him—
she would have checked out his computer, read his
email, probably knew the password for his voice mail
and checked that regularly. But the women Wade had
cybersex with weren't real."

"Because they were on the Internet," Sean said.

"Right. They could have been anyone and anywhere. Whitney could make up fantasies about who
they were, but they weren't a direct threat to her."

"I don't understand how she knew the identities of
the girls on *Party Girl*," Andie said.

"If she had his passwords," Lucy said, "it would
have been easy to log into his profile and see everyone
he chatted with."

"But when did it turn physical?" Andie asked.

"We'll have to ask Wade. Maybe he suggested to
one or more of the girls that they come visit him in
New York. We know from analyzing the patterns of
sexual predators that they first work their victims online. Eventually, photos and videos don't satisfy them
and they escalate. Wade isn't a rapist. I don't see anything in his psyche that he was a predator, but it's the
same escalation. Wade was no longer satisfied with
cybersex, so he asked if they wanted to meet in person. Except for Kirsten, who was seventeen, they
were all his peers, college-aged girls—no one gets
hurt."

The way Lucy said it, Sean knew she didn't believe
that no one was hurt in the sex games Wade and the
others were playing.

"But throw in a psychopathic stalker fixated on
Wade, and suddenly, everyone Wade slept with was at
risk. For a while, Whitney could convince herself that

Wade would come to his senses. She told herself that these girls were cruel to Wade. That they were ugly. That they wouldn't satisfy him sexually. Whatever she needed to believe that justified why he was with them instead of her. She could even pretend they were someone else, maybe even her, because she didn't know them personally."

Lucy flipped through several pages of the sketch-book and stopped on one that was clearly Alanna Andrews. It was obvious to Sean that Lucy had known exactly where it was, probably remembered every image on the pages, and he wondered how long she'd been in here working.

"Alanna killed Whitney's fantasy. Alanna was her cousin. Whitney brought her to parties, took her around New York, and I'd bet money that Alanna met Wade through Whitney. Alanna was Wade's fantasy. She was just as sexually adventurous as he was, but she was a sweet person. She genuinely liked his handicapped brother. She stood up to Wade when he got out of line. He loved her, in his own way, but he wasn't willing to give up his lifestyle. Alanna was young—they were both young—and neither realized that the parties they enjoyed were part of their problem. Wade didn't see the difference between sleeping around and the rave orgies, and Alanna didn't want to share.

"I suspect they were finding a way to get back together. According to Dennis, they were on-again/off-again. Whitney couldn't let that happen. Her own cousin took Wade from her. Her flesh and blood stole from her. Alanna fit in with the Barnetts, but Whitney didn't. The oldest brother, Charles, made that clear when he rescinded her art grant, proving in her mind that she wasn't good enough. But Alanna was? How dare she take Whitney's place as princess of the castle!"

Lucy spoke harshly, as if she knew exactly what Whitney was thinking. Then her voice went back to the well-modulated, cool analyst. "I don't think Whitney planned to kill Alanna. She saw her at the party, and fought with her. Verbally, because there were no serious bruises on the body. She had her portfolio with her—that's why she had the bag with the charcoal residue in it. I don't know why she was carrying her portfolio. Maybe she was coming from a show, or going to draw at the party." Lucy frowned, thinking. She turned to the end of the sketchpad. The images were starkly darker.

Sean said, "That looks like Wade underwater." He reached over and turned to the page before it.

It was clearly Wade and Whitney, naked on a platform bed. Two wineglasses were spilling from their hands and their eyes were open, but blank, without detail.

"I think she was going to kill Wade that night," Lucy said. "Murder-suicide, though she'd convince herself that it was a double suicide, that he would want to die with her."

Andie cleared her throat. "Why didn't she kill Wade? Why her cousin?"

"When she confronted Alanna, she saw hope. If she killed her, Wade wouldn't have Alanna to love. In her warped mind, Whitney thought that if she took away the women Wade was screwing around with, he would come back to her." She looked at Sean. "Did he tell you if he slept with Whitney *after* Alanna was murdered?"

Sean shook his head. "I didn't ask."

"I'll need to analyze the journal more carefully because with psychotics like Whitney, we can't trust everything they write," Lucy said. "They are pathological liars. We need facts we can prove are true, and things we can prove are false, then send the journal to a handwriting expert to help weed through truth and fiction. But I think after Whitney killed Alanna, and no one suspected her, she went to Wade and they had sex. Maybe he was drunk, maybe she was convincing, I don't know. But he realized he'd made a mistake, told her as much, and so she went on to kill Erica Ripley. That was premeditated. She probably followed her for weeks, found the right time, and suffocated her."

"But then Wade didn't sleep with her again," Andie said.

"Right. I doubt he knew Erica was dead until days, weeks later. He'd have been sad, but not as upset as he was about Alanna. He ignored Whitney. They say there is a fine line between love and hate. She began to hate him and herself. The others, Heather and Jessica, she killed out of hate and blame. She blamed every woman who'd had sex with Wade—whether in person or online—and needed to destroy them. And because of his promiscuous lifestyle, she could go to the parties and see exactly who he was with."

Andie sighed, exasperated. "What a piece of work. How do these people function? She sounds like such a raving lunatic that she'd have been caught long ago."

"Psychopaths aren't usually wide-eyed crazies you can point to on the street. It's in their head, the way their brain is wired, or rewired," Lucy said. "When we dig deep into Whitney's background, I suspect we'll find several instances of impulsive behavior, particularly in her preteen years. She was probably a serious kleptomaniac. Arrested for shoplifting, both little things like candy and expensive items like jewelry. She learned to channel her impulsive behavior into drawing, but never truly conquered it. She wants something, she takes it. She wanted Wade, she got him. But she couldn't keep him like she can *things,* so she fell deeper into her psychosis."

Sean said, "Wade denies knowing the last victim, Sierra Hinkle, and I couldn't find her on the *Party Girl* site either."

"She was a random choice. When Wade was arrested, Whitney couldn't allow him to go to prison—she wouldn't be able to see him anymore. She killed the first female she found outside alone. She waited by that bulldozer until someone came by." Lucy turned to Andie. "Did you already send the journal down to your van?"

"No, it's right here."

Andie handed Lucy a leather-bound journal in a plastic bag. Lucy took it out and flipped through it, stopping in the middle. It wasn't what was written so much as the quantity, line after line of small, perfectly slanted handwriting that seemed to blend together after a while.

"Just read one page," she said to Sean. "I think you'll understand her."

"I'll never understand people like that," he said, but took the journal from Lucy.

Tuesday, August 17 Wade left his apartment at 8:36 this morning. He was wearing a white shirt. For lunch he went to Hooligan's. His tight-ass brother was there, thinks he's so noble and rich he acts like a fucking king. Wade went to the Yankees game with his retard brother. Wednesday, August 18 Wade went to the airport with his retard brother. I'm going to miss him so much I cried all night. Two weeks! I don't know where he's going, but I'll find out. How could he leave me for two weeks? Thursday, August 19 I called Wade's office and the bitch wouldn't tell me where he was. I still have a key to his apartment. I went inside, and it smelled like him. I took off my clothes and laid naked in his bed. I put my face in his pillow and remembered when we fucked like rabbits in this bed. He said I was the best. No one turns him on like me. How could he walk away from me? I went to his computer and found his schedule. He took his pet retard to Vancouver, Canada! I can't go, I don't have a passport, why did he do this to me? I can't live without him. I'm going to kill myself. He'll be sorry then. Friday, August 20 I found videos of other girls on Wade's computer. Alanna doesn't satisfy him like I do, otherwise he wouldn't be watching girls get off on dildos. I'll get him back.

"She's been writing in that book daily for over two years," Lucy said.

"She threatened to kill herself," Sean said.

"Turn to the last page."

He did. Whitney's last entry was dated yesterday.

It's hopeless. He'll never love me like I love him. I need to end this horror.

"You think she killed herself?"

"Not yet. She won't kill herself until Wade is dead."

Suzanne stepped into the room. "What did you say?"

They all turned to face Suzanne.

"Wade's in danger," Lucy said. "It's the subtext in the journal. She has several drawings in her sketchpad that show him dead or in pain. She's murderous and suicidal."

"I wish she'd just kill herself and save us all the headache," Suzanne mumbled.

"You don't mean that," Lucy said.

Sean wasn't so sure, but didn't say anything.

Lucy added, "She killed Sierra Hinkle to get Wade out of prison so she can try to convince him to run away with her. If he refuses, she'll kill him."

Suzanne said, "He's still in Rikers, and he's not leaving until his arraignment tomorrow."

"Rikers might be the safest place for him right now," Lucy said.

"I doubt I can convince Wade or his attorney to keep him in prison. But I can put him into protective custody. I'll put someone on his apartment, and we'll escort him from Rikers to his home tomorrow. Tell him to stay put until we find Whitney." Suzanne looked around the room, a pained expression on her face, then said, "Are you almost done in here?"

Andie said, "Thirty minutes."

"Did you find the missing shoes?"

"No, but we found a raincoat with a missing button."

Lucy said, "She took the shoes with her."

"Why?"

"To show Wade before she kills him."

Sean asked, "Why did she take the shoes to begin with?"

"I don't know," Lucy said. "It was impulsive, it doesn't make sense—they're big, hard to conceal, and a direct connection to the victim. Forensics can easily pair up the shoes."

"Maybe she planned on framing someone," Suzanne suggested.

"Possibly." Lucy frowned. "Except not consciously, because Alanna's murder was impulsive and unplanned."

"When I get her in interview, I'll ask her," Suzanne said with complete confidence. "The faster we wrap this up in here, the faster we can find the crazy bitch before she kills someone else."

Suzanne stood outside even though she was freezing. She wanted to forget she'd ever seen the twisted drawings in Whitney Morrissey's apartment. Foolish thought.

There were some cases that stayed with you forever. Suzanne had a few. And this case really hadn't upset her until tonight. It was the raw lunacy on display upstairs that had done it. The insanity and obsession of one woman who drew endlessly, over and over, the face of the same man. Who took her talent and skewed the drawings of women she'd killed. The journal of obsession that the shrinks like Lucy Kincaid would spend weeks analyzing and dissecting.

How could Lucy have spent *four hours* up there? After four minutes, Suzanne had been ready to puke.

She didn't need to know why Whitney Morrissey was a psychopath. She didn't care. She didn't need to see the results of her sick mind. Didn't want to. It was strange: if Suzanne had walked into Whitney's apartment and found a butchered body, she would have dealt with it far better than this.

Sean Rogan emerged from the building and headed her way. Dammit, why couldn't she have just two minutes alone to shore herself up?

"They're coming down."

"Well, congrats on finding your missing girl. You going home now?"

"Tomorrow morning. Unless you need Lucy."

She shook her head. "Unless she can look into her crystal ball and tell me where Whitney Morrissey is right this minute, she's gone above and beyond. And didn't even get paid for it."

"Is that why you do this? For the money?"

Suzanne snorted. "Yeah. For the money."

They were several feet away from the entrance to Whitney's building. Lucy was helping Andie load boxes into the van, checking the logs, making sure they had sealed everything to preserve the chain of evidence. This was going to be a complex legal case, but as soon as they found Whitney, Suzanne's role would be over until trial.

"How does she do it?" Suzanne asked Sean.

"She has me." Sean extended his hand and Suzanne

shook it. He pulled her into a hug. "Take care of yourself, Mad Dog."

He stepped back, grinning.

"Who told you? Hicks!"

Sean winked and walked over to Lucy. He put his arm around her shoulder and kissed her forehead. Suzanne felt a rush of jealousy. Not because Lucy had Sean, but because Suzanne had no one.

She turned, blinking back tears, and called her cop friend Mac.

"Hey, you want to get a bite to eat?"

"It's midnight. I'm on duty at eight."

"Sorry, I just got off."

"Tomorrow, okay?"

"Sure."

She hung up and looked back at Sean and Lucy. He walked her across the street to his car and opened the passenger door for her. Then he got into the driver's side and drove away.

She was going to miss them both.

THIRTY-ONE

Wade Barnett's arraignment Monday morning lasted ten minutes. He was released on his own recognizance. His attorney agreed to all terms: If Barnett cooperated with federal and local authorities in the capture and prosecution of Whitney Morrissey, all charges would be dropped.

Suzanne drove Wade to his apartment. After the arraignment, she had told him what they'd discovered in Whitney's apartment, but she wasn't surprised that he had more questions.

"How long has she been stalking me?" he asked.

"We're still processing evidence. Over two years."

"Years?" He frowned. "I started dating Whitney a little over a year ago, around Thanksgiving. I'd known her casually before that. Was she stalking me *before* then?"

"It appears so."

He sat in the passenger seat of the sedan and stared straight ahead. "It's my fault," he said quietly.

"No, it's not. Give yourself a break."

Actually, Suzanne blamed herself. She hadn't slept all night, thinking about what she could have done differently. She had been so focused on looking for a male killer, she hadn't even considered the alternative.

She'd have to live with it.

Wade said, "I knew Whitney was a wacko, but I didn't think she was dangerous. I ignored her behavior, excused it; I just didn't think she'd hurt anyone. I'm such an asshole."

Suzanne didn't argue. "Maybe you are, but you also have a brother who looks up to you and thinks you're special."

Tears welled in Wade's eyes. "I can't believe he had to go through this."

"If I were you, I'd fire that attorney of yours. He wasn't a good advocate for your brother."

"My mother hired him."

"Well, I'm just saying, he gave Dennis bad advice, and while it all worked out, I wouldn't want that prick involved in my affairs." She paused. "No pun intended."

"How's Ashleigh—I mean, Kirsten?" Wade asked.

"She's going to be okay. She's alive." Suzanne glanced at Wade as they stopped at a light. "You told me you didn't have sex with her. Was that a lie because she's underage?"

"I wasn't lying, we never did it. But—we had this thing going online. You know."

He didn't have to spell it out. It seemed that Whitney Morrissey considered any woman a threat to her fantasy world with Wade Barnett—women he physically had sex with and women he had cybersex with. The depth of her obsession was bordering on insane—but Suzanne wouldn't call her crazy, no matter what she thought of the killer's behavior. Whitney knew exactly what she was doing when she killed those five young women, and she would have to answer for those crimes.

She turned onto Central Park West toward Wade's apartment. "Off the record, Wade, what possessed you to start up the *Party Girl* website?"

"I was just out of college, went to England for the summer and hung out with a friend of mine who'd graduated the year before. Charlie has control over the Barnett Family Trust. I've always resented that I'm on an allowance, and Charlie is a tightwad. It seemed like a legitimate opportunity to make money—sort of Facebook for horny college guys. We sold ads, made a small bundle." He shook his head. "I didn't think there was anything really wrong with it."

"I'm the last person to cast judgment on anyone, but let me suggest that you steer clear of the online sex trade. You can lose control real quick."

"I just didn't think about it."

"Most people don't. Just—think twice next time, okay? You're not the same man you were two years ago."

"I'm not even the same man I was last week."

While Sean went to check out Monday morning, Lucy sat at the small hotel room desk and called Hans Vigo to fill him in on the details of the Whitney Morrissey investigation. She told him what they'd discovered in her apartment, and concluded with, "She takes obsession to a whole new level. Maybe you've seen such pathology, but this was a first for me."

"It's quite extreme. The path she's on—she's going to go for Wade Barnett, you know that."

"Yes. Agent Madeaux put a guard on his apartment."

"Good. Keep him under close watch. You might want to suggest to Agent Madeaux that she hide her agents, so Whitney doesn't think anyone is sitting on him."

"Bait?"

"I didn't say leave him unprotected, but if Whitney fails to see the agents, she'll get reckless and it may be easier to catch her."

"Or it could put innocent people in danger," Lucy said.

"There's always that risk, but with Wade out of prison her priority will be to make contact with him. She was careless with Sierra Hinkle, and she's going to get more careless—and more dangerous—until she's stopped."

"How was she careless with the last victim? Same M.O., no witnesses."

"From what you told me earlier, the victim was found shortly after the murder, while the previous victims were discovered hours to days later. In addition, there was physical evidence left at the scene that the crime scene investigators didn't have before—a button and fabric from a trench coat, correct?"

"That's what it looked like," Lucy said. "We found a matching coat at Whitney's apartment."

"Whitney's going to be extremely frustrated that her plans have been stymied," Hans said.

"Suzanne also had someone check on Dennis Barnett, the younger brother."

"Smart. I don't know that she'd go after Wade's

younger brother, but if she thinks she can get to Wade through him, she might try."

"How could we have prevented this?" she asked Hans.

"I don't understand what you mean."

"In the beginning, what could have been done differently after the first murder so the other four women wouldn't have had to die?"

"That's a destructive game to play, Lucy," Hans said. "I think the primary problem was the crime scene itself. Drugs, alcohol, unlawful trespassing, hidden areas. Easy for someone to slip in and out unnoticed. And because of the setting—outdoors for most of the victims—there is contamination of evidence. Difficult scenes to process. To be honest, I think the first murder was handled poorly from the beginning. I'm not casting blame on the local police, but it should have come out earlier that Barnett had dated the victim."

"Then the police would have looked at him earlier. He would have been a suspect." Then Lucy realized what Hans meant. "And he would have been aware, so he might have taken Whitney more seriously."

"But again, neither of us were there, and if we were, we would only have had the witness statements to go on. If no one mentioned Alanna's ex-boyfriend, then there was nothing for the police to follow up on."

"Secrets are truly dangerous," Hans continued. "Are you on your way home?"

"We're leaving at ten. Miss the traffic both leaving New York and getting back to Washington." She looked out her window from which, if she stood just right, she could see Central Park. The traffic sounds were soothing, far better than the total silence. She was going to miss New York.

"I made a few calls, Lucy."

She didn't have to ask what for.

"And?" Did she really want to know?

"One person on the panel was emphatic that you not be hired. The other two voted to approve the application. But it has to be unanimous."

"Do you know the person?"

"Yes. You won't change her mind. She should have recused herself from the panel."

There had been only one female agent on the panel. "I didn't know any of the agents."

"No, but one of them had worked with Fran Buckley and is still friendly with her. There are some people in the Bureau who don't like the fact that you helped put a former FBI agent in prison. One of them was on the hiring panel."

Lucy was stunned. She'd expected to be rejected because of what happened with Adam Scott, the fact that she'd killed him while he was unarmed. But it was the role—a minor role—she'd had in putting Fran Buckley in prison that had sabotaged her chances?

"Lucy, I hope you'll appeal the decision. If you do, you'll have a new panel. I promise, it will be fair."

Did she want to? Was this still what she wanted?

"Hans, I didn't trust my instincts on the Cinderella Strangler case. My gut told me the killer was a woman, but when I gave my analysis, Dennis Barnett fit the profile as well. He was dragged in for questioning and had a tough time. If I had only stood my ground—"

"Nothing would have changed. Dennis Barnett fit the profile. Until you sit down with a suspect, until you dig deep and understand their psyche, you never know who is capable of murder and under what circumstances." Hans paused, then added, "I read your report. You said everything you needed to, except a conclusion. Your profile was there, but you didn't delineate it. Why?"

"I'm not a profiler. I'm not even an FBI agent."

"But you can be. Both. It's your decision, Lucy. Do you want it enough to fight for it?"

"When I was in Whitney's room," Lucy said, "I mentally stepped back. I can't explain it any other way. It's like my personality wasn't in the room, only Whitney's. I looked at the world through her eyes. In her drawings, everything was perfect—in fact, too perfect. So when she distorted the faces, it was both beautiful and hideous," Lucy said quietly, "Suzanne and the others didn't have the same reaction that I did. There aren't many of us, are there?"

"No, Lucy, there aren't. I'm happy to hear that you can separate yourself from the scene. That's not easy to do."

"I didn't even try. It just—happened. I'll appeal the FBI panel's decision. And if I don't get in, I'll be okay. I've put it in perspective."

"I'm pleased. And good work on the case. I'll see you when you get back to Washington."

Lucy hung up and walked to the window. The sky

had lightened, some blue showing. She felt relieved with her decision.

Lucy's cell phone rang. "I don't have a lot of time," Suzanne said without introduction, "but I wanted you to know I had NYPD check on Dennis and all is well on Staten Island. They're driving by every hour. We have Wade secure. We'll find the bitch."

"Good," Lucy said.

"Come back and visit sometime. I'll show you the city."

"I'd like that. Let me know when you arrest Whitney."

"Absolutely." Suzanne hung up.

Sean returned to the room with coffee for Lucy. She smiled. "You didn't have to get me coffee."

He kissed her. "Yes I did. Who was that?" He sipped his own drink.

"Suzanne. What's that?" She gestured to his cup. Sean didn't like coffee.

"Hot chocolate. Are you ready?"

"Yes. I spoke to Hans. I'm going to appeal."

"I knew you would."

"You did?"

He nodded. "Lucy—"

"We'd better go now or we'll be stuck in traffic when we hit the Beltway."

"I know, but I need five minutes."

His serious tone made her anxious. "What's wrong?"

"Saturday night."

She sat down heavily on the sofa. What had she done wrong? Or maybe his *I love you* had just slipped out and he regretted it. She should feel relieved, but instead she felt cold. "It's okay," she said. "I understand."

He sat down next to her. "What do you think you understand?"

"We all sometimes say things we don't mean, especially in the heat of the moment, and it's not going to change anything." But it would. It would change everything. Because she could no longer trust him.

"Stop it," Sean said. He put his chocolate down, took her coffee from her grip, and placed it on the glass table. He squeezed her hands and said, "I love you. We're not in the throes of passionate sex and I can still state emphatically that I love you."

Butterflies flitted in her stomach. She opened her mouth to tell him she loved him, too, but nothing came out.

He kissed her. "Shh." He rested his forehead on hers. "This is about the condom. Or that I didn't have it on. And I have no excuse. I've never forgotten, not with you or anyone. And I'm not ready to be a dad. I don't know if I'll make a good dad, but if you're pregnant, don't expect me to walk away. Understand? Because I love you, and I'll take the challenge, and—"

Lucy squeezed back tears and turned her head.

"What? Did I say something wrong? Luce—"

"I can't get pregnant. I can't have a baby."

Sean wasn't expecting that answer. He didn't know what to say.

"After the attack seven years ago, there was some internal damage. I had surgery. The doctor couldn't save my uterus."

She'd lived with this truth for years, but hadn't thought about it. When she was eighteen, having children had seemed so far away and unreal that it hadn't affected her, not with everything else she'd had to deal with at the time. And then, she'd been so angry and hurt that she couldn't even comprehend raising a family in such a violent and brutal world.

But now, for the first time, she felt a wave of loss. She wasn't ready for a family now—but even so, she'd never have the chance to have one in the future.

"I'm sorry," she said.

Sean turned her face to his. "Don't tell me you're sorry." He kissed her hard, holding her chin, his hand shaking. "Just, don't." His voice cracked. "I love you. That will never change." He kissed her again.

Lucy held on to Sean. With him, she felt not only strong enough to handle anything, she knew she'd be okay in the end. He was a rock, he didn't budge, he gave her exactly what she needed even before she knew that she needed anything. In Whitney's apartment, he had been an unmoving tower of strength, but didn't coddle her or try to protect her from the cruel truths in Whitney's drawings or writings. He understood without her telling him that any personal emotions would have undone her, so he let her do what had to be done. And afterward, he was still there, ready to listen or just hold her hand.

"You're pretty amazing, Sean Rogan," she said.

"So I've been told many times." He kissed her again, then pulled her to her feet and gave her a tight hug. "You're pretty incredible yourself, Lucy Kincaid."

"So I've been told," she said with a smile.

They stood there in the middle of the hotel room holding each other, neither wanting to let go. Lucy felt a peace she couldn't voice, but didn't have to.

Several minutes later, she kissed him. "We really should go."

They grabbed their bags and left the room. In the elevator to the lobby, Lucy said, "Is there a route home that goes over the water instead of under it?"

"Already programmed into my GPS."

"Thank you."

"The route goes through Staten Island."

"Okay."

"You were upset last night about Dennis Barnett."

"The interview was hard on him, and he didn't have anyone to support him afterward. And now Wade is out of prison, but Dennis can't go see him. And then there's Whitney Morrissey still out there."

"Want to stop by? Check up on him?"

"Suzanne sent NYPD over. He's fine."

"Do you want to stop by?"

"Do we have time?"

"We'll make time."

Wade tried to focus on an ESPN interview with the Yankees coach about the upcoming season, but even baseball couldn't get his mind off Whitney and all the women she'd killed.

He didn't care what the FBI agent said; he blamed himself. He had been so damn selfish and blind to who she really was, but thinking about her behavior now, all the signs had been there.

He'd been a fool to sleep with her after Alanna died. He did stupid things when he was drunk.

His cell phone rang. He almost answered it, but Agent Hansen shook her head and took the phone from him.

"Wade Barnett's residence." A moment later, she handed it to him. "He says he's your brother Dennis."

Wade smiled and took the phone. "Denny. Hey, I'm glad you called me back."

"Whitney is here and she hurt Mom," Dennis whispered. "She wants you to come right now with no one else."

Another voice came on the line. "Come alone, no police, or your retarded brother will die."

Dennis whimpered on the phone.

Wade discreetly glanced at Agent Hansen. She was looking at the view from his window. How much attention was she paying to his conversation? "Sure," he said cheerily. "I can do that."

Whitney gushed, "I knew you would come. I love you so much, Wade. It hurts how much I love you. Hurry."

The line went dead.

Wade looked around his twelfth-floor apartment. How was he going to get out without the Feds knowing? The only way was the fire escape, but could he get out without attracting attention?

He had an idea.

"Okay, Denny," he said into the dead phone. "I'll talk to the FBI and I'm sure they'll let you visit. I'll call you back. Love you, too." He put down his phone. "Agent Hansen, do you think my brother could come over for dinner tonight?"

She said, "I don't see why not, but I'll clear it with Suzanne when she calls in."

"Great. Do you mind if I put on some music?"

"Not at all."

THIRTY-TWO

Sean turned into the exclusive Staten Island neighborhood of Todt Hill, where Dennis lived with his mother. Lucy hadn't expected the sedately grand homes mixed with trees and gentle hills so close to the towering buildings of Manhattan, and the sprawling development in Brooklyn. She liked it here.

"Thanks for avoiding the tunnel."

"It was truly a feat of engineering."

"It's just plain creepy. Aren't you scared of anything?"

"*Scared?*" he said with mock indignation.

"Bad choice of words. You know what I mean."

"Prison. I didn't like the door closing and locking behind me at Rikers and I was even free to leave."

"Most normal people are scared of prison."

He stopped in front of a multilevel house surrounded by trees on a deep, narrow lot near the end of a cul-de-sac. He looked at her. Though his voice was light, his sentiment wasn't. "The only thing I fear is losing you, Princess."

Lucy's heart flipped. She leaned over and kissed him. "You're not going to."

They got out of the car and walked up the short stone path that led to an elaborate curving staircase.

The main entrance was on the second floor, with the first floor housing the five-car garage. Sean rang the bell.

Lucy asked, "Does Kirsten want to see Dennis?"

"After her surgery. She believes he saved her life, and he may well have."

"Good. Telling Dennis that should help him put this whole mess behind him."

Lucy saw movement on the other side of the leaded, beveled glass door. "I saw someone down the hall, just a shadow through the glass."

Sean rang the bell again, taking a slightly protective stance half a step in front of Lucy.

Still, no answer.

"Maybe it was a dog," Lucy said. "A big dog."

"That doesn't bark? Probably his mother."

"Why wouldn't she answer?"

"The police may have told them to stay indoors, not answer the door, any number of security measures," Sean said. "I'll check out the grounds."

"I'll call Dennis," Lucy said.

They walked down the stairs and Lucy stood next to the garage while Sean walked around to the back of the house. She dialed Dennis's cell phone, but on the fifth ring his voice mail came on.

"Hi Dennis, this is Lucy Kincaid, remember me? I'm a friend of Kirsten's. I just wanted to check if everything is okay at your house. Please call me back, okay?" She left her number and hung up. She stared at the house, filled with a nagging sense of dread.

Sean returned. "We have a big problem. Whitney Morrissey is here."

"You saw her?"

"No, but she made her mark. On the wall of one of the rooms is a life-sized drawing of Wade Barnett."

"I'll call Suzanne," Lucy said.

"Let's go to the car. I have an idea."

They got into the car and Sean circled the cul-de-sac and drove past the Barnett house. If Whitney was watching, she'd see them leave.

Lucy called Suzanne.

"Lucy, what's up? I'm in the middle of a crisis."

"Something's wrong at Dennis Barnett's house. Sean and I are here, no one's answering the door or phone, and Sean saw one of Whitney's signature drawings through a window."

"Shit!" She talked to someone in the background. "That must be why Wade took off down the fire escape. I'll call the locals, because I can't get there in less than thirty."

"Tell them to steer clear of the house. No sign of cops. If Whitney's in there—"

"I know. Two, maybe three, possible hostages. You and Sean keep your eye on the house, but don't engage."

"When did Wade leave?"

"Between fifteen and twenty minutes ago. He didn't take his car, so he's probably in a taxi."

Lucy hung up. "She said don't engage. Wade disappeared."

"If Whitney's inside, she'll kill Dennis as soon as Wade shows up."

"If she hasn't killed him already."

Sean turned the car around again and parked two houses up from the Barnetts', around the bend in the cul-de-sac, out of sight. "We'll cut through the neighbor's side yard and enter the Barnett property from the rear," Sean said. "You make your way around to the far side of the garage—you won't be seen from the house, but you'll be able to watch for Wade. Keep him out of the house. I'll find a way inside and assess the danger."

Lucy didn't like that idea. "Be careful, Sean. Whitney is volatile, and won't care who she kills."

"I'm more concerned about you. She seems to hate women more than men."

Lucy considered that. "Women are her adversaries, but so is Dennis because he takes Wade's attention away from her."

"Our goal is to secure the house until the police arrive." He retrieved his gun from the trunk and a small pouch with tools. "If I can get Dennis or his mother out, I will." He kissed her quickly and handed her a .22 pistol strapped into an ankle holster. "Just in case."

She checked the ammo and the safety, then strapped on the holster, but she wouldn't be able to easily get to it under her jeans. She tucked the gun into the small of her back instead.

"When we get home, I'm getting you fitted for holsters," Sean said.

"I have my own gun."

"Which you didn't bring."

"I was following the law. No guns in the city."

"Tell it to the criminals."

They cut through the neighbor's yard around the back of the Barnett property. Sean motioned for Lucy to run low along a path camouflaged by neatly trimmed hedges, which would put her on the far side of the garage.

It took Lucy less than a minute to get into position. When she looked back, she couldn't see Sean anywhere. She wondered how he'd disappeared so quickly.

Near where Lucy hid there was a side door leading into the house. She checked the knob; locked. She moved to the other side so she could watch the road and the door at the same time.

How long ago had she called Suzanne? Lucy looked at her phone. Only four minutes?

An NYPD car drove slowly past the house. Lucy froze, unsure if the officer would be able to see her. The car turned around in the cul-de-sac, then went back up the road.

If Whitney was watching, would she suspect that the cops were coming for her? Were the Barnetts in greater danger?

A taxi pulled up in front of the house a minute later. Wade Barnett got out and strode up the path.

"Wade." Lucy turned toward him as he walked past her hiding spot.

He jumped. "Who are you?"

"Lucy Kincaid. Agent Madeaux is on her way."

"No! Tell her to back off." Wade rubbed his palms repeatedly on his slacks. His temples were damp with sweat.

"Don't give Whitney what she wants. She's dangerous and suicidal. She'll kill your family, then you, and then herself."

He shook his head. "She'll kill Dennis if I don't go in."

"Give the police time to get into position. They have hostage negotiators who know how to handle situations like this."

"No one can negotiate with that nutcase!"

"Shh!" Lucy glanced around. "Please trust me."

"He's my brother. He depends on me."

"Sean is trying to get inside."

"Sean Rogan? You're with him?"

She nodded. "He knows what he's doing. Trust him."

Wade was torn.

The door opened behind Lucy. She reached for her gun, but didn't draw when she saw Dennis. His head was bleeding and he was shaking. "Y-y-you have to c-come inside now," he said. "P-please." His eyes darted to the left. Lucy saw a female hand on his shoulder.

Wade pushed past Lucy and reached for his brother. Whitney peered over Dennis's shoulder. She held a gun at his neck.

"You brought one of your girlfriends?" Whitney said, with a furious glare at Lucy.

"No, I don't know who she is—"

Whitney's eyes teared and she pulled Dennis back into the house. Behind her was a long, wide hall, a laundry room beyond, and a staircase to the right.

"You're cheating on me! Again!"

"No, I'm not," Wade said. He put his palms up. "It's been over between us for a long time."

No! Lucy wanted to scream. When engaged in conversation with Whitney, Wade needed to play along with her as long as possible. It would buy time.

"It's not over!" Whitney screamed, and Dennis let out a yelp as her fingernails dug into his shoulder.

"Pretend!" Lucy ordered Wade through clenched teeth, hoping he understood.

"Where'd you pick up this little slut? In prison? Or is she a cop? You fucked a cop once, you told me."

"I'm not a cop," Lucy said. If Whitney felt threatened, it would make her even more unpredictable. Whitney had the gun, she was in charge. Whitney had to continue believing she was in complete control in order to keep her as calm and reasonable as possible. As reasonable as she could be, Lucy thought, which wasn't comforting considering her history.

If Wade cooperated, Lucy might be able to talk their way out of this, or at least get Dennis to safety. If she could get him out of the house, Sean would have to rescue only Mrs. Barnett.

Lucy considered everything she knew about Whitney. She'd read her journal. She'd studied her artwork. Lucy understood Whitney better than Whitney understood herself. But the killer didn't know that, and if Lucy remained calm and focused, she could use her knowledge to defuse the situation and give Sean and the police more time to get into place.

A hint of a shadow moved to her left. As Wade pleaded with Whitney, Lucy glanced up. Sean was on the roof.

"Let Dennis walk away and I'll come in," Wade said. He stepped forward. "Please, Whitney."

Lucy held her breath, silently pleading for Whitney to let the terrified young man go.

Lucy heard a car door slam up the street. Then another.

Whitney heard it, too.

"Inside! Now!"

"Let Dennis go—"

"Now!" Whitney screamed.

"Just let him—"

"Get in get in get in!" She shook Dennis as she screamed.

Wade stepped through the doorway as Whitney backed up. Lucy reached out. "Don't, Wade, please—" If he went in, he was as good as dead.

"You, too, you little bitch."

"She's not part of this," Wade said.

Whitney ignored Wade. She glared at Lucy and put the gun to Dennis's ear. He started crying.

Whitney pushed the barrel of the gun so hard into Dennis's ear that the sight at the end cut his lobe, which started bleeding. Her finger was on the trigger.

"You don't care about the idiot any more than I do," Whitney said to Lucy.

"You're not letting Dennis go if I walk in there?"

"No, but he can die now or he can die with everyone else."

Time. It was the only thing Lucy had to work with. She followed Wade inside.

Sean watched the scene below him. He knew she had no choice, but he didn't want Lucy in that house. *She knows what she's doing.*

But Whitney was an unpredictable psycho. Sean crawled back up the steep tile roof, wet from the recent storms. The sky was overcast, and the wind whipped around him. The roof wasn't nearly as steep as mountains Sean had scaled, but he didn't have a safety harness. He slipped once and slid two feet before he caught the edge of a tile, which dug sharply into his fingers.

"Slow down, boy," he admonished. If he fell and broke his neck he would be of no help to Lucy.

From the top, where two dormer windows led to the attic, Sean could see four police cars and two unmarked sedans up the street surrounding his GT. He didn't see Suzanne in the mix, but had her ETA pegged for at least another ten minutes. He sent her a message.

Cops not being discreet—get them to back off until SWAT arrives. Whitney has gun. Has Lucy, Wade, and Dennis hostages on main level. Barnett mother's whereabouts unknown. I'm going inside. Tell them I'm one of the good guys.

The window was locked. Sean rolled out his tools and picked up his glass-cutter. Being trained under two veterans—his brother Duke and Duke's partner, JT Caruso—had given Sean a wealth of skills most civilians didn't have.

He gently pushed in the glass at the bottom so he could pull it out in one piece. He doubted anyone downstairs would hear the breaking glass, but he wasn't taking chances. He reached in and unlocked the window. It was stiff from disuse, but eventually it opened with a screech. Sean grimaced at the noise, slipped through, and listened. He heard nothing in the house below—no shouting, no gunshots, no one running up the stairs to confront him.

His eyes adjusted to the dark, dusty room. He found a light switch, but the bulb was burned out or missing. On the far side was an opening that led to a staircase. He shined his pencil-size flashlight and found another switch. A ceiling light illuminated the stairwell and a door below.

Sean walked down along the edge of the wooden stairs hoping to diminish the sound of creaking steps. He carefully cracked open the door to assess the landing. It was the second floor, near the end of the hall. The many hallway doors were closed. When he was confident there was no one there, he stepped out, quietly closing the door behind him.

He heard a voice on the main floor below. By its panicked and shrill tone, it was Whitney.

His phone vibrated in his pocket. He checked the message.

SWAT is en route, ETA 4 min. I'm 9 min out. Talked to the lieutenant, and cops will secure and hold. Stay put.

Sean ignored the last comment. He pocketed his phone and walked down the carpeted hall to the top of a double-wide curving staircase that led to a marbled foyer below. The voice echoed.

"We could go to an island," Whitney said, sounding delusional. "Wade, we need time alone. With no one to interfere."

"Okay," Wade said. "Let's go. You and me, right now."

The voices were coming from almost directly beneath Sean. That meant they weren't near the front of the house. He sent Suzanne a message to that effect, and started down the stairs. Almost immediately he realized that if he continued, everyone in that room would be able to see him. He got on his knees and looked through the railings. The room was a den with two narrow windows looking out into the side yard and several evergreen trees.

He couldn't see Lucy or Whitney, but Wade stood next to a sofa where an unconscious older female lay. There was blood on her head.

He silently went back up the stairs, gave Suzanne the information, then checked the rest of the floor for a second staircase. He thought in a house this big there'd be another way down, but there wasn't.

He would have to take his chances.

THIRTY-THREE

Sean had seen only the art Whitney had drawn on the wall of the den, but Lucy saw that she'd been hard at work. Dozens of drawings were strewn around the room and taped on the walls. They were rough, hurried, and incomplete, without her usual meticulous attention to detail. These had a sharper, almost frantic texture to them. But the subject was still obvious: Wade Barnett.

Wade stood next to his unconscious mother lying on the couch. "Let's do it, Whitney. Right now," Wade said. "I have the money. We'll go to Martha's Vineyard. My family has a place there."

Lucy had been watching Whitney carefully. She was using Dennis as a shield of sorts because Dennis was being compliant. She kept one hand on a shoulder, and used the gun to poke him when she wanted to make a point.

Whitney was on edge, but she wasn't stupid.

"I saw the cops driving by, Wade. I told you not to call them! How could you betray me *again*?"

"I didn't tell the police."

"I don't believe your lies anymore!" she screamed. Dennis jumped and she hit him with the gun. He cried, and urine seeped through his pants down to the floor.

Lucy saw the embarrassment and horror on Dennis's face.

Whitney wrinkled her nose. "What is that smell?"

Dennis mumbled, "I'm sorry I'm sorry."

"It's okay, Denny," Wade said, taking a step toward his brother before Whitney turned the gun on him.

"Stay right there!"

"Please let him go to his room. He'll stay there, I promise."

"Your promises mean shit!" Then her voice and face softened. "It's going to be okay. I figured out the problem in our relationship. It was because on September thirteenth I told you I didn't want to go to the Yankees game."

Wade looked confused, but Lucy remembered the journal entry. It was from seventeen *months* ago. Whitney still remembered the exact day. Lucy had to get her to keep talking.

"I didn't even see you in September," Wade said.

"Yes, you did! No. The year before, remember?"

Wade's face paled. "Yes, I remember." Wade wasn't a good liar. Whitney was going back and forth too fast, from angry to calm. Lucy needed to keep her calm. Dennis was sobbing, and it was clearly grating on Whitney.

Lucy asked, "What happened that day?"

"Wade said, 'Let's go to the Yankees game.' And I said, 'I don't want to.' And he was upset and we did what I wanted, but that's where I went wrong." She turned to Wade, suddenly looking the personification of innocence. "I'll always go to the baseball games with you. That's why you fucked Alanna, right? Because she liked baseball. But you don't need her anymore because I love baseball. I know every stat of every player. Try me."

"Whitney, I don't—"

"Ask me a question!"

Lucy asked, "How many world series have the Yankees won?"

"Twenty-seven!" Whitney smiled. "The last one was 2009."

"What number was Babe Ruth?" Lucy asked. She watched the gun in Whitney's hand. That finger playing with the trigger made Lucy extremely nervous.

"Three!" Whitney said. "It's retired. And Roger Maris was number nine. Reggie Jackson was forty-four, and—"

Wade interrupted her. "Okay, I believe you."

Lucy shot him a look of frustration. There would have been nothing better than for Whitney to spend the next twenty minutes reciting baseball statistics.

Whitney frowned. "I'm so sorry."

"I forgive you."

"You don't mean it."

"Yes, I do," Wade said, dripping with exaggerated sincerity. "I forgive you for everything. For the baseball game, for killing all those women—"

Lucy tried to cut him off. "Whitney, who's the manager for the Yankees?"

But Whitney wasn't listening to her. She said, "Women? You mean those druggy whores who thought they were better than me? They tricked you. You didn't know better, didn't realize they were witches casting a spell on you. The only way to break the spell was to get rid of them."

Whitney said to Lucy, "Get me that bag." She gestured to a duffel bag on the floor near the door. Lucy hadn't noticed it before.

Lucy walked slowly over. Out of the corner of one eye she saw a flash of movement down that hall, then nothing. Sean? SWAT?

She bent and picked up the bag. It wasn't heavy. She returned.

"Empty it out."

Lucy unzipped the bag. Inside was a collection of mismatched shoes. Her stomach rolled as she turned the bag upside down and the shoes fell to the floor. Two spike heels, one black and one silver; two flip-flops, and a silver flat that matched the shoe on Sierra Hinkle's foot.

"That's what's left of those bitches," Whitney told Wade. "And you did it to them. You killed them."

Wade was overcome at the evidence of Whitney's crimes. "Whitney, what—why? Why did you kill them?"

"To save you."

"Their shoes—you're sick. You're insane."

Lucy tried to interrupt.

"Whitney, we can solve this now. Let's talk about—"

It was as if Lucy hadn't spoken. Whitney said to Wade, "I'm the only sane person here! I need you, we have to be together or I'm going to die." She kicked the pile of shoes. "They walked all over you. Used you."

Wade glanced at Lucy, eyes wide, at a loss for words.

Whitney's eyes narrowed. "Why do you keep look-ing at *her*?" She waved the gun in Lucy's direction. "How long have you been screwing her? Was she one of your *Party Girl* bimbos?"

"No, I never met her before today."

"A one-night stand?"

"No!"

Mrs. Barnett moaned from the couch and tried to get up. Wade knelt by her. "Mom, it's Wade. Are you okay?"

She didn't respond, but her eyes were open and blinking.

Lucy turned to Whitney, easing her way between Whitney and Wade. Dennis was tracking her with his eyes. She wanted to reassure him, but there was noth-ing she could say.

"Whitney, you're hurting inside, I can see it!"

She nodded. "I love him so much. I can't think of anything but him. I breathe for him. I need him."

"I see that." Lucy thought back to the journals and the repeating themes she wrote about. They boiled down to one thing: need. Whitney's sole focus was Wade, and she'd convinced herself that without him, she was no one. "Wade needs you. He's been reckless and irresponsible without you."

"I know. He was arrested for drunk driving, he lost his license, he even threw up outside the Yankees game during the playoffs last year."

"You followed me there?" Wade exclaimed.

Lucy looked at Wade and whispered through clenched teeth, "Shut up!"

Whitney let go of Dennis, who fell to the floor. She

took two steps toward Lucy and hit her on the side of the head with the gun. Lucy stumbled sideways and fell to the floor, her vision cloudy.

"Don't tell him to shut up, you fucking bitch!"

Lucy tried to get up, but the pain made her nauseous. Blood from a head wound dripped to the floor. She lay back down to gather her strength.

Dennis cried out, "Lucy!"

Whitney pulled Dennis to his knees. She held the gun to the back of his head.

As her vision cleared, Lucy saw movement by the double doors. Dark blue Nikes. Sean. She focused on breathing to dull the pain. Blood dripped on the carpet, but even minor head wounds could bleed a lot. She didn't think it was serious.

Whitney glared at her with fury. "This one's like all the other witches you fucked. Are you fucking her, Wade?"

"No."

Lucy slowly eased herself into a sitting position. Her vision started to clear.

"Whitney," Wade said, "I'm so sorry. I'm sorry I hurt you. I'm sorry I didn't see that you were suffering. How can I fix this? What can I do?"

"Love me!"

"Okay."

"You're lying!"

"What do you want from me? Whitney, give me a chance, I'm begging you! Put down the gun and I'll make everything right."

"You can't! I knew you couldn't love me if you had all those fucking sluts at your beck and call. They didn't need you like I do. Please forgive me."

Wade looked at Lucy again, lost and confused, and she nodded at him, hoping he understood she wanted him to continue to tell Whitney what she wanted to hear.

"I forgive—"

But Whitney had noticed the nonverbal exchange between Wade and Lucy, and she reddened, shaking with her rage. "You lied to me! You told me you didn't know her!"

"I don't. I met her today."

Whitney hit Dennis. "Who is she? How do you know her?"

"Lucy," Dennis squeaked.

"I'm okay," she told him, sitting up and leaning against the desk.

"Tell me!"

"My name is Lucy Kincaid, I—"

"I didn't ask you!"

Dennis said, "S-she's a p-p-p-"

"Spit it out, you idiot."

"I'm a private investigator," Lucy said.

Whitney was confused and curious. Lucy hoped the police had a plan, because she was running out of ideas. She explained. "I came to New York looking for a runaway."

She willed Wade to keep his mouth shut.

Whitney asked, "How do you know her, Dennis?"

Lucy shook her head slightly when Dennis looked at her. "I-I-I—forget."

"You are such a retard! You're the problem. Wade can't commit to me because of *you*. His stupid brother. His can't-do-shit idiot *brother*!" She hit him with the gun.

Wade took two steps and Whitney waved the gun at him. "Don't come any closer."

"Don't hurt my brother!"

"Tell him to answer the question. Dennis, how do you know her?"

Dennis didn't answer, and Lucy knew it was to protect her. She said, "I'm not a cop, but I've been helping the police."

Whitney stared at her. "How?"

"I'm working with a private investigator, but I don't have a license. I'm a criminal psychologist, helping the police."

Whitney shook her head. "A shrink? You think you could analyze me? You think you know me?"

"Yes, I do."

Whitney seemed intrigued as well as angry. Lucy hoped SWAT was in place, because she only saw this turning bad.

"Then tell me why I killed those girls."

Whitney was issuing a challenge. Lucy said, "They had Wade's attention so you killed them."

"So simplistic. You don't know me at all!"

Lucy continued quickly. "Because Wade went to bed with you after you killed Alanna, you thought he'd come back to you after you killed the others, too."

Whitney turned to Wade. "You told her about that? You said you didn't know her!"

"He didn't tell me," Lucy said, "I figured it out."

"I don't believe you!"

"You took the shoes, I think—" She didn't know.

Lucy didn't understand why Whitney took the one shoe.

Whitney laughed. "You want to know why?"

"Yes, I do," Lucy said.

"Because Alanna ran and lost her shoe. I didn't notice, but when she was dead I had to get out of there. I found her shoe on the stairs and I didn't want anyone looking for her. So I grabbed it and left. And then . . ." Her voice trailed off.

"You took the other shoes for what? Luck?"

"Yes, that's right. No one even thought I killed Alanna. Wade made love to me. It was glorious. Heaven. So the next time I made sure to do it exactly the same way."

"You killed your own cousin?" Wade said.

"She was a cheap, ugly, fucking slut."

With a growl, Wade rushed her.

Whitney jerked toward him, surprised, and her finger clenched the trigger.

The bullet hit Wade in the stomach. Blood seeped through his shirt. He staggered back several steps.

Dennis cried out. He dove toward Whitney. She backhanded him and he fell, bleeding.

Whitney turned to Wade, eyes wide and wild. "No no no!" Whitney screamed. "I love you, Wade!"

"I hate you," Wade said through clenched lips. "Go fuck yourself!"

She screamed and turned the gun on Dennis. "It's your fault!"

Sean kicked in the door, gun out, drawing her attention—and her gun—away from everyone else in the room.

A window broke. Whitney's body jerked twice.

A dark hole appeared in the back of her shirt, spreading until her whole back was a deep, dark red. Blood dribbled out the side of her mouth as she crumpled to the floor.

Silence descended as every eye in the room went to the body. It seemed to last for minutes, but when SWAT rushed the room, only seconds had passed.

"We need an ambulance!" Lucy yelled. "Wade was shot in the abdomen."

Sean was at her side when she crawled over to Wade. Dennis took Wade's hand. "You're going to be okay," Dennis said, repeating the mantra.

"Denny." Wade coughed.

Sean ripped open Wade's shirt and pressed his hands to the open wound. "Medics!" he called.

A SWAT guy knelt on one knee next to Lucy. He had a small medical bag and took out a thick pad of gauze and cotton. "I got it," he said to Sean and took over the first aid.

"Paramedics are already on site waiting for us to clear the scene. Is there anyone else in the house?"

"No," Sean said.

Lucy went over to Mrs. Barnett. "Where are you injured?"

"Head," she whispered.

Lucy inspected the wound. The cut was dry and not bleeding anymore, but her graying hair was sticky with blood. "We have a head injury here, probable concussion."

"Are you a doctor?" the SWAT medic asked.

"No, I've only had some first responder training."

Sean stared at her. "I don't think there's anything you don't know how to do."

"You could have gotten yourself shot," she said.

"But I didn't."

"Tell me you knew SWAT was in place."

"I knew they were coming."

Lucy let out a long, pent-up breath.

Sean frowned at the blood on her head. "You need medical attention."

"I'm fine." When he began to argue, she said, "Really. I just need to clean up."

"Me, too." He wiped his bloody hands on his khakis.

The paramedics brought in a stretcher and equipment. "Clear the room! Stat!"

Lucy pulled Dennis's hand from Wade's. "You have to let them do their job," she said. "Come with me." When Dennis didn't move, she said, "Let's get you cleaned up, Denny, okay?"

Wade said, "Go ahead, Denny."

He nodded, looking lost and bewildered. With tears in his eyes, he looked at the paramedic and said, "Don't let him die. He's my brother."

"Not on my watch, kid."

Lucy led Dennis past Whitney's dead body. Dennis stared at her, bewildered. Lucy wasn't going to forget today anytime soon.

Sean followed them out to the porch. Suzanne was coming up the stairs and waved. Lucy sat Dennis down on a bench and said, "You're safe here. I'm going to talk to Agent Madeaux, okay?"

He nodded, dazed. A medic came up to him. "I'm going to look at your head, all right?"

They left Dennis with the medic and met Suzanne

at the top of the stairs. "Looks like I missed all the fun," she said. "I heard Wade is down. How bad?"

"The paramedics are inside," Lucy said. "He was shot in the abdomen."

"What were you doing out here? Did you think she'd show up here?"

"I was concerned about Dennis after the interview yesterday. He was so upset. I wanted to let him talk about it if he wanted. And Sean had news for him about Kirsten. She's having surgery tomorrow and hoped to see Dennis at the end of the week. He saved her life last weekend. We wanted to tell him in person."

"At least that's one happy ending." They stepped out of the way as the paramedics brought Wade out.

"How is he?" Sean asked.

"Lucky," the paramedic said. "I think he's going to make it."

Dennis stood, wobbly.

"Whoa, son, let's sit you down," the medic said.

"I gotta go with my brother. Please."

The medic looked at Lucy, and she said, "I think he should go with him, if there's room in the ambulance."

"I'll see what I can do." He helped Dennis down the stairs.

Suzanne turned back to them. "I'll need to debrief both of you, but I'll be stuck here for a while."

"We'll stay another night," Sean said. He led Lucy over to the bench where Dennis had been sitting. "I'm getting my first-aid kit. Or I'm taking you to the hospital."

"Get the kit," she said.

Sean jogged down the stairs, stopping to talk briefly with the SWAT leader. He almost looked like one of them. Except he didn't have the big gun or the bulletproof vest. He jumped in and risked himself time and time again. That's who Sean was. He'd never let someone else suffer if he could stop it.

Suzanne sat next to Lucy. "You have your hands full with that guy."

"I sure do."

"You're lucky."

Yes, I am.

THIRTY-FOUR

Three Weeks Later

Sean pulled Lucy down the hall and into Kate's office. He quietly shut the door. Lucy barely suppressed a giggle, then forced herself to eye Sean sternly.

"It's my belated birthday dinner," she said, raising her eyebrows in mock indignation. "Don't you think everyone will notice that we snuck off?"

Sean kissed her. "I don't care." He kissed her again, drawing her lips into his, wiping the giggle from her face. She was trying to keep it light; Sean was turning it serious.

"What is it?" She didn't know why she was nervous. All she could think about was New York, and Sean telling her *I love you*. She wanted to hear it again, yet the thought of hearing it again terrified her. How could she be so confused? It wasn't as if she were debating whether to date Sean or not. She couldn't imagine her life without him, not anymore. She had twenty-five years under her belt without Sean Rogan, but the thought of walking away from him scared her almost as much as his declaration of love.

"You can't say no."

"I can't?"

"Nope, you can't, and I mean it."

She smiled, a bit nervous, but she trusted him. "Okay, yes."

"You don't know the question."

"I trust you."

He smiled slyly and she became even more nervous. "Yes to anything?"

"Sean—just spill it."

He reached into his pocket and for a split second she thought that he was going to give her a ring. That he was going to ask her to marry him. She wasn't ready for that, not yet.

He pulled out a tri-fold brochure.

"We've been talking about going away practically since we met," he said. "Now, we're going. New York didn't count. I already made reservations for the first week of May—I know, it's two months away, but I have that job in Texas and I can't get out of it. Believe me, if I could—"

"Yes."

"Yes what?"

"Sure. May sounds great."

"You didn't ask where."

"I trust you."

He smiled and drew her into his arms. "I think *'I trust you'* is your way of saying *'I love you.'*" He kissed her.

"Sean—"

"Shh. I know you love me." He kissed her again, then grinned. "Who wouldn't?"

She smiled. Maybe she did. She certainly didn't want to be with anyone else. He made her happy. Sean gave her a sense of normalcy that she hadn't had in seven long years.

And she trusted him.

The door opened. Patrick cleared his throat.

Sean put one arm around Lucy's shoulders. "What's up?"

After they'd returned from New York, Patrick had seemed to accept her relationship with Sean, though they hadn't discussed it.

"I'd like to talk to my sister," Patrick now said.

Sean didn't move. Lucy took his hand and said, "Sean."

He kissed her before walking past Patrick with what might have been called the evil eye.

"Why does he always have to be so stubborn?" Patrick said, shutting the door behind Sean.

Lucy just laughed.

Patrick stepped up and hugged Lucy. "I'm proud of you, sis."

"Thank you." She didn't know where this was coming from. "You okay?"

"Of course," he said. "I'm just going to spit it out. Sean's my friend and my partner, but I don't think he's good enough for you, and I don't think I ever will. I wouldn't pick him for you, because I think you need someone stable and mature."

Lucy's heart twisted. "Patrick, don't—please."

She didn't want to have to choose. She didn't want the pressure of picking her brother or Sean. Patrick was family. But Sean . . . she wasn't walking away.

"It's okay. I guess I didn't say it right." Patrick ran both hands through his hair, exasperated. "You care for Sean, and you're a big girl. It's not my choice who you date. I'm working through that. I guess I was jealous. I came here to be closer to my sister, and then

Sean waltzes in and takes over. It's his way, I know that, but I don't want to lose you."

Lucy smiled and blinked back tears. "You never will. I love you so much, Patrick." She hugged him tightly. "Thank you."

"He makes you happy, doesn't he?"

She nodded. "And he makes me laugh."

They walked back to the family room, where Lucy's family and friends were gathered. She was so blessed. With these people in her life, how could she fail? She could—and would—take on the world because she had a foundation that was wonderful and rare.

Sean walked over to her and took her hand. He kissed it. He was nervous, Lucy realized. Even in all his cocky arrogance, he was insecure about his relationships.

She tilted her head up and kissed him. In front of her friends and family. She was uncomfortable with public displays of affection, but the one small kiss said more than any words could.

Noah Armstrong had been standing unobtrusively across the room. Now he walked over and handed Lucy a letter. "Hans wanted to be here to give this to you, but he couldn't get away."

It was the same type of envelope as the one that had carried her rejection letter four weeks ago. The day after she'd returned from New York City, she'd appealed the decision of the FBI oral interview panel. She had been granted a second interview in the neighboring jurisdiction. While Lucy was pretty certain that Hans had had something to do with the fast response, he had assured her that the panel was fair and unbiased. That acceptance or rejection would be the panel's sole decision.

She looked at Noah, pained, not wanting another rejection, not tonight when she was so happy.

He smiled. "Go ahead."

She opened the envelope and unfolded the letter.

Dear Ms. Lucy Kincaid,

The Federal Bureau of Investigation is pleased to inform you that you've been accepted into the FBI Academy, having passed all written, oral, and background checks. Please report at 10 a.m. Monday, May 9, for a medical physical, and to your training officer, Special Agent Noah Armstrong in the Washington D.C. Field Office, at 9 a.m. Monday, May 16.

The next opening in the FBI Academy at Quantico commences in August. Provided you pass your physical, you will be required to report on Sunday, August 14, before 2000 hours.

Congratulations.

Sean picked her up and swung her around. "I knew it," he said.

"You had more faith in me than I did." She looked around, smiling, trying not to cry. "You all did. I won't let you down."

Read on for an excerpt from
IF I SHOULD DIE
by Allison Brennan

Published by Ballantine Books

FBI recruit Lucy Kincaid hadn't realized how much she'd needed a vacation until she and her boyfriend Sean Rogan checked into the Spruce Lake Inn in the Adirondacks. However, after less than twenty-four hours, she felt the tension of the last few months miraculously wash away in the beauty of the mountains, the serenity of the blue lake, and the purity of the fresh air.

Only a faint, nagging fear that such unadulterated bliss must be paid back marred an otherwise perfect weekend.

"So quiet this morning," Sean said. They'd had the resort pack a picnic lunch and were taking a five-mile hike to another small lake. They hadn't seen anyone since they left the lodge.

Sean had been planning this vacation practically since they first became involved four months ago, and he had not overlooked a single detail. He'd flown them into a private airport in his single-engine Cessna. The flight alone would have kept Lucy tickled for days. Then, he'd taken her to the lakeside cabin he'd rented at the resort—far enough to make them believe they were in the middle of nowhere, but close enough to the main lodge that they could eat dinner, or use the weight room, or walk a mile into the quaint old mining town down a tree-lined country road. And last night after a romantic dinner in town, they'd made love. Lucy had wakened in Sean's arms, with him smiling at her.

She was in heaven.

"Yep, it's nice and quiet," she said. "No traffic, no television, no news."

"I meant you. You're quiet. In fact, you look apprehensive."

"Not at all." She took his hand.

"Luce?" he said, staring at her with his probing blue eyes.

"What?"

"I know what you're thinking."

"Do not."

"You're thinking about all the things you need to do next week before reporting to FBI headquarters."

She laughed. "You're wrong."

"Really?"

He didn't believe her, so she told him the truth. "I'm not used to relaxing. The last time I took a vacation was with Patrick over a year ago. We got snowed in at a ski lodge with a dead body and a long list of suspects."

"No dead bodies here," Sean said, barely restraining his grin.

"You're teasing me."

He kissed her. "Am not."

They continued their walk down the mountainside. The scent of pine and spruce reminded Lucy of Christmas. A wet winter had given birth to a vibrant spring, and everywhere life bloomed: wildflowers, new leaves, and critters. In twenty minutes they'd seen white-tailed deer, rabbits, and a wide range of birds.

"I'm going to get spoiled." Lucy stopped to watch an eagle soar across the sky.

"You mean I'm not already spoiling you? I'd better get a move on."

She rolled her eyes. "I probably shouldn't say anything, your ego is big enough, but I missed you when you went to Texas."

"I knew you would," Sean said. He pulled her into his arms. "I missed you, too, Princess." He kissed her. "You could have come with me."

"Maybe I should have, to keep you out of trouble." But she shook her head. "It was better you weren't distracted."

"But you're my favorite distraction." He kissed her again, this time slowly, methodically, taking his time with her lips, making her body sag and lean into him. Lucy had once thought weak knees from a good kissing were only in books; now she knew better.

He smiled, his brown hair falling across his forehead, his dimple making his natural charm irresistible.

"The outdoors makes you glow," Sean said.

She laughed. "Is that a line?"

He grinned. "Do I need a line with you? Seriously, I want to take a picture."

She groaned. "I hate having my picture taken."

"Then you go up ahead and I'll take it when you least expect it."

"Impossible, now that I know you're playing with your camera."

Because it made Sean happy, Lucy did what he asked and continued along the narrow path several feet ahead of him. She almost tripped over an old wooden sign that was camouflaged by new growth of moss and ferns. Bright orange paint caught her eye.

She squatted and lifted the sign out of the plants, pulling hard since some of the leaves and roots had wrapped around the stake.

DANGER!
ABANDONED MINE
KELLEY MINING CO.

Sean clicked a picture with his digital camera, then pocketed it and helped Lucy free the sign.

"I didn't know there were mines right around here," she said. "Didn't Abel say they were on the other side of town?"

They'd chatted with Abel Hendricks, the inn owner, when they'd first arrived.

Sean scanned the area. "They could come out this far, I suppose. It's not my area of expertise."

Lucy feigned surprise. "You mean there's something you don't know?"

"Is that a challenge? Because I could spend the next three days learning about mining and earth science if you want."

"I like you ignorant," she teased, knowing Sean prided himself on being smart.

"Them's fighting words." He reached out and tickled her with his free hand.

She yelped and jumped back. "We should put the

sign upright. It's here for a reason. We don't want someone wandering off the path if they might get hurt."

Sean looked around the immediate area. "I don't see where it's supposed to be. It looks like it's been lying here awhile." He set down the sign and took out his cell phone.

"You have reception?" she asked.

"Barely, but I'm just marking the coordinates so we can inform the Forestry Department, or whoever takes care of these things. It probably fell in a storm."

He pocketed his phone, then picked up the sign again. The soil on the path was too hard to get the stake deep enough to keep the sign upright, so he moved off the trail and tested the ground.

"Here's good," he said. He pushed down on the top of the sign as hard as he could, and the stake went in a good ten or so inches. "We'll find out who to talk to when we get back to the inn. I wouldn't mind learning—"

A sharp cracking sound cut through the field. Lucy watched in horror as Sean's legs buckled and he disappeared from view, his startled cry echoing in her head.

"Sean!"

Lucy started to run to where he'd fallen, then stopped.

Abandoned mines.

She dropped her backpack and got down on her hands and knees. She felt around the damp soil, taking care with each inch forward. "Sean? Answer me!" she called.

Silence.

She moved to the edge of the hole Sean had fallen in. She quickly pulled off the leaves and dirt and plants that had accumulated on the top of a boarded-up mine shaft. The boards were rotted and broken, and a hole in the middle showed where Sean had fallen.

"Sean!" she called into the hole. "Answer me! Tell me you're okay!"

All Lucy heard in response was the echo of her own voice.